INTERRUPT

Also By Jeff Carlson

The Frozen Sky

The Plague Year Trilogy

Plague Year
Plague War
Plague Zone

Short Story Collection

Long Eyes

INTERRUPT

Jeff Carlson

Published by 47North
P.O. Box 400818
Las Vegas, NV 89140

ISBN-10: 1612183646
ISBN-13: 9781612183640

For Diana

ADVANCE PRAISE FOR INTERRUPT

"Let's be honest: Carlson is dangerous. *Interrupt* is riveting, high concept, and so real I felt the fires and blood. Thumbs up."
—Scott Sigler, *New York Times* bestselling author of *Pandemic*

"*Interrupt* is an edgy, exciting thriller full of adventure and surprises. This book has it all—elite military units, classified weaponry, weird science, a dash of romance, and horrific global disasters. Carlson writes like a knife at your throat."
—Bob Mayer, *New York Times* best-selling author of the *Green Berets* and *Area 51* series

"Terrific pacing. Dimensional characters. Jeff Carlson delivers everything and more in a killer thriller. You won't put this one down."
—John Lescroart, *New York Times* best-selling author of *The Hunter*

"I've been a fan of Carlson's work since he unleashed his nanotech on the world in *Plague Year*. This new book is *exciting*. *Interrupt* is a quantum leap in storytelling. I love the concept unreservedly. Love the writing to the point of jealousy. Carlson is so ridiculously talented, he makes me want to poke my eyeballs out. *Interrupt* is a phenomenal read."
—Steven Savile, international best-selling author of *Silver*

"An extremely exciting global thriller. Jeff Carlson's *Interrupt* is based on strong science and a dangerous new scenario that reminds us of our sun's instability, the consequences to our planet, and how powerfully influenced our species may have been when we first began in the Paleolithic. The ideas fly as fast as jets. This thriller has brains!"
—Kim Stanley Robinson, Hugo and Nebula Award-winning author of *2312*

ACKNOWLEDGMENTS

This book is a work of fiction. All of the science and weapon technologies are real, although I've taken some liberty with our current level of comparative genetics. What if is an intriguing question, but there is no firm evidence yet to link the Neanderthal genome to modern human conditions, only compelling theories.

The notion that autists exhibit stronger traits of Homo neanderthalensis than "normal" people was not my invention. Fascinating discussions of this idea can be found in articles in Science, Science News, the New York Times, the Los Angeles Times, the databases of the National Center for Biotechnology Information, and on the websites and forums of www.rdos.net, www.wrongplanet.net, and www.aspiesforfreedom.com, to name just a few.

For their generous help and expertise, I'd like to thank many people, including James Han and Bridget Swift with the Joint Genome Institute; Ben Bowen, Ph.D., at Lawrence Berkeley National Laboratory; James Noonan, Ph.D., Department of Genetics at Yale; Michael Stein, M.D., with Diablo Clinic Research; Seth Shostak, Ph.D., senior astronomer with the SETI Project and author of the spectacular memoir Confessions of an Alien Hunter; Captain Chris Earl, U.S. Navy; Commander Thomas Korsmo, U.S. Navy; Lieutenant, Colonel Brian Woolworth,

U.S. Army Special Forces; Lieutenant, Colonel Brian Lihani, U.S. Air Force (ret.); and, as always, my father, Gus Carlson, Ph.D., former division leader at Lawrence Livermore National Laboratory.

Other experts wish to remain anonymous due to the sensitive, sometimes classified aspects of this book. You know who you are. Thank you.

I'd also like to express my appreciation to John Koziol for sharing his skills in the ways of computers and software; Robin Burcell for her experience with DOJ programs, databases, and facial recognition software; Jack Welch, Ph.D., Professor Emeritus of Astronomy at Cal Berkeley; Charles H. Hanson, M.D.; and Penny Hill, super genius.

My editor David Pomerico is like Thai food—fiery, evocative, nutritious, and good. Working with him is a pleasure. Katy Ball, Justin Golenbock, Patrick Magee, and Jill Taplin are also integral to the team at 47North. They brought years of experience and great insights to *Interrupt*, which means this novel is partly theirs.

Also a tip of the hat to my agents on all sides of the continent, Donald Maass, Cameron McClure, and Jim Ehrich. These guys are like Batman—a team of Bat People—well-equipped and poised to strike. Having them on my side is awesome.

Most of all, I'd like to thank my wife and sons. They're remarkably patient with me and supportive of my writing.

Enjoy!

INTERRUPT

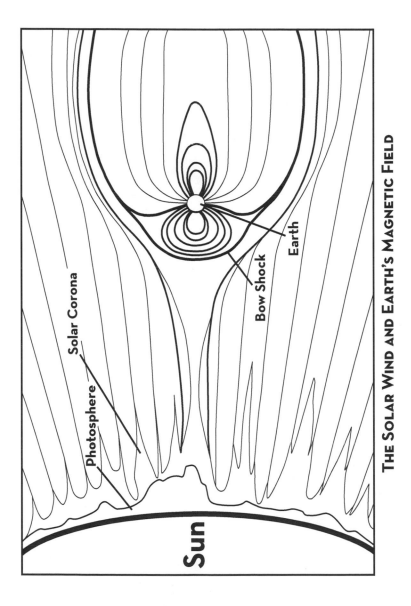

The Solar Wind and Earth's Magnetic Field

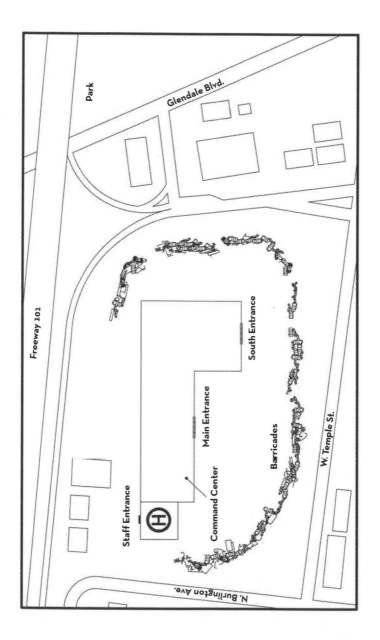

Park

Glendale Blvd.

Freeway 101

South Entrance

Main Entrance

Barricades

Staff Entrance

Command Center

W. Temple St.

N. Burlington Ave.

SILVER LAKE HOSPITAL

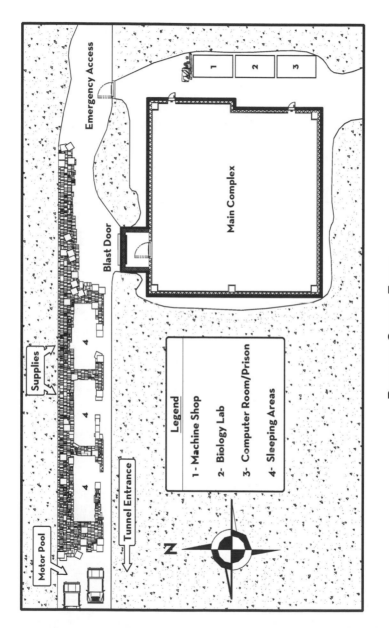

BUNKER SEVEN FOUR

PROLOGUE

. . . .

27,000 B.C.
SOUTHERN FRANCE

Nim's tribe always hunted in packs. Their world was too dangerous for anyone to walk alone. Even his scouts traveled in threes, and those men never left the valley beyond sight of their camp. The instinct to stay together was as powerful as the urge to breathe.

Sunrise touched the valley as Nim led five hunters over a ridgeline, each man glancing back in turn. Below them, the horse-skin tents of their home had dwindled to six small specks. Now the shallow contours of the land separated Nim's pack from the tribe entirely.

"Follow me," he said.

It was more than the law. It was the best Nim could offer them. He put himself in front as much as possible, shielding his people.

The wind was cutting on the ridge. No trees grew from the earth, only patches of short grass and isolated shrubs. The wind tugged at their bodies, rushing southward as they moved east.

The men ignored the cold. If they reacted, it was to tighten their formation even more, using each other for warmth as they jogged into the barren steppe plains.

They did not speak. There was no need. Nim worried about En's leg and Han's cough—En had wrenched his knee six days ago, and Han's throat had bothered him much longer—but they would have sent other men in their places if they thought they couldn't keep up. Nor did anyone ask where Nim was going when his direction and pace began to change, slowing, sprinting, then slowing again. They kept their eyes down to search through the rock and brittle earth.

Silence was a survival trait. In the cold, each breath whipped away as white gusts of fog. Talking made their lungs more vulnerable. They trusted Nim to guide them.

It was a dreary world. Gleaming through the clouds, only the sun wasn't gray or brown or dark green. Nim was less attuned to color than to the shape of the land, which varied sharply. Mountains filled two horizons. The men themselves were brown in every way, brown-eyed, brown-haired, clad in tan skins and leggings. Their faces had been burnished by the weather where their skin was exposed between their manes and beards.

Skirting a lake's ice-rimmed muddy shore, Nim found reindeer tracks. "Good," he said.

Unfortunately, the adults of their prey weighed several hundred pounds with antlers and stamping hooves. Three of his men ran with limps. Han had a withered forearm he'd broken twice. Every hunt was a risk.

Nim led his pack north—upwind from the reindeer. Scents and sounds carried for miles because there were so few of either. Nim hoped the smell of his pack would drive the reindeer toward the mountains.

The mountains were important because the foothills acted as a wall. Nim used box canyons for traps or stampeded the animals over cliffs, anything to minimize his casualties. Only twenty-six of them had survived the winter. Five were children. Three women were pregnant. That was it. They were aware of two other tribes living in the south, but otherwise Nim's people were alone.

Discovering new tracks ahead of him was like stepping on knives. Nim felt a sharp thrill of fear. "Stop!" he hissed, looking downwind first in case they'd walked into an ambush.

Man-shaped footprints had disturbed the pulverized rock—fresh tracks—intruders.

The sun was higher now, dull white behind the clouds. Snow gleamed on the mountains. Nim paced slowly over a wide area, examining the ground. Then he made his decision.

The reindeer had shied north to avoid the other men, so he took his hunters east. East was away from the herd but away from home, too. Han grunted his approval as they ran from the other men's tracks, recognizing Nim's intent.

Soon they hooked northward again, maneuvering behind the enemy.

Twice they found more footprints where the other men had followed the wider trail left by the reindeer. Each time Nim adjusted his course, threading through the terrain. He was careful never to cross the highest points, which would allow him to see but also to be seen. The wind was enough. He had their scent, so he stalked after both targets.

Finally, he spotted one of the intruders near the base of a hill. Nim dropped into a crawl with his best knife in hand. Each of his hunters carried several blades of flaked granite in addition to clubs of horse bone.

"Be ready," he said as a second intruder joined the first.

The other men touched the earth again and again, clumsily examining the herd's spoor. They were hideous. They had small heads, flat faces, and pebble noses. One had diseased-looking hair that was yellow and thin. They were taller than Nim with longer legs and arms.

He knew of them from his father's legends. His father had called them Dead Men because they uttered nonsense if they spoke and because their tools and clothing were pitiful efforts like things imagined by ghosts. The Dead Men even walked like spirits, with strides as long as the reindeer.

Nim's pack had caught up because the Dead Men appeared to need a lot of rest, which was good. For any advantage the Dead Men possessed in height and reach, Nim's hunters compensated with their stamina. His people were stronger. They had natural armor in the dense bone of their foreheads.

The Dead Men were Cro-Magnon men, the early race of *Homo sapiens*.

Nim and his tribe were Neanderthals.

"Now. Before they smell us," Nim said. He stole sideways against a crease of bedrock. Han and En came after him while the other three stayed behind. They would attack in two prongs, although they were outnumbered.

Nim didn't need to see all of the Dead Men to know there were eleven. From their tracks, he'd learned a great deal about them. The Dead Men wore leather wrappings like his people, but they had smaller feet and didn't push as hard into the earth. They were insubstantial.

To his eyes, their movements also lacked focus. As they traveled, the Dead Men meandered with the same flighty behavior as the reindeer, never holding position. Nim didn't like it. Everything his people did, they did with unity.

The adrenaline in his veins felt loud and good as he ascended the lee side of the hill. Near the top, the wind increased. Nim was acutely aware of each gust sweeping his skin with the oxygen-thick scent of the glaciers.

This is our land, he thought.

Beside him, En wore a feral grin. Han flexed his bad arm in a repetitive, habitual motion that Nim found calming.

"Go," he said.

They charged over the hill. The Dead Men were exactly where he'd expected, kneeling at a spring. One fell backward in shock. The rest scattered to Nim's right, where they would meet his other hunters. . . .

But their speed was breathtaking. Nim's pack had no chance to engage the Dead Men, not even the one who'd fallen. Han got in a single slash of his knife, opening the Dead Man's shoulder before the Dead Man sprang onto his long legs and ran.

"Haaaaaaaaa!" Nim shouted, chasing them with his voice.

His father had defended this territory before him. Nim would find the enemy camp and kill them in their tents if necessary. With luck, the Dead Men would return to their tribe and leave, taking their women and children. Why did they keep coming?

Seconds later, Nim saw the Dead Men sprinting up a hill to the southeast. Han laughed and sank his knife into the mud by the spring, rubbing off the enemy's blood.

Nim had only superstition to explain what happened next. The moment Han's knife cut the earth, the sky sputtered and dimmed. It was as if Nim blinked with his eyes open. Darkness buzzed inside his mind.

Magic, he thought. *Evil.*

Something in the daylight had undergone a profound change. The sun flickered. Then there was pain. When Nim could think again, he found himself on the ground, his cheek bloodied by a rock. The hunk of granite obscured his sight.

Nim shoved himself upright. His hunters sprawled nearby, dazed. The Dead Men must have unleashed a power beyond comprehension. Nim had no proof the Dead Men were to blame, but he trusted his hatred of them. He remembered how the sky had dimmed. Those shadows had been worse than any eclipse, unnatural and silent.

He swung his head to look at the sun. Was its light changing? Terrible currents roiled the clouds on the horizon, turning the sky black. The storm would reach them soon.

He realized instantly how this magic would tip the balance between his kind and the Dead Men. If his people couldn't think during the shadows, they would be helpless.

"Get up!" he said.

En was the first to stand. Nim's heart surged with defiant strength.

"Track the Dead Men and kill them," he said.

The sun flickered again. Nim sagged to one knee, fighting it. The shadows felt like a club smashing him. He went blank, woke, went blank, and woke again. Each moment of clarity lasted seconds, allowing him no more than glimpses of his surroundings.

When it stopped, his environment had changed wildly. Rain fell through the dark of night. He was alone. Freezing water swirled at his feet, coursing over an open field where the hill had been. Other things had changed, too. His belly was as tight as if he hadn't eaten for days. When he felt his cheek, the wound had scabbed. His senses screamed that he'd moved across the land while forgetting everything he'd done in coming to this place. It was two or even three nights later.

Nim's feelings of loss were gut-wrenching. He howled in rage for his tribe.

"Where are you!?" he cried. Then another black bolt seared through his mind, and this assault did not stop.

The Neanderthals' time had come to an end.

PART ONE

RISE

I

· · · · · · · · · · · ·

LOS ANGELES

Emily's vision went white as she drove down West 4th Street. For an instant, she thought the sky had flashed with lightning, but the air was clear and perfect like most summer mornings in California—and when she blinked, a red car was swerving into her lane. The front of her new black Nissan Altima crunched against the other vehicle.

Emily shouted, "Oh!"

The jolt wasn't hard enough to set off her airbags. She'd barely been going twenty-five between two stoplights, but that was enough to ruin her entire day at six in the morning.

Fortunately, she had an arsenal of bad movie dialogue for any occasion. "It looks like I picked the wrong week to quit sniffing glue," she said, stunned, trying to laugh at her misfortune. Had she been blinded by the sun reflecting from the glass face of a building?

Her next thought was work. *I'm going to be late*, she thought, reaching for the files on the passenger seat. Impact had caused a landslide. She grabbed at her lists of IgA proteins and the nonconfidential summaries written by her biology team.

Down the block, a horn blared. Much closer, someone was yelling. Emily glanced at the mini-mall on her right, where two men knelt over someone else in front of a McDonald's.

Her view was obstructed by the cars lined up for the drive-thru. If the men over there were mugging the third guy, it wouldn't be the first crime she'd witnessed in L.A., but she stepped out of her car anyway. It was the right thing to do.

Emily Flint was twenty-seven years old, small, and trim. The low heels of her work shoes clacked on the street as she stood up, safe inside the V of her open door and the car itself. She didn't think anyone could see her as she steadied her nerves by straightening her charcoal skirt and white blouse.

The sun rose over the tall, square shapes of the business district. It cast sparks on steel and glass. *That must be what got me,* she thought, but she couldn't convince herself.

The two men at the McDonald's were helping the fallen man. Other people were arguing in the drive-thru where a blue Toyota had bumped another car. Somehow they'd all been distracted at once. Everything about the busy street felt wrong.

Emily had set her alarm for five a.m. on one of the biggest days of her career. Now her eight-month-old Altima was banged up, not to mention the hours she'd waste on the phone with her insurance. She'd planned to deliver the envelope in her purse this week, too. She couldn't let it wait.

The envelope held a $3500 check for a catering hall. Her wedding was scheduled for September 1. If she didn't get the deposit to the caterers by Friday, their reservation would be cancelled. Then what? Everyone would think she was dragging her feet. But she wasn't. She was busy with work, and she and Chase were basically married already, sharing most of their finances as well as their tiny apartment.

Here we go, she thought as an older man emerged from the red car.

A truck rig eased down the street behind him. It probably wouldn't fit past his car. The old man was pale, and Emily said, "Are you okay?"

"Sorry!" he said. "I'm sorry."

"I think there was an earthquake. Someone else crashed in front of the McDonald's," she said before the truck horn bellowed. The enormous machine was ten feet away. Emily jumped half out of her skin.

A guy in sunglasses leaned through the cab window. "Hey, move it," he said.

Emily wanted to be clever. This jerk was too comfortable bullying them, but she couldn't think of anything good, so she went for loud instead. "Bite me!" she yelled.

The words surprised everyone, including herself.

"Jeez, lady," the trucker said. He disappeared into his cab as Emily put her hand over her mouth. The older man gaped at her. Then the two of them laughed. It was a good moment, unexpected and fun, until the truck's air brakes squealed.

"Let me help you move your car," she said.

Fifteen minutes later, Emily drove away. She'd lost a headlight and the steering felt sticky, but her engine seemed fine. So were her tires.

On the next block, she saw another wreck, a three-car collision much uglier than her fender bender. An ambulance was on-scene. Two paramedics helped a man with a bloody scalp as Emily drove past, feeling an uneasy blend of empathy and creeping fear.

So many accidents, she thought. She reached for her files again, then put both hands on the steering wheel as if the comfort she wanted wasn't in those printouts.

Emily led a group of computational biologists at DNAllied Inc. In three hours, the company expected her to announce a billion-dollar breakthrough. They'd scheduled a major media release at One California Plaza, an elegant downtown skyscraper, which meant anyone in her right mind would have finalized her presentation by now. The catch was she'd heard back from a collaborator at Yale at the last second. He had experimental data sets that would improve her results on multiple levels, so yesterday she'd restarted her programs from scratch.

Her boss was going to shoot her.

The Altima definitely had a shimmy.

"Sometimes I feel like my life is an earthquake," she said as a strand of smoke rose in the distance, barely visible between two buildings. Talking to herself was a bad habit. She grabbed her BlackBerry.

"Hey, babe," Chase said through a tick of static.

"Hi." Her reception was only at two bars. Weird. "Did you feel the quake? Either it was pretty big or I picked the wrong week to quit drinking again."

"Right." He was used to her goofball humor and had gotten pretty good at deflecting it. Chase Coughlin was a thirty-two-year-old M.D. with a crushing schedule of his own. Tuesday was one of his days off. "I didn't feel anything," he said.

"I had an accident. The car's a little smashed in. I don't know what's going on, but I saw two other crashes and a fire, I think."

"Did they check for whiplash?"

"I'm okay. I'm just really, really late and I don't want to spend the money on the car."

"Me either."

That was Chase. Good or bad, he told you what he thought. Maybe all surgeons were the same, disinterested in anything except their own assessment of a situation. Emily had a harder time working through her problems—this problem especially.

Chase was good-looking and confident and completely unfair about how many household chores were her responsibility. Emily did the shopping. Emily fetched the dry cleaning. Yes, Chase made more money, but he also carried more debt from his student loans. The truth was she'd been having second thoughts.

"I've got to go," she said.

"Wait. Where are you?"

"I'm downtown," she said. "The car's still driving and I don't have time to deal with it today."

"I know. I'll get it to the shop for you."

"Would you?" Relief softened Emily's doubt. Chase was a good guy, really. He was just such a *guy,* more interested in sports, sex, and sandwiches than in tedious junk like keeping their lives organized.

As she turned into the entrance of the Plaza's underground garage, Emily made up her mind. She would FedEx the deposit to the catering hall.

He said, "Your extra keys are in your dresser, right? I'll figure out a tow truck. We can catch up for lunch."

"Love to. Bye."

She heard an ambulance wailing when she opened her window to punch the TICKET button at the gate. The hospital where Chase worked was ten minutes from the Plaza. DNAllied was about an equal distance away. They often met for tacos or sushi. Both of them spent more time at their jobs than in their apartment, which might have contributed to the uncertainty she'd felt.

The sirens echoed from the next block over, howling through the gaps between the buildings. But the same sound was also to her left. Another emergency vehicle was on the move somewhere else in the neighborhood.

A chill slithered up the back of Emily's neck. *It's like the whole city is coming apart.*

She drove into the garage. At 7:05 a.m., the top level was packed. She descended to the second level to find a space. Then the elevator took forever.

DNAllied had booked a fourth-floor conference room with a gamut of visual aids from dry-erase boards to HDTV monitors. Their media director was testing short clips of 3D animation and other mock-ups when Emily walked in.

It was 7:21. She had her laptop slung over one shoulder and her other arm loaded with paperwork. "Good morning," she called, looking for her boss. A knot of men sat in the front row by the podium.

Raymund Esposito was fifty-one and resembled a beach ball in a yellow tie. He banged against his chair when he jumped up.

"Emily!" he said, not *Dr. Flint*, chastising her for the benefit of the other men in the room. He'd been on the warpath even before she trash-canned her results and started over, because they didn't see eye to eye about what she was doing.

Emily motioned for him to walk with her to the podium. She thought she had a new argument that was sure to convince him, although it would take some fancy footwork.

She started off cautiously. "Hi, Ray. I'm late."

"I've been here since the day started in New York," he said. "The board is very concerned about your email."

"I'm sorry you're caught in the middle," she said, wondering if she might move from this small surrender to her new tactic, but Ray was absorbed in his misery.

"There is no middle," he said. "They're right. You're wrong. I think they'd pull you from the media release if your name wasn't on the agenda."

"Let me show you something," she said, taking a seat.

The conference room had high-speed Wi-Fi, and her laptop was loaded with state-of-the-art encryption. What it lacked was the muscle to process the staggering amounts of data associated with her project. Like everyone at DNAllied, Emily used a secure shell to remotely access the exascale cloud allocations at the University of California, Los Angeles. UCLA's supercloud clocked in at .001 exaflops—billions upon billions of floating-point calculations per second—which was a supremely beautiful number.

Nevertheless, the old mantra held true. *Garbage in, garbage out.* The computer wasn't smart. She was.

Next-generation biologists like Emily combined degrees in bio-physical chemistry with excellent programming skills, which had led to the hottest trend in genetics: data mining, data integration, and predictive models. She did lab work, too, yet it was her ability to sift through the results of hundreds of other labs that put her at the front of the pack. Pure research was necessary, even prestigious, but the money and power were in applicable science.

In her field, that meant gene therapies. Medicine. Emily worked in biomarker discovery, targeting the reasons behind hereditary diseases and other genetic miscues. What they understood, they could fix. Her team was on the verge of eradicating an entire spectrum of neurological disorders including autism, ADHD, Alzheimer's, and bipolar disorder.

Accessing the university's supercloud, Emily typed in her username and password. Her log-in failed. She must have mis-keyed either *EFlint* or *Capricorn421* while Ray hovered over her.

"Our guy at Yale is topnotch," she said as she tried again. "His SNPs data on the Pelat find changes everything." She spoke the acronym like a single word, *snips*, for single nucleotide polymorphisms.

"Pelat had nothing to do with your biomarkers," Ray said.

"That's not true."

"We should be rehearsing your speech."

"Not yet. Let me show you."

Last summer, mountain climbers in France had unearthed the remains of a man near the base of Mount Pelat. Less than half the body had been preserved by the ice, but police were quick to realize he'd been murdered by a blow to the skull—and that he was Neanderthal. The mummified tissue had been a godsend for geneticists. Years ago, rough sequences of the Neanderthal genome had been performed using fossilized bone samples, but Pelat offered organs and skin as good as anything taken from a living man, which made all the difference in the analysis of protein-signaling networks.

"Pelat could be our holy grail," Emily said. "We've been using chimpanzee samples for the same reason. Their expression patterns—"

"It doesn't matter."

"It does. Their protein and metabolite expression patterns are different than ours! I don't think you realize how much we can do with orthogonal data sets. If I have enough information, I can tell you anything. We're on the cusp on resolving so many issues in a single model."

"Listen," Ray said. "I need to ask you straight out. Are you working up the data for a prenatal vaccine?"

"No."

"The patents belong to the company, not you. The board is enthusiastic about your work, but you have to remember you need approval instead of striking out on your own."

"I know."

"That's not what you said in your email. Then you started your programs all over again."

The email, she thought. *God save me from the email.*

In a moment of high energy, Emily had dashed off a note about the ultimate goal of her research. Apparently she'd used an exclamation point. The email was passed up the food chain, where someone decided she must be a fire-breathing socialist on a crusade.

Yes, she wanted to save lives. She loved the idea of helping people everywhere, but to think she wanted to give everything away for free was ridiculous.

Emily liked money. Who didn't like money?

Her stock options gave her a personal stake in DNAllied landing the interest of a major pharmaceutical company, after which she could pay down Chase's loans and move them into a better apartment, but the board was afraid she intended to speak out against her own project.

"I'm sorry I sent the email," she said. "All I meant was we aren't done yet. We'll never be done, not in our lifetimes."

"That's right." Ray pounced on her words. "That's exactly right. We take it one step at a time, which means we stay on track. The infant and juvenile therapies come first."

"But we could be refining our data for those therapies *and* the prenatal vaccine. There's no reason we can't do both."

"There is," Ray said. "This is about managing our resources. We can't have our best minds running in a thousand directions at once, and it's not your job to choose where or how we're most productive."

It made her queasy to think they'd dissuade her from the real cure. A single vaccine for pregnant women would be a gold mine. The board wanted more. They wanted diamond mines. The fact of the matter was that weekly shots for afflicted children and adults would be many, many times more lucrative than giving expectant mothers a single inoculation to protect babies against a wide range of disabilities.

"There's an easy solution," she said. "I know how we can make DNAllied the priciest thing on the market."

Ray grimaced. "Emily—"

"If we give one subset of my data to the right people, they can design the vaccine. There's a team at the University of Texas. They're primed to jump on this. They probably won't develop it as fast as I could, but maybe I can consult a bit. Then the vaccine goes to trials. They make eighty billion dollars. Most of that money comes right back to us and we also get the accolades, the good will, and the proof this stuff works exactly like the melanoma gene therapies out of UCSD in 2010. If we have real-world evidence from—"

"Emily, enough. I see what you're trying to do and it's commendable. This is about your nephew." The look in Ray's brown eyes was shrewder than she would have guessed. "You don't want anyone else to suffer like him," Ray said. "It's a noble cause. Honestly. But how old is he now? Eight? He's exactly who you'll save by developing our juvenile therapies, and he's your own flesh and blood."

That was a cheap shot, she thought.

"The important thing is to help the people who need it," Ray said. He was parroting the company line, which sounded great. *Help the people who need it.*

In the meanwhile, what if their own kids were born with preventable disorders? Their greed had a blindness she couldn't resolve. If their own children grew up autistic or bipolar, what good were an extra gazillion dollars in stock?

"Here we go," she said, looking down to hide her anger. Her log-in had finally been accepted, and she navigated her way through the UCLA server to her files. There were two. The third was only a progress bar at ninety-eight percent. "Let me show you how the Pelat data changes our simulations."

"We're using your original sims today," Ray said.

"The new results are done."

"They haven't been vetted, and we're not rescheduling this event." Ray's voice was stern with a hint of exasperation.

He was being fatherly now, she realized, and he'd cast her as the overexcited young fool. Emily wanted to forgive him. Ray was protecting his job. He had retired parents to support and two sons, one in the Air Force, another in college. Her project wasn't the only reason he was on edge. His first boy was a weapons loader in South Korea, where the military had been on alert for weeks. Ray was worried.

I guess I should be, too.

DNAllied was already doing the dance with Pfizer and Enring Corp., two of the heavy hitters in Big Pharma. The board wanted a bidding war. The miracles Emily envisioned couldn't come fast enough.

Even if Pfizer or Enring bought in, her team at DNAllied was several months from their first drug trials. She could accelerate the process by sinking her time into the infant and juvenile therapies, but she wanted to stay with her vaccine. She didn't have six months to spare. Other labs were pursuing identical lines of research, and a prenatal vaccine might be worth consideration for the Nobel Prize for medicine.

"Just tell me I'll have free rein after today," she said. "I've earned the right to move in new directions."

"Absolutely not," Ray said. "You're the one who started this, and you're the one they want to see it through. What's wrong with that?"

He must have seen the dismay in her eyes.

"Listen," he said. "I'm not supposed to say this. The board brought up the possibility of firing you if necessary."

"That's insane. I did all the work."

Legally, the patents were theirs. Her data, her simulations, the biomarkers—her contract said everything she did on company time was proprietary.

Should I get a lawyer? she wondered. *All they want are their drugs. They don't care what else I can accomplish.*

"I went to bat for you," Ray said. "I told them you're a team player, but you're a little ball of energy. A genius. I told them you're like our own little Einstein."

Emily forced a smile, but inside, she chafed at *little*. Worse, her laptop dropped the connection to UCLA. "Wait," she said.

"What's up?"

"I lost everything."

"Don't give me this, Emily."

She flashed Ray a look, hoping it was clear she wouldn't kill her own data on purpose. But for the first time, she wondered if she should sneak her files to another team. She corresponded with other labs every day. Getting her data out wouldn't be hard.

She logged in again as Ray took the chair beside her. He smelled like deodorant and sweat. She opened one of her files. It should have begun with a series of bipartite graphs showing the abundance of specific peptides in autistic males. Instead, she'd received half of her data feed.

"This isn't right," she said with an unpleasant heat in her stomach. She laid one hand on her midriff as if to contain the feeling.

Somehow her new files had been corrupted. DNAllied's laptops were loaded with firewalls and crypto. The university's supercloud was equally secure. A virus was unlikely. What did that leave? Either she'd experienced data transmission errors or someone in the company had sabotaged her results.

My God, Emily thought. *What else could go wrong today?*

2

· · · · · · · · · · · ·

LOS ANGELES

I n the kitchenette tucked behind the conference room, Emily stood
by the sink with her older sister Laura. Laura's eight-year-old son, P.J.,
sat in the corner with a Nintendo 3DS game. Both women held handfuls of note cards.

The power flickered, and Emily glanced at the lights as the microwave beeped, automatically resetting its digital display. "Is that bad
luck?" she asked. "I'm having bad luck today."

Laura smiled. "You can't get out of this, Em."

"I'm serious."

"You're stalling."

An hour and a half had passed since Emily's fight with Ray. The
media event started in ten minutes. Through the wall, Emily heard a
hubbub of voices. She paced nervously while Laura leafed through several cards prepared in Emily's handwriting.

Laura was gorgeous. Her dark blond hair was more honey-hued than
Emily's straw-colored ponytail. The diamond stud earrings and smoky
eyes didn't hurt, either. Laura exuded a casual, unflinching maturity

Emily tried to emulate. Since they'd been kids, she'd wanted to emulate nearly everything about Laura.

Will you be proud of me? she thought.

Detached from the women, P.J.'s silence made an odd counterpoint to Emily's restlessness. Laura rarely allowed him to play his 3DS because it could be an ordeal to separate him from the game. P.J. resisted to the point of shrieking.

Now the thin-limbed boy set his 3DS in his lap, ignoring the rousing sound track of *LEGO Indiana Jones*. Was he staring at the wallpaper?

"Let's practice one more time," Laura said.

Emily gestured at him. "Are you sure?"

"Yes. He's fine, Auntie Em."

The nickname rankled and pleased Emily. She wasn't a wrinkled old lady like Dorothy's aunt in *The Wizard of Oz*, but the movie had always been one of their favorites.

The good news was she'd recovered her statistical models from UCLA. A few minutes ago, the IT guys at DNAllied had texted Ray and Emily to explain what they thought had happened. The ECC circuitry in DNAllied's server—error control and correction—appeared to have been fooled by corrupted line transmissions that met the circuitry's parity tests. For several seconds, Emily's data packets had been dropping bits in between UCLA and the Plaza. Then the problem stopped, although Laura said she'd read some nutty stuff on her iPhone this morning.

The net overflowed with stories of hackers and worms. Credit cards had been declined everywhere on the West Coast for twenty minutes. Emily wasn't sure what to think. First her car, then her computers. If she gave in to Ray's demands and made no mention of a prenatal vaccine, today would be a complete disaster.

"I need to ask you something," she said.

Laura shook her head and raised the note cards like an axe. "Straighten up. You're slouching."

"Sir, yes, sir, sir," Emily joked. But she did as she was told and lifted her shoulders. "Thank you for coming in this morning," she said, smiling at an imaginary crowd. "Your press kits contain links to hi-def presentations. I'd like to touch on several highlights, then field any questions you may have."

"Slower," Laura said.

"My colleagues and I have finished a comprehensive study in functional genomics, reaching into mankind's distant past in order to study who we are today. More specifically, we focused on the causes of one of society's most tragic epidemics."

Settling into her speech, Emily stole another glance at P.J. while Laura's gaze was on the note cards.

Her nephew was autistic. Auntie Em believed she could save him. She'd gone into biology for other reasons, but P.J. had become a large part of what motivated her.

"Hold on," she said, stepping toward him.

"You cheater," Laura said.

P.J. didn't turn as Emily approached, taking the game from his lap before it fell to the floor. "Here you go," she said.

Did his gaze dart toward her face? Maybe. She did not receive the smile she'd hoped for. Interacting with P.J. could be like talking to someone through a fog bank. There were glimpses, which made their relationship all the more poignant. P.J. was someone she'd lost too many times. From one day to the next they would be apart, together, then apart again.

Emily wanted to ruffle his hair, yet stopped herself, putting his feelings before her own. Most of the time, P.J. didn't like physical contact— but he'd detected something in how she'd paused.

"Four thousand seventy-four," he said.

"What's that?"

"Four thousand seventy-four," he said.

Autistic children had trouble reading expressions and body language. They responded to different cues. Emily wondered what he'd meant until she realized, *That's how many dots there are on the wallpaper.*

His talent for math ran in the family. She shared the same knack. On good days, he was capable of solving multiplication tables that would stump a high school senior.

"P.J., you're so awesome," she said.

He had been seventeen months old when he faded. Until then he'd been an active little bug, grasping and walking and beginning to make silly noises like words. Then his gaze turned inward. He stopped talking. The change was a horrific trauma for everyone in the family, especially Laura's husband, Greg, who eventually—right or wrong—put the blame on himself.

In developed nations like the U.S. and Europe, autism rates had skyrocketed, increasing 700 percent since 1996. More than 1 percent of children were being diagnosed with autistic spectrum disorders.

Was there an environmental factor, a sudden genetic drift, or both? The first might cause the other. The world's drinking water was laced with new chemical compounds and trace metals. Pharmaceutical agents, pesticides, flame retardants, and dioxin were all measurable in the biosphere, some of it transient, most of it everlasting.

Originally, Laura had seized any number of explanations for P.J.'s condition. Several advocate groups had filed lawsuits, insisting vaccines such as MMR caused autism. After dozens of studies, solid evidence said vaccinations weren't at fault—but it was an emotional issue, because if there wasn't an outside source, the cause must be something in the parents themselves. Research showed a powerful genetic basis for ASD, a term used to encompass autism, Asperger syndrome, Rett syndrome, childhood disintegrative disorder, and PDD-NOS, pervasive developmental disorder not otherwise specified.

Even with Emily's data, several steps remained before anyone could determine if ASD was caused by rare mutations or by multi-gene interactions of common variants. One thing she knew for sure. Ninety percent of the risk of ASD was inherited.

One factor was older moms and dads. The father's sperm were less active, the mother's eggs had aged. Laura was eleven years Emily's senior because Emily had been a late surprise for their parents. Greg was six years older than Laura. In the modern age, people delayed parenthood to pursue their careers or simply to avoid the responsibility.

Emily's personal fear was mixed with defiance and shame. She wanted kids. Chase said he did, too, but neither of them wanted to rush into diapers and a minivan. And if they waited a few more years . . . Her family genes were suspect.

Walking back to Laura felt like walking a tightrope. Emily didn't want her sister's life, which was something she could never admit.

She blurted other words instead. "I need to know what to do," she said.

"What do you mean?" Laura asked.

"I have two speeches. Those notes you're holding are the company version. But there's another one." Emily grabbed her handbag. She opened it and showed Laura a second set of note cards. "They only want me to say part of what I should say. I didn't tell you because, uh, I've been working on more than gene therapies for babies and kids."

Laura stared at her. "Are you in trouble?"

"Yes. It's a prenatal vaccine. It would stop anyone from ever being born with ASD."

"What about people like P.J.?"

"We've talked about this before," Emily said quietly. "There will be complications with juvenile therapies. By their second year, kids are establishing their permanent neurological makeup even if some pathways are underperforming or missing altogether. The therapies . . . They'll change him, Laura. He'll become a totally different person."

"Isn't that what we want?"

At least right now you two can get through the day, Emily thought. *P.J. would have to relearn everything, maybe even how to walk or use the toilet.*

But you'll be angry if I say so.

She understood Laura's hope. Sometimes P.J.'s pixie face lit up. On his best days, Laura was able to coax him into sharing what he saw inside his head, stammering through discussions of his favorite toys and snacks. And if he lost his talent for math, Laura would gratefully trade that ability if P.J. gained new social skills and normal awareness.

"We'll help him, too," Emily said. "That's what my boss wants me to focus on. But our company will make plenty of money if we tell people we're also refining our data for a vaccine. Selling out to Enring Corp. shouldn't be the main point of the media release."

"Maybe your boss knows what he's talking about."

Emily was shocked. "What?"

"It sounds to me like you're doing good things either way," Laura said. "You don't have any patience, Em. You never did. Why can't you finish the gene therapies first?" Her smile was gentle, even pitying. "You know I'm right."

"I guess," Emily said. *You're wrong,* she thought. *If I don't make my data public, they might bury the vaccine for years.*

But if she used the media conference to say what she wanted, she would lose her job. They'd probably hit her with a lawsuit. Even if she walked away free, even if another company hired her, DNAllied owned her statistical models. She would be forced to start from scratch if she could re-create her data at all, and once again the prenatal vaccine would be delayed or lost.

Her idealism had a price. She'd made her deal with the devil. Now she was locked in.

Worse, she'd shared her apprehension with Laura. She felt disloyal for not making P.J. her first priority.

Laura turned away from her. She used P.J. as an excuse to rebuff Emily, walking across the room to her son, but she couldn't have hurt Emily more if she'd slapped her.

"P.J.?" Laura said. "Sweetheart? Let's go to the bathroom before Auntie Em is ready for her talk."

He didn't answer. Emily couldn't speak, either, her insides whirling as Laura glanced back at her. For a long moment, the two women studied each other in silence.

"What are you going to do?" Laura asked.

Emily nodded, trying to reassure her sister. She wanted to say, *I'll do it your way.* Instead, she thought, *We'll see.*

NORTHERN CALIFORNIA

"W̶e may be in trouble," Marcus Wolsinger said as he shut the door to the control room. Dust and flies were anathema to their electronics, but Marcus closed the door harder than necessary in frustration.

Most of his staff had yet to return to their desks. They'd been up for thirty-six hours straight before last night. Marcus was exhausted, too. Nevertheless, he'd woken early to call the East Coast and Colorado. His mind hadn't allowed him to rest. He wanted to get back to work. He needed his staff.

Steve Church was the only person in the shoebox-shaped room, a small, prefabricated structure. The walls were aluminum and glass. The furniture consisted of six cheap desks and eight good chairs, although each desk held its own computer and expensive flat-screen displays.

"I told everyone to be here," Marcus said.

Steve looked up from his Mac. Even with the AC cranked to a frosty sixty-eight degrees, Steve was bleary-eyed, and Marcus wondered if his friend had slept.

"I just got off the phone with SWPC," Marcus said. "They think I'm crazy."

"They're right," Steve said.

"Nothing's wrong with our software."

"There must be."

Marcus shook his head uneasily. "Two observatories confirmed our data. It's the satellites that can't hear it. And if we move past the idea that we're getting false reads, we may be in trouble."

Marcus and Steve were senior astronomers with the Hoffman Square Kilometer Field, a radio telescope array in the mountains north of San Francisco. Marcus was black. Steve was white. Otherwise, Marcus felt like they might have been brothers. Both of them were in their mid-forties, although they dressed like kids in T-shirts and jeans. Steve had a crop of beard stubble he'd let go for two days. Marcus wore a BEAM ME UP pin given to him by Steve's wife, harking back to a time when they'd been as fresh as the crew of *Star Trek*. Now both men had potbellies (Marcus more so than Steve) and receding hairlines (Steve more so than Marcus), and yet their relaxed appearance could not mask the intensity he felt.

Marcus took the computer beside Steve. He began to type, then, half-consciously, he paused to survey the desktop.

Marcus had a touch of obsessive-compulsive disorder. He was notorious for rearranging the junk on any desk into neat geometries—keyboard, mouse pad, sticky notes, pens. He shaved when Steve did not. He changed his socks when Steve did not. His ex ridiculed him for being an anal robot, but that he'd brought order to her life was precisely why Janet had been attracted to him in the beginning.

He aligned three pens and a binder with a cold, stale cup of coffee. Then he rattled on his keyboard, opening the files he'd developed since sunrise.

Outside the control room's broad windows, the brown California hills were a stovetop warming in the sun. None of the worn, dirty peaks of the Coast Range lifted higher than five thousand feet, and the landscape consisted of weeds, brush, and scattered oak and pine trees. Their array was more commanding. The terrain was dotted with thousands of white six-meter dishes identical to those used for commercial television. The Hoffman Square Kilometer Field and another like it in Australia were the cutting edge in radio astronomy, with more channels and capabilities than anything else on the planet.

Marcus pointed at his files. "The signal creep is subtle, but it's there," he said. "I think the sun is experiencing a rise in microflares."

Steve answered with tired irritation. "We anticipated a lot of background chatter when we built the array. What if the software is creating patterns that don't exist?"

"Our system's one hundred percent. The programmers and I ran a dozen integration checks."

"It would be better if those guys were here."

Marcus shrugged. Their lead programmers lived in Silicon Valley. They'd consulted with him online despite his connection failing twice. The net had been spotty all morning. Marcus had asked them to drive to the array but was met with excuses. No one wanted to stay in the mountains. Their programs often ran for weeks, so the site staff were a few postdoctoral kids in their twenties. Marcus and Steve had only made the trip up from the San Francisco Bay Area because they'd discovered more junk noise than usual in their data during the past week.

The noise was escalating.

Marcus found that disturbing.

"Look." He opened a series of waterfall plots on his computer. Each plot—a square graph—was a cascade of color-coded lines, a snapshot image of the broad spectrum of electromagnetic radiation analyzed by the array. "There's an irregular but upward trend," he said. "The electrostatic bursts in Earth's magnetic field have hit one plateau after another."

"Why isn't SWPC forecasting a solar storm?" Steve asked.

"They're still gathering reports from the satellites."

"The sats would record the flares."

"No." Marcus shook his head. The Space Weather Prediction Center in Boulder, Colorado, was where the National Oceanic and Atmospheric Administration monitored solar activity, but Marcus had grown accustomed to the role of the devil's advocate. He could be ruthless about proving his ideas. "These are microflares," he said. "The satellites have inferior hardware, software, and data storage."

"I'm not convinced."

"We're seeing something new. Something deeper than surface activity."

Most of Marcus's self-respect stemmed from his career, which had begun with the SETI Project before he was asked to join ES2, an innovative new venture to explore the reaches of space. Unfortunately, a lot of people belittled the Extra-Solar Earth Search Program and everything associated with it. Science fiction had made sure of that. The public thought aliens were a joke. They expected bloodthirsty monsters. Steve's caution was understandable. He wanted to make sure they didn't embarrass ES2, whereas Marcus was more willing to trust his intuition.

"If we could go further back, the trend would be obvious," Marcus said. "It's easy to extrapolate our readings."

"So everything you've said is just a hunch?"

"No."

One of the challenges in radio astronomy was the sheer volume of incoming noise. The universe was unimaginably vast, although Marcus sometimes felt as if he could grasp a complete model of its ancient, busy clockwork in his head.

Every day, tracking one hundred million frequencies in a tiny portion of the sky, the Hoffman Square Kilometer Field listened to 800,000,000,000,000 bits of data. Their computers discarded 99.999 percent. They didn't have the capacity to retain so much information, much less analyze it. No one did. For the time being, the engineers who'd designed the array had leapt far ahead of the processing power of any computer. It was like asking a blind old man to sort through the voices in a jam-packed football stadium.

"I know this isn't how you wanted the array to make its first big splash," Marcus said. "Me neither. But even if the microflares stop, this could be an important discovery. And if the flares don't stop . . ."

Earth's sun was a remarkably mild G-class yellow star. Life had flourished on their planet because of the sun's benevolence, although the most tranquil star was still a star, a ball of hydrogen gas so massive it was collapsing under its own weight.

As the sun burned, it crumpled and pulsed. Beneath its erratic surface violence, it maintained a slower, deeper cycle from stormy to simmering and back again, a cycle from solar maximum to solar minimum. The process took roughly eleven years—but eleven years ago, everyone had been astonished. The solar maximum hadn't happened. Instead, they'd borne witness to the calmest period in recorded history.

Given the abnormally long minimum, experts predicted the oncoming max could be severe. During a solar max, the sun was more likely to produce sunspots. From these spots came solar flares. Some were bursts of X-rays and radio noise. More lethal were coronal mass ejections, clouds of charged particles much larger than Earth. Fortunately, most CMEs spun off away from their planet. Others brushed by or collided head-on, overloading electrical grids and telecommunications systems. In 2009, the crash of Air France 447 was thought to have been caused by a fluctuation in Earth's magnetic field above South America, killing two hundred passengers and crew.

Marcus gestured for Steve to take his place at the computer. "I'm sending our files to SWPC," he said. "If you want to correct anything, now's your chance."

"Okay, okay." Steve rolled his eyes, defeated.

Marcus scooted back in his chair. Steve slid over. He began studying the plots in detail while Marcus reexamined the data himself, searching for errors. There were none.

As he worked, Steve changed the subject. "How's it going with Roell?"

Marcus's son had been visiting for his summer trade-off between Marcus and Janet, so he'd come to the array with his father. But their relationship was . . . complicated.

"He's mad at me," Marcus said. "I should have left him at home."

"Sometimes you want to strangle 'em." Steve had two children himself, although they were younger than Roell, aged thirteen and eleven. "Try not to be too hard on him or yourself," he said. "I read somewhere teenage minds are different than ours. I mean physically different. Their frontal lobes haven't developed. They're more impulsive."

Marcus nodded.

At seventeen, Roell was interested in two things, girls and balls, which sounded like a bad joke, but it was an honest assessment of his son, who lived for basketball and football. Marcus couldn't help feeling exasperated. That he hadn't been more involved with Roell's school activities or Boy Scouts was a constant regret.

"Christ," Steve said, reacting to the computer screen.

Marcus felt his insides flip-flop. "You think I'm right."

Steve hesitated. He gazed at Marcus with a troubled expression. "I'm going to call my family," he said. "Then let's wake everyone up and get 'em back at the computers. We need to figure out what's going on."

Minutes later, Marcus hurried through the station's hallway. The building consisted of two prefabs joined in a T. The control room and a small lounge formed the extremities. The hallway led down the spine of the T to four compact offices and storage closets. Marcus had arranged two cots in one office, planning to bunk with Roell until Roell asked to move. A ranch house stood near the station, but Marcus and Steve hadn't wanted to impose on the site staff by evicting anyone from a real bed.

The office Roell had chosen stank of athletic shoes. He kept the window shut and his Air Jordans off, yet it wasn't necessarily a bad smell when Marcus knocked on the door and leaned in. The room smelled like a healthy young animal.

Roell sat in his sleeping bag with his iPhone, his lean body folded around the gadget as his thumb worked at its screen. In the dim room, with the blinds drawn, the phone illuminated Roell's face like a spotlight. That must have been part of the appeal. Marcus had seen enough of his son's texts to know his conversations amounted to *What up* and *Nuthin.* Nevertheless, texting seemed to fulfill the boy's need for attention.

"Come to the control room with me," Marcus said.

"I want to go home. To Mom's."

"You like computers," Marcus said. "We're networking with some of the greatest technology in astrophysics. IBEX. Hubble. Let me show you."

"Have you seen what's happening in the real world? The Chinese are bracketing our guys."

"Right."

Most of the news lately had been focused on the Marines, who'd returned to Vietnamese soil after forty years, this time in support of the communist government. Vietnam, Korea, and Japan were all potential flashpoints in America's standoff with China, but Marcus wished Roell wasn't so attracted to the drama. The boy's fascination was strange. He played at being involved in gangsta rap, imitating those self-centered posers, and yet Roell was equally excited by the new, loud, patriotic tone sweeping the country. Was that because the soldiers had body armor and guns? Or did he enjoy the primal feeling of us-against-them?

The media had created fan clubs for the war, which wasn't a war, although it made great material for TV, blogs, Twitter, and Facebook.

Facebook! The relentless updates were motivated by ad revenue and subscription rates, which Roell was too naive to realize despite wanting to be so streetwise.

More important, Roell's dyslexia didn't slow him on the net. The boy's ability to bang through his favorite sites and half-coherent text messages were proof to Marcus that he should apply himself harder in school, but they'd butted heads on the topic too many times, so Marcus tried again.

"Something's happening with our sun that we can't explain," he said. "If our data's correct, the solar wind is accelerating—"

"Nobody cares, Dad."

"They should. If the sun—"

"Check it out." Roell held up his phone to display a photo of a plucky U.S. sailor gazing at an ocean. "Our guys are in trouble, and all you care about is outer space."

Marcus stopped himself from barking a response. When he was younger, Roell had loved *Star Wars* and Bionicles. He'd read the books with his father, watched the movies, and papered his bulletin board with drawings of Jango Fett and LEGO robots.

"I'm not trying to scare you," Marcus said, trying to scare him, "but the sun shouldn't radiate like this unless it's pre-nova. Do you know what I'm talking about? The sun gives off a lot more than visible light. Among other things, it emits an outgassing of charged particles called the solar wind."

"Uh-huh."

"Here's the spooky part. The surface of the sun averages ten thousand degrees Fahrenheit—but above it, the corona runs as hot as five million. That's like a lightbulb making the air around it hotter than the glass. It violates the second law of thermodynamics. The sun's gravity is so extreme, it should pull the solar wind back into itself, but the corona superheats the wind beyond the point where gravity can hold it."

Marcus didn't add that no one fully comprehended how. Science also couldn't explain why the solar wind hit its topmost speeds. One model proposed co-rotating regions within the solar wind where expanding rings of charged particles smashed into each other, creating shock waves as fast as twenty-five hundred kilometers per second.

Even in normal conditions, the levels of ionizing radiation striking Earth could rise or fall by a factor of thousands. What would happen if the sun's magnetic field was entering a phase in which it relaxed or stiffened? Either phenomenon would allow larger, more frequent blasts of charged particles to escape . . .

"Come with me," Marcus implored his son. "At the very least, you can get your messages, okay?"

Cell transmissions weren't permitted in the area. The array was so sensitive, it registered the tiny electrical pulse generated by starting a car. Roell was free to access his social networks on their computers, which used landlines, but Marcus had insisted Roell turn off the wireless functions on his iPhone.

"Fine." The boy pulled himself from the sleeping bag.

Marcus pretended not to watch as he dressed. Jeans. Sports jersey. Roell was a great-looking kid. They'd done that much right. Roell had Janet's cheekbones, which gave him a regal look despite the loose jersey, as if he was too good for any clothes.

He had deep black skin unlike his father's. Marcus had three white ancestors in his family. They were Roell's ancestors, too, but no one would ever guess. The difference was another unspoken source of tension between them. Skin color was important among Roell's classmates and on the street.

The street was where Roell had learned his slouch. Walking through the hall, he scuffed his ninety-dollar basketball shoes on the cheap carpet. ES2's money had gone into the array. Roell grunted in disapproval at the cramped lounge with its faded couch, but he lingered in front of three Coke and snack machines rigged to dispense their goods for free. Janet had allowed him to develop a craving for sugar and caffeine loaded with chemicals that would rot his bones.

"Take two," Marcus said generously.

Roell was caught off guard. He'd expected an argument. Instead, he grinned and selected two cans of Mountain Dew.

Marcus led him into the control room, where Steve had been joined by the postdoctoral astronomers who worked on site. The four of them were gathered around one computer, murmuring together. To Marcus, their nervous energy was palpable.

"S'up," Roell asked Kym Vang, a round Laotian girl in her twenties.

Marcus intervened before Roell could embarrass them further. He sat at another computer and Roell took the chair beside him. "We're sharing our feeds with Space Command," Marcus said. "Last night I talked with an Air Force general."

"That'd be a cool job," Roell said, allowing the faintest glimpse of the wide-eyed little boy Marcus remembered. He bumped Marcus's leg with his knee, leaving Marcus pleased by the casual contact. Those few seconds were a victory. It was progress. Roell might be poking fun, but he was also proud of his awkward old genius dad.

One of ES2's primary investors was AFSPC, the United States Air Force Space Command. AFSPC and NORAD were interested in phased array technology for tracking foreign satellites. Military involvement was off-putting to some of their other supporters, like academics, but they needed the funding and gleaned new expertise from the arrangement.

To Roell, this meant Marcus was working with the most awesome of the awesome—the guys with missiles and laser beams.

"What are they saying?" Roell asked.

"Nothing yet. No one knows how to classify some of the activity we're recording. Gamma radiation is up, X-rays, ultraviolet."

"Nobody's ever seen anything like this?"

"It depends who you ask," Marcus said, downplaying his concern. "When I was your age, everyone would have said G-class stars were quiet and stable. Then twenty years ago, they found nine that regularly produce superflares."

"Like how big?"

"Like as much as a hundred million times larger than the worst flares we've seen, which is good."

"What would happen?"

"It won't. If superflares had occurred in our solar system, we'd see flood plains on Jupiter's moons where the ice melted and refroze again."

Marcus didn't add that closer to the sun, Earth's atmosphere would have been ripped away. No one believed there was life more complex than microbes on the planets orbiting S Fornacis or Groombridge 1830, two of the main sequence yellow stars known to produce superflares. Something had gone wrong inside those stars—something Marcus was afraid was occurring to a lesser degree within Earth's sun—yet he pretended he wasn't worried.

"This is just a particularly bad solar max. It will alter a lot of our assumptions, but let me tell you a secret. We don't know as much as we like to think we do."

"That's for sure," Roell said, never missing an opportunity to assert himself.

Marcus smiled ruefully. People had been counting sunspots since Kepler's and Galileo's first observations in 1607 and 1612. Since then, nearly forty cycles from solar max to solar min had been well-documented, and yet their oldest records barely established a pattern over four centuries.

Four centuries were a blink in the lifespan of a sun. Increases in the velocity and particle density of the solar wind might be normal occurrences.

"Right now our array is working double-time," Marcus said. "We're listening to the sun, too. We can't avoid it. But if we can confirm the same activity in other G-class stars, we'll have a better idea what to expect. Tweaking our software to listen to their solar winds was easy. It's combing through each signature for microflares that takes an hour or two."

"This is all you see?" Roell asked, pointing at the waterfall plots on the computer.

"Yes. That's a star system called Xi Ursae Majoris. It's not a good candidate, but it's in the sky right now, and we're being thorough."

Xi was twenty-seven light-years away, so everything they heard was twenty-seven years old, which was how long it took electromagnetic radiation to travel so far. In many ways, astronomers were like archeologists, always reaching into the past. For Marcus, that was the appeal, the patience required, the concentration and skill.

The wait was too much for Roell. He drummed his fingers on the desk, no doubt re-creating some popular new song. The noise was a distraction, but Marcus said nothing until he noticed a disapproving glance from Kym.

"Roell, stop," he said.

"What?"

"The banging. Stop."

Across the room, Steve said, "Marcus?" His voice held a note of surprise.

We've got a hit! Marcus thought. He couldn't help flashing Roell a look of triumph before he turned to Steve—but his friend pointed at the window. Fat dust tails had lifted from the dirt road leading to the array.

A car drove into the field. Another followed it. The array had no gate or security features. The cost of running several kilometers of fence around the dishes had seemed excessive, not to mention contradictory to the open, public stance of the ES2 Program.

"I didn't think anyone else was coming," Kym said.

"No," Marcus said.

"They're moving too fast."

Anyone associated with ES2 would have slowed to fifteen miles per hour. The few roads inside the array were asphalted, but twenty dishes stood along the entrance. ES2 employees knew better than to throw rocks from their tires. Nor did they get company cars. Both vehicles were new white Chevy sedans. Either the new arrivals were driving rental cars or they'd come from someplace with a motor pool.

It's not a news team, Marcus thought. *There's no broadcast van.*

"Let's see who it is," Roell said.

"Stay here," Marcus said, earning a scowl from his son. He looked at Kym. "We're feeding our data streams to the net, right?"

"Of course."

Marcus left his computer and pushed through the door of the control room into the lounge. Outside, he heard the cars pull up to the building. Their doors opened and banged shut as he exited into sunlight.

Five men and a woman had poured from the vehicles. Two of the men wore Army uniforms. The others were dressed in business suits. Marcus had never seen any of them before, but the woman greeted him by name. "Mr. Wolsinger," she said. "I'm Rebecca Drayer with the NSA."

· · · · · · · · · · · ·

SOUTH CHINA SEA

ieutenant Commander Drew Haldane stepped onto a dark catwalk on the towering edge of the USS *America*, a new Ford-class super-carrier. His watch read 00:06.

She's late, Drew thought.

Ship's time was synched with Hanoi, fourteen hours ahead of San Diego. It was the middle of the night on this side of the world. The *America* was blacked out. So were the rest of the ships in the strike group. Few stars sparkled through the cloud cover, and yet Drew couldn't ignore the huge drop from the 03 Level, no less than six stories above the waves.

The ocean clashed with the ponderous movements of the ship. The *America* was larger than many skyscrapers if those buildings were laid sideways, displacing one hundred thousand metric tons of water. Drew felt the conflict between the ocean and the *America* in the swirling updrafts of cold salt air against the hull. Damp wind brushed his hair.

He was thirty-three, hard and fit. The young woman who joined him was twenty-five. Her hourglass physique looked neat and crisp in her uniform as she ducked the storage canisters bolted overhead. This sponson—a narrow, open catwalk beneath the flight deck—was crowded with gear. It was also exposed to the weather, which made it unpopular with the crew and an ideal place to meet.

Lieutenant Junior Grade Julie Christensen stepped close to Drew, starlight gleaming in her brown hair. She smelled like clean laundry, a good, fresh, feminine smell.

But this wasn't a romantic interlude.

"The satellites are up and down, sir," she whispered. "We're getting a lot of static. That's why you went red. Most of the conventional systems pulled through, but special ops were the first to go."

"That's scary as hell."

"Yes, sir."

"How much of the solar activity is real?"

"I don't know. I'm sorry, sir."

Sunspots routinely disrupted global communications, but military satellites were far more expensive than civilian equipment and hardened against solar flares. Drew wasn't buying it. He assumed the sunspots reported by the Armed Forces weather service were a rusty lie to minimize any appearance of weakness.

He said, "Did the Chinese launch anything new?"

"No, sir."

That means they already have a pulse weapon in orbit, he thought. What if they were targeting U.S. frequencies specifically? The best estimates he'd heard put the U.S. military at least a decade ahead of China with narrowband transmissions. China shouldn't know about ROMEO at all.

Could they have hit the right frequencies by accident?

Drew didn't look at Christensen as he considered his options. They weren't supposed to be friends, and their meeting was outside normal protocol. He was an aviator. She was a communications officer on the flag bridge.

If they were caught, it might blow their cover. Tonight was their first encounter in person. Drew had read her file back in the States, nothing more. The two of them had no relationship except that when his sat phone went dark, dropping its link, Christensen was his fail-safe to re-establish contact with the Pentagon.

Nevertheless, Drew was a warrior and an athlete, extra-attuned to his body and his surroundings. That he felt attracted to this bright young woman was predictable—but from the way she stood too near, her gaze flickering from his eyes to his mouth, he thought she felt it, too.

They were paired in a unique way. Aside from himself and Christensen, Drew had been told only one other ROMEO agent was aboard the *America*, which meant the three of them were alone on this foreign sea. They needed to protect each other.

"We were picking up a lot of interference today," he said. "New stuff. I think the Chinese have a ground-based weapon plus whatever they've got in orbit."

He had a flash drive and handed it to Christensen down low against her hip. Her gaze connected with his as their fingers touched.

"You can send this for me?" he asked. She would need to be careful when she uploaded his data through the ship's normal transmissions.

She nodded. "Yes, sir."

"We'll need to meet again."

"I can get away whenever you want me," she said.

Good, Drew thought. With her neck-length brown hair and freckled nose, Christensen was achingly cute. Her eyes were enormous hazel pools in the dark. Drew glanced away, although beyond the catwalk was utter darkness. He didn't need to see the strike group to know the ships were there, like a floating city.

Within the *America*, the *Harry S. Truman*, and the carriers' support craft, hundreds of men and women reached in every direction through radar, sonar, and other sensors, creating an electronic umbrella around the fleet.

The umbrella had been compromised. The Chinese attack on U.S. satellites was more than a prelude to war. It was the first shot. And if China could selectively hit the U.S. intelligence agencies' encrypted communications net, they must also have the capacity to paralyze the strike group in a wink.

What else can I do? Drew thought.

He'd been sent to Vietnam to act as additional eyes watching for new weapons tech in the battlefield: bio, nano, cyber, pulse.

The race for EMPs had become a top priority. Electromagnetic pulses were an unstoppable method of crippling technology-dependent militaries. Every circuit and computer chip was a weak point. Most of their systems were hardened, though not EMP-proof.

Both sides could generate an electromagnetic pulse with a nuke, but missile launches were impossible to hide. Even if one side managed to outwit the other, nuclear attacks would create untold amounts of fallout, most likely enough to poison both sides of the world. Clean EMP weapons like high-powered microwaves or loop antenna devices were the answer.

"I—" Drew said.

He heard boot steps on the deck.

Christensen pressed herself against him, stretching up to cover his mouth with her own. She startled Drew. Then he wrapped his arms around her.

She was pretending they were lovers. Drew wasn't above making the most of their predicament. He ran his hand down her side into the curve of her waist as they kissed. She didn't fight him. He thought she was smiling.

Sexual relationships were forbidden. Four thousand men and women couldn't be locked together without some mischief, so fraternization between two sailors might be overlooked on land, in port. Good order and discipline were the rule at sea—but smooching was a lesser crime than espionage.

The boot steps walked closer, then stopped. "Hey, break it up," said another man, a chief petty officer making rounds. He passed a red-lensed flashlight over their torsos, yet deliberately avoided their faces. He didn't want to see who they were.

Drew turned to the CPO as Christensen slipped away. "Sorry," Drew said.

The CPO looked at Drew's flight suit, a green one-piece made of fire-resistant Nomex. Pilots never wore anything else. The suit identified Drew as one of the elite groups aboard the ship, and, while the CPO wouldn't report them, he might gossip.

Christensen was gone. The CPO had done the gentlemanly thing.

"Appreciate it," Drew said. Then he ducked inside through one open hatch and another, moving into the dry, recycled air of the ship.

The steel corridors were empty. Christensen hadn't waited. Drew headed aft because she would have gone forward. Then a man rounded a corner behind him and four more appeared in the direction he was walking. Had they seen her?

Drew was due to launch. He'd follow up with Christensen later. The wardroom was also on the 03 Level, and he beelined for it, making a hole for the other sailors with the ease of habit. They turned their shoulders and passed without touching. Their footsteps were light on the white-tiled deck.

The voices behind him were also quiet, although Navy personnel learned to work and sleep through anything. The catapults and thundering jets on the flight deck could be heard throughout the ship. Even so, the best sailors tried not to disturb each other.

Drew's guilt felt like a brand. He and Christensen were Navy in every way, loyal and competent, and yet they'd deceived the good people around them.

If the other crew members were the ship's blood, he was a white blood cell. They had the same purpose, but he was fundamentally different. These were men and women who would die for each other. They were a team.

I should warn them.

Unfortunately, he had his orders. Christensen probably outranked him, too. She wore j.g. insignia, but she was the one on the bridge. ROMEO would want her to call the shots even if she said *sir* to Drew.

She kissed me. Why? We could have been holding hands or hugging when that dude came along. But she kissed me.

Feeling harried and distracted—and glad—Drew entered the wardroom's familiar noise. Despite its low ceiling, the wardroom was a wide space with faux wood paneling, real linen, silverware, and dozens of aviators and crew. On an HDTV tuned to ESPN Classic, the Chargers and Steelers slugged it out.

"There he is! That's the guy!"

The brash voice of Lieutenant Ted Buegeleisen caught Drew before he reached the buffet. *This is the last thing I need,* he thought, but he allowed himself to be waved over.

"You love me, you love him," Buegeleisen declared. Sharing his table were two female helicopter pilots. One was brunette, the other sandy-blond. She wore a ring, which hadn't stopped Buegeleisen from chatting her up. It never did.

"Bugle" was Drew's friend and partner, again on multiple levels. Drew flew a two-man EA-18G. Bugle was his electronic warfare officer and a ROMEO agent, a tall, happy guy who considered himself catnip with the ladies. In reality, Bugle was a six-foot-three horse-faced dork. Drew had difficulty imagining a less likely prospect for a secret agent.

"Did you know this maniac saved four people from a deck fire?" Bugle asked the women.

"How's mid rats tonight?" Drew said. Going on one in the morning, they were served midnight rations left over from dinner, but Bugle was not to be deterred.

"It's true," Bugle said. "You're looking at him. A few years ago we had a fire on the *Lincoln* when some idiot was sneaking cigarettes by the fuel hoses."

Drew left their table to grab a tray, two hamburgers, and a scoop of canned pineapple. He wished he was more like Bugle, fuzz in the brain, peaceful at heart, although he realized some of his disquiet was purely physiological.

The *America* and the *Truman* split every twenty-four hours into two "fly days" of thirteen hours each, creating some overlap at midnight and at noon. Drew's launch cycle was the second. He expected to fly from two a.m. to four a.m., but it was tough to eat when his belly thought it should be asleep and even tougher to sleep when his body thought it should be in the sun. Three weeks ago, Drew had been stationed in Guantanamo. Five weeks ago, he'd been in Seoul. His biorhythms were more out of whack than those of the crew members who'd already been with the *America* in San Diego.

Could that explain the tick of anxiety in his head? Despite everything he'd said to Christensen, he had no evidence of a Chinese attack.

"This cowboy ran into the fire four times!" Bugle said as Drew returned with his tray.

Christensen. Drew recalled the warmth of her body as he sat down and dug into his chow. If she was like him, she was lonely. ROMEO training meant less downtime, less dates, less family, less everything.

He admired her dedication. Twenty-five years old and a ROMEO agent . . . What had caused her to give up any semblance of a normal life? Were her motives like his own? Drew hadn't gotten over his sister's death—maybe he never would—but personal scars weren't the main reason people chose to serve.

"Every time he comes back with someone else!" Bugle said. "We've got two jets on fire and smoke as thick as water, but he keeps going back in."

"No way," the brunette said.

"Bugle makes it sound good," Drew said. "The smoke wasn't as thick as water."

"It was like the Amazon!" Bugle insisted.

Drew laughed. *He's an idiot, but he's my idiot,* he thought. Bugle's blabbermouth style was the perfect disguise. The two of them had been last-minute additions to the crew, yet they'd made fast friends across the ship with Bugle taking the lead on the social scene.

ROMEO was a clandestine division of the Defense Intelligence Agency, a hand-picked group trained to blend with standard forces. Bugle claimed that was why they were code-named after the greatest secret lover of all time. ROMEO wasn't an acronym. Bugle said they were supposed to get intimate with their shipmates. Drew believed there were similar groups called ALPHA, BRAVO, and so on.

"I'm sorry," he said. "We need to fly."

"We'll see you later!" Bugle said. Both women chuckled at the eagerness in his face.

For Drew, the waiting was the hardest part, waiting and wondering if he could rely on anyone else. Once he'd quit accepting things at face value, life had grown complicated in a hurry. Maybe they were all spies.

As he and Bugle bussed their trays, six men rose from other tables. Would he know if any of them were Central Intelligence or National Security operatives?

A pilot named Giles jostled Bugle's arm, faking the tough guy. "Watch it, fuckface," Giles said, and Bugle responded brightly with "No thanks!"

Everyone handled the anticipation differently. Giles and Bugle fed off each other's noise. Other men turned inward, like Drew.

The eight of them crossed the ship into the PR shop, an oversized storage locker lined with naked pipe and conduit. Giles cranked the boom box as they suited up. Drew tried to let the rapid-fire guitars erase his mind. It was better to be loud—better to be amped.

Christensen will have new orders once we're back, he thought. *If we make it back. China has decent aircraft, and a lot of 'em. It won't be like pounding the shit out of Iraq.*

If a pulse weapon burns our planes . . .

Drew grabbed his flight helmet and filed into the ready room, where the squadron duty officer handed over a weight chit. Drew scrawled his name before selecting a 9mm Beretta and two spare clips from the table.

"Next time I want a bazooka," Bugle said.

"You *are* a bazooka," Drew said, a rare crack for him, and Bugle laughed and punched his shoulder.

Every day Bugle wanted something different, a machine gun, a flamethrower, a fast horse. Clowning let him shrug off the superstition that they might need their sidearms.

A pistol was ludicrous compared to the missiles carried by an EA-18G, more so given the 20mm Vulcan cannon and five thousand pounds of ordnance on a normal F/A-18 fighter. No man would need his Beretta unless he was shot down in enemy territory, which was why they were also handed blood chits—waterproof sheets printed with the American flag and, in the spidery symbols of Vietnamese, Simple Mandarin, Complex Mandarin, and Cantonese, a short phrase that translated as *If you help me, my government will repay you.*

Four of their eight guys were spares. The *America* would launch two 18Gs piloted by Drew and Giles for their mission, launch a fighter escort in case either of the first two planes developed problems, then either recover the fighter or farm him out to another cycle. The fourth two-man team was an on-deck spare. Combat operations were predicated on the assumption of casualties, and yet as Drew led their group from the ready room, he found clarity at last.

They ascended behind the tower that held the flag bridge. In the dim shine of the sodium lights, Drew traded fist jabs with Giles and Wade as they walked to their jets.

"Rock 'em," Giles said.

"Beautiful night," Bugle added, and Drew nodded, breathing the sweet stink of jet fuel. He wasn't aware that he was grinning.

The ROMEO shrinks said Drew's self-assessment was too simple, but he thought he knew himself. He was the older brother of a girl raised by a single dad, an uneducated joe who'd worked fifty-hour weeks to make time-and-a-half in a paper plant in St. Paul, Minnesota. Their father was a good man. He'd destroyed his hands and his back to provide for them. Drew had tried to be the dad, too, cooking and folding laundry, watching over Brigit's homework, her boyfriends, and her ambitions to play soccer and piano.

The Navy had become his surrogate family, although the ROMEO profilers were right. His loyalty was more than the desire for a home. Drew felt more than he wanted to, remembered more than he wanted to, and years ago he'd hoped the Navy might be a way to toughen up and prove himself.

Now he was lying to his friends for all the right reasons. It was crucial to prevent intercepts and to preserve the status of shadow forces like ROMEO. If not for his double role, he wouldn't have learned about the threat of a pulse weapon—but because of ROMEO, he was forced to withhold his information.

That felt like betrayal.

He hated it.

5

· · · · · · · · · · · ·

LOS ANGELES

Partway through her media event, Emily had a death grip on the podium and swallowed again to relax her throat. She hated public speaking. DNAllied's media director had done a nice job, promising the major television, print, and web outlets the scoop of the week. The hall was packed with news teams.

Was her mom watching on TV?

"We share ninety-eight percent of our DNA with chimpanzees," Emily said, "and ninety-nine point seven with Neanderthal man, which makes them an excellent sounding board for comparative genomics."

Laura stood with P.J. in the back of the conference room. Uncharacteristically, Emily avoided her sister's gaze.

"*Homo sapiens, Homo neanderthalensis*, and chimpanzees are similar creatures, yet our cousins adapted to the same world in different ways," she said. "Some of their adaptations are less effective. Some are more. Among chimpanzees, for example, the incidence of most forms of cancer is twenty percent less than in *Homo sapiens*, whereas we believe *Homo neanderthalensis* was more susceptible than our own species."

Emily paused one last time. She'd brought both sets of notes to the podium. This was where the two diverged.

Was her nephew worth more to her than unborn strangers? What about the thousands of other families with autistic children who needed help?

Emily decided she had to save them first. She would read the company version. Even this speech was loaded with hazards. She didn't want to sound tactless or cold-blooded, but she expected controversy.

Lifting her chin like a boxer, Emily said, "Chimpanzees are also far less likely to develop cognitive disorders. Their resistance to these disorders includes Alzheimer's disease, dementia, bipolar disorders . . . and autism."

Some people stirred among the media, such as the business writer from *Newsweek* and the woman from the local ABC affiliate. Emily had been warned that a few in particular would resist her findings. This was more than a hot-button issue. She was playing with evolution and some of the most incendiary questions of their time.

The subject was also intensely personal for her, not only because of Laura and P.J. Because of her mother. Maintaining family tradition, Jana Flint had raised her girls in accordance with the Catholic Church, and she didn't always accept Emily's career choice. No one could say or do anything that would hurt Emily more than Laura's disapproval, but she'd been on thin ice with her mother for years.

Six reporters had their hands up. One man asked, "Miz Flint, are you implying—"

Emily tried to stay on track. "We want to use those differences to our advantage," she said. "At DNAllied, we've developed and certified an extensive database of specific gene sequences that will lead to individualized cures in millions of people."

"Are you implying there's a connection between cancer and intelligence?" the reporter asked.

"It's not that simple."

"But you just—"

"Okay, please," the media director said. "Doctor Flint is happy to answer questions. Let's take them one at a time." He pointed away from the aggressive reporter to someone who looked like a safer bet, a man with sleepy eyes and a mustache.

The new man said, "Has there really been any research done into chimpanzees with Alzheimer's? Or depression? How would you know if a monkey has memory loss or was bipolar?"

"The same as with people," Emily said. "Several well-designed behavioral studies have tracked both domesticated chimpanzees and those in the wild."

Another reporter said, "Will your database be made public?"

"Yes," Emily said. "DNAllied believes this information is too valuable to families all over the world to sell or license it."

"How much will these gene therapies cost?"

"That I don't know," Emily said.

The first reporter stood up. "Miz Flint, Miz Flint, this therapy, you're going to use chimpanzee and Neanderthal DNA in people?"

"I'm not involved in the medical aspects of—"

"Isn't that what we're talking about? Splicing animal genes into human beings?"

"Yes," Emily said as the lights flickered.

Everyone looked up. Several of the camera and sound crews frowned at their equipment. Emily already had a stomach full of butterflies. Now her thoughts turned paranoid.

What's happening? she thought, and yet she soldiered on.

"Microscopic amounts of clean, tailored genetic material can be used to provide people with healthier lives," she said. "It's sterile and painless, like a flu shot. There's no reason to be afraid. In any case, our gene therapies are somewhere in the future. It might be years. What we've accomplished so far is to establish a broad knowledge base of disease-prone and corrective sequences."

"But your database could be used to screen for those disease-prone sequences right now, couldn't it?" the reporter asked. "And, uh, selecting children based on how they score?"

Selecting was code for *aborting*, Emily realized. Numbly, she hoped her dad hadn't been able to find the right channel in her parents' house in Santa Barbara. Otherwise her mom had probably fallen out of her chair.

"I'm sorry, who are you with?" she asked. She wanted the reporter to say FOX News or *Christian Family Digest*, anything to taint his accusations with the mark of the religious right. He ignored her, scribbling in his notebook as the media director signaled Emily and leaned toward the podium.

"Let's focus on some of the incredible technology Doctor Flint has been using," the media director said.

Emily stepped back with relief.

"Projects of this scope often begin with Illumina sequencing equipment and Fibonacci structural mass spectrometers," the media director said. "Our first goal is to . . ."

Emily barely heard, looking at the back of the room.

Staring at the belligerent reporter, Laura's spectacular blue eyes were drawn into angry slits. Emily thought she also saw disgust in the face of a female reporter. Did this woman know someone who was sick or handicapped? If she was a science writer, she probably dealt with goons all the time.

It must be aggravating to watch these events taken over by people with repressive agendas, Emily thought.

Her mother was among those who called themselves pro-life. Despite having married Emily's father, who was less devout, almost indifferent to organized religion, Jana Flint opposed abortion rights and also spoke out against contraception. Maybe her ardency on these topics had been fueled by her shame at falling in love with someone outside the Church.

Emily's faith was a quieter thing. She didn't believe what she was doing was wrong or evil. If every speck in the universe was God's creation, studying His workmanship must be part of the mystery. Free will and intelligence weren't traps to avoid. They were gifts. And yet . . .

What if other people used her data in ugly ways?

Finally, the press conference was over. Ray and the media director wanted to compare notes in a private office, but Emily asked for a minute in the kitchenette with her sister.

"You did the right thing, Em. You really did." Laura hugged both Emily and P.J.

Inside, Emily felt as stiff as the boy. *I hope you're right,* she thought, wondering how many women would give birth to autistic children while DNAllied suppressed her vaccine.

Breathing in Laura's perfume, she remembered the prenatal visits to which she'd accompanied her sister. Neither of them doubted Laura's baby would be perfect. The worst health concerns in their family were three aunts with high blood pressure. That hadn't stopped the OB/GYN from encouraging Laura to undergo standard screening for conditions such as Down syndrome or spina bifida. Unprompted, the OB/GYN had also given them the hard sell with a story about her cousin whose son had Down's.

"He was always happy," the doctor said, "but even as an adult, he couldn't tie his own shoes. He needed constant supervision and medical care until he died at thirty-eight."

The OB/GYN's opinion was firm. Nonviable children should be aborted. The screens weren't able to test for ASD, however—not yet—much less determine which children might be high-functioning versus those who would be low. If those predictions became reliable, where did anyone draw the line?

I can't imagine our lives without P.J., Emily thought, and yet Laura and Greg were better off than most parents. They lived in West Hollywood, a golf course community where they owned a house with a yard, unlike the cramped apartment complex where Emily lived with Chase in Pasadena. Although they easily covered their expenses for physical therapy and special ed, the stress of having an autistic son had added to the fine wrinkles and dark, permanent smudges of exhaustion around Laura's eyes. Too many families didn't have the money for special assistance.

Maybe I really should steal my data for the guys at the University of Texas, she thought. *They can say they developed those results on their own. Simultaneous discovery. It happens all the time. DNAllied won't be able to track it back to me.*

With a prenatal vaccine, no one would suffer—not the children, not the parents—but Emily didn't want anyone else to refine her work.

Her possessiveness wasn't a matter of her ego or her guilt.

She wanted to keep a secret.

Her statistical models held the prospect of something more controversial than any vaccine. In comparing the protein expression patterns of *Homo sapiens* to those of Neanderthals and chimpanzees, Emily had uncovered a disconcerting trend she hadn't shared with anyone at DNAllied, much less Ray or the board.

What would her sister think?

Emily had found a genetic time bomb buried deep within modern man. The fuse was burning. And she wasn't sure if making it public would do more harm than good.

Letting go of P.J., Laura smiled at her son. Then she paused. She hugged Emily again and kissed her cheek, misinterpreting the worry on Emily's face. "Don't be upset about that reporter," Laura said.

Emily ducked her eyes. "I won't."

"Some people are always going to be upset," Laura said. "That's their problem, not yours. You're helping children. Never forget it."

"Thank you," Emily said. But her heart was unhappy.

I still haven't told you the whole truth, she thought.

6

· · · · · · · · · · · ·

NORTHERN CALIFORNIA

The noon sun glared through the windows as Marcus walked from the control room into the lounge. Roell and Agent Drayer followed him. Marcus turned on her, hoping to push her farther from their computers with his voice.

"This is illegal and stupid," he said. "Our lawyers will file an injunction."

He'd hardly slept since driving to the array three days ago. His nerves were tight, and his blood felt like dirty water. Given the choice, he would have concealed his frustration from Roell, but he refused to let his son out of his sight with armed men posted in the control room and the parking lot.

He'd learned Agent Drayer was a desk jockey like himself. Her specialty was signal analysis, which was why the National Security Agency had sent her to the array. They expected Drayer to verify Marcus's readings and to ascertain whether or not he was faking his data. Her fellow agents were also analysts and techs. The two Army soldiers had been sent to quash any inkling of causing trouble.

"We can fight you in court," Marcus said.

"Mr. Wolsinger," Drayer replied, always *Mr. Wolsinger.* She was formal and dry. "Unless you have something new to—"

"Our lawyers have contacted the media. Thousands of our supporters worldwide are posting about your takeover on the net."

"I understand."

Between the two of them, Marcus and Roell outweighed Drayer by three hundred pounds, but she wore her authority like it was sewn into her dark suit. She reminded him of Janet. Drayer was white, in her late thirties, tall and thin, but Janet's composure had always been his favorite thing about her even when she used it against him.

Wrestling with his anger, Marcus took a step toward Drayer. He would protect the array with force if he was able. She must have seen the impulse in how his posture changed. Her eyes widened. So did Roell's.

Marcus treasured the excitement in Roell's expression. The boy was impressed with his father, so Marcus was louder than necessary for Roell's benefit.

"The work we're doing now is pivotal," he said. "By shutting us down—"

"You're in operation."

"If we can't share our data with other observatories, it's inefficient and—"

"Mr. Wolsinger. You have your phone lines, and your assistant seems to be coordinating fine with other installations."

"She's wasting time she could direct elsewhere."

"It will have to do. Our country is nearly at war."

Drayer had a habit of lifting her chin when she spoke. The gesture was superior and irritating, and Marcus gritted his teeth.

"There are tactical advantages in hoarding our intelligence," Drayer said. "The more data we gather about what's happening, the better we can deal with it, and it would be irresponsible to share our information in ways that can be intercepted by the enemy."

"You can't hide the sun!"

"China doesn't have the facilities we do."

Marcus's defeat was another feeling that reminded him of Janet. It was linked with every humiliation and loss from their divorce. "Are we prisoners here?" he asked.

"No. If your staff wants to leave—"

"We're staying. We *built* this place," he said, letting Drayer see his possessiveness. Then he said, "My son should go home."

"What?" Roell said, "Dad, I don't—"

"You're going."

"I can help! You said I could help."

Now he wants to stay, Marcus thought. The arrival of real-life government agents must have been the greatest thing that ever happened to Roell, but he didn't want Roell mixed up in legal issues. He was acutely aware of Drayer's gaze moving back and forth between them, analyzing Marcus's failures and Roell's disobedience.

"You're going," Marcus said.

"Shit." Roell stamped out of the lounge, banging down the hallway.

Marcus glanced at Drayer. She nodded slightly, either confirming her permission for Roell to leave or acknowledging Marcus's quandary. Did she have children? She wore a wedding band, although it was smooth platinum and lacked a diamond, not even a chip, being utterly functional like everything about her. Even if Drayer was a mom, she couldn't guess what she'd done to him.

Marcus had won this fight, protecting his son, but he wasn't sure at what cost to their relationship.

Roell wasted no time throwing his stuff into two duffel bags. Marcus reached to take one, but Roell grabbed everything and stalked back into the hall. Marcus followed.

Outside, Roell paused. An Army corporal stood on the ramp for handicapped access. Sunlight gleamed from the endless dishes of the array, and, much closer, from the cars lined against the station.

"Call me when you're at your mom's," Marcus said.

Roell walked to a green Toyota Prius, dumped in his bags, and climbed into the passenger seat. Marcus knew it was wrong to call Janet after their son was en route, depriving her of the chance to protest. What if she had plans for drinks or dinner with her boyfriend?

The main thing was Roell's well-being.

"Hurry back," Marcus said to the driver. The Prius belonged to one of their postdocs, a white kid named Chuck. Chuck wanted to stay, too, but Marcus had said he'd consider it a personal favor, and Janet's home in Palo Alto was barely four hours away.

"See you tonight," Chuck said.

Marcus waved, although Roell wasn't looking. His gut hurt from sleep deprivation and coffee. He needed food, but he didn't know when he would ever sleep.

He returned to the office where Roell had bunked. No one else should get stuck with cleaning, although he realized tidying up was also a way to say goodbye.

Behind him, Agent Drayer knocked on the open door.

"Mr. Wolsinger," she said. "We have a call from back East."

Why had she come instead of one of his assistants? Was she was trying to be courteous? They would be working alongside each other for the foreseeable future, so Marcus supposed he should accept her olive branch. "Let's go," he said, brushing past.

They walked down the hall together, uncomfortable and silent.

Marcus had spent years feeling bitter after his divorce, but, for once, there was no solace in delving into his work. When he reached the control room, he found Steve, Kym, and one of Drayer's men. Her other agents were in the adjacent room with the servers. They'd started to install network monitoring software that Kym muttered was a jack, as in *hijack*. Soon the NSA would be a permanent presence, limiting their outside contacts and recording every move.

Nevertheless, Steve was bursting at the seams. "Marcus!" he said. "You need to see this."

Across the room, Marcus caught a glance from Kym. Drayer went straight to Steve, making certain she didn't miss anything, while Marcus pretended to yawn and let Drayer pass.

Kym took him aside with a whisper. "Why are you reading about ice caps and lava beds?" she asked.

Marcus's heart leapt. "I'm not," he said.

"Uh." Kym's dark gaze didn't move to Drayer, and Marcus liked her for being so perceptive. She said, "We just got twenty-six file attachments from NOAA."

"Delete them for me."

"Even if I did, everything stays on the servers, where these guys'll find 'em as soon as they check your traffic. Sorry. But I saved the files to a thumb drive."

"Good enough. I'll tell you about it later," Marcus said, offering Kym his full confidence.

She smiled before he hurried across the room. Maybe she'd bought him some time. Possibly he could bargain with it. He needed to regain control.

Joining Steve and Drayer, Marcus said, "What've we got?"

Steve didn't let their tension affect his enthusiasm. "Goddard's reporting similar microflares from half a dozen F- and G-stars, and they're barely a quarter of the way through their logs," Steve said. "We're sure to see more."

"What does that mean?" Drayer asked as Marcus said, "What's the longest span?"

"Eight years," Steve said.

"One of you needs to explain what that means," Drayer said.

"I'd like to make several calls," Marcus told her.

"First you talk to me." Drayer answered too quickly—she didn't mean it—but he would try to hold her to their bargain when he wanted to contact Australia and Japan.

"Show her," he said urgently.

Steve tapped at his keyboard. The smattering of instant messaging windows on his screen were blotted out by eleven hi-res images, each of which began to jerk through its own slide show. Most of the images looked like speckled blobs of white Jell-O set against backgrounds as black as obsidian, although a few were distorted like jellyfish or wind-swept ghosts. No matter their shape, every image expanded or fell inward during the short, repeating video loops.

The sight caused an unpleasant, forlorn emotion in Marcus. He felt as appalled as when the doctors explained his mother was sick.

He found his voice. "We have a friend at Goddard, the Goddard Space Flight Center near Baltimore," he said. "That's one of the places where they perform ground control for the Hubble Telescope."

Drayer pointed at the screen. "Those are stars," she said.

"Correct. Goddard's been crunching data on thousands of main sequence G-class stars like our own."

"Why do they look like bubbles?"

"Those are heliospheres. There's one around our sun, too." Marcus cupped his hands as if holding Roell's basketball. "The solar wind creates a sphere of gas that pushes out past Pluto into deep space. We know a lot more about it since NASA put up the Interstellar Boundary Explorer. They've been mapping the termination shock, where it stops."

"Okay," Drayer said. "So what?"

"It's collapsing."

Once activated in high Earth orbit in 2008, IBEX had required a mere six months to map the heliosphere, which stretched twenty billion miles across. IBEX completed its initial run so swiftly because the storms within the termination shock produced energetic neutral atoms, many of which sped back to the sun.

The IBEX team had expected to see variations in the particle flux. The heliosphere was no more a creaseless ball than was the sun itself, but they'd predicted these variations would be minor. Instead, they'd discovered an enormous rift where the heliosphere was buckling under interstellar pressures.

In 2008, this dent had been 50 percent deeper than anyone could explain. Years later, it had continued to sink inward as soft spots appeared in other places.

Some of the collapse could be attributed to the long solar minimum. With any decrease in the solar wind, the heliosphere would weaken—but after closely analyzing the rift's rate of decay, IBEX was able to put a rough date on its origin.

The heliosphere had been shrinking for thirty thousand years.

"Look at the candidates they sent us," Marcus said. "The heliospheres of these stars are rapidly bleeding away or expanding. There's an undeniable pattern."

"Why hasn't anyone seen it before?" Drayer said.

"They have. We didn't think it applied to us."

"Aren't those stars identical to the sun?"

"More or less. But thousands of others aren't exhibiting microflares."

"We don't know what's happening yet," Steve said.

"I think we do," Marcus said. "I think there were times when our sun burned more powerfully than anyone's realized, and it's about to start again. Now."

Drayer touched the cell phone on her belt as if to call for help, perhaps subconsciously.

"Don't let him scare you," Steve said. "In stellar terms, *now* doesn't mean right now. It means during the next ten thousand years. Even if he's right, the sun won't change for centuries or millennia."

"What if it does?" Marcus said. "If the solar max increases drastically, it could last for years. You can't argue with their data."

Steve laughed. "It's revolutionary, and the whole phenomenon will have your name on it—our name," he said, sweeping his hand through the air as if to include everyone who'd ever worked for ES2.

Kym was typing at her keyboard, but she looked at Steve, then turned to Marcus. From her expression, she was clearly conflicted. She wanted to share Steve's excitement. But there was also fear in her eyes.

Marcus felt the same cold dread.

In a few minutes, if he could sneak a phone call, he'd warn Janet to meet Roell and stock up on food and bottled water. Batteries. She should pull as much cash as possible, too, and fill the tank in her car. What else?

Sunblock. Hats. People would strip the shelves of both as soon as the first TV interview said this morning's flares might become a way of life.

Marcus wished he'd kept Roell with him, but Roell would be safer at Janet's, wouldn't he? There were no doctors within thirty miles of the array, much less police or grocery stores. He felt a cold glint of dismay as he considered how many people might require medical help.

"Who are you reporting to?" he asked Drayer.

"Director Schories."

Marcus didn't know who that was. "Does he report to the president?"

"Yes."

"Call him. Call everyone. If we're lucky, we still have time to brace for this thing."

7

· · · · · · · · · · · ·

SOUTH CHINA SEA

rew's headset crackled with Bugle's loud voice: "Watch that turbulence!"

"I got it."

"Their fuel line's jumping like a snake!"

"I got it." Drew wrestled his jet into position against the rough predawn air, his engines howling. Overhead, the larger bulk of a KC-45 tanker bobbed in the same pockets of chop. On this side of the world, it was 4:38 a.m. Predawn was typically a quiet hour, but today the atmosphere was in turmoil. Trailing from the tanker's port wing, fifty feet of semi-rigid hose snapped in the wind.

Drew failed to connect. "Damn it," he said, peeling back.

"You're losing your touch," Bugle marveled. He was speaking on their ICS, the internal communications system. Bugle sat behind Drew in their EA-18G, a constant voice in his ear like a guardian angel— or a devil.

The sun formed a yellow spark on the ocean's blue horizon. Far below, to the north, the contours of Vietnam and China were a green-

and-brown horseshoe of coastlines against the multi-hued sea. White sand. Green surf. The darker expanses of deep water were spotted with the wake lines of tiny ships.

Drew might have scrubbed his refueling effort or delayed until they could climb to higher elevation, but they were already at 30,000 feet, an altitude that was normally above the weather, and both aircraft were moving at 300 miles per hour, a speed that let them slice through normal turbulence. Strike control hadn't wanted to call off the KC-45 that flew out of Cam Rhan Bay with two fighter escorts. The *America* had fewer planes in the sky than it needed, so everyone was running double cycles. Drew needed to return to his sector.

Equally pressing were the orange bulbs on his warning and caution lights panel. His heading indicator and his artificial horizon were out, systems failures that had popped up since he'd launched three hours ago. Drew could fly his EA-18G without either system, but the malfunctions could be lethal if there were more.

How much abuse can she take? he thought.

An aircraft was always a *she*, a lover, not a tool. Their ladies were suffering. Three F/A-18s and another 18G had been downgraded from flight-ready on the *America*. Twice that many were undergoing emergency repairs. Various small burnouts were disabling their jets.

Steady, he thought, rising to a trail position off the tanker's port wing. Unfortunately, the big tanker was doing everything except holding still.

In flight, an 18's fuel tanks were accessed by a probe extending forward from the starboard side of the aircraft. It was all very sexual. The pilot was supposed to slip the probe's nozzle into a basket at the end of the tanker's refueling hose. This morning Drew felt like a rhino lumbering after a butterfly. He brought his jet up, then banked left and up again to chase the whipping hose—

The probe fit into the basket with a *clunk* that he felt throughout the aircraft. The amber light on the fuel pod turned green. His fuel gauge began to rise as JP5 rushed through the line into his jet and the tanks in his wings.

"Nice work," Bugle said.

Another E/A-18G held position on Drew's left, his wingman, 501, crewed by Giles and Wade. Set above and behind the tanker were its escorts, two USAF F-35s. Both types of aircraft were narrow, clean-edged darts, each one racked with more firepower and computers than many Third World cities.

Drew felt a twinge of pride at the sight. Comparing their jets to Chinese MiGs was like putting a Ferrari alongside a Subaru. *But that's if our aircraft are in one piece,* he thought. *We've got to find China's EMP and shut it down. They're beating us without even trying . . .*

The green light on the fuel pod went amber. Drew detached and slid to the right wing of the tanker, buffeted by the wind.

Meanwhile, the guys in 501 rose for their own refueling effort.

Drew thumbed the ICS. "Your turn to work again," he told Bugle. "We need to find something for Julie."

"Christensen," Bugle said.

"Say again?"

"Yesterday you were calling her Christensen, dude."

"Shut up," Drew said, thinking, *Shit. He's right.* When had he stopped thinking of her as *Christensen* and allowed her to become *Julie* in his head?

The sky was definitely brighter now. The sun would light them up in minutes, which was good. They couldn't trust their scopes. Phantoms and blind spots filled their radar, but in daylight, Drew could see for miles.

The Carrier Strike Group was a spectacular sight in the South China Sea, a nearly landlocked body of water between Vietnam, China, the Philippines, and Malaysia. Worse, China's primary naval base was on Hainan Island, a broad hunk of rock protruding from China's southwestern coast like a fist aimed at Vietnam's side.

Not every ship was friendly. The coastlines were crowded with dhows—fishing boats, civilian craft, and ferries—any of which could be packed with explosives. Nor were the Chinese warships far away. The enemy had walked three of their destroyers to the edge of the U.S. strike group, almost daring to intermingle the two fleets.

If there was shooting, it would be a meat grinder.

Julie was aboard the most valuable target.

She was a distraction he couldn't afford—a distraction he was glad to own. It had been too long since he'd felt like he might belong to anyone except Bugle and their fun, well-established friendship.

"Five Oh One's complete," Giles radioed through a burr of static.

Drew slid to starboard as his wingman came off the tanker. To Bugle, he said, "Giles just bought us another three hours, so let's make something of it. I want a hard read."

"I'm not out here to piss in a hose," Bugle said, referring to their relief tubes.

The Navy spent upward of sixty million dollars apiece on their aircraft, yet hadn't come up with anything more comfortable for a toilet. *Leave it to Bugle to talk up the experience,* Drew thought, shaking his head in disgust and admiration.

Could I ever be more like him?

They dove toward the *America*'s northeast perimeter. Below, the ocean was torn by whitecaps. Drew scanned the dawn sky as well as watching his screens. A normal 18G was modified with one million dollars in electronic warfare systems. With every mission, Bugle also jacked in two ROMEO black boxes worth an additional two million dollars.

Three million bucks hadn't been enough. They didn't have conclusive evidence. Meanwhile, the world media was peppered with news about the solar max. Power outages had occurred in Denver and New York. Apparently it was a natural event, but Drew refused to accept this explanation. His superiors didn't, either. They were trained to think the worst. They needed proof. Until then, they couldn't even accuse the Chinese of using an EMP, although it was slowly picking them apart.

The perfect weapon, Drew thought.

Somehow they needed to turn the tables. It might be possible to jam the EMP if they understood its frequencies or nailed down its location. In the meantime, his first priority was to help the *America* and the *Truman* maintain the controlled zone into which no enemy assets could be allowed.

Because so many weapons were supersonic, this battle space was huge. The two aircraft carriers held the center of the controlled zone while nine Aegis destroyers, three cruisers, and two replenishment ships held station over an area of several square nautical miles. SH-60 Seahawk helicopters and buoys helped them hunt for enemy submarines, as did a classified number of their own attack subs.

The *America* and the *Truman* couldn't ignore conventional threats, a fact that worked in China's favor. Reacting to Chinese forces kept the Carrier Strike Group preoccupied, so not only did China feint at the *America* with ships and aircraft, they constantly adjusted their surface-to-air defenses on land and among their navy, shutting some off, turning others on.

"I'm picking up two Big Bird radars," Bugle said, meaning two enemy SA-20 missile systems were tracking their aircraft.

"I see 'em," Drew confirmed.

"Six Oh Two, this is Five Oh Four," Bugle said on the radio, calling the E-2D Hawkeye plane acting as their control. "SA-20 active, bull oh four oh for seventy. SA-20 active, bull oh four five for sixty-five."

"Roger, Five Oh Four," the Hawkeye said. "Be advised we have two bogies out of Rex. Current position is bull three oh five for seventy-five. Hot. Heading one eight five."

That's straight at us, Drew thought. "Copy," he said, wondering how close the Chinese pilots would fly.

Every second was a new game of nerves, a game in which the People's Liberation Army Navy demonstrated they had blood like cold steel. Drew gave 'em that much. It was his highest praise, no matter if the swagger of the PLAN was all anyone had expected.

Vietnam had leapt at the opportunity to gain a friend against their most traditional enemy. As far as they were concerned, their war with the U.S. had been with a passing invader, but they'd been fighting China for two thousand years. They were determined to prevent the Chinese from assuming total control of southeast Asia.

Hainan Island was a metropolis of ship-building facilities, dry docks, and ports for China's southern fleet. The island was also riddled with subterranean channels, allowing PLAN submarines to put to sea undetected. U.S. Command wasn't positive how many subs the Chinese had deployed, in part because PLAN surface craft made as much noise as possible, sometimes to the point of having their crews bang on their ships with wrenches and pipes.

ROMEO believed Hainan's ship-building activity was a cover for exotic weapons research. Orbital surveillance couldn't penetrate the busy throngs of troops and machinery, and the island's burrows were hardened against sonar and magnetic scans.

"Suppose the EMP isn't on Hainan?" Drew said suddenly. "The Chinese do everything they can to keep us from getting close. Maybe it's more sleight of hand."

"The mainland's too far away," Bugle said.

"Not if their EMP's on the coast. You need to isolate the next pulse so we can tell Christensen where to look."

"I thought we were calling her Julie now," Bugle said.

Drew ignored him. "We keep putting our attention on Hainan and coming up empty," he said. "What if it's so obviously the right place, it's wrong? On the coast, they could truck an EMP from one disguised location to another. They—"

"I'm picking up that new signal again," Bugle said.

"Show me where."

"It's gone."

"Let me patch through to—"

"It's back."

"Six Oh Two, this is Five Oh Four," Drew said on his control freq. "We're getting a lot of noise. I'm breaking north to see if we can pinpoint a source."

"Affirmative, Five Oh Four. Single group BRA three zero zero for fifty. Twenty-nine thousand feet."

That meant the Chinese MiGs weren't backing off, but Drew rocketed away from the U.S. ships instead of avoiding the enemy fighters. It took seconds to reach the fleet's northernmost edge, where he settled into a new track with Giles and Wade in a combat spread about a mile off his port wing, heading west now instead of straight at Hainan—but at 480 mph, they'd be on top of the Chinese MiGs in a heartbeat if either set of planes altered course.

I should have said something to her, he thought.

Trying to escape the memory of her hazel eyes made him reckless. "Let's get closer," Drew said, banking his jet into a nose-high climbing turn.

"Sure," Bugle said. "That way the fuckin' bad guys can make quick work of us if they've got a fuckin' death ray."

Drew grinned. Was there anyone else he'd prefer to have at his back? "You must have slept through the theater brief," he said. "The Chinese aren't the bad guys, remember? They're co-claimants for oil and fishing rights in international territory."

"This whole thing is nuts," Bugle said. "We're wasting half as much fuel trolling around as anyone will ever pump out of the ocean floor."

Drew had heard the same complaint aboard ship. It sounded smart, but it wasn't true. "They think the oil deposits would feed mainland China for twenty years," he said. "Besides, nobody's here for oil. This is about national sovereignty. China filed with the ICAO years ago to run aircraft on Taiwan's side of the Taiwan Strait. Then they did the same thing with Vietnam. It's been one provocation after another."

"Uh," Bugle said, obviously flabbergasted at Drew's motormouth.

"Here's the real irony," Drew said. "Between our consumers, labor forces, and energy markets, the U.S. and China generate a full third of the world economy. That's right. You couldn't separate us if you tried, but politically—"

"I'm reading a signal that's off the charts!" Bugle yelled.

More of Drew's electronics went dark. "I lost my radar," he said, checking the rest of his displays.

Should I report an in-flight emergency? No.

"No, we're okay," he thought out loud as Bugle said, "The pulse is gone."

Drew looked for the enemy fighters. He glanced across the sky for Chinese missile launches. An EMP could initiate an assault, taking down the aircraft that would protect Julie and the *America*. But he saw nothing. To his left, Giles and Wade remained airborne.

He radioed the E-2D Hawkeye first. "Six Oh Two, did you feel that? I think we were hit by a pulse weapon."

"Negative," the Hawkeye answered. "Negative. Stand by."

Drew radioed Giles and Wade with practiced calm. "Five Oh One, say your status?"

Silence.

"Five Oh One, do you copy?" Drew banked toward his wingman as he switched to his ICS and said, "I lost my stores management systems."

"Backseat is good," Bugle said, meaning he had operable links to the ALQ-218 and NGJ electronic warfare pods on their wings. "Look."

They'd flown so close to the other jet, Drew saw Giles working frantically inside his canopy.

Giles pointed at his helmet and gave a thumbs down. Then he pat-ted his console, made a fist, and flicked open his fingers. He was RTB—return to base. Giles's aircraft peeled away from Drew, lurching once in an alarming, uncontrolled motion toward the water far below.

Drew raced after them. He wanted to pursue the Chinese pulse weapon, but Giles and Wade needed him to be their voice.

"Six Oh Two, this is Five Oh Four," Drew radioed the Hawkeye. "Five Oh One is RTB NORDO. He's taking the lead. He has a problem with flight control."

"Those sons of bitches!" Bugle said.

"Stay cool. We're fine."

But if they were hit again, Drew didn't know if either plane would stay in the air. Could he block a line-of-sight pulse from Hainan or the coast? One jet might save the other, so Drew decelerated as Giles flew toward the fleet. He hoped to cover Giles with his own plane.

The sun rose through the haze on the horizon. Daylight changed the ocean's hue as Drew followed Giles through a line above the USS *Hoyer*, a cruiser on the *America*'s northeast perimeter.

Then the sky shattered with a white snap. The light dazzled Drew despite his visor, burning an imprint of the *Hoyer*'s lean shape into his eyes.

"What the hell was—!"

Bee bee bee bee bee bee. His radar altimeter was screaming. He was almost in the water. An instant ago, he'd been at 2500 feet, running above the *Hoyer*. Now he was at 1500 with the broad waves of the ocean directly below his aircraft.

Behind him, Bugle yelled, "Pull up! Pull up!"

Drew shook off his confusion and hauled on the stick, bringing his jet into a climb. "Where are Giles and Wade!?" he shouted as his radio filled with chatter and blaring static.

Three or four voices emerged from the noise:

"Rampage Four One Eight is in the water! Rampage Four One Eight is in the water!"

"Do you copy—"

"—systems down—"

Drew didn't see Giles's plane as he struggled for safe altitude, slamming through a rough current of wind to 2500 feet. Nor could he find the *Hoyer*. It was gone.

Other U.S. ships lay in front of him.

He identified the *Samuel Grant*, an Aegis destroyer that should have been on the west side of their battle space. He hadn't merely lost altitude; he'd leapt forward more than three miles; and he couldn't explain the jump except to think—

"Break left break left!" Bugle yelled.

From his peripheral vision, Drew saw a flitting black shape above to his right. He threw his plane into a sheer turn. The intruder ripped past. Jet wash slammed into Drew's aircraft and pulled at his wings. He lost control, his pulse thudding in his head.

That was a Chinese MiG, he thought. *We're under attack.*

· · · · · · · · · · · ·

8

LOS ANGELES

"Sorry I'm late!"

Emily looked up to see Chase slipping through the noisy sandwich shop. At 1:33 p.m., the lunch rush was over, but Sandoval's was always popular. Emily had fended off two groups who wanted her table, pointing at a second iced tea she'd bought for Chase. She'd also put in his sandwich order. It was the least she could do after he'd delivered a rental car to the Plaza for her, then brought her Altima to the dealer before driving back again in his Lexus.

She set aside the plastic chit #74 she'd been given at the counter and rose to meet her fiancé. Chase was worth the wait. Thick-chested, dark-haired, he carried himself well and wasn't shy about public displays of affection. Emily met him with a full-body embrace.

Their kiss grew hotter than she'd planned. She was aware of three women laughing at the next table as she nuzzled Chase. *Let them look,* she thought. She was glad to be young and in love.

At last, she broke it up.

"Think you used enough dynamite there, Butch?" Chase asked, using one of her best movie lines against her.

Emily flushed. She was more pleased that he was playing her game than embarrassed by showing off, but now she felt conscious of the crowd. She sat down after tucking a stray yellow bang behind one ear.

Chase took the chair across from her. "How was your media thing?" he asked.

"Mostly good."

"Bad?"

"No, it was good," Emily said before he could start battering at her in his relentless, intelligent way. "I didn't say anything about a prenatal vaccine."

Chase looked at her in silence. Was he disappointed?

She was saved by the man at the counter. "Seventy-three and seventy-four!" the man shouted.

"Ham, no cheese or mayo," Emily said, showing Chase their order number. He was an L.A. boy through and through, barely able to bring himself to eat carbohydrates, although they met here regularly because it was near the hospital.

She wasn't alone in watching Chase walk to the counter. He turned heads at the next table, too. All three women were well-dressed professionals in their mid-thirties. Emily touched her lipstick to hide a frown.

She'd met Chase at a convention on hereditary diseases where he'd swept her off her feet with a speed that was unlike her. They'd made out on the first date, slept together nine days after that, and almost two years later Emily remained uneasy and excited to be riding this express train.

Chase got too much silly-headed attention from the female staff and patients at work. That was a temptation. Would he give in to it in another five years? He was losing his hair, which had receded at both temples. Emily thought it made him look grown-up, but Chase was inse-cure about it, always glancing into mirrors to fluff and primp. Would he become more likely to have an affair if the thinning didn't stop?

I can be everything you want, Emily thought, staring at him as he returned with their tray. "Thank you," she said, flashing a smile that was as much for the women at the next table as for him.

Chase didn't miss the byplay. He glanced sideways, then sat down. "So tell me about it," he said, digging into his sandwich. "Sorry. I've got thirty minutes."

Emily toyed with her food as she told him about her morning and the meetings afterward at DNAllied. "That reporter would have eaten me alive if I told him what I really think," she said.

"You mean your up-curve?"

"Yes."

"You made the right call. They had more than enough to take in without you rubbing their noses in it. Besides, why write one paper when you can write two?"

Emily nodded.

"I'm serious," Chase said. "You need to announce the rest of your data before anyone else starts talking about race-related mutations."

"Ethnocentric variations," Emily corrected him. That was her best effort at saying the same thing inoffensively. Race played a major role in individual risk factors. No group was exempt. African-Americans had elevated rates of sickle-cell disease; northern Europeans, cystic fibrosis; and Caucasians of all stripes were more likely to have children diag-nosed with ASD than blacks, Hispanics, Asians, or multi-racial parents.

But what if Laura never talks to me again? she thought.

According to her statistical models, an unmistakable dual trend existed in most demographics. Cancer rates were increasing even as cognitive disorders became more common, and the asshole reporter had been fundamentally correct in one thing.

"You have new evidence that reduced apoptosis is a major factor in brain size," Chase said, prompting her.

"I don't want to make it political," Emily said.

"It's not. It's science."

"The implications are too easy to twist around," she said. "People will make it ugly."

"Some people," Chase said.

He was derisive, but Emily felt miserable about her results. She said, "Some of it *is* ugly, Chase."

There were scientists, even doctors like Chase, who believed technology kept alive more and more individuals who would have died in other ages, thus weakening the gene pool with traits as slight or as self-destructive as myopia, IBS, diabetes, or schizophrenia.

Emily wasn't so certain. Evolution had never been an organized, step-by-step process like those goofy charts of a fish who became a reptile who became a monkey who became a man. Life was loaded with dead ends and miracles. Natural selection took generations to produce new characteristics that might be lost in recessive genes, then reappear centuries later. The deterioration of humankind was one explanation for the rise in children who were cancer-prone, depressive, or autistic, but Emily wanted no part of reinforcing this theory, because the most glaring solution was straight out of Nazi Germany. Eugenic programs. Genocide. It was unthinkable.

Some people would refuse her cures. Many families championed their sons and daughters with ASD. They said autists were different, not inferior. The more militant groups claimed the condition represented higher evolution because of the savant skills a tiny percentage displayed in mathematics, musical ability, or other talents.

Emily knew her media release would bring a lot of heat. Even before today, she'd received hate mail on her company email. Some people reviled her merely for writing on the subjects of autism and biotech.

"Here's the thing," she said. "My data suggests ASD is a throwback to prehistoric modes of consciousness. Whether that's better or worse isn't a value judgment I'm prepared to make."

"You don't have to."

"I do. If I publish something that says the genetic markers for autism are homologous to specific sequences in Neanderthal DNA, it's like playing catch with a gun. Somebody will get hurt."

"Are you talking about your mom?"

"I—" Emily shook her head.

He's always surprising me, she thought. Was he encouraging her to defy her mother? Chase had charmed her parents by attending Christmas services and Easter Vigil with her mother and talking football with her dad. Emily was pleased to think he'd choose her over them. He could be such a politician himself, wooing both sides.

And yet . . . her success would be his own. Chase might gain even more traction at the hospital if his wife was a Nobel contender.

Do you really love me for me? How much of it is because of my job?

"Sometimes I wish I'd never gotten into this business," she said.

"What are you talking about? I'm proud of you," Chase said. "You made the right choice today. Rocking the boat would be stupid. The vaccine can wait. Maybe it takes longer than you want, but either way, you win. This isn't about right or wrong, babe. It's right and right."

Emily smiled. "So you don't care if . . ."

"Better health means better lives for everyone," Chase said. "I see it daily, people spending all their money and time just to stop hurting. You're going to change the world."

"I know." Her smile faded.

"Your gene therapies are just the beginning."

"We have to be very, very careful how we talk about intelligence," she warned him. "Everyone assumes you personally support any theory you advance."

And it gets worse, she thought.

Long ago, offspring with greater reasoning had become more likely to thrive. They'd passed their intelligence on to their children—but at a steep cost. The gap in cancer rates between chimpanzees and *Homo sapiens* appeared to be due to how each species' cells self-destructed, a biological process known as programmed cell death or apoptosis.

Cancer and cognitive dysfunction represented a bizarre seesaw. *Homo sapiens* produced neurons at a much higher rate than chimps. The flip side of the coin was that human beings also failed to destroy cells as quickly.

In the end, men had conquered the planet. A higher cancer risk was never an evolutionary pitfall since most cancers didn't manifest until after people reached reproductive age. From a standpoint of sheer efficiency and species propagation, it was an excellent trade-off.

"I wouldn't know where to start with a new paper," Emily said. "There are so many variables."

"Name one."

"I'll give you three," she said. "Dietary, lifestyle, and environmental factors are all at play in comparing chimps' cancer rates to ours. For one thing, high caloric diets are a massive trigger, especially diets rich in sugar. We'd need to separate out how much of the incidence of cancer is predicated on obesity."

"So you don't expect funding from Burger King," Chase said. "So what?"

We're so different, Emily thought with an appreciative smile. She valued his support, but thrashing out her plans with him could be exhausting.

Chase didn't understand how badly her trends were muddled. Nor was cancer a single disease. People tended to group more than two hundred unique pathologies under the term *cancer* and yet the fascinating truth was humankind appeared to be regaining the cancer resistance of their cousins in unconscious, involuntary ways.

One benefit of Down syndrome was tumor-suppressing genes on chromosome 21. People with Down's had a wildly reduced incidence of most malignancies, as did those with many other cognitive diseases—but not autists.

ASD seemed to have no correlation with low cancer rates, yet overall the data was bewitchingly suggestive. Was the rise in mental disorders the first step in evolving into a more cancer-resistant human? Why would that happen? Could it be in response to the pollutants they'd dumped into their environment?

"My little worrier," Chase said, reaching out to stroke her forearm. "Just do your work. Some people are always going to get their panties in a bunch."

"You sound like Laura."

"Yep." Chase knew Laura was in his corner, and he knew Emily had a high regard for her sister's opinion.

Does he know I've been having doubts about us?

"Thank you," Emily said. "I mean it. You're really working all night?"

" 'Fraid so."

"I love you," she said, feeling inordinately fond of her arrogant, educated husband-to-be. They made a good team. "We should elope right now," she said. As she spoke, she realized she wasn't entirely kidding.

Chase saluted her with his glass of iced tea. "Your mom would kill us."

"I don't want to wait. We . . . We could start our honeymoon tomorrow. Tonight." Emily laid her hand on his thigh under the table.

Chase stared at her. "You're not serious," he said.

"Aren't I?"

She was a bit stung by the alarm in his eyes. Chase had always been bolder and more spontaneous, which were traits she admired. Either he had his own doubts about their marriage or he feared crossing her straightlaced mother.

Did she enjoy upsetting her mom? No. Her career choice was not a second child's act of rebellion, trying to get her parents' attention. Her mom should have been proud of her even if the Church frowned upon reproductive sciences including biology and genetics.

She gave Chase an impish grin, teasing him, testing him. "I want to do it. Road trip. Vegas. We'll save at least five grand."

"Emily, let's wait."

"You're just mad you didn't think of it first," she said. Letting him off the hook, she laughed out loud.

"Besides, you need time to get your next paper together," Chase said.

Maybe he was right. In many ways, her trend analysis was even more intriguing than her work developing gene therapies. Her data definitely needed more scrutiny. The nature of humankind was changing.

But what are we becoming? Emily wondered. *And why?*

She was halfway home when she left the 110 on the first off-ramp she saw, drove under the freeway, and took an on-ramp heading back in the direction she'd come.

Speeding south toward DNAllied, she was frustrated by the traffic. At 3:32, the 110 had clogged with the afternoon commute. At least her rental car, a Nissan hybrid, was even nicer than her Altima.

She didn't want to lose her job, but she couldn't ignore her belief that DNAllied would bury her data for a prenatal vaccine. *I can't be that selfish,* she thought. *I have to do it. I'll pirate my own data for the guys at the University of Texas.*

"Arrg, I'm a pirate," she said, trying to keep up her courage.

What if Ray was still at work?

The DNAllied building was on South Union Drive in a light industrial neighborhood between downtown L.A. and West Hollywood. Emily slowed as she reached her off-ramp and merged into the city. The radio was playing an awesome Taylor Swift song. That felt like a good omen, but as she sat at a traffic light, her windshield glowed with bands of purple and red.

What in the world? she thought, leaning over her steering wheel.

The radio was suddenly reduced to static. The clear sky erupted with color. Then her vision exploded with blinding white shapes and ghosts.

The next thing Emily knew, she was staggering through her own small hell, moving on foot on the black asphalt of a street. Her cheek felt bruised. Her sleeve was torn. Other people walked around her, many of them crying or yelling. Somewhere a dog barked. At first, the people's voices were confused. Then the yelling grew louder.

Where am I? she thought.

Office buildings, a Sizzler restaurant, and storefronts lined the block. Motionless cars surrounded her. Emily recognized the street as West 6th. She was two hundred yards from the freeway. She saw her rental car down the block.

Most of the abandoned vehicles were in clumps, joined by fender benders and bang-ups. A blue sedan had gone through the glass front of a convenience store. No one appeared to be driving, although she heard a few engines running.

As she watched, an old Buick nudged past a smaller car and rolled several feet before crunching into the side of an SUV. No one sat behind the wheel. The Buick must have been left in drive. But not everyone had left their vehicles. Some people, disoriented, seemed to be trapped or unable to open their doors.

The mayhem reminded Emily of her crash that morning.

It's happening again, she thought, sorting through her broken memory. *But what's happening!?*

9

. . . .

SOUTH CHINA SEA

rew hauled his jet up into the sunrise, twisting his head from side to side. The *Samuel Grant* lay below. A second Aegis destroyer was also in sight. His gaze left the ocean for the sky. What if more enemy fighters were inbound?

The Chinese MiG had just swept overhead, passing Drew at a downward angle as he climbed to 3000 feet.

We're too low, he thought.

To the west, the dark landmass of Vietnam had brightened in the sunrise, its coastline emerging from shadows to brown and green. Yellow light glistened on the always-changing surface of the ocean. Then the MiG slammed into the water.

"Shit," Drew said. He'd had nothing to do with the other pilot's death, but the sight filled him with dread. He thumbed his radio. "Six Oh Two, this is—"

"Missiles four o'clock high inbound!" Bugle yelled.

Drew forgot everything else. He dove for the ocean again as Bugle relayed their position and status on their control frequency, yammering through as much data as possible in case they were hit.

"This is Five Oh Four we're under fire from bandits inside our screen I think in sector ten we're fielding an EMP attack repeat a major EMP attack!" Bugle yelled as Drew accelerated into a steep turn to his right, firing chaff and flares from his aircraft's belly. With luck, the air-to-air missiles behind him would retarget the incandescent chaff.

"No good! Still tracking!" Bugle screamed.

Drew punched more chaff and flares, executing a thirty degree cut left.

"Now they're at seven o'clock!"

Drew reached 1100 mph as the missiles closed in. The G forces were a smothering weight. It crushed Drew against his seat. Fortunately he was layered in gear, each component blending man to machine. The Nomex sheath of his G suit was packed with air bladders that expanded under acceleration, pushing the blood up from his legs and abdomen into his chest and head, where he needed it, while the form-fitting straps of his torso harness secured him to the KOCH fittings on his seat.

The pressure felt like being squeezed under the heel of a giant boot, but Drew was familiar with this pain. He was more stunned by the gleam of purple and blue reflecting in vast pools across the ocean.

"Here they come!" Bugle screamed.

As he leveled out at 75 feet, Drew glanced up, taking his eyes off the water.

The morning sky was full of color, a light show very different than his whiteout. The atmosphere appeared to be painted with immense waves of blue and violet—an aurora—something he'd never seen south of Anchorage or Helsinki. The South China Sea was near the equator, well below the Tropic of Cancer. Auroras at this latitude were impossible.

There wasn't time to wonder. Nor was there room for it inside the tight, deft hurricane of his mind, which was practically empty of thought. This close to the brink, Drew was no more than his instincts.

He punched a third round of chaff as he hauled his jet into another shuddering climb to 500 feet, 750, 1000 . . .

The missiles exploded behind him. Drew felt the concussions against his aircraft—felt himself still breathing—his heart beating—and he laughed inside his mask with the invincible glee of a naval aviator.

It didn't last.

"Nice work! We have bandits at ten o'clock high!" Bugle yelled. "Chinese fighters!"

"Weapons hot," Drew said as he touched his fire control system.

"They're going for the *Grant*."

"Shit—"

Drew's radar page and armament load indicator were out. With these systems malfunctioning, safety checks might prevent him from firing his missiles, and an EA-18G was not a fighter. Drew had self-protect capability in two AMRAAM missiles, but no gun. Electronics filled the space in his nose where an F/A-18 would carry its Vulcan cannon.

Buffeted by storm winds, he leveled out at 1500 feet and raced for the *Grant*. The sky was in chaos. Beneath the warm, gauzy light of the aurora, the U.S. planes were scattered. Many of their ships had also peeled off course, the precise formation of the Carrier Strike Group dissolving into a more crumpled shape. A few of their warships had turned toward the *America*. Others were drifting away.

Orange streaks of fire ripped from the *Grant* into the sky as Drew approached—Tomahawk missiles intended for the enemy ships—and he saw its 20mm Phalanx guns blazing, too.

The gunfire struck one of the Chinese fighters. The MiG lost a wingtip and part of its nose. Then the rest of its wing disintegrated and it tumbled, plunging toward the water.

Much closer, an American helicopter lay upside down in the ocean, rocking in the wake of the *Grant*. The destroyer hadn't altered course to avoid the bird, much less slowed to help, which meant the whiteout hadn't been limited to the sky. It had affected everyone in the Carrier Strike Group.

It affected the Chinese, too, Drew realized.

To the north, smoke lifted from the bump on the horizon that was Hainan Island. He'd supposed this fire was caused by U.S. missile strikes. What if it was another crashed Chinese aircraft? The first MiG should have blasted him. Drew had been a sitting duck at close range, naked to guns or missiles. Now he believed the MiG hadn't been in control even before the Chinese pilot spiraled into the water.

In fact, Drew wondered why the missiles fired at him had come from *behind* that Chinese plane. Those weapons had been released by another enemy fighter and could have locked onto their own man instead of Drew.

They're as confused as we are, he thought as he banked up and over to chase the surviving MiG. The maneuver was pure reflex. His brain might have been finding excuses for the enemy, but his body—his training—acted to kill.

Behind Drew, Bugle was also working at high speed. Bugle's radar page was functional and he yelled, "I brought you on target! He's locked!"

The Chinese MiG dodged across the strike group, attempting to lose Drew.

But the MiG was outmatched.

"I said he's locked! You got him!" Bugle yelled.

Drew hesitated, allowing the other aircraft to slip away for a heartbeat as they roared together through the sunrise. He believed the Chinese had started the fighting, but it was a misunderstanding. They were all victims.

And yet if he let the MiG escape, the enemy pilot might hurt people on his own side.

"Yaaaah!" Drew shouted, squeezing his trigger.

The missile didn't release.

"The computer dropped the designation! You need to—" Drew shouted as he pulled his trigger again. This time, the AMRAAM launched.

Bugle's lock was true. The weapon went supersonic and curved after the MiG, impacting its tail. The plane tore apart in a fireball. No one ejected. Drew knew he'd killed the man, but he quashed his feelings as he veered around to return to the north perimeter.

He saw one MiG engaged with three F/A-18s. The MiG wouldn't last. The bigger obstacle was the Chinese surface-to-air missiles that arrived from the coast, slicing past the aircraft. American fighters ruled the sky, but for how long?

Drew raced to join them, shouting at Bugle, "Jam those SAMs before someone gets hit!"

"I'm working it!"

Were the Chinese ships also off course? One of their destroyers looked like it had increased its speed, careening toward the U.S. fleet.

The whiteout wasn't an assault, Drew thought. The light had been something else. But the situation was already out of hand. Both sides believed the phenomenon was a weapon, and now their skirmish was devolving into war.

The danger in any escalation was larger than one man's life. Drew was less afraid for himself than for his entire nation, because their attack subs would be safe from the EMPs beneath the water.

What did the subs' crews think was happening? They should be able to detect the madness above them—the missile launches from the surface craft, the fighters and helicopters splashing into the ocean—and if communications were out, the sub commanders would activate their final orders.

Drew swung his jet away from the fight. If anyone noticed, it might look like cowardice, but he poured on the speed as he ran for the *America*.

Bugle yelled at him on their ICS. "What are you doing? We can't leave our guys—"

"I need a line to the flag bridge!"

"We have to go back!"

"Get me Christensen on the bridge! Now!"

The electromagnetic interference was so strong that their radios might not work at a distance. Closer, Bugle should be able to punch through on the frequency they'd preset with Julie.

"Romeo Two, this is Romeo One," Bugle said as Drew's gaze cut across the fighters he'd abandoned on his flank.

What if we're too late? he thought.

Their subs were called boomers because their end purpose was to deliver their Trident II missiles, each of which packed a very large boom of 475 kilotons. If those men believed the Chinese had decimated the fleet, if the sub crews were unable to contact any U.S. assets whatsoever, they would fire on Hainan and other targets across the mainland, hoping to vaporize China's missile bases before the enemy launched their own warheads.

Drew had seen the computer projections.

A nuclear exchange was unwinnable.

He would be responsible for it. The first warning that China was developing an EMP weapon had come from him. The data had been inconclusive, but he'd attached his opinion to it, believing the worst.

What if the impression he'd relayed from the field was the deciding factor?

Below, the air was mottled with smoke trails and clouds, some white, some black, all of it snarled by the wind. Drew's eyes picked out a small debris field where a fighter had hit the water, leaving only a few fragments on the surface and iridescent fuel. Among the ships, more Sea Sparrow and Tomahawk missiles whipped into the sky while their 20mm Phalanx guns blurred through thousands of rounds per minute to prevent enemy weapons from reaching the strike group.

But something got through. The *McCray* took a missile toward its stern belowdecks, which lifted apart in a fiery spray of metal and human beings.

"No!" Drew shouted as his headset brought Julie Christensen to his ears.

"Romeo One, Romeo Two," she said.

"The EMPs aren't a weapon! Stand down! Stand down!"

Her voice was riddled with static. "Say again, Romeo One?"

"We have to tell both sides to stand down!" Drew shouted. "The electromagnetic pulses we're fielding are not a weapon! Both sides—"

The sky went white.

Drew woke up with his head thick with pain and a sense of plummeting. When he was a kid, he'd loved roller coasters and other rides like the elevator drop. For a moment, he thought he might be that thrill-seeking child again. It was a bittersweet feeling, both happy and lost.

Then his vision cleared. His aircraft was knifing toward the *McCray*, the destroyer that had been gutted. Columns of greasy smoke lifted into the wind from its ruined deck. Drew's left wing would clear the ship's tower by a matter of ten feet, a distance that shrunk to nothing as the breeze floated him in its direction.

He could eject. Instead, he stayed put. There were dozens of sailors in the tower, so Drew shoved his hand against his stick. Nothing. Too many of his systems were dead.

"C'mon, c'mon!" Drew tried to tip his wings and use the wind like a kite. Then he noticed the quiet behind him. "Bugle?" he asked.

No answer.

"Bugle!"

The smoke enveloped him, but he missed the *McCray*. Then he burst through and the ocean loomed in front of him like a surging desert. At his speed, every rolling dune would be as hard as concrete.

Drew set his head back. He also arranged his knees so his thighs laid flat against the seat pan. Their seats were self-contained, one thousand–pound constructs nestled inside the jet itself. Rocket motors would launch them from the aircraft at speeds exceeding 300 mph, more than enough to break a man's neck or shear off his limbs if he was out of position, but Drew couldn't wait for Bugle to acknowledge.

He yanked his eject handle. They were thrown from the cockpit a microsecond before they hit the water. He felt something clip his head, cracking his visor. A part of the aircraft?

Drew only knew that he went up. Then he separated from his seat and his chute deployed.

The wind raked across the ocean. It jerked Drew sideways and swirled him up and back, driving him at a low angle toward the waves. The air was damp against his face where his helmet left his cheek exposed.

Bugle's parachute would deploy even if his friend was unconscious. Meanwhile, their seat pans would splash down first and float nearby, attached to their KOCH fittings on a line. Each pan was equipped with a survival kit with an individual raft, rations, drinking water, and a flare gun.

Drew tried to look for Bugle as he fell, but he was in the water too fast—cold, heavy water. His survival vest inflated automatically and bobbed against his chin and arms.

Drew activated his beacon and a radio signal for retrieval, but he didn't expect a helicopter any time soon. The signal would be lost in the electromagnetic noise, and, worse, the fight raged on above him, the sky split by missiles and aircraft.

How many friends were dead?

Where was Bugle?

Drew shoved off his cracked flight helmet and kicked at his boots. The laces were tied too tight. There wasn't time to duck into the water to pry or cut his boots free.

He was five hundred yards from the *McCray*. Each wave carried him up and down. At the top of one swell, he saw life rafts and people in the water. Maybe he could help. He reached forward to swim—

It happened again. Drew didn't know how or why he was affected, only that his consciousness seemed to flicker in and out. His mind stuttered through a flurry of images like snapshots, each one brighter than the last as the sun rose. The first thing that stayed with him was a fire trail overhead; an odd wave running against the current; the taste of salt and smoke.

The snapshots ended. Drew could think again. He turned his head at a new sound, the blunt rushing bass growl of a ship. The noise was the Chinese destroyer he'd seen near the edge of the U.S. fleet. He'd drifted farther from his people during the whiteouts, and the enemy ship bulled past him on a collision course with the *McCray*.

As he coughed and struggled in the destroyer's wake, Drew wondered if the destroyer had been deliberately aimed at the *McCray*. In their coherent moments, the Chinese crew might have decided to inflict as much damage as possible even if it meant suicide.

"Stop!" he yelled.

No one could hear him, but now that Drew was out of the fight, he felt all of his terror and grief. Was there any way Julie had been able to share his warning that the EMPs weren't man-made?

Look at them, he thought. He understood the enemy's decision. There was honor in it. A suicide attack was better than being captured or killed while they were helpless, but it was a mistake. He would have told them if he could.

The silhouette of the Chinese destroyer ran tall against the glowing sky. Then it plowed into the *McCray*, filling the sunrise with explosions.

The ocean was on fire.

LOS ANGELES

Pain stopped Emily in the congested street. She'd cut her toes on broken glass.

I'm barefoot, she realized.

The road was littered with empty shoes. Everyone had taken off their heels, shoes, sandals, and boots. Why? It was an unnerving sight—the abandoned shoes scattered in the street where people had been.

Almost as disturbing, Emily could smell cinnamon and her grandmother's favorite perfume, which was impossible. Nanna had been dead for years. How could she smell her perfume?

The sky bled with strange light.

"My leg!" someone shrieked among the cars ahead of her. "My leg! My leg!" It was a man, but agony had ratcheted his voice into a high, brittle keen.

Oh God, Emily thought, looking for him in the milling crowd. Was he pinned?

Then she heard a more horrendous sound behind her: the deafening roar of an airplane. All around her, people screamed as the gray bulk of a passenger jet slashed overhead. It looked like it was upside down.

The plane disappeared beyond the elevated line of the interstate where the freeway formed an overpass above West 6th. Beyond the freeway, cyclones of fire and smoke billowed above the city. Emily saw chunks of debris. She thought she saw seats and people. Metal. Dust. A second later, the earth trembled.

Nearly lost in the noise, Emily heard a creak of metal as a green SUV teetered on the guardrail of the freeway overpass. Smoke rose from the freeway, too, where the traffic formed brutal pileups. Beyond the guardrail, Emily saw the rooftops of dozens of vehicles—a truck's gaping windshield—a man waving his arms—and the undercarriage or wheels of two cars that had flipped.

I was doing seventy up there, she thought with dull shock. *I was doing seventy before I reached my exit and stopped.*

Somebody was inside the teetering SUV—a woman in a business suit. She scrabbled back from the windshield, shoving at the driver door.

The SUV plummeted thirty feet with the woman inside.

Emily felt as if her heart dropped at the same time. She almost sat down, unable to breathe.

"My leg!" the man yelled.

She couldn't help them both.

The man was closer.

Forcing air into her chest, Emily turned to pick her way through the vehicles. She stopped again as her gaze turned west. Two threads of smoke curled from the cityscape. Laura lived in that direction. Emily was frantic with silent prayers and disbelief.

Please, God. Please.

A teenage girl grabbed her arm and shouted, "Help me! My dad! Please help!"

To Emily, the girl's voice felt like her own thoughts. She followed her into the cars. The girl wore a short skirt and knee socks and ran with a funny limp because she had one leather boot on, just one, like she hadn't been able to pull it off when everyone else removed their shoes.

The asphalt felt warm against Emily's skin and she thought, *I don't get it. Our shoes? What could—*

They didn't run far. The girl led Emily to a dark-haired man in his fifties who slumped over the wheel of an Acura TL. He was dead or unconscious. A stroke? One of his eyes was a crimson egg, bulging and bloodshot. The pupil didn't react even when Emily's shadow crossed his face, but she decided to administer CPR.

"Let's get him out of the car!" she said, gesturing for the girl to help her with the man's weight. They dropped him on the road. He was still wearing his shoes.

He didn't have time to take them off, Emily thought as she checked his airways, then bent to put her mouth over his open lips. First, she said, "Try the engine."

She blew into the man's mouth and straightened up to press her palms against his heart. One, two, three, four. Chase could have done better. Was he okay? Chase should be at work. Silver Lake was closer than Laura's house, but the road was blocked with stalls, and Emily couldn't carry this man to the hospital.

"It won't start!" the girl shouted. She couldn't have been older than fifteen. Emily wanted to check the key herself, but she tried to breathe life into the girl's father again and—

She blacked out.

When she woke up, she was cowering with two women and four men against the brick face of an office complex, looking at the street through a few trees and a short ornamental brick wall. All of them were coughing, filthy, and scratched.

Smoke and dust obscured most of the street. Above, through the haze, the sky burned with red light. Everyone flinched as a swarm of birds darted alongside the building and then vanished.

Emily smelled her grandmother's perfume again. It seemed stronger than the smoke, and she realized her brain was generating false signals. She was also unsettled by her vertigo, a sense that the ground was sliding beneath her even though both she and it were motionless. Her balance was shot. Her head ached.

Another truth went through her like a knife. The seven of them had huddled together like family, the men stretching out their arms, not to corral the women, but to shield them. Like the teenage girl, who was gone, these people were strangers to Emily, and yet there was real intimacy in their postures.

"Where . . . ?" someone said.

They came from every walk of life. One man wore rough jeans and a work shirt—maybe a landscaper. Another wore gym clothes. The other two wore business shirts and slacks, no jackets. Emily and another woman fit the same white-collar description.

They were hiding from a second plane crash. As the wind opened a pocket in the haze, Emily saw a huge tailfin jutting through the demolished ruins of several buildings down the street, fires licking at the debris.

How many planes had been above LAX and Burbank when the sky lit up? Dozens? More?

What if they'd all gone down?

"Let me go!" one of the women screamed, reacting even more strongly than Emily. This woman's blouse was open, the shoulder yanked off. Was that why she panicked?

The woman fought out of the group as two men pulled back, bewildered and chagrined. Emily believed they had good intentions.

"We've got to get off the street!" Emily yelled.

"My family—" a man said as the other woman shouted, "Josh! Josh!" She ran into the sea of cars, recognizing someone. The man also sprinted away and Emily was left with three survivors.

Some aspects of the street looked completely normal—the Taco Bell beside an auto shop, a UPS store, more office buildings—but the fires and the standstill traffic had turned the city into another world. The screaming was the worst. The human sounds of despair rose and fell but never ended.

There was another body sprawled in the street. The man wasn't visibly hurt. He wasn't bloody or burned, but he lay with his arm hooked beneath him in an unnatural position, and his eyes looked like empty white glass.

Something was killing people besides car crashes and fires.

My head, Emily thought. What if some of them were hemorrhaging or experiencing fatal seizures?

She wasn't going to wait to find out. "I work down the street!" she yelled. "It's a new building. Earthquake proof. I can get us inside."

"Where are we?" the landscaper asked.

"The corner of West 6th and Valencia. I work here."

They responded to her certainty. "Show us," a businessmen said.

Laura's house was only a few miles past DNAllied, but it might as well have been a hundred. Emily couldn't imagine wading through forty blocks of smoke and cars, and Laura's house was a two-story ranch home made of wood. It wasn't anyplace to take shelter.

"This way," Emily said.

Two of the survivors went with her, not the third. Emily looked back.

"This way!" she shouted.

A pistol shot cracked somewhere in the smoke. Then the buildings echoed with the chatter of an automatic weapon.

"Oh shit!" The landscaper fled into vehicles, leaving Emily and the businessman.

Three young black men burst from the haze. They wore red ban-
dannas on their arms or foreheads. Gangbangers. One of them swung
a boxy little gun. Another carried a revolver.

Emily had no time to hide. Two of the gangbangers ran past, but
the one who'd zigzagged closest to her slowed down and lingered, grinning even as his friends yelled at him. "Forget it, Trey!"

He was in his twenties. He had great teeth, straight and bright.
Striding toward her, he said, "Hey there, swee—"

Emily rammed her bare foot into his groin and dropped him. Karate
lessons. As he slumped to his knees, fighting to stay up, Emily wrapped
her small hands into a single fist and threw her weight into his jaw, snapping it. She felt his bones crack as pain lanced through her forearm.

He let go of his revolver. He flopped down as the weapon clattered
on the asphalt. Emily hesitated, eyeing it, but she'd have to get too close
to grab it.

He pushed himself up, groaning through a bloody drool of spit.

Emily turned and ran.

She was alone.

In the smoke, Emily passed two cops warily chasing the gangbangers. One policeman had his arm in a combat sling.

Why were they fighting? There was nothing to loot from the business district except computers and a little money. The young men hadn't
carried anything except their weapons. Emily supposed they'd been
driving through, then left their car with their guns and ran into the
policemen.

Should I go with the cops? she thought. She'd taken first aid classes
at Chase's insistence, but the cops probably had better training. And she
was afraid.

At the intersection of West 6th and Union Drive, she turned north.
DNAllied was set back from the street by twenty feet of grass, and, in
front, by its fenced parking lot. Emily had once described the archi-
tecture to a friend as post-post-post-postmodern. It didn't fit with the

four-story office buildings on either side. It wouldn't fit anywhere. Faced with concrete ribs and black glass, DNAllied was a single-story structure arranged like a hexagon around a central courtyard.

Emily hurried to a side door and saw people inside the tinted glass. She wasn't sure who. Then she reached the door. It was locked. She didn't have her pass card. Her purse must have been in her car, so she punched her code into the electronic lock instead. It didn't work. She pounded on the glass.

The noise drew attention from inside, where her boss, Ray, was shouting at two men. They turned and walked to the door.

All three of them were wearing shoes.

Are they arguing about whether or not to help me? Emily thought as Ray grabbed one man's arm. The guy shrugged him off. Emily recognized him as Dale Upton from IT, someone she knew and liked, but Dale wasn't fighting with Ray about who to let in. Ray was trying to stop him from leaving.

Dale opened the door and ran out, barely glancing at Emily.

"Wait!" she yelled, but she couldn't bring herself to go after him. She pushed inside as Dale's friend ran, too.

Had the building protected them? The structure was made of concrete and its windows were energy-efficient, double-pane, UV-proof glass. With the lights out, even this entry hall was gloomy despite the beige tile floor.

Ray pulled the door shut behind her and locked it. "Was there a bomb?" he asked.

"I don't know, I don't know," Emily said, her voice accelerating. "It happened at least twice and there were planes falling down and the sky— The sky is *red*—"

They hugged each other, the middle-aged man and the young woman who'd never been anything more to each other than coworkers. Worse, they'd been adversaries, but now Emily was glad for Ray's girth.

He was solid and reassuring. She breathed in his deodorant with her cheek pressed against his chest.

Outside, someone thudded into a car with a hollow *bang*. Emily and Ray jumped.

It was happening again. Emily could see at least twenty people in the street, maybe thirty as the smoke shifted. All of them staggered drunkenly. No matter whether they'd been running or limping or carrying an injured friend, everyone seemed like they'd been hammered by an invisible force.

It only lasted a second. Then the people outside changed again. They looked up, regaining their equilibrium, beginning to move once more, but now there was a distinct change in their actions.

"Look," Emily said. "Ray? Look."

"I—I don't . . ." he stammered.

Her skin crawled with revulsion and stress. "Move away from the window," she said, leading him back a few steps. Every muscle in her body had tightened, ready to run, and yet she felt hypnotized by the street outside. Unable to look away, Emily and Ray bumped against a potted plant and stopped, clutching each other. Fortunately, they were concealed by the dark glass.

The people outside lacked focus. Before, everyone had moved with urgency. Now Emily was reminded of a school of fish or the agitated birds she'd seen. Walking slowly at first, then gathering momentum, the people outside banded together into knots of four or five, gazing inward at each other. They seemed more interested in following each other than in looking around.

Some of them dropped the objects they were holding—a briefcase, a jacket, a fabric med kit from a car.

They congregated in groups strictly divided along racial lines, whites with whites, Hispanics with Hispanics, a black woman alone. There was no mixing. Everyone was shoeless, but that didn't appear to be a common denominator. They discriminated against each other by the tones of each other's skin, the most basic visual cue available.

I was one of them, Emily realized. Her group had done the same. All of those people had been white, although she hadn't thought anything of it at the time.

Now she felt like she didn't even know herself, and she might have screamed except for the memory of the woman who'd panicked. Where was that woman now? Outside? Somehow the realization helped Emily control herself.

"I need to find my sister," she said, her thoughts bubbling with horror for Laura and P.J. and Chase and their friends and parents and—

"Stay inside," Ray said. "Emily. Listen to me. We need to stay inside."

"We can't just stand here. Did you try the phone?" She separated herself from Ray and stepped deeper into the building.

Shadows filled every corner. Several computers were on, fed by batteries. The silent gleam of their monitors added to the surreal, lonely feeling that these offices were a place she'd never been before. Over and over, the computers' emergency systems went *beep beep beep* from every side.

Her skin prickled with grime, and her bangs were loose, the blond strands dark with soot. The heat had left her thirsty. Her arm ached from hitting the gangbanger. Bruises throbbed in her shins and knees. But the physical pain was good. It felt better than her yammering fear.

The phones were out.

So was the Internet.

Ray's cell phone got nothing.

Emily found a battery-powered desk radio, but it squealed with static. "Maybe, um, maybe we can . . ." Ray said.

Emily lowered the radio's volume, then left it dialed to the local news station. Would they hear something soon? Anything?

A windstorm rumbled through the street, blowing the haze away in curtains. The wind peppered the glass with grit and trash. A fist-sized object smacked one window and disappeared again. *Krakrak!* The noise was like something outside trying to get in. Every muscle in her body was clenched in terror.

Then the wind stopped. Rain splattered down.

Just as quickly, the rain quit and a thick fog blew in. It swirled and moaned against the building, speckling the glass with moisture.

Ocean fog in June? Emily wondered.

Another flock of birds darted past. Two or three hit the glass and fell dead as the rest swished and spun and were gone.

Despite the overcast, despite DNAllied's insulated glass, the air grew warmer. Emily raked her fingers through her filthy hair and damp scalp. How much hotter must it be outside? Ray's pink face was dotted with sweat.

"The break room," she said. "It has a TV. We—"

Four ghosts appeared in the fog.

"Oh God." Emily ducked behind a desk, waving frantically at Ray. Had the people outside seen them? Her eyes felt as wide as lightbulbs as she peeked around a filing cabinet, but she couldn't stop herself from looking. What if they'd walked right up to the glass?

The foursome moved abnormally as they went by, taking short, erratic steps more like animals than human beings. Then they were gone.

Emily stood up, wondering how long she and Ray could stay inside by themselves.

In the break room, the TV screen was broadcasting snow. She left it on as they examined the cupboards and the refrigerator for food. Chips. A banana. Two take-out boxes of Italian. The vending machines were loaded with snack bags and Pepsi, but the machines were dead without electricity.

Emily went to the sink and lifted the faucet handle. The water was running. Emily drank until she was nauseous and gestured for Ray to drink, too. "We should fill everything we can find," she said.

He nodded, but he made no effort to locate a janitor's bucket or other containers.

She topped off every cup she found in the cupboards, small or big, dirty or clean. Then she pulled the stopper and filled the sink, too.

What if the fires spread?

The rain and the fog could have extinguished the littlest fires started by stovetops or car crashes. The wind would drive the largest burns inland to the east—and so much of the city was concrete and steel. They might be okay.

Emily sat beside Ray and monitored the radio as it squawked and hissed. They couldn't see the street from the break room, which was a relief at first. It also made her nervous.

What else can we do?

"It's something in the sky," she said. "Ray? If it was a biological agent, I'd be infected. It got me while I was outside. Then I would have communicated it to you."

"Not necessarily," he said.

"What if we wave and yell at those people? What if they come inside and they're okay, too?"

"You don't know what they'll do."

"*I* wasn't dangerous. You saw them. They're slow. Confused. I think it's affecting their ability to think."

Ray shook his head.

"The building protects us," she said. "There must be other survivors who are okay, people in other buildings or parking garages. We need to find them."

"Don't be an idiot."

She wasn't going to let him stop her. "It's something in the sky like from a nuclear bomb! You've seen those movies, right? Except the effect is still going on. Cars won't start. There's no power."

"Bombs don't work like that."

"It started this morning," she said. "My laptop was scrambled. Then the lights started flickering. The news said there were sunspots. Maybe we can shield ourselves! We need metal. We could make helmets." Emily got up and paced away from the table, but stopped to protect her toes. At the very least, she needed to look for Band-Aids and a pair of shoes.

"We should wait," Ray said.

I can't, Emily thought. *My family's out there.* But she could see in his demeanor that he would resist if she tried to make him go outside. He was too cautious, too good at managing risk. It was how Ray dealt with everything. Maybe she could change his mind if she found something that worked.

"I'm going to look around," she said.

Walking through the building alone, her pulse felt too loud in her neck, as if her heart were in the wrong place. She took one step and then another, touching the skin beneath the collar of her blouse.

You can do this, she coached herself. *You can.*

She reached the front entrance and looked out. There was a shoulder bag lying on the steps by the door. Emily thought she recognized it. She leaned forward to see if—

Her vision filled with white pinpoints.

She threw herself backward, cracking her elbow on the tile floor as she scrabbled away.

In the hall, she stopped, grateful for her sanity. She clung to the floor and sobbed. Maybe she should have known better. The lobby was faced entirely with clear glass, not tinted, and the roof lifted to form an arch above the door. The effect was penetrating that wall. If she'd needed more proof, her brush with the outside was enough. Something in the air or the sky was affecting people's brains.

Emily stood up, wiping her cheeks. She entered another stretch of cubicles and looked at the desktop computers. If she ripped the plastic off one of the towers, she thought she could bend the steel manifold inside to form some kind of headgear. Or she could use the metal shelves in the supply room. But how would she cut them?

By habit, she'd walked toward her own office in the southwest part of the building. Along the same wing were more offices with windows to the outside—double-pane windows protected by the ribbed overhang of the roof.

Emily treaded carefully to the last door.

DNAllied was situated partway up a long, mild slope in the terrain. The last office looked out across several blocks of L.A. and West Hollywood.

The fog had lifted in tendrils and veils. The weird lights in the sky seemed to be gone, leaving only the sun. It glared through the mist onto the cityscape. She saw no moving cars, no planes, few people, only the tireless black fingers of smoke rising from six locations.

Her gaze was drawn to a small group about two blocks away—a group of four people walking with direction and purpose. Their postures were different than the light-footed gaits of everyone else. So was the way they'd formed together like a battle line of soldiers. But they weren't in uniform. They seemed like another random collection of people, one man in a sports coat, another in a purple-and-yellow Lakers jersey.

They wore shoes.

They were multi-racial—three white, one black—the only mixed group she'd seen, although they were exclusively male.

"Ray!" she shouted. "Ray!"

A fifth man emerged from the standstill traffic and approached them. He was also white. He held a split chunk of wood like a club. Emily thought one of the four called to the fifth man. This person was smaller than the rest, a boy. His head undulated on his neck as he conveyed his message.

The fifth man mimicked the boy's peculiar head movement as he joined them, perhaps hooting one word.

Emily was struck again by the normality of so much of what she saw—the elevated, colorful signs of a Shell station and a Circle K, a restaurant, an apartment complex—but the glass face of another building had been punched in by a delivery truck, and the other survivors on the street shrank from the organized group.

Everyone moved in that flighty way except these five men, which emphasized the willful, almost predatory manner in which they carried themselves.

Behind her glass, Emily raised one hand reluctantly, caught between hope and dread. *Why aren't they affected, too?* she wondered. *What's different?*

"Ray!" she hollered. "Ray, my God! Come here! Ray!"

Why didn't he answer? She almost left the window to check on him. Then with a decisive movement, she banged on the glass. But the men outside were down the block. They couldn't hear.

Emily turned and rummaged through the two desks in the office, looking for a flashlight. She realized she should check the emergency supplies. They performed earthquake drills twice a year. Emily sprinted down the hall, skipping awkwardly to save her toes. She opened a supply closet and rifled through the printer paper and ink cartridges for an orange duffel bag. Then she ran back to the window with a fat halogen light.

The group strode past her building on West 6th Street, continuing east with the wind. Emily smacked the glass again. She flicked her light on and off, on and off.

One man noticed her flashlight from the corner of his eye. He rocked his head in that odd motion, sharing two words with his friends. Two sounds. No more. In unison, they turned to stare at her. Emily froze, unsure if she'd made a mistake.

She saw now that all of them were armed. Each man held a hunk of wood, a long pole, or a tire iron.

The boy was their leader. Lean, light-haired, he stayed in front, his head shifting alertly as the group walked through the cars.

As they moved closer, Emily realized with a chill that some of their clubs were bloodied. Red spatters covered one man's chest. Another's cheek was smeared. Who had they been fighting? More gang members?

Emily was still making sense of the gore on their crude weapons when she brought her hand to her mouth, overwhelmed by the most acute shock of all.

The boy in front was her nephew, P.J.

11

. . . .

NORTHERN CALIFORNIA

The change in Earth's magnetic field seemed to be increasing. That was Marcus's first thought as he shook off the effects of another interrupt. This time he'd lost two hours. His watch was gone, but he was able to judge how long he'd blacked out by the daylight streaming through the window. It was midafternoon.

Marcus put his hand against the wall to steady himself, dripping with sweat. He was in one of the offices. The desk had been overturned and there was paperwork scattered on the floor beside the computer monitor, keyboard, phone, and two couch cushions from the lounge.

Something else didn't match. Marcus saw three phone cords looped neatly on the carpet with a thicker, darker computer line—but this room only had one phone. He also thought he smelled Janet, his ex. The scent was rich and feminine, and he was embarrassed to discover he was sexually aroused. That was a part of his life he'd neglected in recent years.

"Hey!" he yelled, wondering where the others had gone. Silence. Then he heard a faint *tik, tik tik* like footsteps. The noise surrounded him.

Tik.

The sound lifted the hair on the back of his neck. Was there someone creeping in the hall? On the roof?

Marcus bent to grab the desk lamp. Its shade had been torn off when the room was trashed, and the bulb was shattered. Now the short lamp made a good club.

Tik tik.

He couldn't explain what was happening. He'd expected massive geomagnetic storms, but not unconsciousness—except he hadn't been unconscious. He seemed to walk and act during the interrupts without memory of what he'd done.

Suddenly he lowered his weapon. The "footsteps" were the sound of the station expanding in the heat. The prefab building was mostly aluminum and plastic, but it had wood facades that were swelling in the sun.

The temperature had risen significantly. Ten degrees? More?

He felt nauseous. His left shoulder throbbed and his hand ached. Was this a precursor to a heart attack? The interrupts might be especially difficult for a man like himself, a middle-aged desk jockey.

That smell . . . His brain was misfiring, generating tricks of memory and other sensory illusions. Janet wasn't here.

Where was Roell?!?

The thought cut through Marcus like a bullet. He lurched across the room to the door. The hall was dark. Marcus padded softly on the carpet, afraid, but then he rejected the feeling.

"Steve!" he yelled. "Kym!"

Had he called Roell before the first interrupt? Any kind of warning would have been better than none.

Roell probably hadn't made it halfway home. The drive down to Janet's house in Palo Alto would have taken four or five hours depending on traffic. With luck, Roell hadn't been so badly hit. The phenomenon wouldn't be the same everywhere. Marcus believed the interrupts occurred in pulses dependent upon a complex interaction between the flares, the solar wind, and the Earth's magnetic field.

He needed to get to a working phone and a car. If there was any chance he could find his son, he'd take it.

Where were his keys? Steve's might be in his room. Kym had kept her BlackBerry in her desk. The thought gave Marcus direction, and he increased his pace an instant before he stopped and stared.

The station lounge was filled with perks like Blu-ray and Wii, the big couch, the Ping-Pong table, and free soft drinks and snacks, all provided by Doug Hoffman, the dot com gazillionaire who'd put up half of the funding for the array.

The lounge had been destroyed. The door to the small entry room was propped open by the TV, which lay on the floor, and the couch was stripped. The vending machines' glass faces were smashed open. Why? The machines were rigged to dispense everything for free, but even if he'd been gathering supplies before the last interrupt, why bother with tiny bags of chips and candy? There was real food in the kitchen and in the two ranch homes on-site.

Someone had flown into a rage in this place.

Marcus Wolsinger stared at his own hands as a slow breeze pushed through the doors and touched him, invading the building with heat and dust. The knuckles of his left hand were swollen. He was right-handed, but there were small cuts on that palm, too, and his shoulder and back hurt down to his tailbone. Was he responsible for the vandalism himself?

"Steve!" he yelled.

A footstep whispered in the shadows behind him. Marcus whirled, raising his fists.

Agent Drayer looked shaken and angry. Her jacket was gone and her blouse was ruffled, missing two buttons. Marcus saw a faint dab of red at her nostril. She'd had a nosebleed.

"Where is everyone?" she asked.

Her tone set him off. Her voice was accusing, as if the interrupts were his fault. "I don't know," he said.

"I thought I heard someone outside," she said.

"It's the station settling in the heat."

"I heard voices. There's a house across the field, right?"

I sent Roell away because of you, Marcus thought. He would have kept his son here if the NSA hadn't arrived, and then maybe Roell would be safe. They'd be together.

"We should—" Drayer said.

Marcus walked away. She could stay or go. He didn't care. But as he eased through the glass, a crumpled shape in the entry room turned his head. Just as the door from the lounge into the entry room was propped open by the TV, the entry room's door to the outside was held open by a body. Marcus cringed, feeling cold despite the hot wind.

The TV concealed most of the body except for its hand. The fingers were white. They looked like a man's.

"What do you see?" Drayer asked.

She walked after Marcus as he altered his course.

What if the man was Steve?

Marcus shaded his eyes as he neared the lounge's windows. Maybe the man on the floor should have been more important, but his gaze was drawn outside.

The sky was too bright, nearly cloudless except for a thin white membrane with vast bowls and gaps punched through it. Ferocious storms were alive in the atmosphere. Marcus wondered how long he had before the turbulence rocked downward and scoured the low peaks of the Coast Range. The land was baking with thermals. This close to the cooling expanse of the Pacific, would they see tornadoes or hurricanes?

He was relieved to find the body was one of Drayer's soldiers. Drayer knelt to check the man's vital signs, revealing a hideous contusion on the side of his face. He'd been struck so hard the skin had split in several places. The cheekbone beneath had caved in, yet there was very little blood. The man must have died instantly.

Drayer glanced left and right. She was looking for his assailant or maybe the weapon that had killed him. Marcus was more interested in the soldier's gun belt. The holster was empty. The man's shoes had been stolen, too, which was weird.

Marcus stepped past the body. The sky was mesmerizing. He bumped against the wall when he started down the handicapped access ramp.

Then the railing zapped him. "Ah!" he shouted.

"Are you all right?" Drayer asked.

"Don't touch it. Static charge."

"What does—"

Marcus strode toward the cars lined up alongside the building. If Drayer didn't get it—if one warning wasn't enough—too bad.

Every step felt like a mile beneath the hellish sky. Again and again he squinted back at the station's door, feeling vulnerable and lost. The third car was his own. The silver Accord was four years old, his one luxury since the divorce. He didn't have his keys in his pocket, but he'd kept a spare in a magnetic box hidden inside the rear bumper.

Marcus didn't reach for it. The solar flares were putting enough energy into the planet's surface that metal objects were storing electrical charges, especially those insulated from the ground like vehicles on rubber tires.

How many joules could the steel frame of a car absorb? That would depend on the duration and strength of the flares. But he saw a solution.

Five cardboard boxes sat against the station, supplies unloaded by Drayer's team, possibly food or camping gear. The contents couldn't have been too important because the boxes had been left outside.

His shoulder protested as he yanked at the nearest box, ripping three feet of cardboard from the lid.

"What are you doing?" Drayer called.

Then he returned to his car. A lizard scurried out from beneath it. The dry fields of the array were home to squirrels, rabbits, birds, and these swift little reptiles—but the lizard was sluggish, even crippled. Its legs twitched as it tried to run. Was that a coincidence? Or was this lizard also suffering some lasting effect of the interrupts?

Distracted, Marcus nearly laid his hand on the car.

He jerked back. *Stupid!* he thought. *Everything is different now. Don't be stupid.*

He needed to prevent his body from becoming a conduit for the charge. The rubber in his shoes was probably enough to protect him, but if it wasn't? If he burned?

Marcus felt fresh beads of sweat pop out of his skin as he set his cardboard down and knelt on it. He reached under the bumper and felt along the warm steel.

Nothing happened.

With his key safely in hand, he stood up and glanced at the thousands of dishes spread across the terrain. Most of their lines ran underground, and the dishes themselves were hardened against electromagnetic radiation, but how much could they take before they short-circuited?

Hopefully the pulse had been its most intense in the mountains, sparing Roell and the largest cities. If the phenomenon had hit lower elevations, if Roell had driven far enough to reach the Bay Area, the danger he faced would be infinitely worse. Metal doors and stairwells, power lines, fences, every one of these things was a potential hazard, some dissipating their charges into the earth, others storing it like lightning.

Marcus placed his cardboard by the driver door and stepped onto it. Then he entered the car, making certain to keep his shoe on the cardboard until he lifted his foot after himself.

Drayer was watching. Did she realize how far apart they really were? If he grabbed his cardboard, he could stop her from getting into the car unless she ripped off another piece. Even that wouldn't do her any good as soon as he was moving . . .

The engine wouldn't start.

Marcus tried the ignition six times, but the battery or the starter was dead. More likely, the Accord's computer chips were fried.

He didn't need to decide whether or not to take Drayer along. He stepped out onto his cardboard. The two government sedans were much older than his car, maybe ten years older. They would have less electronics, which meant he might get one running.

"Do you have your keys?" he called.

Drayer shook her head. What was she doing? Going through her pockets? No. She'd touched her belly like she was ill.

Marcus walked closer. Drayer stepped back. Confused by her reaction, Marcus held up his hands. Did she think he'd grab her?

"Will someone come for you?" he asked. "More agents or soldiers?"

"Yes, " she said. "Maybe. This isn't a localized event, is it? Is this happening everywhere?"

"That's right."

"They'll be overwhelmed," she said. "If it's nationwide . . . We're in the middle of nowhere. I wouldn't hold your breath for a helicopter if that's what you're thinking."

"I'm going to the control room," he said.

The station didn't seem to provide any proof against the phenomenon. The walls were too thin. But the world outside was hot and bright. Marcus preferred the shadows.

At the top of the ramp, he summoned enough dispassion to search the dead man's pockets for keys or a phone. He found nothing. Drayer made a gesture as if to carry the body inside, but the shattered glass on the floor was treacherous even without lugging the man's weight. Marcus's shoulder hurt too much, and Drayer was too small. Not like Roell.

Roell hated school and he had trouble with his father, but he was made for physical challenges. As early as Under 7 soccer, Roell had been taller and faster than anyone else on the field, most of them Caucasian. Some parents questioned whether he wasn't actually nine or ten.

They were so upset they said this in Janet's hearing, implying that she'd lied about Roell's age to let him compete against smaller kids.

It was no coincidence that 65 percent of NFL players and more than 80 percent of the NBA were African-American when African-Americans made up less than 13 percent of the U.S. population. Blacks had evolved on wide-open plains. They were built for running—for long-range hunting and war—whereas whites had adapted to the comparatively close-in environment of Europe's mountains and ice. Blacks often possessed greater musculature and stamina. Marcus was glad now for any advantage for his son.

They entered the control room. It hadn't been demolished like the lounge, but even their backup power was out. He had no success with the emergency batteries or the generator system. The phone was no good, either.

Drayer put the handset back in its cradle and said, "Do you have a cell phone?"

Marcus had found Kym's BlackBerry. "It's dead."

"We should look for mine."

"Do it. Go."

"You need to help me," she said.

"I'm busy." Marcus walked to the electronics room. He opened the door to absolute darkness, letting in a dim shaft of light. The room was a twenty-by-forty windowless box lined with racks of signal converters and other hardware. It was the strongest room in the station, a cinder-block vault.

It also functioned as a Faraday cage. Their construction crews had embedded the walls and ceiling with layer upon layer of chicken wire and 5mm copper sheeting to shield the array from the electromagnetic noise created by the systems inside.

If the electronics room would protect him from the interrupts, a Mac sat in the corner as well as the laptop plugged into their servers by the NSA. Marcus needed to restore power with their generators. Then he'd have everything he required for command applications. Outside, the dishes themselves acted as passive receivers. Except for their signal amplifiers and repositioning motors, the dishes needed no electricity—and the interrupts were so strong, amplifiers were unnecessary. Nor was there any reason to realign the dishes since Earth was engulfed by the phenomenon.

With the electronics room up and running, Marcus could make the array live again.

But my son, he thought. *My God, my son.*

Roell might be lost to him. If people everywhere had been unconscious, there would be unattended stovetops. Even if the cities weren't consumed by fire, millions of refugees would separate Marcus from Roell.

He was unable to call or text. Their cars wouldn't start. He could hike down from the mountains to search for his son, but the nearest town of any size was thirty miles away. Hiking that far might take two or three days, even weeks if he lost his mind with each interrupt.

If anyone will survive, it's Roell, he thought. *He's young. Strong.*

His other option was to sift through the solar activity for a pattern. He might be able to predict the next interrupt. Forecasts could be the best way to help Roell. If they reestablished communications . . . if Drayer's people came for them . . .

Marcus didn't dare plan any further, because he knew in his heart that if the phenomenon didn't stop, he was unlikely to see his child again.

Drayer had followed him to the door.

"We should be safe in here," Marcus said. "This room is heavily shielded."

"You think it's coming back," she said.

Marcus avoided her gaze, unwilling to waste time convincing her. He moved to the nearest rack and began stacking the smallest components. This room would be especially crowded if they found Steve or the others, but they needed to carry inside food, water, lights, a bucket for a toilet, and as many phones as they could grab in case service was restored.

"What happened to us the last time?" Drayer asked. "Do you remember?" Her voice was hard again—accusing—but when Marcus looked up, her eyes were afraid.

"No," he said.

She stared at him. Then she nodded. "I'll look for my phone. Car keys. How long do we have before it happens again?"

"I don't know. Not yet."

Drayer left and Marcus brooded as he worked alone, struggling to tamp down his relentless guilt.

I'll find you, he promised his son.

12

. . . .

LOS ANGELES

Emily stood transfixed as P.J. reached up and tapped on the window with his bloody crowbar. The tinted glass was all that separated them, but P.J. wasn't looking at her. He watched the tip of his weapon, his blue eyes smoldering.

Four men stood behind him. Each one held his head down, chin to chest, eyes up. It was a predatory look, dangerous and strange, and yet their faces were utterly calm.

Emily's heart beat so hard she was shaking. From the outside, she knew, the heavy tint reduced the windows to mirrors. Their own reflections must have been more visible to them than her silhouette.

Screeeeeee. His crowbar traced across the glass, testing it. Then he drew his arm back to strike.

"Wait!" Emily cried.

P.J.'s gaze snapped to her, and he paused. Did he recognize her? *Could* he recognize her?

The feral intelligence in his eyes was unlike anything she'd seen in him. This wasn't her nephew. Emily didn't understand how that was possible, but someone else was walking inside his body.

Laura's house was four miles away. The boy Emily loved wouldn't have been able to hike four miles, much less cover that distance in an hour.

Why had he come here?

He'd never visited her workplace. Even if he had, he probably couldn't have followed the directions by himself.

What if Laura sent him to me? she thought, grasping at the hope that her sister was alive. But in truth, she was even more afraid for Laura if Laura had been confronted with this new boy.

P.J. was breathing oddly. Everyone in the group breathed the same way, not in unison, which would have been even more disturbing, but each man inhaled with a flare of nostrils, then exhaled in a gust from his mouth. Slow breath in, quick air out. It reminded her of something.

There wasn't time to study them. P.J. scraped his crowbar up the window again. Emily jumped as the metal crossed her face, then stopped with her body half-turned to run.

They didn't care about her.

Sick with adrenaline, every muscle twitching, Emily stayed at the window as P.J. touched his crowbar over five points like a constellation. *What in God's name is he doing?* she thought. *Is he—*

He was singing.

Another man raised his voice in harmony, piping one note in response. A second man matched him. Then a third. Each of them bobbed his head with strict timing like different parts of one choir. P.J. was the conductor, directing them with his crowbar and his lilting voice.

"Nnnnn mh," P.J. sang with a *tap* on the glass.

The man beside him answered, "Hhn."

"Nnnnn mh," P.J. sang, *tap tap* again on the glass.

"Hn," the next man sang.

Emily realized he was touching his own reflection and indicating his friends. *They're identifying each other.*

It was an astonishing notion. Her fright blended with superstitious awe. These men were strangers to each other—that was her best guess—and yet they'd changed like P.J., which had made them comrades. Who were they?

Then the sky shuddered.

P.J.'s group slumped onto the lawn, his crowbar rattling against the window as they fell. Outside, faintly, Emily heard a great squall of terror. Thousands of people were screaming, disoriented and hurt. The sound prickled her arms with gooseflesh.

She rushed to the glass. P.J. and his men were dazed, barely moving, although three different people ran into the street. Others kept shouting where she couldn't see them.

What if P.J.'s group was more sensitive to the effect than everyone else?

I could bring them inside, she thought.

None of DNAllied's windows were designed to open. Emily glanced at a fire extinguisher recessed in the wall. The fire extinguisher should be heavy enough to break the glass, but they might need the building longer than she wanted to believe. Bashing out the window would be foolish.

One of the men struggled to his feet, the guy in the Lakers jersey. He had sandy hair and close-set eyes—and there was blood on his shirt. Could she trust him?

Emily pounded her fist on the glass. "You have to get inside!" she yelled. "Can you hear me!? Get inside!"

He looked up, but his eyes were foggy.

"There's a door around the building to your left!" Emily yelled. "I'm coming! I'll help!"

She ran down the corridor, then dodged through an office space packed with cubicles. There was a fire exit around the corner—

"Emily!" Ray said. He dropped the desk chair in his arms and lumbered into her path.

She gaped at the exit. He'd constructed a barricade with three desks and a hunk of cubicle paneling, blocking off the glass wall.

"The light stopped!" she said. "We can go outside."

"No one's going outside."

"We have to move this stuff!"

"Emily." Ray grabbed her arm, red-faced and sweaty. He was past his prime, but he outweighed her by eighty pounds even if most of it was fat. He was also two inches taller.

"Everyone's okay!" she said.

His hand squeezed tighter. "Quiet."

"Ow. Ray—"

"Be quiet."

Someone else had entered the building. Emily heard a man's voice. His words were firm and quick. What was he saying?

She and Ray stared at each other as new tension leapt between them. Then he turned toward the voice, dragging Emily with him. She didn't yell or fight. She didn't want to make any sound that would alert the intruder.

Ray's fingers were painful on her arm, and he smelled like fear— but as they approached the break room, the intruder's voice was disrupted by a roar of static.

Emily laughed, an uneven sound of excitement. The voice they'd heard was the radio. It said: "Guard stations wherever possible with police and firefighter units. I repeat, all military per—"

More static.

"—and emergency—"

Static.

She pulled her arm from Ray's grip. "My nephew is out there!" she said.

"The Army will find us. You heard him."

"Ray, other people are all right! We're not the only ones and you can't lock me inside!" she yelled, coiling herself into a karate stance.

Twenty minutes ago, they'd embraced each other. Now a quiet part of Emily wept at the unfairness of what they'd become. Was this who they really were? Barely more than animals?

Outside, a horn was blaring. More distantly, they heard a deep crashing noise as if a building had collapsed. How close were the fires? The idea of being caught in an inferno made her shout again. "We can't stay here!" she yelled.

"If the Army—"

The static from the radio became an ear-splitting squawk as both of them stumbled, suddenly woozy. Ray fell to his knees.

It's back, Emily thought. For a second, the building hadn't protected them from the return of the effect. She saw her chance.

She sprinted from the break room before Ray regained his feet.

In the street, the air spun with storm winds. The world outside was a kaleidoscope of shadows, dust, and one flash of unobstructed daylight.

Emily didn't pause at the fire exit. Ray would catch her if she stopped. Besides, no one stood waiting at the glass. If they'd come to that door, she was too late, so she ran for the corridor where she'd seen P.J.

He was gone. So were his companions.

Emily raised her hand to the window. She scrubbed angrily at the wet streaks on her face. She would have given anything to be with Laura or Chase. Her parents. Anyone. Were they alive?

She looked at the city through curtains of ash and smoke. Hidden in the gloom, she noticed the sun had begun to sink toward the west horizon. It was early evening, and the realization gave her new hope.

Maybe the effect would end when the sun went down.

13

- - - - - - - - - - - -

NORTHERN CALIFORNIA

There was another interrupt, Marcus thought as consciousness returned, but he was more preoccupied by the insistent drive of his muscles and spine.

He was making love to a dark-haired woman. She lay on her back on the blue carpet, spreading her knees wide for him. His cheek pressed against hers. His nose was tantalized by the pleasant musk of her hair and her welcoming body.

At first he wasn't sure if it was a dream. His hips thrust between the open fork of her thighs as she moaned and rocked her pelvis up to meet him. She climaxed. Daylight shone through the window as she held him and shuddered. They were in the same office. None of the mess had been cleaned, although the overturned desk had been shoved against the door as if to protect them from anyone in the hall.

The woman was Rebecca Drayer.

"Yuh, you," Marcus stammered in confusion, then fear. His head cleared like he'd been electrocuted.

The change in Drayer was total and abrupt. As she regained her senses, placing herself, she recoiled. But she was pinned beneath him. Marcus jerked away, hurting himself as he withdrew. His erection wilted.

Drayer screamed, "What are—!?"

She swung her fist at his face as she scrabbled away. She barely connected with his jaw, but Marcus accepted the blow. Drayer's hands went to her groin and her breasts, seeking pain or blood, covering her nudity as she sat up. What she found was evidence of her own sexual excitement.

"Can't, we can't . . ." she stammered.

In her cheeks and in her chest, the high blush of her passion deepened into shock. Then she went white-faced with humiliation, horror, outrage.

Marcus realized he was staring. He brought his palm to his eyes, trying—stupidly—to give her privacy. They were too close together. He stayed on his knees, not wanting her to feel threatened. She scrambled to her feet.

"I don't know what . . ." he said.

"I was . . . You . . . HELP!" Drayer yelled as she stepped back from him. The door was on the other side of Marcus. He saw her gauge how much room she had to run around him.

Could she drag the overturned desk away from the door by herself? Should he offer to help?

Floundering for the appropriate response, Marcus hid his privates with his hand. His testicles throbbed as if he'd been kicked. Where were his pants?

Drayer kept her arm across her breasts and her other hand over her groin, her expression tortured by bewilderment and loathing.

"HELP!" she yelled.

"I wasn't . . . assaulting you." Marcus stumbled through his words.

"HELP ME!"

No one came running. No one shouted back. The station was silent.

Drayer's eyes blazed as she ducked to the floor, sorting through the clothes strewn among the paperwork, the phone, the lamp. She was prepared to fight him if necessary.

"It was the interrupt," Marcus said. "We were . . . different."

Drayer grabbed pants and a shirt. She bundled the clothing against her belly and stalked past him, less interested now in concealing her body than in fleeing from him.

The desk stopped her. She latched onto a corner and dragged. A leg caught on the carpet. Drayer grunted and then screamed in dismay, hindered by the ball of clothing. She wouldn't let go of it. She tugged at the desk and gained an inch.

"Let me help you. Please. Let me help." Marcus found his jeans and yanked them on. Then he approached her as delicately as possible.

Drayer flinched. She couldn't look at him.

He pulled at one of the desk legs. The desk slid a foot from the door. For the slightest microsecond, Drayer's gaze flickered toward his face, conveying anguish and panic—and relief?

She fled into the hall.

"Drayer!" he shouted, but even that felt wrong. *Rebecca.* Did her friends call her Becky?

He felt dehydrated, bruised, and ill. Were those physiological reactions to the interrupt or caused by his shame? Drayer was married. The two of them were strangers. Having sex together was akin to rape, although she'd been an eager participant.

Why was I doing that to her?

Then, more insidiously: *Why was she letting me?*

Marcus wanted to close the door and hide.

He blamed Drayer for his decision to send Roell home, but now she must feel like she was carrying her own curse. He needed to help her.

He needed her to help him. Who else was alive? Why hadn't anyone answered when she screamed?

He hurried to get dressed.

In her rush, she'd abandoned her undergarments. Marcus couldn't imagine taking her white panties and bra with him. He nudged a paper file into a heap with his toes, burying the cotton lace. Then he averted his eyes. He put on his shirt. He couldn't find his socks.

His head was sluggish. He had a pounding migraine. His soul felt undone by sympathy and guilt.

As always, he took comfort in the habit of analysis.

We made love before.

After the last interrupt, what he'd assumed were memories of Janet had, in reality, been physical traces of Drayer. They'd kissed or rubbed each other until she woke up and ran. Then they'd investigated the station and the cars together. Had she recalled the first time or, like him, had she retained only vague impressions until now?

Marcus surveyed the mess they'd ignored and the desk they'd used for security when the door itself was unlocked. During an interrupt, they were clearly unintelligent, screwing like animals when their families needed them.

How much do we remember? Is it possible that I feel like the station is important even if I don't know why?

He ran his hand over his face. His beard stubble hadn't increased since morning, and he doubted he would shave if he wasn't interested in fixing the array. He assumed it was still the first day. Good.

Then he had another unsettling thought.

He hadn't orgasmed, although he'd been close. He'd certainly ejaculated traces of sperm. He hadn't worn a condom. He worried if she was on the pill or the patch or had an IUD.

Forget that for now. Find her. Make sure she's okay.

Where is everyone?

A forbidding sense of déjà vu encompassed Marcus as he stepped into the hall. The last time he'd walked through the station's dark interior, he'd found a dead man . . .

The wind rushed over the building.

Outside, a door creaked back and forth.

"Don't come any closer," Drayer said. Her pale face waited for him in the doorway of the next office. She was dressed again, her black hair tied in a knot. She seemed to have regained her composure. "Don't you come near me," she said.

Marcus's face burned. "I'm sorry."

She was a formidable woman, a professional through and through. Like him, she'd drawn on her training and her intellect to reassure herself. Of course she felt violated. She must feel petrified, and she resented her weakness. She said, "What's happening to us?"

Words spilled out of him. "I think we lose our short-term memories with each interrupt. When the pulse hits, it erases or stunts our personalities. We forget who we are. Then it stops. But I think the effect lasts several minutes after the event. It probably interferes with our memories from several minutes prior as well."

"That doesn't explain why you . . ."

"I'm sorry."

"We . . ." Drayer shook herself. "People may be injured," she said. Her voice was strong. She did not ask more questions. She gave him a command. "We need to find everyone and see if they're okay," she said.

"Good idea." Marcus would have agreed with anything. He didn't want to fight. He wanted to ask if he'd hurt her physically, but he was leery of setting off a new firestorm of accusations.

She touched her forehead and her dark, sweaty hair. "My head," she said. "I'm not sure where to look. Where would they go?"

"The ranch house. The electronics room. I don't know. But they would have heard you, heard us if they were in the station." He tried again to apologize. "Drayer, I'm sorry. I didn't want to . . ."

"It won't happen again."

"I know," he said, although it was useless to promise. Whoever they'd become during the interrupts, they'd freely chosen to make love. He wanted to hurry past her to the lounge and the control room, but he hesitated, reluctant to move toward her. "It's not too late to jury-rig the computers and a generator," he said.

She was skeptical. "You think you can use the array to predict the next flare?"

"That's what we agreed to do."

"It didn't work."

"We must have been caught outside the electronics room," he said. "It doesn't make sense to go searching through the hills or the ranch house. Everyone will come here if they can."

"Not if they're injured."

"We may not have much time before there's another interrupt. If we're in the open . . ." Marcus left his words unspoken. The implication was cruel, but it was true.

By her silence, he knew Drayer understood.

If we're caught in the open, we may become mates again.

Drayer gestured for him to take the lead. Marcus's eyes widened. He hadn't expected her to defer to him. She was a federal agent— but she wasn't James Bond. She was a desk worker, a computer analyst. Equally important, she was unarmed. He was larger. They didn't know who or what they'd find. Marcus was also more familiar with the station.

He went first into the gloom.

Drayer followed him, keeping her distance yet getting closer as soon as he was ten feet ahead. Their circumstances were insane. She clearly didn't want to be with him. She also didn't want to be alone. And what options did she have? To run outside? What if there were more dead bodies or murderers or rapists?

The last doorway in the hall was a gaping mouth. Outside, the wind groaned. Marcus's heart jackhammered in his chest.

He crept forward like a man in a nightmare.

At the door, he peeked in. It was a storage closet. One shelf had been cracked, bowing in the middle, leaving an avalanche of ink cartridges and reams of paper on the floor. Marcus didn't know what he'd expected. Someone waiting to attack?

He stopped at the end of the hall, quivering with tension.

"What is it?" Drayer hissed. "What do you see?"

In the lounge, the damage had increased. The windows had been shattered like the vending machines. The door to the outside was still propped open by the TV, but the dead man was gone. Someone had taken him. Most of the broken glass had been swept against the wall, leaving small shards on the carpet.

"Hello!" Drayer shouted. "Hello!"

Marcus stared at her as she picked barefoot through the glass to the open windows. He tried to match her bravery. He went after her, yet angled to one side, giving her room.

They stared outside.

Squinting in the sunlight, Marcus peered at the ranch house across the field. He couldn't tell if anyone was inside. Where were Steve and Kym and the rest? Had they wandered off into the mountains? The hot wind smelled like dust and dry grass, a good smell, which heightened his anxiety.

Drayer's expression conveyed a sense of being overwhelmed again. He wanted to say something, but what? His head churned with strain and fear.

The low alpine environment would never be ideal for survival. In summer, it was at its worst with too little water and nothing to forage except a few edible plants, squirrels, and deer. If they were forced to subsist without their intelligence, they were doomed.

But that was in the future. At the moment, Marcus grappled with another conundrum. Why had Drayer joined with him instead of one of her agents? Because he was different from the others? As the only black man at the array, Marcus was superficially unique. During an interrupt, his dark skin might be an attractant. Maybe the impression they'd made on each other before the solar flares—no matter if arguments were the basis of the impression—had felt like some kind of bond in their animal state.

And what if we're territorial? he thought. That could explain why the others were missing. Maybe he'd chased them off. Or maybe *he* had been driven from the better home in the area because he looked different.

If so, why would Drayer stay with him?

She turned to him and repeated the most important question. "What's happening to us?" she asked.

Marcus seized on the opportunity to push his emotions aside. "Your brain is an incredibly complicated electrical organ," he said. "It has a biochemical process that produces as much as twelve watts every second every day."

She nodded.

"Our self-awareness depends on that energy. Our minds are the result of fifty billion neurons working as a single unit. I think we're taking enough electromagnetic radiation to interrupt some parts of the whole."

"Then we're going to die," she said. "We'll start losing our hair and throwing up."

"From radiation poisoning? Maybe not. Not inside." Marcus found his resolve. He turned from the sun-washed landscape and walked toward the control room.

"Stop," Drayer said. "I need to find my people."

"They'll come here if they're . . ." *If they're alive,* he thought, but he didn't want to keep frightening her. "Help me first."

They couldn't afford to be enemies.

"Please," he said. "We need to protect the array. Our friends will come here if they can. We'll look for them as soon as we can."

Drayer grimaced, but she walked after him.

Inside the control room, they found one of the computers on the floor. Another was missing. Marcus hurried to disconnect the last Mac and hauled it into the electronics room, where he was startled to find more work accomplished than he recalled.

The missing computer was inside with three cases of canned food and snack bags and Gatorade and Pepsi. Two flashlights. Batteries. A desk fan.

"I don't get it," Drayer said. "Why didn't we hide in here instead of the office? There's food. It's safe."

Marcus set the computer on a rack. He switched on one of the flashlights and swept the beam over the narrow room. "This is why," he said. "No windows. It's dark. There's nothing we recognized as useful, just a lot of machines."

"Here," Drayer said. She passed one of the plastic quart bottles of Gatorade to him, then cracked another for herself.

The sugar smell of the drink made him dizzy with thirst. Marcus coughed as he gulped it, spilling some on his chest. He didn't stop until the bottle was half empty. Then he capped it and walked back into the control room, realizing there was another reason why they might have left this part of the station during the interrupt. The control room was a dead end. They'd have nowhere to retreat in a fight.

"Let's get one of the generators and as much fuel as we can carry," he said. "We also need to punch an exhaust line through the wall. We can look for everyone while we're outside."

"Maybe one of us should stay in here," she said.

"Come with me. Please. I'm scared as hell," he said, admitting his own vulnerability.

It was the right thing to say.

"Me, too," she said.

They studied each other. Warily, he compared her to Janet. At thirty-four, Janet was younger than Drayer, almost too young to be the mother of a seventeen-year-old. She could be fickle, even cold, whereas Drayer was more mature, more deliberate.

"I need to be able to trust someone," she said. "I want to trust you."

"You can."

Drayer hesitated for a beat. Marcus had to fight to meet her stare. Then she said, "You swear you can get the array working?"

"We can."

She nodded. "Let's go."

14

· · · · · · · · · · · ·

NORTHERN CALIFORNIA

As they ventured into the sunlight, neither Marcus nor Drayer looked at each other. They stared at the landscape. Nothing moved except the wind, which murmured through the array, lifting dust and bits of grass and leaves. The debris flashed and swirled. Long clouds warped the sky. Three hundred yards away, the shed with the generator sat beside the residential home. The windows were empty eyes.

Unnerved, Marcus thought, *Is anyone waiting there?*

At the base of the nearest dish, the low weeds rustled like a hand or a snake.

"Watch out!" Marcus said. He jumped back.

Drayer jumped with him—but the noise was two small lizards, moving clumsily.

"Sorry," Marcus said. "I'm sorry."

Cold-blooded life must be affected much harder than we are, he thought. Humans were adept at shifting from hot to cold and back again. Lizards couldn't regulate as much energy.

"We should find hats and sunglasses and wear as much sunscreen as possible," he said. "My guess is skin cancer and cataracts were always a major problem once we got down from the trees."

Drayer froze again. Marcus turned to see what had alarmed her. But she was looking at him. She wanted to get away from *him*.

"What are you talking about?" she said.

"The jungle would have protected us from most of the ultraviolet. I mean the canopy of leaves and branches."

Drayer backed away. Her face was stricken, and Marcus felt a jolt of panic that she would leave him to the wind and the endless white dishes.

"Wait," he said. "I'm okay."

"There's no jungle here!"

"I mean millions of years ago," he said. "The jungle canopy would have protected us from most of the ultraviolet when we were first evolving into early man. This has happened before. This has always been happening."

The sky fluttered, and they both glanced up.

Drayer's voice quieted as she reached a decision. "I don't understand," she said. "But I don't think you're crazy."

Her words affected Marcus more strongly than he could have imagined. He nodded.

They began walking again.

He wanted to reward her confidence in him. He said, "The sun puts out a lot more than visible light. Some of it is lethal radiation, nuclear radiation, but the sun also emits a constant flow of charged particles called the solar wind."

"If it's constant . . ."

"Our sun is unstable. You saw the microflares we were tracking."

"Yes."

"The flares aren't the issue. They don't affect us directly. But in our last readings, the solar wind had quintupled. Earth's magnetic field and ionosphere are being distorted."

"I don't know what that is."

"The ionosphere is our upper atmosphere. It forms a giant bubble around us, but our magnetic field is dozens of times larger than Earth, especially the tail on the night side away from the sun. Right now the whole thing is wobbling. There must be furrows and bumps larger than the planet itself. They collide. That creates shock waves."

Drayer said nothing. Maybe she was trying to picture it.

Marcus grappled with his own thoughts. The atmosphere typically absorbed radiation of the smallest wavelengths such as gamma and X-rays. Now every layer of the sky was oscillating. There might be places on the surface where living things were burned down by invisible death, but he said, "What's hitting us is mostly intense electrostatic noise and magnetic fluctuations. It's not lethal radiation, it's just noise. I don't mean noise like you can hear. I mean energy bursts."

They'd reached the shed, a broad cinder-block cube much like the electronics room inside the station. The doors were locked.

Marcus looked at the nearest home, but he couldn't bring himself to investigate. One of the windows was shattered. What if there were more dead bodies inside?

Six paving stones sat in front of the shed, forming an entrance for the rare times when it rained and the mountains turned to mud. Marcus wrenched one of the stones out of the dirt, then used the stone to bash the lock off the steel door.

They went in. The air was stale and warm.

Marcus assessed the four DuroMax 4500-watt generators, which were held to the floor by brackets, not permanently mounted. Each generator was an orange chunk of machinery cradled in black handlebars. He disconnected the power line from one and began loosening the wing nuts that secured the floor brackets.

"I don't know enough about the brain to say what's being inhibited," he said. "It seems like most of our executive function is gone. Logic. Memory."

"Our frontal and temporal lobes."

"Yes," he said, impressed with her again. "The good news is the pulse won't be consistent over the whole planet, not at first. For all we know, it's still happening, but we're in an unaffected area. If we can calculate the safest spots, some of them might be fairly consistent, nodes where magnetic anomalies prevent the shock waves. People might be okay there."

"You said 'Not at first,'" Drayer said, finding the bad news he'd hoped to disguise in the good.

"I think the shock waves are increasing."

"So the safe spots . . ."

"There won't be many of them, and they might not last."

Marcus had the generator free. He hefted one end of the machine and gestured for her to take the other side. It weighed a hundred and thirty pounds. Drayer struggled with it, but Marcus stopped her.

"Let's leave it for a minute," he said. "We'd better see how much fuel we have."

They walked behind the shed to a dozen steel drums of fuel. Even one was probably too heavy for them to carry, although an old jeep was parked nearby, a 1980s model GMC built before cars were equipped with computers.

Marcus wondered if Drayer would want to leave if they got the jeep running. Maybe he should hide the key if he found it . . .

"Can you hotwire a car?" he asked.

"What? No."

He tentatively put his fingertips on one fuel drum, afraid it held a static charge. But it was okay. Sitting on the bare earth, the drum had dissipated whatever charge it had absorbed into the ground.

"We'll have to roll it across the field," he said. "Let's move the generator first. I don't want it damaged if there's another interrupt."

We, I, he thought, noting the difference in his words. Janet had accused him of starting too many of his sentences with *I*. That needed to change.

He grunted in discomfort when they lifted the generator, hurting his back. Drayer didn't complain. They lugged the machine across the field in the dry wind and the heat. Marcus tried to keep to the oblong shadows of the dishes.

Something moved at the corner of the station.

"What was that?" Drayer said.

"A person. I saw him. Let's put the generator down."

Whoever they'd spotted should be friendly. The only people in the area were Marcus's staff and Drayer's agents—but too many aspects of their lives had changed. A cold, disconnected calm filtered through Marcus as he walked toward the station, analyzing every detail.

There was no one at the corner.

Marcus glanced back at the generator. He didn't want to carry it inside until he was sure they weren't walking into an ambush.

"Go," Drayer said, taking the initiative. They had no weapons, much less a gun. Nevertheless, they approached the door the way Marcus had seen federal agents assaulting bad guys on TV, covering each other. He watched the windows while she went to the door. Then she stood ready until he joined her.

Inside, Marcus picked up one of the boxy game consoles on the floor. *I can throw it if I have to*, he thought, liking its corners and light weight.

Drayer grabbed three Coke cans for missiles. Marcus took another.

They wavered between moving down the hall or heading into the control room. Drayer probably wanted to avoid the office. It would always remind her of what had happened. In any case, Marcus's goal was to protect his electronics.

A man coughed in the control room.

Marcus signaled Drayer. He raised his clumsy weapon, ready to protect her. Then they went through the door together.

Steve Church sat at a desk like a crumpled shadow.

"Steve!" Marcus said. "Steve?"

Steve didn't lift his gaze from the desktop. His thin hair was curled with sweat. He gripped his armrests like he thought he'd float away. Dirt smudged one cheek.

"He's hurt," Drayer said as Steve mumbled, "They did this to us. We found them."

Marcus shook his head. "What are you talking about?"

"We never should have been looking in the first place. Don't you remember?"

"No."

Steve looked up, wide-eyed, ignoring Drayer. His tone was victorious. "I can show you," he said. "Where are the computers? Did they take them?"

"I don't think—"

"We found them! Sentient life in Ursa Major. They did this to us. There was a carrier wave. The signal . . . I can still hear it. Like music."

"Goddard detected similar microflares in a lot of places," Marcus said. "That's it. There was no artificial signal."

"They did this to the sun to blind us."

Could he be right? Marcus wondered for a split second. But . . . no. No. Steve's ravings were delusional paranoia. Even if they'd discovered an extraterrestrial signal before the first interrupts, Steve wouldn't have any memory of it. Worse, Steve seemed to think aliens were stealing things right here in the station or among the array.

"Come with me," Marcus said, although he immediately regretted the words. He couldn't replace the computers if Steve smashed them for some reason. "We're bringing a generator and some fuel into the building. You can help."

Drayer looked at Marcus and frowned. She clearly shared his concern.

"Let's get you something to drink," Marcus said to Steve, setting his hand on his friend's shoulder. He turned to Drayer. "Can you get him something to drink?"

She didn't move, and he saw the question in her eyes. If it came down to it, who would he choose—his colleague, who was deranged, or the woman he barely knew, yet had slept with? The trust they'd forged was so tenuous.

"Please, Rebecca," Marcus said, using her given name for the first time.

Drayer nodded. She went to the electronics room, fetching Gatorade and several snack bags. Marcus sat beside Steve as they devoured the nuts and chips. Drayer kept her distance.

In that quiet moment, Marcus tried to think ahead. The electronics room would be a very temporary shelter even if they had unlimited food and water. He and Steve might be able to rig a portable Faraday cage on the jeep. They would need metal and a welding torch . . . Maybe they could find their way into caves or a bomb shelter. Then what?

Marcus realized he was making himself feel as demented as Steve. *Get up,* he thought. *Get moving.*

He left his chair. "We can eat when we're done," he said. "Rebecca? Steve? Come on."

They returned outside. Marcus held one of Steve's arms and Drayer held the other as Steve tottered between them, unhappy and distracted. Dusk was settling over the mountains.

"It'll be dark in an hour," Drayer said.

"They did this to us," Steve muttered as Drayer added, "The sun will be on the other side of the world. We should be safe."

"I'm sorry, I don't think so," Marcus said. "You have to realize, the initial shock waves are larger than the distance between us and the moon. Then our magnetic field echoes and pulses. It's everywhere."

They reached the generator. Marcus guided Steve to one side of it. Before he lifted the other end, he glanced at Drayer. He wished he could console her, but she deserved the truth.

"Nighttime won't be any safer than the day," he said.

15

• • • • • • • • • • • •

LOS ANGELES

Twilight darkened the city as Emily completed her preparations to leave DNAllied. Sitting on the tile near a barricaded door, she checked her laptop again, memorizing the numbers displayed on its screen. It was June 14. The summer solstice was eight days away. Daylight in southern California would average nearly fifteen hours for the next two weeks with sunrise at 5:45 and sunset a few minutes after 8:00 p.m.

"Fifteen minutes," she said mostly to herself.

"You should wait," Ray said. "The Army will come. The police. Somebody."

"Help me."

"No."

Ray wouldn't meet her eyes in the white gleam of the laptop, which Emily closed to reduce its light. She didn't want to attract attention from outside, where distant flames cast an orange-red glow against the nearest buildings. Worse, another fire burned just a hundred yards down the street—a small fire tended by human shapes.

"You're making a mistake," Ray said. "Your family . . ."

"Help me," Emily said. "Please." She didn't want to hear it any-more. Ray kept saying her family would want her to be safe, but he was only trying to justify his own cowardice.

Emily couldn't stay. Yes, she hoped to find Laura and Chase, but there was another reason to go. Emily had a theory about what was happening—an unlikely, fantastic theory—and yet the evidence was too compelling.

She was determined to find out.

She double-checked her sneakers, a pair of men's running shoes stolen from a coworker's desk. They were too big, so she'd stuffed the toes with extra socks and laced them tight.

She also had a backpack loaded with snacks, water bottles, a first aid kit, a radio, AA batteries, and mace. There was pepper spray in her front pocket, a map of the downtown area in her back pocket, and a heavy flashlight to occupy one hand. She wore clear plastic lab glasses and a leather jacket despite the heat because the roads would be littered with ash and wreckage. She hadn't forgotten the gangbangers or P.J.'s crowbar, either.

Her jacket pocket also held a blood collection kit. There were more in her backpack. Emily had enough VacuCaps to draw samples from two hundred people.

"I'm leaving," she said, gesturing at the barricade. Ray didn't move and she said, "You don't want anyone to know you're in here, right? If I have to pull those desks away by myself, it'll be noisy."

"Just wait."

"Ray—"

"What if you don't come back?"

That's what he's really afraid of, Emily thought. She actually smiled, feeling protective of him. It was a welcome emotion compared to her anxiety.

"If I have to come back, I will," she said. "And if I find help, I'll send them for you."

At sundown, everyone would turn normal again. Emily was sure of it. She had to be sure, because if she was wrong, what difference did it make if she was fine when everyone else she knew was gone?

She planned to cross the city during the night. At worst, she'd cover it in stages. If necessary, Emily hoped she could make it from one safe place to another, leapfrogging her way to the hospital and then to Laura's house even if the journey took two or three nights.

Ray didn't realize his terror was amplified by his own immobility. The thought of being caught by the effect made Emily shiver, but she would take that gamble in order to help her family. If she could draw her blood samples . . . If the hospital had emergency power . . .

Emily believed the military would use Silver Lake as a base if they'd come into the city. Hospitals were priority assets in any disaster. The Army might have working communications, and, equally important, most of Silver Lake's fourth floor was dedicated to oncology research labs. DNAllied had the equipment she needed—but without electricity, the DNAllied building was useless.

She also wanted Chase. Oh, how she wanted his self-assurance instead of Ray's stubborn attitude.

She got up and began to haul the furniture from the door. They'd stacked desk chairs on top of the heavier desks. She removed one and nearly dropped another before Ray joined her.

At last, the exit was clear. Emily returned to her backpack and the crude armor she'd devised. She planned to wear a helmet even after the effect had stopped. Maybe it would help. What if she was trapped in the open at sunrise?

The helmet was bulky, but it was her best effort, ripping the guts from two computer towers and keeping two steel panels, banging the corners into shape with a fire extinguisher. Then she'd cinched both parts together with shoelaces. Two fins would rest on her shoulders, although she couldn't expect them to keep the helmet in place. Velcro ties needed to be wrapped around the outside, one as a chin strap, the next across her forehead. It wasn't a process she could manage alone.

"Ray?" she asked, holding up the straps.

He joined her on the floor. Emily paused before donning her helmet. She'd avoided sharing her theory because Ray was upset, but he was right about one thing. If she didn't come back, someone else had to carry on. Ray could preserve her notes in case the Army really did rescue him in a few days.

"I wrote down where I'm going and everything I've seen so far," she said. "Here." She handed him three folded sheets of paper. Her pack held a duplicate copy along with several flash drives protected inside an Altoids tin. "We also have backups of my statistical models in my office. UCLA's supercomputer is probably okay, too, if we can reach it."

"Why would you go there?"

"The data, Ray. Our gene therapies. They'll need it."

The two of them waited in the growing dark, flashlights off, laptop off, gazing at the street outside. It had been maddening to be so limited in what she could see or hear—because of that it had taken all day to figure it out.

"They're cavemen," she said.

"What are you talking about?"

"They're not zombies, they're cavemen! Look at them. They work together. There's a social structure. They're just not very sophisticated."

Thirty people had set up camp in a gas station down the street, using the mechanics' bays for shelter. The men had found weapons among the many tools, and the building was surrounded by an open parking lot, which made it easier to guard. There was probably food in the cashier's office and water in the restrooms, although Emily cringed at the idea of drinking from public toilets. Maybe they'd figured out the sinks.

"I've been studying them," she said. "They're not stupid, they're more primitive. They're literally like primates. I'd give anything to know what's happening to chimpanzees and the great apes. Are they also acting weird? Are they the same?"

"I don't . . ."

"Those survivors remind me of chimps. They don't talk much, definitely not as much as you'd expect people to argue during the end of the world. Most of their communication seems to be gestures or simple sounds."

Ray shook his head.

"P.J.'s group was different—more organized," she said.

"You're imagining things."

"You didn't see him, Ray," she said, worrying that more imagination was exactly what they needed. Ray's lack of flexibility wouldn't accomplish anything except heavier barricades at the doors.

He wanted to ignore the signs. She couldn't.

All mammals had the same bump of nervous tissue they'd inherited from the reptiles—the brain stem—a primordial glob at the top of the spine. It was the most basic part of them. Eat. Sleep. Reproduce. Fight. Emily believed everyone caught by the effect was limited to the brain stem and the occipital lobes, which processed visual input. They probably retained some function elsewhere throughout the brain, although this activity must be sporadic except in P.J.'s kind. And if some people were cavemen, her nephew was . . .

Emily could barely admit to herself what she was thinking. She recognized her own inclination to explain any trait as genetic, but she might be one of the few people left with the education to fit the pieces of this puzzle together. How many other biologists, anthropologists, or scholars were still alive, much less protected from the outside?

The primitives' main objective was food. They foraged through the landscaping for leaves and bark, which seemed inedible, and yet Emily saw them chewing on this greenery as well as the fruit and bread they found in surrounding buildings.

This group was strictly Caucasian. Two other groups had appeared only to retreat after a show of yelling and mock combat, thrashing at the air with their hands.

The streets of L.A. must be overrun with survivors. Dividing themselves into rival packs only created new obstacles, and yet all three groups had assembled themselves along ethnic lines. The first intruders had been Hispanic. The next group had been black. The primitives were racist in the truest sense of the word, using skin colors like uniforms.

They understood fire, too. Two hunters had returned with a bowlful of embers, nursing this heat into flames against the outside of the garage. They had no concept of the gas pumps or the propane tank nearby. Nor did they care that they were permanently stripping the area of fuel, killing trees for bark and branches, uprooting brush. Late in the afternoon, they'd cooked a dog, piercing hunks of its carcass on metal shafts.

Emily and Ray had also seen two primitives copulating on their knees right in front of everyone else, a man in his thirties and a girl, maybe sixteen.

She was the teenager Emily had tried to help near the freeway. Emily recognized her striped knee socks. Watching them, Emily had flushed with horror, but the girl made a show of laughing as she pushed her rump against the man.

Emily had been relieved when Ray coughed and walked away, leaving her alone at the window. Did he think she was gross for staying to watch? She needed clues. Odds were the girl hadn't known the man before, so what had set them off? A look? A scent? More than once Emily had felt a glint of attraction for a stranger herself; a tall man on the sidewalk; a nice face in the car beside her at a stoplight. It was just an impulse, easily repressed—but early in her research, Emily had read studies involving specific brain injuries, like in car crashes, when people went through their windshields. Survivors with poor function in their frontal lobes were often disinhibited.

The primitives seemed to lack self-restraint, and yet the girl was underage. Wouldn't sex hurt? Maybe she'd faked her enthusiasm in order to stay with the group or to avoid a beating.

As a mother, Laura was obsessed with child molesters and perverts, even saving a DOJ map on her computer. Statewide, California had more than eighty-five thousand registered sex offenders. Laura assumed twice as many hadn't been caught or had yet to act, satisfying themselves in other ways. Even Chase liked soft-core movies with threesomes or other things Emily wouldn't do herself, and he was educated and clean and decent.

Laura said porno was the biggest industry in the world after food and guns. Viagra made huge money for the same reason. Even after men's bodies failed, she said, their brains lusted—and Emily knew too much biology to disagree.

Most animals would not breed beyond the limits of their environment. Human beings had responded to other pressures. In the slow, global struggle for dominance, one nation or faith against the rest, larger populations tended to prevail. Natural selection had led to a race of men and women hardwired for sex, but it came with a dark side.

Emily had been able to find mace and pepper spray so readily because the other women in the building, like her, were afraid to walk the short distance from their cars to the office without protection. Now, when the effect stopped, how many girls and women would discover themselves with unknown partners? In some ways, Emily was more afraid of suffering the same fate than of being hurt, which turned her thoughts back to P.J.

"There's obviously a cognitive difference between normal survivors and P.J.'s minority," she said. "We're sure to find a genetic variation."

Ray shuffled through her notes. It was a dismissive gesture.

"We might be able to cross-reference their blood samples with medical and school records to see if those men are autistic or otherwise mentally handicapped!" she said. "And if we can identify them, we'll save lives. I don't mean because we should put them in jail. We know the cure even if we need time to develop it. Our gene therapies might stop his kind from attacking everyone else."

"It's dark," he said suddenly.

"We—" Emily stopped. There was no use pretending anymore. The sun had gone down, but the human shapes in the street hadn't changed. She peered at her watch. Her slim DKNY digital had quit working before she was safe, but she'd found a wind-up Invicta and clipped it to her wrist.

8:12.

"No," she said. She'd been fooling herself because the sky remained brighter than it should be, glowing with the auroras.

Disappointment took her breath away. If the effect never ended, if it wasn't sunlight that caused it but something else . . . Emily slumped down, defeated and furious, beating her hands on the white tile floor.

An hour later, she stood sleepless at the glass. Only a few of the primitives remained around their fire. The rest had gone inside the garage while these four stood guard.

Ray dozed in a chair behind her. They were both exhausted, but Emily felt like waking him to apologize. More and more, it looked as if the two of them would be forced to endure together. Could she repair their relationship?

"You should help me," she murmured. "Why can't you—"

The silhouettes around the fire fell down. One man toppled into the edge of the flames. His hair caught fire. Then everyone stood up again as other people emerged from the gas station, yelling in confusion.

It was 9:24 p.m. Emily put her thumb on an iPhone, typing Laura's number. There was no signal. She had the radio beside her, too, but it continued to squawk and buzz except for one loud screech of words:

"—shill law. In all cases—"

Martial law, she thought. The voice sounded like the same man as before. Was it a recording? If so, who knew how long the message had played or if there were organized police or soldiers left to monitor the broadcast.

"What's going on?" Ray asked.

"They're awake. It stopped."

The burning man thrashed as another guy fought with him, smothering his clothes, but the yelling was much bigger than thirty voices. The sound carried over the city like a high, moaning wind.

"I'm going out there," she said.

16

. . . .

LOS ANGELES

Emily crept away from DNAllied as men shouted in the night. Their voices were an intimidating sound laced with despair and rage. Gripping her flashlight, which she didn't dare turn on, Emily looked back at the door. It wasn't too late to run inside before Ray rebuilt his barricade.

She hid behind a concrete planter as the wind made a muffled noise against her helmet. Each breath tasted like smoke. To the east and north, the fires gave off dull roars like ocean surf. The sky was black with clouds. There were no auroras.

Four shadows ran through the street in front of her, picking their way through the stalled traffic. "Don't touch them!" a man said. "Don't touch them!"

What was he yelling about?

Emily stayed behind the planter. Hiding was selfish, but she didn't want to lead anyone into DNAllied. She had to protect their computers and equipment. Ultimately she'd come outside to meet people, but she felt like a rabbit in a zoo where the cages had been opened. She was small and weak. Too many other survivors would be dangerous.

She ran to a Jetta that had stopped halfway on the sidewalk. She crouched there, then scurried to a minivan and knelt again.

Shoes littered the street—a white shirt—someone's phone. It took her a moment to realize the minivan was contributing to her fear. When she leaned too close, her hair lifted inside her helmet. She'd felt the same bad energy alongside the Jetta.

Emily stood up. "Oh my God," she said.

The city block formed a long, high canyon pooled in darkness, but the faint light of the fires reflected from the glass and steel of dozens of vehicles. Thousands more waited beyond them in the night.

Were the cars electrified by the effect? As a computer scientist, Emily knew basic engineering. Electricity traveled easily through water. Human beings were mostly liquid. Her sneakers had rubber soles, but she'd put her knee on the street when she hid beside the minivan. That simple act might have been a death sentence.

Already her resolve was fading as she hesitated in the dark.

It had occurred to Emily that the summer solstice and long hours of daylight might have something to do with the effect. She hoped Earth's tilt was a factor, because it could mean that only the northern hemisphere was in trouble. Help would arrive faster if people were safe below the equator, but even if Brazil sent an army, they wouldn't have enough men to stabilize more than a few cities.

You're on your own, she thought, willing herself forward.

The hospital was eleven blocks from DNAllied, practically a straight shot up Union Drive. Emily was going there even if she had to do it ten feet at a time.

She stepped around the minivan and paced toward the next vehicle. The crashed cars had rolled onto the sidewalk here, too, which left only the lawn of an office complex. She climbed through a hedge, then fell hard onto a patch of river rock.

Hidden by the brush, she heard more people behind her. Three shapes appeared in the night. One was sobbing—a woman. The other two seemed to be men. The first growled, "If that guy comes anywhere near us, I'll kill him!"

His friend's voice was more panicked. "Did you see what he did?"

"I'll kill him!"

They slowed in the middle of the street.

Say something, Emily told herself. At some point, she needed to take a chance. She needed allies.

She stood up.

But the trio moved away. They'd only paused to find another opening through the cars. Not quite chasing them, Emily marched twenty feet before she ducked into hiding again, this time against a thin pair of birch trees. Then she ran another fifty feet, stumbling through more empty shoes before she took cover beside a slick yellow Mustang.

She was heading northeast in the direction taken by P.J.'s group. Ahead, she saw a tall billboard advertising a popular kids' show about living, talking flowers. A huge round outline in the corner was one character's petals.

Could this giant picture have drawn P.J.'s group up Union Drive? Because they were curious? Five hours had passed since she'd seen them. By now, P.J. could be anywhere, but there would be others like him.

If she found them, would she have the courage to draw the blood samples she needed?

"I think it's okay," a man said behind her.

Emily leapt up. She banged her head against the Mustang, then wobbled in pain.

Other voices followed the first, hissing, "It's a girl—"

"—on her head?"

Two flashlights cut across her body as Emily scrambled onto her feet. She yanked the pepper spray from her front pocket.

"Whoa," a man said. "We won't hurt you."

Ten survivors had emerged from the office building's underground garage, many of them tapping at cell phones and PDAs. Only a few of the devices had lit screens. The other gadgets were dead.

They were normal people. Their skin color ranged between white, black, and brown, which calmed Emily more than she would have believed.

Most of the group quickly sorted through the abandoned shoes and shoved on anything that would fit. Others gaped at the burning sky. The few women stayed behind the men except for a black-haired lady in her forties. She pushed in beside their leader, carrying a broken-off mop handle like a spear.

"Does your helmet work?" she asked.

"I thought . . ." Emily made a helpless gesture. "The effect might come back."

"No way," the leader said. "It's dark."

They've been having the same argument as Ray and I, she thought.

His face was bruised at the hairline. Had he been hurt in an accident or a fight? At least two more of his people were wounded. One had a scraped cheek. Another man's arm was crudely bandaged in a spare shirt. Emily could only guess what they'd been through with no food or water except what they might have found in a few cars inside the garage, no lights except car lights, and no way to look outside. Their hours underground must have been ugly and claustrophobic.

"I need to get to the hospital," Emily said, hoping she could convince them to go with her. She also wanted blood samples. She needed a control group.

"There'll be a million people at the hospital," the leader said. "We have to find food before the sun comes up."

"I heard a radio broadcast," Emily said. "The Army is trying to put together emergency stations. The hospital will be one of them. Can you—"

All of them dropped when a gunshot echoed through the street. Much closer, they heard a rustling noise in the sky that made Emily push herself even closer to the ground until someone said, "Birds. The gun scared up some birds."

They stood up again. "Let's move," another man said.

"You can stay with us," the leader told Emily, openly studying her. "But we're going for restaurants and stores."

He wasn't looking at her body. He was examining her helmet, lab glasses, and flashlight. If she ran, would he chase her?

"I'm a scientist," she said. "I work in gene therapy. I think I know what's happening and I need to get to a radio, the Army, anyone who's still organized."

"Gene therapy," he repeated.

"I think I know why some people can think and talk during the effect—why they attack the rest." Too late, she realized these people knew nothing about P.J.'s kind. They had been underground, and anyone who ventured outside either hadn't come back or remembered nothing of what they'd seen. "I'd like to take blood samples from everyone here," she said.

"We don't have time for this," the leader said, motioning for her to come closer.

Emily backed away. "I need to get to the hospital," she said. But before she ran, she tried her best to warn them. "Don't touch the cars."

"She's crazy," someone said.

The leader nodded. "I want that flashlight," he said an instant before he stopped and looked past her.

Other survivors had ventured into the street with three flashlights, talking in a loud hush. Emily saw the dynamic change among her smaller group. One man stepped forward, waving his arm, but the rest shrank back as if preparing for a fight.

Then a flashlight popped in the street, bursting apart with a metallic *snap*. It cast a searing white arc like lightning before its owner fell.

There were screams. Everyone stumbled away from the crackling light, but as they fled, two more survivors spasmed and dropped.

The cars were deathtraps—people were being electrocuted—and Emily turned and ran from both groups.

"Wait!" the black-haired lady said. "I'll come with you."

They hurried into the dark. The other woman was short and wore a business suit that couldn't hide the extra pounds on her waist, but she seemed competent and tough.

Emily was grateful. "Don't touch the cars!" she said. "Are you wearing shoes?"

"What difference does—"

Emily clutched her arm and looked down. The lady wore mismatched sneakers she'd scavenged from the street. "The insulation could save your life," Emily said. "I think those people were barefoot."

Ahead, a third mass of dark shapes filtered through the cars, many of them calling to each other. Others babbled or wept. Everywhere on the block, new people were merging with the distraught survivors who'd spent the day in the sun. That would complicate Emily's mission. She was also going the wrong way. The majority of these survivors were headed south.

Walking against the human tide, Emily paused more often than she wanted to, allowing other people through the openings instead of forcing the issue. If someone pushed her into a car . . . If everyone understood the danger, and men used their weight against her . . .

They paused near the bulk of a van. "My name's Michelle," the black-haired woman said.

"Emily."

"Are you really a scientist?"

"Yes."

They started walking again. Emily kept her flashlight off and hid it down against her leg. What if someone jumped her for her equipment? Some of the people around them had put on bike helmets. One man wore a Raiders helmet, probably an office trophy. Others had wrapped their heads in tinfoil or strapped pots or mixing bowls to their heads.

This group was loaded with supplies. They had water jugs from office coolers, briefcases, satchels, and a man on a stretcher. Someone grabbed Emily's pack and she tried to twist free until she saw it was Michelle.

As they cleared the mob, Michelle called back to the strangers. "Where are you going?"

"West," a man said. "Get away from the fires."

If the wind stops, the fires might come back this way, Emily realized. She wasn't sure if the storms would let up, but new fires could start any time and carry through the city. They would be safest on the coast. Unfortunately, Emily didn't believe private homes or condos would be sturdy enough to shield them from the effect. The steel structures and parking garages of the business district might be the only places to hide from the sun.

A body lay in the street. More garbage. Glass. Three stragglers knelt together among the cars, praying. Then a woman lurched out from behind a truck. "Have you seen my daughter?" she cried. "My daughter! Paige Lundgren! She's twelve years old, brown hair, I think she wore a pink shirt today!"

Emily's mouth worked, but the woman was already moving toward someone else in the dark.

"Oh God," Emily said.

Michelle agreed with a sympathetic noise. "Do you have kids?" she asked.

"Fiancé. You?"

"Divorced. I hope that bastard is—" Michelle broke off and said, "The fires look like they're east of us."

They'd reached an intersection where the four-story buildings dropped away to smaller shops, parking lots, and a Jiffy Lube. Beyond a line of trees, Emily glimpsed orange flames and heavy smoke.

"The wind is definitely moving that way," Michelle said. "The fire must have crossed in front of us. You're thinking we stay on Union until we get to West 3rd or Beverly?"

"Wherever there's a way through," Emily said, switching on her flashlight. The organized groups were gone. Even the stragglers seemed to have dwindled.

They made better time with the light until they found out why everyone had disappeared. First there were cars with blistered paint. Next they saw one that had exploded, throwing its doors. Farther on, the vehicles were blackened hulks. Emily didn't want to enter the debris, but the buildings on either side were impassable wreckage. The air reeked of scorched rubber and plastic.

"Maybe we should go back," Michelle said.

"Shh." Emily cocked her head, listening to the murmur of a lone, repetitive voice.

"Annie?" the hidden man said. "Annie? Annie?"

"We could catch up with those groups," Michelle said as Emily held up one hand to stop her.

"We need to see who's over there," she said.

Michelle protested. "No! Listen to him."

"Annie?" the man said. "Annie?"

Emily had accepted that finding P.J. and his kind would be next to impossible. They'd disappeared into the crowds of other survivors now that everyone was awake, but if she was right, all of them would exhibit severe forms of ASD. She'd been looking for anyone who fit that description, no matter if everyone was half-insane with trauma. They were all acting strangely. But it might be the loners she wanted.

"Help me," she said.

She couldn't sneak up on him. Their footsteps crunched in the street. Michelle kicked a small object that banged away in the dark. Emily jumped, and yet the bodiless voice didn't change.

"Annie? Annie?"

They had good reason to avoid him. What if there was another event? It had been half an hour since Emily left DNAllied. Throughout the day, there had never been a quiet period longer than ten minutes. If the effect was going to return, it was overdue . . .

And if he was like P.J., if he turned violent at the same time Emily and Michelle lost their intelligence, they would be easy targets.

17

· · · · · · · · · · · ·

LOS ANGELES

Emily walked closer to the hidden man, feeling Michelle tremble beside her. He looked like the boogeyman, a short, distorted shape behind a four-door sedan. Its blue paint gleamed in the halo of her flashlight.

His voice was raw and monotone. "Annie? Annie?"

He sat slumped with his legs sprawled out before him, one foot rocking back and forth. His sneakers fit well. He hadn't found these shoes. They belonged to him. Did that mean he'd been inside until the effect stopped or was he like P.J.?

Emily shoved her light at him as she moved around the car, needing to see his face.

A young man in his twenties squinted at her with a mouthful of blood. His forehead was also smashed. Then his eyes rolled like a startled horse, and he leaned away from her. To him, *she* was the boogeyman. Behind her light, her head must have looked inhumanly thick.

"Wait!" Emily ripped at her chin strap. "Wait."

She knelt to his level and set her helmet on the street. The young man kept his face averted even as his gaze darted almost at random, stealing glances at Emily with his peripheral vision. He held an open cell phone, a pink phone that didn't look like it belonged to a man.

His fidgeting and the way he avoided her eyes were typical of autists, but Emily needed more than that to make a diagnosis. He was obviously afraid. He was hurt.

"My name is Emily and this is Michelle," she said.

His voice was too loud. "Can you help me find Annie?"

"Yes."

"No," Michelle whispered behind her.

Taking the young man with them would be a monumental complication. Could he walk? The two of them might barely be able to carry his weight, but Emily wanted people to help P.J., so she would help this young man.

She gave the flashlight to Michelle. Then she dabbed at the young man's face with the cuff of her jacket sleeve, covering her scheme with this kindness. "Are you all right?" she asked. "What happened to your face?"

"I need to find Annie."

Each of her collection kits held thirty VacuCaps, slender, sterile, two-inch vacuum tubes capped with butterfly needles. They were "purple caps" and contained an anti-coagulant called EDTA, which would prevent the blood from clotting.

Emily took one and removed its plastic sheath. She jabbed the needle into the inside of his elbow. The tube instantly drew itself full and she withdrew it from his arm.

"Ouch," he said.

Emily discarded the butterfly needle, then replaced the self-sealing VacuCap in her kit. Ideally she would refrigerate the blood in order to slow the degradation of its ribonucleic acids. RNA was fragile. If the proteins she wanted to sequence were destroyed, this sample would be useless. But she could only move so fast.

She helped the young man to his feet. "Let's find Annie," she said, relieved that he could walk. "Don't touch the cars. Are you listening to me? Don't touch the cars."

Before they left, Emily glanced down at her helmet. She wanted to put it on, but hiding in her armor might damage her fragile rapport with him. She doubted the helmet would stop the effect in any case, although it might protect its wearer in combat.

"Michelle?" she asked. "Do you want the helmet?"

"Yes."

They led him back to the intersection of Union and Beverly, where they turned west. If this fire had swept east, they might be able to navigate around the burn . . . but two blocks later, they were met with ruins again.

"We could spend all night backtracking. I think we need to go through," Emily said, pointing north up Burlington Avenue.

Michelle was resigned. "All right."

Despite her lab glasses, the ash stung Emily's eyes and made her cough. Exploded cars were a larger problem. A chrome talon slashed Emily's thigh and she cried out. Moments later, the wind filled with the smell of cooked meat. "Don't look," Emily said, shepherding the young man around six or seven bodies.

Three buildings had fallen into the street, dropping huge, charred dunes of brick and drywall across the motionless traffic. Emily cut both hands scrambling up a loose hill, then hurt her back pulling at the young man. Were these cars also electrified? Most had sagged on melted tires, bringing their frames into contact with the road, and Michelle wasn't hurt when she slipped and banged against one.

The young man slowed them down. He was difficult. "My phone should be in my right front pocket," he said. "This phone isn't mine. My phone should be in my right front pocket."

Emily's impatience with him made her think of Laura and P.J. Then she felt wistful and sad. Exhaustion threatened to stop her. She wanted to sit and rest.

They staggered out of the debris at Court Street, a neighborhood of low-income apartments and student housing. The fire hadn't jumped to the next buildings here. They had only the cars to contend with. There were no refugees, although they heard dogs barking and distant gunfire.

The gradual rise in the street leveled out. Beyond a series of duplex apartments, the sky glowed. Emily's chest swelled with emotion when she realized the light was too steady and white to be a fire. The hospital had electricity. The emergency station was real.

"We're almost there!" she said with a wild grin at Michelle and the young man. But as they rounded a family restaurant where Chase liked to get BBQ, her elation gave way to hopelessness.

Silver Lake formed a stout, two-tiered L with the long wing reaching seven stories. The shorter wing was five stories high. The hospital cradled its main entrance and its largest parking lots on its south side within the crook of the L. Smaller outcroppings grew from the west end, including a third-story helicopter pad.

Yesterday, the structure had been faced in mirrored glass. Tonight, the middle of its pristine surface was bashed apart. Had a rescue chopper missed the pad? Several windows on the lower floors were also cracked or destroyed. They looked as if they'd been shot out.

The hospital had become a fortress. Its parking lots were ringed with barriers, soldiers, and thousands of people. Somewhere a bullhorn shouted above the noise.

Emily turned off her flashlight. She did it to hide them from the other refugees, but losing its light was demoralizing.

"We'll never get in," Michelle said. "We should've stayed in the parking garage."

"They'll let me in and I need him if I'm going to run more tests," Emily said. "We'll say you're his sister, my sister, whatever they need to hear."

The hour they'd spent together felt like a lifetime. Michelle represented the only stability Emily had seen since stepping outside, and Michelle had proved heady and loyal.

"Please don't leave me," Emily said.

The three of them walked toward the riot. Emily kept one hand on the young man's arm. She held her flashlight like a club.

Michelle gasped as four men charged toward them. But the men ran past. More shadows sat on the sidewalk. Other people had broken into the nearest buildings, invading offices and a sandwich shop. Were they making camp or searching for supplies?

"They're turning everyone back," a woman said.

Emily didn't answer. Most of the crowds appeared to have formed at the southern face of the hospital where the big red EMERGENCY sign stood above the ER. Elsewhere, the mob was thinner. Emily led her companions toward the west side. She knew the doctors and nursing staff had private parking and a private entrance behind the lower, three-story addition on the west end beneath the helicopter pad.

The soldiers had used existing fence lines wherever possible. The rest of the barricades consisted of commuter cars, vehicles that men could roll or push from the parking lot after shooting out the tires and allowing the frames to come in contact with the ground. Some of the cars were upside down. The barricades were staggered with gaps, but gunshot bodies sprawled in most of the holes where refugees had attempted to run through and were killed—and the dead refugees made effective barriers of another sort for the soldiers waiting on the other side.

The crowds would have been an excellent place to gather blood samples. Many people were barefoot or wore mismatched shoes. There were plenty of others in normal footwear, but wearing shoes wasn't enough of a clue. She would need to look at them, talk to them, and there was no time.

The young man fought Emily as they pressed into the mob, and she lied to him. "Annie's here!" she said. "She's here!"

Floodlights glared on the far side of the barrier, glinting in the blood and reflecting through fractured windshields. The soldiers standing in the light wore helmets and black vests over their camouflage uniforms. More interesting, Emily noticed two soldiers with ropes tied to their waists. They also held their rifles in a funny way with the shoulder straps looped around their forearms.

They're expecting another event, she thought. *Then someone inside will drag them back into the hospital.*

On the west side, a gate had been left between the overturned cars, although there were no less than fifteen soldiers in this space. All of them were roped. One man, an officer, was attempting to converse with the screaming survivors. People waved money at him—a cross— photographs—but he let no one through.

"Okay, stay close!" Emily yelled to Michelle, shouldering past an old man and then a fat woman with blood speckled across her blouse. Emily wanted to bring them, too. But she looked away. "I'm a doctor!" she yelled. "I'm a doctor!"

It got her to the front, although the young man lagged behind. She almost lost her grip on him as people jostled and banged against her.

She showed her blood collection kit to the officer. "My name is Emily Flint and I work in the labs!" she yelled. "You can check with Chase Coughlin or Bonnie Watkins or Marvin, um, Marvin Castillo!" she said, rattling off every name she could remember from Chase's coworkers. "Bonnie is the head of surgery! I do blood work for her and I need to get inside!"

"I'm a doctor, I'm a doctor!" another man began to shout.

"I need ID!" the officer yelled at Emily.

"I don't have it! I lost everything! I found these kits in an ambulance and I've been testing as many survivors as I can! I know why some people kill others during the events! There have been attacks here, too, right!?"

Emily held the officer's gaze as his eyes widened in surprise. She was getting better at lying, using her face as well as her words.

"Okay, you're in!" the officer shouted.

"I need this patient and my lab assistant to complete my tests!" she yelled, yanking at the young man. He broke free, scaring her, until Michelle shoved him to the front.

The officer waved them toward one of his soldiers. "Sanchez, find out where these people need to go!"

"Thank you," Emily said, but the officer didn't notice.

"Get back!" he shouted at the mob. "Go! Find shelter! There's no more room! Find shelter!"

She didn't envy his job, nor could she do anything for him or the other soldiers except feel respect. They'd kept the hospital safe when it might have been submerged in turmoil, but this responsibility was a harsh one.

Sanchez untied himself and led them into the building. Was he a sergeant? Emily didn't know what the stripes on his shoulder meant.

They hurried into a corridor where the soldiers' ropes trailed inside. The corridor was empty and the lights were on emergency power. Less than one in three bulbs was illuminated.

"Sir, do you have a radio?" Emily asked. "Where's your boss?"

"Colonel Bowen is on Level Two, ma'am," Sanchez said. "I don't know about communications."

Emily realized the corridor was deserted because it was too close to the outside. The ropes trailed in bunches to a pair of offices on either side. Both doors were open, showing eight soldiers drinking or eating from canteens or plastic pouches of food. They would drag their buddies inside if there was another event.

How many refugees had been allowed in? The hospital was the size of seven football fields stacked on top of each other, but the top floors might not be proof against the effect, and the outer rooms surely weren't, either, especially where the glass been destroyed.

In another fifty feet, Sanchez rounded a corner into a mass of yelling people. Emily heard the crowd and braced herself, making sure she didn't lose Michelle or the young man.

Protected by grown-ups, thirty children sat on the floor, some bleeding, others with burnt hands or faces where they'd contacted fences or cars. Every side room boiled with overworked medics and the repulsive stench of human guts, urine, and smoke.

The four of them pushed through the mayhem in fits and starts until Sanchez reached a stairwell. Refugees filled the steps, too, sitting on the right-hand side. Most of them appeared to be okay until Emily realized they couldn't see, not because they'd been injured, but because they'd lost their glasses or contacts. The stairwell was a blind ward.

"Is there water?" one man asked as Emily hurried by. Others prayed over an open Bible. She heard crying and bickering.

Sanchez led Emily, Michelle, and the young man to a second-floor hallway. Most of the wounded lining the hall wore uniforms—police, firefighter, Army. It wasn't as loud. There was more discipline. The second floor was where their stronghold began. Emily felt encouraged.

Sanchez crossed into the main bulk of the hospital and delivered them to a command center in the administrative offices. The cubicles were adorned with personal items like family photos and plants, but the desktop computers were off. Uniformed men and women centered around a few Dell laptops and a vast note board they'd rigged above their computers, jamming pencils and two combat knives into the drywall to hold their lists and sketches. Emily recognized an L-shaped drawing of Silver Lake's exterior with a bumpy oval inked around it to show the barricades.

Sanchez approached an officer near the front of the room. "Corporal Sanchez from the west entrance, sir," he said. "This woman is a doctor. She knows something."

The officer was in his thirties like Chase and had thick brown hair. He nodded to Sanchez. He was on the phone—a regular phone—and Emily felt a fresh burst of energy at the sight. Where was he calling? Was this Colonel Bowen?

Emily combed both hands through her hair, wanting to make herself presentable. She needed to be taken seriously even if she was filthy with ash and sweat.

"Bring them back," the officer told the phone. "If the roof won't hold . . . Right. Close all the doors you can and bring those men down to the fifth floor."

Emily's excitement faded. He was talking to other people in the hospital, not a military base or Sacramento or Washington, D.C. His phone was a closed circuit inside the building.

He hung up. "I'm Captain Walsh," he said.

They brought me to a second-in-command, Emily thought. She couldn't let him dismiss her. "I'm a geneticist with DNAllied, and I think I can tell you why some people turn violent during the events," she said. "I can tell you who to watch for."

Walsh's gaze shifted to Michelle and the young man. "Who?" he asked.

"It's complicated." Emily resisted glancing at the young man herself. Suddenly she was afraid they'd start shooting anyone who was handicapped. Had the situation gone that far? *Yes*, she thought, recalling the bloody corpses among the barricades.

She needed to be very, very careful what she told them.

"My data is untested, but this building has state-of-the-art labs in the oncology wing and specialists who can consult with me," she said. "In the meantime, we need to get a warning out."

"Who are we looking for?"

"I have a genetic profile, but it's just a theory. I've been working with next to nothing. Do you have a radio?"

"The sat links are intermittent," Walsh said. "We're getting more data than we send out, but if we put it on a loop, enough will get through for other people to string the message together."

"How long will that take? We need help!"

"Don't count on it," Walsh said. "There are no helicopters, no trucks, and very little armor. If you have information that can protect us, tell me now."

Emily hesitated.

"Help isn't coming," Walsh said.

18

. . . .

SOUTH CHINA SEA

Drew's thoughts bled out of a nightmare and coalesced around the medic leaning over him. An IV line reached up from Drew's forearm. Beyond the medic, Drew had a blurred impression of a concave metal ceiling lined with struts and wiring. His eyes felt like they were full of sand, but this was a familiar place. He was inside a C-17 Globemaster III cargo plane. The deck vibrated beneath his back, bumping in heavy turbulence.

He tried to sit up. "Did we launch?"

The medic held him down. "Welcome back to the living. How's your head?"

"Did we launch our nukes?"

"No. The fight's over for now. Six of their ships are down and two of ours, the *Collinson* and the *McCray*."

"Where's my partner?"

"I don't know. Just rest."

"My eyes hurt." Drew's face was blistered and swollen.

The medic examined him quickly, flashing a penlight over his eyes. "Looks like superficial keratitis," he said. "You were in the water for three hours and in and out of the pulse the whole time."

Superficial, Drew thought, grasping at that first word. He knew guys in the docks who'd developed welders' keratitis, permanently impairing their vision with corneal burns.

"You'll heal in a day or two," the medic said. "Just rest. We're forty minutes from Japan and activating all agents."

He's with ROMEO, Drew realized, peering left and right after the medic had gone. He heard people talking, but everything was lumps and shadows, which terrified him. He would never fly again if he couldn't see.

He remembered an enemy destroyer striking the *McCray*. After that, nothing. There was no way to land a C-17 on a carrier, which meant he'd been brought to shore and loaded aboard in Vietnam. Somehow they'd fished him out of the ocean. The EMP must have let up. Chopper crews had put their lives on the line to save him and others.

It was intolerable to be helpless. Drew pushed himself onto his elbows, blinking furiously.

The fuselage was two hundred feet long, a bare tube crowded to capacity. On his right, people began to sit up as the medic walked among them, his hands moving from a pouch on his hip to their IV lines—if they had a line—or to their arms if not. He was injecting them with disposable hypodermics. But not everyone was waking up.

The Marine on Drew's left lay motionless, although his eyes were open. Most of his chest was swaddled in bandages. Drew said, "You okay? If you want, I can shout for . . ."

He's dead, Drew realized.

Nearby, another Marine sat on the deck, recovering. Drew spoke to him urgently. "Are you okay?"

"Got a fuckin' headache and a broken arm, but that's better than most guys," the Marine said. "You?"

"Day at the beach."

"Yeah." The Marine laughed, sharing Drew's need to make any sort of conversation in this flying morgue.

"All right, listen up!" a woman hollered at the front of the plane. "Listen up! This is a DIA flight with every agent we thought we could pull. Come here. We're short on time. Most of you have been doped to the gills because we don't have the personnel to deal with wounded."

"Nice," the Marine said.

Drew pulled the IV shunt from his arm, freeing himself even as he glanced at the dead man beside him.

They'd been stacked in the plane like cordwood, optimizing flight time by leaving the wounded in deep, healing comas. Had bad reactions killed some of their own people? Drew was sure the knock-out and wake-up drugs weren't FDA approved, but this sort of treatment was exactly what they'd signed up for.

He braced himself to stand in the turbulence. The Marine rose, too. They moved forward with twenty others. A limping man nearly fell when the deck dropped abruptly. Drew and the Marine caught him. Then a smaller disturbance caused people to sidestep or move back.

Even with the grit in his eyes, Drew recognized Julie Christensen's lithe movements. Joy was an unusual emotion for him. Most of his life, he'd been too serious—too alone—but he didn't need to figure out what to say. Julie kissed him right in front of everyone.

"Whoa," the Marine said.

Behind him, a louder voice said, "Yeah, that's our super secret handshake."

Drew turned from Julie's heat. "Bugle!" he said, feeling a different joy. His friend's height was easy to spot in the crowd. Drew concealed the fact that he could barely see, holding out one hand as he kept his other arm around Julie's waist.

Bugle clasped his hand and leaned in for a chest bump, playing it cool. "Dude, you look like shit."

Drew didn't let him go. Especially after so much death, it seemed important to express the bond he felt. "I didn't think I'd find either of you," he said, noting that Bugle's face wasn't red or burnt. Why not? Had Bugle kept his flight helmet on during their time in the water?

Julie's hazel eyes danced, taking in Drew's blisters as she lifted one hand to caress his cheek. She paused, then set her fingers on his chest.

Drew was aware of other people staring. "This is nuts," he whispered. "We barely know each other."

She shook her head. "I've read your file, too."

Then you know my sister died on her bike when a guy blew through a stop sign, he thought. *Because I was too busy to drive her.* His reflex was to pull back, protecting that old wound, but something in Julie's expression stopped him. Was it forgiveness? He squeezed her again and said, "You—"

"Move it!" the officer called. "Let's move!"

They walked with Bugle and the Marine to the front of the plane, where thirty operatives had sat or knelt to make room for others to stand behind them. Drew couldn't make out the officer's insignia, although he assumed she was Air Force.

"Eight hours ago," she said, "Earth's magnetic field was struck by X-class solar flares. The result was a sustained worldwide EMP. Recently the pulse has been intermittent, but we don't know enough yet to make predictions. It might stop altogether. It might not. We're pulling back. Communications are shot, but we've managed to convey to the Chinese that we're in retreat."

Julie noticed Drew squinting. She turned to him silently and he shook his head.

The officer had set a laptop on her stand. Drew could see that much. The orange-and-brown blurs on its screen might have been China's shoreline.

"The *America* and its strike group are hunkering down," she said. "For the most part, they're reporting they're safe inside their ships. Even better, our subs are one hundred percent operational."

Drew glanced at the fuselage as Bugle muttered under his breath, "Oh, shit."

Most of these operatives weren't aviators, so maybe they didn't know. The *America* was built to withstand the electromagnetic pulse of a nuclear near miss, its vitals shielded within tons of steel, but aircraft were constructed of lightweight aluminum.

If the EMP came back, they would fall like a rock.

"Most of you are alive because we received early reports that the Chinese were testing a pulse weapon in theater," the officer said. "Based on those warnings, yesterday we brought in four specialized aircraft and other gear. That's lucky for you because the pulse hasn't stopped. It's still happening. This C-17 is one of the very few aircraft in flight anywhere in the world, but the decision was made that you're worth the investment. We need you back home."

Then we're safe from the EMP, Drew thought, extending his hand to Bugle for a fist jab. They deserved to celebrate. Without their data, ROMEO wouldn't have sent these planes, so in a sense they'd saved themselves.

The officer began a slideshow of images. Drew eased closer to her, leaving Julie. He needed to follow this briefing if he was going to have any value, but he was clumsy. He stepped on a Marine who was sitting down, then bumped another man as the officer displayed MRI and CT scans of several human brains—or the same brain in different states.

"The pulse is having an extreme cognitive effect on anyone caught in the open. According to our doctors, the first indications are temporal lobe seizures," the officer said, touching her own temple. "This is where the skull is its thinnest. From there, the seizures spread."

"Sit down," an Air Force captain hissed at Drew.

Behind him, Julie also moved into the crowd. She caught his arm and murmured, "What's wrong?"

Drew took her hand, drawing her attention from his face. "I'm fine," he said.

If he told her how badly his vision was affected, would she report him? The medic had said his eyesight would improve. He couldn't chance being downgraded from flight ready.

"The seizures are very similar to epileptic activity," the officer said. "Reasoning, prioritizing, short-term memory, all of these areas of the brain shut down. There's a dramatic personality shift."

She brought up a video of a blank-faced man, a policeman, shambling across a city street jammed with vehicles. Shoes off, hat off, he fumbled stupidly with an open car door in his way. He only needed to pull it shut, but he pushed and pushed until finally he clambered over the door onto the hood of the car.

No one in the plane spoke, sharing one another's horror and disbelief.

"Our losses may be bigger than in every war we've fought combined," the officer said. "Our forces in Afghanistan, Vietnam, Korea, Japan . . . Seventy percent are AWOL, wounded, or dead. Stateside, our casualties are in the millions."

Drew could barely imagine that sudden combat that must have erupted among those who were still conscious. In Vietnam, the Marines would be fighting their allies for the old tunnels of the Vietcong and for the modern steel-and-concrete buildings in Ho Chi Minh City and Da Nang. In Afghanistan, NATO forces would have made frontal assaults on the caves of the Taliban, not only to clear every stronghold of insurgents, but to occupy those rocky holes themselves. Elsewhere, American soldiers must have run for the urban areas of Seoul, Tokyo, and Baghdad, struggling for room in those cities' lower levels and basements.

"We've lost fifty billion dollars in civilian satellites," the officer said.

"Telecom, weather, science, it's all gone. Most of our military net survived the first few hours, but now we're down to our RADIUS series. Even those are vulnerable except when they're in protect mode, so we're rationing our eyes and ears. Radio is out. Landlines are out. We're bringing you home because you're trained to operate on your own—forever, if necessary—with no resources except what you find yourselves."

But are there enough of us? Drew wondered. Four planeloads of black ops and Special Forces weren't enough to accomplish more than a few missions across North America.

"We need to outlast this crisis," the officer said. "The Chinese threat hasn't gone away."

"Ma'am?" the Marine said. "If they can't see, either, now's the perfect time to launch against their command and control."

"That's nuts," Julie objected. "If we're experiencing electronics failures, our targeting systems might go, too. We couldn't be positive where our missiles would land."

"The nukes are hardened against—"

"We might not even get a full launch, just enough to make the Chinese counterstrike! You need to think about—"

"Enough," the officer said as the small crowd rustled and muttered. It was the first hint of disharmony among the tightly disciplined ROMEO agents.

Drew didn't doubt that in other places, the people with the launch codes were having the same argument. He understood the Marine's aggression. Everyone had lost good friends and squad mates, and their families were in danger back home.

"We haven't ruled out the possibility that the solar activity is manmade," the officer said, "which means China's satellites and radar systems may have been ready to survive the pulse. If so, we're at a huge disadvantage."

"You think they started the flares?" a woman asked.

"China has put billions of dollars into their exotic weapons programs. They definitely have the launch capacity to send a package into the sun. Look at this."

The officer brought up a new window packed with file names, then initiated it. Her laptop rolled through dozens of still shots of different men in a strikingly similar pose, hunched forward, their arms lifted away from their bodies with a fence post, a pipe, an axe, a bat. All of them were American by the look of them—men in jeans or slacks or shorts—a Cleveland Browns jersey—and their poise was completely unlike the confused policeman in the video.

"There are ongoing reports of attacks among the survivors," the officer said. "It's happening in every city, every state. We're losing lives and resources to our own people."

"They're all white," Drew said for Julie's benefit, demonstrating that he could see.

The officer glanced at him. "Almost," she said. "Early data suggests they're either Caucasian or mixed Caucasian descent. The majority of these attacks are happening in North America, Europe, and Australia."

"How do we know that if our sats are down?" Julie asked.

"We're still in contact with our allies and with China. Enough information is getting out. The incidence of these attacks is four hundred times less among Asian, African, and Hispanic populations."

"Then we're missing some key data or it's not the EMP that's causing it," the Air Force captain said. "There are no racial differences in the human brain."

"You're not the first to say that," the officer said. "It's possible the Chinese are underreporting their own issues, or there may be a trigger we haven't identified yet. Something they put in our water. Something in our food."

Drew grimaced. Historically, the People's Republic had worked very hard to regulate the outside world's perception of their nation. For decades, they'd claimed there were no homosexuals in China, no famine, no political dissent. But if they were experiencing the same attacks now, and hiding it, they were setting themselves up for all-out conflict with the United States. Too many people had died.

"We're trying to capture some of the assailants," the officer said. "Unfortunately, there are complications. Our cities are on fire. We have a limited number of air assets. We're also treating these men as biohazards in case there's a chemical or biological contagion at work."

"What about facial recognition programs?" Julie asked.

"We've run our imagery and fingerprints in the few cases any were recovered," the officer said. "No luck there, which means they're not criminals or known terrorists—or military or law enforcement. The only hit was from a civil database in Michigan. One man was printed for a part-time job in child welfare, but that's not much to go on."

The plane rattled again and she raised her voice.

"All we know is these attacks are persistent and organized, and they're not happening on Chinese soil. We think it's a weapon."

Then we're at war, Drew thought.

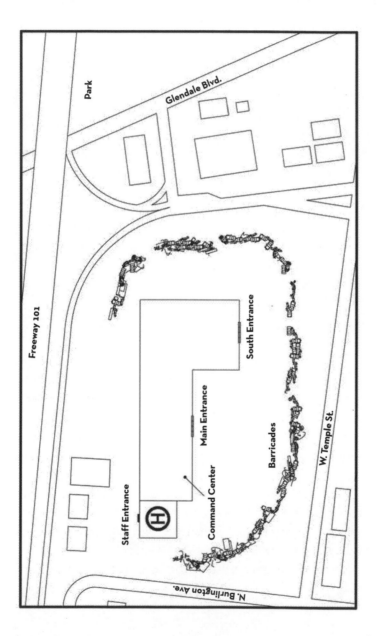

Park

Glendale Blvd.

Freeway 101

South Entrance

Main Entrance

Command Center

Barricades

Staff Entrance

W. Temple St.

N. Burlington Ave.

SILVER LAKE HOSPITAL

19

. . . .

LOS ANGELES

In the hospital's makeshift command center, Emily paced from side to side in a tiny space between two desks. She wanted to project conviction and expertise, but her body betrayed her.

Two doctors stood with Colonel Bowen. Pulling these men from their duties had taken more than an hour, giving Emily too much time to worry, because Captain Walsh insisted she wait here with Michelle and the young man. "It's not safe," Walsh said. Outside, there had been more gunfire, and raised voices constantly passed through the hall. They were barely in control of the hospital.

Emily had been reduced to asking every paramedic or nurse she saw about Chase. She kept thinking he would walk through the door. Waiting for him was torture, but first she needed to convince these men to give her every resource available.

"We need a larger sample base!" she said, holding up her collection kit.

One of the doctors was a dark, harried man in his forties. "I don't see the point," he said, looking at Emily with impatience, even scorn. "Let me get back to work."

"Stop," Bowen said before the doctor could leave.

National Guard Colonel John Bowen was a tall, hefty man in his sixties. The only chink in his resolve was his flexing hands. His fists kneaded constantly at his sides, for which Emily forgave him.

Bowen said, "You think the difference in the people outside is genetic?"

"Yes."

"That doesn't make sense," the doctor said.

"It does! The repetitive or restricted behaviors that characterize ASD become an advantage during the effect. I've seen it myself. They're more coherent, more focused than everyone else."

"Even if that's true, there's no way to take samples during the flares," the doctor said.

"We'll do it now," Emily said.

"You can't test your theory for the same reason. It's a catch-22. Everyone is either safe in here or they're lunatics if they're outside."

"We have some capacity to monitor the grounds outside," Bowen said, gesturing across the busy room.

In a corner, three Guardsmen had slung rifles from their shoulders, doubling as security as they worked at their laptops. Beside them, Michelle waited with the young man, who sat with his head down, picking incessantly at the back of his left hand.

Bowen said, "If we have to, we can send the boy out and watch him."

"No!" Emily said.

"Miss Flint," Bowen said. "You're right. We need to understand what's happening, and he's what we have available."

So we saved him just to turn him into a guinea pig, she thought with fresh guilt.

"I don't have time for this," the doctor said. "Right now most of our lab techs are matching donor types and trying to keep up with the demand for blood, and they're doing it in hallways and bathrooms. It would be wrong to make them—"

"Listen to me," Emily said. "ASD affects some of the most central parts of the brain in ways we still don't understand, the cerebrum, the amygdala. It also creates local overconnectivity in the cerebral cortex. Brain weight, volume, and head circumference all tend to be greater in autists."

"That's a huge generalization," the doctor objected.

"An excess of neurons might allow them to maintain some function where we don't," Emily said. "The effect causes us to lose our higher thinking. Adults with ASD already have weak connections between the frontal lobes and the rest of the brain, which could mean they're ready for it. By our standards, they don't associate well. There are abnormalities in their orientation to stimuli, novelty detection, language and face processing, working memory . . . The list goes on and on."

The second doctor frowned. "She's right that autistic individuals tend to use different portions of the brain, not just for motor function but for the default network."

"What does that mean?" Bowen asked.

"The default network is the large-scale brain network involved in social and emotional processing," Emily said. "It's unusually diffuse in adults with ASD, and yet they have intact connectivity of the task-positive network. There's an imbalance toward goal-directed thinking and sustained attention, which plays into compulsive and ritualistic behaviors."

She pointed at the young man, who continued to pick at his hand even though the skin was irritated and pink. The parallel between the young man's self-stimulation and Colonel Bowen's fists was intriguing. In normal people, such fidgeting was called a nervous tic, whereas in autists, it was deemed a sign of their condition. But the two behaviors were closely related.

"Autists also tend to lack empathy for others," she said. "They're unable to internalize what other people are feeling."

"You think that's why they attack us?" Bowen asked.

"In their altered state, yes. A study in 2007 reported nearly two-thirds of children with ASD exhibiting tantrums and one third had a history of aggression, especially in those with language impairment. They were frustrated. Alienated."

All three men were watching her closely now, and Emily used their attention to center herself. She stopped pacing.

"What if they've always been impaired because they were trying to use both aspects of their minds?" she asked. "Compared to us, they're overequipped. They have the unique, autistic regions of their brains in addition to the more normal sections, which shut off during the events. Then they're more focused than ever. The confusion they've always felt is gone."

"Too much of what she's saying fits," the second doctor said, but Emily glanced away to hide her uncertainty.

This is it, she thought. *This is where they'll really resist what I have to say. And maybe they're right. We don't have a lot of evidence yet.*

"For twenty years there's been a spike in children born with autistic spectrum disorders," she said.

The first doctor shook his head. "That's debatable."

"The increase is seven hundred percent."

"If you were a physician, you'd know that most of this so-called epidemic is easy to explain. Awareness and detection have both improved. We've broadened our criteria for diagnosis. Parents are also taking advantage of social programs for autism, which is where all the money is these days. No one is *retarded* anymore."

"You're wrong."

"I've been in medicine my whole life and seen things change. Everyone is *autistic* now because families have learned to play the game with government handouts."

"Broadened criteria accounts for twenty percent of the spike at most," Emily said, but she saw no point in arguing with this idiot. Colonel Bowen was who she needed to convince, so she turned and held Bowen's gaze. "What if the increase was a reaction to our environment?" she asked. "I'm not talking about MMR vaccines or flame retardants in baby blankets. I mean what if autism is an evolutionary response to solar activity?"

"That's absurd," the doctor said.

"There are any number of animals who use or respond to Earth's geomagnetic field. Birds and insects. Deer. Cows. Crocodiles. Dolphins. We like to ignore it, but the fact is human beings are just animals, too. Our brain tissue is suffused with magnetic crystals, especially in critical regions like the cerebellum and cerebral cortex. Biomagnetism is how bees and fish navigate so accurately. Birds use it to migrate. But no one's ever explained why people have magnets in their heads."

"The amount of magnetite in the human brain is infinitesimal," the doctor said.

"That could be part of why people change! If we're subjected to overwhelming magnetic fields—"

Bowen ended the debate. "I want as many lab personnel on this as possible," he told the first doctor.

"Right now we're saving lives," the doctor said. "You can't expect us to let people die."

"We'll start with anyone who matches your profile," Bowen told Emily. Then he turned to the doctor. "You probably have an hour before my squads come back inside. Get as much done as you can with the wounded, but prep your labs. I want this done fast. Is that understood?"

"Colonel, we can't—"

"Is that understood?"

Emily tried to appeal to both doctors with a separate request, letting all of her love and dread show in her face. "Have you seen Chase Coughlin? He's an attending. He should have been on shift today."

"I don't know," the first doctor said as he left the command center.

Emily started after him. "I should help in the labs," she said to Bowen, afraid that her real intent was transparent. She wanted to set up her blood work, but first she planned to look for Chase.

"Wait!" a soldier yelled. At the same time, all of them stopped and looked up as if responding to a larger voice. Emily felt like she was using a new sense, a sixth sense, to perceive an invisible change in her world.

Then it was obvious. Static etched its way across the computer screens as the lights flickered. Outside the hospital, silence fell. The distant noise of the crowds vanished.

Below, a new, louder sound rose from the ground floor as panic spread through the refugees inside.

"Lock the building down!" Bowen shouted. "Lock it down! Put reinforcements at every stairwell and make sure the hospital staff has protection! We might need extra men downstairs!"

"Our radios are out!" another Guardsman yelled.

Emily retreated to Michelle's side and clutched her friend, watching the door with wide eyes. Were some of the survivors inside also changing? Not every room would be proof against the effect. And if a few men turned violent, how long before the place was torn apart?

Bowen swept the room, finding Emily. "I need you," he said.

She stepped forward.

Bowen led her to the bank of laptops manned by three of his men. His fists flexed and bunched. "Will it stop?" he asked.

"I don't know," she said.

The laptops had recovered from the first surge of the effect and were clear now. Six of the screens showed grainy green-and-white video. Four were close shots of the parking lot or the barricades. Two were longer views of the city. Emily recognized the streets south and east of Silver Lake. A seventh camera merely showed the distorted yellow glare of a floodlight.

The other lights either shut off automatically or burned out in the effect, she realized. Their cameras were using night vision.

The people outside were primitives. They banded together in eddies and clusters, sorting themselves. Here and there, loners or twosomes separated from the mob. It was like watching sand blown by the wind. There was an eerie grace in how they drifted and found each other.

The groups began to reach critical mass. Some of them challenged each other, hollering and shoving, but their displays of aggression did not seem to escalate—not until there was a flurry of motion at one point beyond the barricades south of the hospital. People began to run.

Emily pointed. "We need to move this camera!"

The Guardsman manning the laptop looked at Colonel Bowen, who nodded. "Number four doesn't have much range," the Guardsman said, his shoulder bumping Emily as he lifted a handset. "Remote Four, this is Bravo. You still there?" He turned to Emily. "Where are you trying to look?"

"To your left. Up. Zoom south past those cars."

"We're going to lose a lot of resolution."

"Enhance it," Bowen said.

"I'm sorry, sir. Our software's doing everything it can."

The screen shifted with unbearable slowness, drawing out the tension in Emily's veins. Earlier, listening to Bowen's soldiers, she'd learned how the cameras worked. It was useless to mount electronics outside. Nor could they post men at the windows with binoculars or rifle scopes. The hospital's exterior wasn't proof against the effect. Instead, Bowen's engineers had rigged a series of mirrors in seven places. In each case, the outermost mirror could be shifted only slightly, with wires, to provide the cameras inside with new angles. Otherwise they were blind.

"Holy shit," the Guardsman said as the image finally lifted enough to see what had scattered the primitives.

Eight men stalked north toward the hospital. They carried clubs and shared a distinct, confident bearing. In fact, Emily recognized the slight figure leading the group. P.J. "I see him!" she said. "The boy in front."

We've crossed paths twice now, she thought. *Is that because he's constantly on the move? The first time, at DNAllied, he might have been drawn up my street by the billboard. What is he looking for?*

Now, it seemed, the hospital lights and the crowds had attracted him.

"That's my nephew," she said. "He lives near here." The idea clicked as she said it out loud. "This is his home ground."

"Your nephew," Bowen said.

"Yes. He's autistic. He's the first one I saw acting differently."

Bowen cursed, leaning all of his weight very close to Emily when she tried to avoid his eyes. His voice was rigid with anger. "What else haven't you told us?" he said.

"I didn't think it mattered."

"How many people are autistic in North America?"

"Uh." Emily despised herself for answering.

She didn't want to make P.J. the bad guy, but she'd already crossed that line, and Bowen was right to ask. There must be small bands like P.J.'s everywhere in the world, like an army that rose up and disappeared again with each event.

"The last few years, rates have been reported as high as one in every hundred births," she said.

Bowen stared at her, and, briefly, Emily saw him falter. The math was unavoidable. "There are five hundred and twenty million people in Canada and the U.S.," he said.

"We don't know if all of them will turn! High-functioning autists probably don't have enough of the necessary neurological differences. There are so many variables. I could be totally off base."

"If you're right, we might be up against five million enemy combatants," Bowen said like a man on the brink.

Emily raised both hands to stop him. "What if it's only ten percent? Either way, a lot of them will be babies or children. You don't have to assume we're dealing with millions of adults."

"Sir, I can move a sniper team to a window," another officer said. "We've rigged some armor. It could be enough for our men to crawl—"

"Don't!" Emily shouted. "We don't know enough yet."

"Try it," Bowen said to his officer.

"Colonel, please. We need to capture them."

Bowen relented. "If your shooter can get into position, his orders are to shoot to wound," he told his officer before he glanced back at Emily. "Tell me what they're doing."

P.J.'s head movements were identical to what she'd seen earlier today. His companions mimicked his bobbing and swaying. An explanation was on the tip of her tongue, but she was too stunned to sort cleanly through her thoughts. Then she remembered the anthropology papers she'd read as part of her work with her collaborator at Yale.

The genetic shift she'd unearthed in her statistical models . . . What if those trends weren't the degeneration of *Homo sapiens* at all, but the resurgence of variations that had been successful in a different age? If the human race was evolving in response to changes in the sun, they could be resurrecting an earlier set of forms and instincts that had served them well in prehistory.

"Those men are singing," she said. "It's another language. An old language."

"My team is in place," the officer told Bowen.

There was no time. The soldiers were ready to fire. Could she stop them from killing P.J.?

"I think they're Neanderthals," she said.

20

. . . .

LOS ANGELES

Wait," the boy said, listening more to himself than to the noisy, burning darkness. He trusted the quiet responses within himself as much as his eyes and ears. For him, inside and out were nearly identical, creating an equilibrium that he would never question or try to explain.

It served him especially well in this chaos.

The sky was a mess of black clouds and blowing ash. The wind reeked of strange smells, and the earth was equally confusing. The wreckage was static compared to the roiling sky, but the buildings and cars were more alarming because of their permanence, seemingly larger than the wind overhead.

The boy stood motionless for several breaths, measuring the city and the sounds of hurt men and women fleeing him. He was reassured by his pack's formation. Eight hunters. One circle.

He led them into an open patch beside a truck. None of them understood the vehicle, how it was made or what it was for, but no one questioned him. In many ways the men were extensions of the boy, bound to him as certainly as his own hands and feet—and by moving sideways, they concealed themselves from the Guard sniper no human being could have possibly detected inside the hospital more than two hundred yards away.

Emily sighed, her tension breaking as P.J. disappeared from their cameras. "I've lost visual," the officer said, pointing at a WHOLE FOODS delivery truck on his screen.

Now they can't shoot him, Emily thought, but she felt a new spike of adrenaline when another Guardsman said, "Sir, unless that truck's full of something a lot heavier than groceries, our man can fire through it."

"No. Stand down," Bowen said. "Miss Flint? What the hell are you talking about?"

"They're singing."

"What?"

"Play it back. Watch how they communicate. They're singing." *At least, they're trying to sing,* she thought. *Waking up in our world must be a thousand times more shocking for them than it is for us.*

Bowen gestured to a Guardsman. "Can you play it back on another computer without losing the live feed?"

"Yes, sir."

Bowen turned to Emily. "Explain."

She wished she'd found Chase. He would have supported her. Fighting the stew of anxiety and foreboding in her heart, she said, "There have been excellent studies comparing Neanderthal physiology with other primates. Their larynx was positioned at the top of the throat, higher than ours, more like what we see in monkeys and apes today."

"They're not cavemen. They're regular people," an officer said.

"Look at them!" Emily pointed at a laptop where an eight-second clip was followed by a twelve-second clip. Both short videos played over and over in a loop, showing P.J. hoot and a man's reply. "I know they're in modern human bodies, but they're practically choking when they talk. They don't have the right throats for it."

"Do we have any directional mikes?" Bowen asked.

"No, sir."

"Apes can't make the same variety of sounds we can," Emily insisted. "Neither could Neanderthals. You see them in movies as big fat stupid monsters, but we've proven they had language and culture. Most of what they said was very basic in any case. They didn't need phone numbers or ATM codes. Happy. Sad. Excited. Scared. That was enough for them. Some anthropologists believe Neanderthals might have been intensely emotional, so they didn't use words like we do. They hummed and sang instead."

Bowen frowned at her, his voice trailing off as he glanced back at the video. "They do look like they're . . . No. He's right. I don't believe you."

"Then what else are they doing?" Emily asked. Her tone was challenging. "P.J.'s group hasn't had time to develop or relearn a language, but they're communicating. That's why they're ahead of us out there."

"Follow me," the boy said before he left the truck. His voice held a sharp, unfeminine pitch that carried over the noise of the city.

The others in the pack used the same lilting tone when they spoke, warning each other as they shifted north through the debris and abandoned cars. "Watch out," one man sang, sidestepping a fallen bumper. Another man repeated the sound. "Watch out," he sang, avoiding a body sprawled in the darkness.

The boy was drawn by the lights inside the hospital. To him, the structure resembled a cliff face made of unknown materials. He did not comprehend steel or glass, but he followed his restlessness toward the building, curious and mistrustful.

He perceived danger in this place. He also saw opportunity. That was why his pack stayed on the move. Their roaming was more than the impulse of nomad hunters. The boy understood that mere instants ago, many people had gathered in this place—most of them enemies—but his pack was not only exploring the land to find water and food. Their high voices were also a signal to their own kind.

As they swept through the wreckage, a stooped shape emerged from the blowing dark. Nothing needed to be said. By the man's posture, by the very fact that he'd approached the group, the boy knew this man belonged to him.

Emily's skin crawled as she watched P.J. She strained to comprehend, but he was so *alien*. Goose bumps rose on her forearms and the back of her neck.

"I have them on Camera Three," the Guardsman said.

"Damn it," Bowen said. "They found another one."

"Most of the differences between us were cosmetic," Emily said. "There are only three hundred proteins that *Homo sapiens* and Neanderthals don't share—three hundred out of billions. There was interbreeding. The best evidence we have today is that we were separate species, but we come from a common ancestor. We were cousins."

"So they're inside us," Bowen said.

"Some of us. Yes. Mainly people of European and Middle Eastern descent."

"One of them looks Hispanic to me," an officer said.

"We've been interbreeding, too. Do you realize how many generations have come and gone since the Neanderthals disappeared? It's been thirty thousand years."

"Then we won't be able to assess who's who without your blood samples," Bowen said.

Emily heard his self-doubt. Worse, he obviously thought her lab work would be too cumbersome to help him defend the building. "I'll come up with something we can use in the field," she said. "You don't—"

"They're killing him!" the officer said.

On the screen, two of P.J.'s followers stepped forward and clubbed the new man.

They crushed his skull with two overhand blows. He fell. They hit him again and again and again. Then it was finished.

"Follow me," the boy sang without looking back.

He'd taken longer than he might have in testing the newcomer because, uncomfortably, his pack was an even number. He had a compulsion toward threes. He didn't know why, but his instinct was to organize his people in trios. With eight of them, this was impossible, so he'd nearly allowed the newcomer to join the pack. But the newcomer had been a half-man. His voice had been wrong, his posture, his expression.

The boy knew who was one of them and who was not. No one looked like they should, yet correct behavior was ingrained into everything they did. Voice and visual cues superseded physical appearance.

The blood on their weapons was not entirely from their enemies. The boy had also rejected two other half-breeds. One had been female and even more valuable because of her gender, but he could not accept impurity. He would always attack.

He moved toward the hospital.

Emily shivered with horror and grief as the Guardsman asked, "Why did they kill him? He was singing, too."

"He wasn't right enough," she said. "I told you. They're hybrids. Not all of them will have the same neurological makeup."

"That's good news for us," the Guardsman said. "They'll fight each other along with everyone else."

Something snapped inside her. "You son of a bitch. Those are people out there just like you and me. What if someone in your family is—"

"Take them out," Bowen told the officer with the handset to the sniper team.

"No!" Emily said. "There has to be another way."

"As far as I can see, we're at war," Bowen said.

"We can talk to them." She hated that her tone was pleading, conflicted, helpless, while Bowen's was flat and certain.

"You can't go out there," Bowen said.

"Maybe we can," Emily said. "Your armor—"

"It's a two-man box that weighs three hundred pounds," Bowen said. "No one's carrying it outside. We can barely move it to the window."

At the same time, the officer reacted to a voice on his handset. "This is Kingsnake Eight Five," he said.

Is he relaying the command to shoot? Emily thought with fresh panic. "I can cure them!" she said.

"Wait," Bowen told his officer.

"I might even be able to make us immune to the effect so we can think outside, but I need them. We need data. There's no way I can tailor my gene therapies without them."

Someone spoke again on the officer's handset, and the officer looked at Bowen. "What are your orders, sir?"

"They're coming toward us because they're curious," Emily said. "What if your sniper uses a flashlight? Even better, we can turn the lights on and off at one of the exits. They might come inside to investigate. Then we grab them. If you shoot them now, even to wound, they'll just bleed to death out there and the ones who get away will remember what you did!"

"Goddamn it," Bowen said. "Hold your fire."

On the laptop screen, P.J.'s group stalked closer alongside the barricade of cars, only visible through the gaps. Would they venture inside?

As soon as they were protected from the effect, they should turn into their normal selves again. If so, she would have her nephew back, but how far did he need to come into the hospital before he woke up?

"Thank you," she said.

"I'm not doing this because he's your family," Bowen said. "Major, let's get a team on the lights at the entrance on the south wing. Try to signal those men outside." He turned to another officer. "Do what we can to identify them."

"I'm on it, sir." The major picked up a phone as the other officer's screen filled with still shots isolated from the video file, low-res close-ups of individual faces.

Emily's gaze was riveted to the live feeds as waves of light began to flash at the end of the hospital's short, southern wing, casting shadows across the vehicles sitting neatly in the parking lot and the sturdier line of the barricades.

The light caught P.J.'s group in a space between two cars. They ducked out of sight. For a moment, Emily scanned the laptop screens, wondering where they'd gone. Then she saw them moving again, skirting east along the barricades.

"Come on," she whispered. "Come on, P.J."

The boy stayed in front as they crept east through the glare and shadows. Each man held an arm up to protect his face. Walking into the yellow light was like finding the sun on the ground. It was menacing and bizarre, and the boy shielded the men with his own body wherever possible. He did this in the truest sense of self-sacrifice, without ego, only pride in his kind.

Then he checked himself. The light defied understanding, but the winking was deliberate. The pattern he saw in the busy on-off-on was man-made.

Was it a trap? Would the light hurt?

"Wait," he sang, leading his pack into a shallow concrete drain between two sections of the parking lot. "Down." Hidden in this small crease, they knelt together beneath the wind, the ash, and the city's overwhelming heights.

Emily spun on Bowen. "Stop!" she said. "Don't flash the lights anymore. Just leave them on."

"You heard her," Bowen said.

One of his Guardsmen lifted his handset as Emily said, "We're overdoing it. They're more sensitive than we are, and they're already disoriented by our world."

"You . . ." Bowen frowned. "You say that like they're from somewhere else."

"That's right." Distracted by the video feed, Emily prayed for her nephew to start moving closer again. *Don't go*, she thought. Then her gaze left the video for the still shots, and what little hope she'd held onto gave way to sorrow.

If anything, the change in P.J. had increased. His face was an expressionless mask except for his eyes. His eyes were deep, baleful gems that leapt with purpose. If he felt lonely—if his group had any sense of being outnumbered—it didn't show.

He looked pitiless, even serene.

"A species wouldn't adapt to anything as a natural part of their environment unless it was constant," Emily said. Her voice was hushed. "Our two races must have diverged during a period of off-and-on flares. The Neanderthals rose to prominence during the effect, whereas *Homo sapiens* evolved for normal conditions."

"You mean the sun has always been doing this," Bowen said.

If modern man had unknowingly reacted to subtle changes in solar activity, that would explain the increase in autistic children during the past decades. The Neanderthal had risen again within them as if welcoming the acceleration of the solar wind.

It was the worst possible news. What if the effect continued for years?

"But it will stop," Emily said. "It's because the flares stopped that the Neanderthals died off. They're a niche species. They're made for the world when it's like this. The extra brain mass and overconnectivity . . . I remember a study in 2011 that showed incredibly similar activity in autists' brains. Between their frontal and temporal regions, there were only eight genes that differed greatly. But in everyone else, more than five hundred genes showed differing levels."

"That's how they know each other," Bowen said.

Emily nodded. "If I had to guess, I'd say they've tapped into some sort of ancestral memory. They may be less individual we are."

She studied her nephew's face again.

"I'm not sure how much of P.J. is left in there," she said.

His name was Nim. The pack identified the boy by this low hum because it was the intonation he used the most himself. *Nnnnnnnn mh.* Each of them had their own sound.

Unfortunately, nothing else was familiar. They were eight men out of place and time, and the boy hesitated, which was unlike him. Too many of his reflexes had no correlation with his surroundings, so he interrogated the pack as he'd done repeatedly tonight.

"Nim," he sang, conveying his own health and certainty.

"En," a man answered, *Hnnn.*

"Nim," he sang.

"Han," the next man hummed, *Hnnnh.*

The base personalities of the pack were with him as always. They were rooted in each other and their ancient drives. For their kind, self-awareness consisted mostly of verifying a shared mental state. The Neanderthal brain was built wholly upon hypermnesia and intuition, reinforcing these tools in each generation until even their psyches were fixed. Nim was their decision maker. The others supported him. It was a simple model that had made them an efficient, dominant species for tens of thousands of years.

Nim wasn't surprised to live again. His thoughts were too rudimentary to gnaw at himself with such abstractions, although he was dismayed by his puny size. He'd been a child before, but never with such spindly arms and legs.

His subconscious had pushed his body for every available shred of strength, tearing ligaments in his thigh, distending the muscles in his arm. Pain was less important than stamina when the pack was in danger.

Nim could not understand the lights, which were steady now, but he'd gleaned the truth that this magic was man-made. Therefore the Dead Men were near. He remembered them like he remembered every element of his biosphere. The congested city could not have been less like the desolate terrain of the Ice Age, yet Nim was limited to one response.

This is our land, he thought, not in discrete words but in stabs of emotion. It was as if his own blood spoke to him.

He lifted his hand to the swirling ash. Black flakes touched his palm. He looked from the hospital to the orange glow on the horizon farther east. Then he gestured twice, once in the direction of the flames, once at Silver Lake.

"Burn," he sang.

The pack rose and fled into the night to retrieve torches from the distant inferno.

21

. . . .

LOS ANGELES

Dawn lit Silver Lake. Sunlight intruded through windows and hall-ways, coloring the interior. On the ground floor on the main building's north side, Emily walked toward Waiting Room 1 in a daze. She didn't want to go inside Room 1, but she didn't feel as if she had any choice. There was nowhere left to go.

An old woman stood by the door like a minister or a ghoul.

Good morning, Emily thought, intending to greet her with a useless pleasantry until the old woman said, "He promised the world will end in fire! The rainbow is His sign it won't be flood again."

Emily stared at her. "I know the Bible," she said.

"Fire!" The old woman was at least seventy, rail-thin and gray, yet dressed elegantly in a sapphire-colored suit. "Look at the sky! You'll see Ezekiel's wheels and fires exactly like the rainbow. Fire, not flood, that was His promise."

"Leave me alone."

The longest day of Emily's life had stretched into morning. It was 4:57 a.m. She felt groggy and strained. She was excited, too, because her lab work had gone well. She'd finally caught a break. Colonel Bowen couldn't send his men outside to collect blood samples, but during the previous calm they'd taken six prisoners—six men who'd been found among the injured refugees with bloody hands and wounds of their own.

The men looked like they'd been fighting. Also, five of the six wouldn't answer questions or make eye contact. A quick-thinking sergeant had brought them inside to prevent more attacks. Then the men were forgotten until rumors spread among the soldiers during P.J.'s feint at the hospital.

Emily's sample base had been sitting under her nose all along. Statistically, six men were insignificant. She needed hundreds more, but the soldiers had given her something to work with in addition to the young man she'd found with Michelle.

Isolating their white blood cells in a centrifuge had been a matter of minutes. Next she'd run those samples through an Illumina sequencer for light RNA seq tests, a meticulous job that took hours. Then she'd loaded her results into Silver Lake's computers and walked away to let the data process.

She needed sleep, but she couldn't rest. She couldn't stop. She couldn't leave. So she'd come to the hospital's prep area like someone under a spell.

Waiting Room 1 was a windowless space where families could sit while their loved ones were in surgery. The walls were hung with soft paintings of flowers and mountains and black-and-red posters detailing legal support for the uninsured, although most of the tables and chairs had been thrown into a pile to clear the floor.

Thirty or more bodies lined the carpet. A few appeared to be sleeping. The rest were bent or contorted, a jumble of white eyes and teeth and gnarled hands.

"All of our sins, our pride and arrogance," the old woman said. "The Lord has shown us what happens to the righteous and the unrighteous alike. This day has come and He will judge us."

"You think God is doing this to us?"

"It's the end of times."

"Then why don't you go outside!" Emily snarled at her. "If this is what God wants, why don't you go out there?"

The woman smiled sadly. "It's not me you're angry with," she said.

Embarrassment propelled Emily through the door. The old woman wasn't to blame for the carnage. She was trying to be loving and good, but Emily felt like she would implode if she didn't yell at someone.

Why are they keeping them in here? she wondered. *As evidence?* She'd been told the hospital's morgue—the refrigerated morgue— had been crammed with food taken from the building's cafes and vendor carts, but tossing corpses into the waiting room wasn't much better than leaving them where they fell. Bodies couldn't be kept at room temperature.

"I forgive you," the woman said behind her. "Jesus can, too."

My mom must be thinking the same thing, Emily thought.

Her mother's faith had grown more severe after P.J. was born. Sometimes Emily felt like her devotion was a way to avoid the hardest questions. For Jana Flint, the morals of every situation were carved in stone. She didn't try to look for solutions. She said P.J. had been born with ASD to teach them patience and grace, the implication being that his condition was also meant to punish Laura, or all of them, which Emily believed was cruel nonsense.

In the past few years, Laura and Emily had let their weak modern faith slip away almost completely. Laura was too busy with P.J. to go to service except at Christmas, and Emily was more interested in her work.

What if that had been an incredible blunder? She'd been so absorbed with her accomplishments and Chase and now . . .

Now . . .

More bodies had been stowed in the lounge than she'd realized. To her untrained eye, it was difficult to sort out the damage done to these people. Some of it looked accidental like burns and crashes. Others appeared to have been intentionally hurt. Emily saw blunt trauma wounds and a horrible gash on a woman's back.

She reached the end of the room without finding Chase. She turned to hurry out, making a ragged sound like laughter.

Then she froze. Chase had been so badly beaten she'd walked past him. Maybe she'd fooled herself, ignoring clues like his blue scrubs; his nice hands; his size.

Emily went lightheaded with sorrow and denial. *They didn't know,* she thought. *They said they didn't have him on the list and I was so sure.*

She had to sit down.

Gasping, crying, she reached for his cold hand. He'd been here all along. In her mind, he'd been alive, lost somewhere in the pandemonium inside the hospital—but in reality, he'd probably died before she left DNAllied. Shouldn't she have felt something?

Sometimes she despised her own genius. She'd let herself become preoccupied with new data and theories while her man lay dead in this stinking room.

We're supposed to get married, she thought. *We'll buy a house. We'll have a boy and a girl. They'll go to school. We'll work and save our money and do well and love each other. We'll vacation in Hawaii and Europe.*

We're supposed to grow old together.

She wanted to think he'd been killed saving other people. He was thick-chested and strong, and the hospital was like his home. He would have defended it.

"There, there," the old woman said from somewhere far away. Emily became aware of her again as she crouched at Emily's side. "He's gone to a better place," the old woman said. "There, there. He's in the Lord's arms."

Emily sobbed. "I d-don't . . . I . . ."

"Let's pray. We can pray for them all."

I don't believe there's a big white man in the sky who's going to welcome anyone home, she thought, savage with grief.

In her bitterness, she recalled a historic Catholic church her family had visited on the East Coast when she was a teenager. Set in tile more than fifty feet across had been the face of a Christ as blond as Emily and with eyes even more blue, an implausible appearance for a Jewish carpenter born on the shores of the Mediterranean.

Depictions such as this were an easy argument that gods were made in man's image, not vice versa. Emily and Laura had secretly discussed the subject many times before family dinners or Church events with their mom, and yet now it struck her—

Some people believed in evolution, others in the guiding hand of a Creator.

What if they were both right?

Emily reeled at the implications, because the solar flares were a reminder that life on Earth had been shaped by a force much greater than the planet itself.

Men had indulged in sun worship for millennia before Christianity absorbed those old faiths, transforming their rites and symbols to fit the new religion. The yellow disk of the sun became halos. Celebrations of the spring equinox and winter solstice turned into Easter and Christmas. For anyone who'd studied history, it was clear that man's attempts to explain his existence had evolved through the ages . . . but what if primitive sun worship had been based on something real and accessible? Then they'd forgotten. They'd revised the story.

And now our violent and jealous God has returned, she thought, weeping over Chase's bloody corpse.

"Don't fret," the old woman said. "Don't fret. He's with the Lord. You can be, too. Your salvation is in the Lord."

"Yes. Thank you."

"Pray with me," the old woman said.

"I—" *It can't hurt*, Emily thought.

Could praying actually help? Some monks and holy men were able to reach such states of self-possession, they slowed their own hearts or went days without food. What if that level of concentration could somehow guard them against the effect? Praying might be a natural attempt to focus their minds.

"The Lord is my shepherd," Emily said as the old woman joined her in the Lord's Prayer, which had been imprinted upon Emily years ago in Sunday school. "I shall not want."

The ritual calmed her pain.

Then she remembered another of the Bible's ancient myths. *The tower of Babel*, she thought. The legend told of a race of men struck down from above, left senseless and unable to communicate with each other. Had that been an isolated event? How long did it last?

Before she left, Emily reached for Chase's hand again. She wanted to keep his class ring.

I'll wear it with my engagement ring, always.

She took off her own ring, slid his larger band on her finger, then replaced hers. She wanted to kiss him goodbye, but she couldn't look at his bludgeoned skull.

I love you, she thought.

Emily went to the lists of known dead before searching for food. The emptiness inside her went beyond hunger. It seemed more important to write his name. Chase deserved their respect, and she was furious that he'd been dumped in the waiting room like garbage.

The third-floor nurses' station was one of the many places she knew inside Silver Lake. Typically she met Chase at restaurants or didn't see him until he came home, but a handful of times, she'd surprised him while he was on shift. Thanksgiving. Valentine's Day. Chase worked many holidays, and Emily enjoyed rewarding him with fun things like flowers, two slices of pumpkin pie, or a peek inside her blouse. Once they'd made out in a stairwell.

Her memories faded as she blundered through a knot of police and medical staff.

"Watch it!" a cop said.

The third floor was being used for post-op recovery. At five in the morning, it was also a safe place for off-duty soldiers and cops to rest. The voices around her were low and tight except for one man shouting in a private room.

Everywhere, people slept in the halls.

At the nurses' station, seven men and women filled a space meant for four. Two of them had functioning laptops. The rest were sorting handwritten notes, struggling to organize a deluge of new charts.

They glanced up as Emily stopped by the three clipboards pinned to the wall. One man seemed to recognize her. He reached for his phone. Emily ignored them. She was certain she was a mess, red-eyed and disheveled. Her outsides matched her soul.

First P.J., now Chase. What if Laura was gone, too?

The clipboards held the truth. Dozens of names had been scrawled on the white sheets with stark, irrefutable power. Adding his name would be like carving his tombstone. It might be the only testament Chase received.

Where would they bury him? Beneath the trees in the parking lot? Even if the flares stopped, no one had time to dig more than a few mass graves.

Emily took one breath and then another. Somehow she closed her hand on the magic marker tied to the first clipboard. She removed the cap. It was blue. Most of the handwriting on these pages was a well-practiced cursive, small and neat. She wrote his name in large block letters as masculine as possible.

Chase, Michael Coughlin, M.D.

"Miss Flint!" someone yelled. "Miss Flint!"

Mrs. Coughlin, she thought. But it would never be.

The yelling man was Captain Walsh. He'd brought two soldiers as an escort.

"Here," Emily called.

Walsh jogged through the crowded hallway. "Colonel Bowen needs you in the command center," he said. His men roused the sleeping cops and Guardsmen. The noise level increased as everyone grabbed their weapons.

"What's wrong?" Emily asked.

"They're back," Walsh said.

"Is it the same group? My nephew?"

"We're not sure yet. There are more of them."

"That's probably where they've been all night—looking for each other. How many?"

"Almost thirty."

Emily hurried after Walsh into the milling soldiers. She glanced back at the clipboards, torn between her heartbreak and her sense of duty until she discerned something in Walsh's stone face. He wanted to hide something from the men around them.

"What aren't you telling me?" she asked.

"Most of them have torches. They're flanking us on the east and south," Walsh said, lowering his voice, but in his words, Emily heard the old woman's prophecy.

The world will end in fire.

22

· · · · · · · · · · · ·

LOS ANGELES

On the second floor of the hospital's west end, Emily rushed into the command center with Walsh. She felt like a burning car that had crashed and bounced and—in seconds—might crash again.

Bowen stood at the bank of laptop screens with his officers and Guardsmen. "We're sitting ducks," he said.

In the gray dawn, beyond the parking lot and barricades to the southeast, their cameras showed running groups of three and six. Fire gleamed in every man's hand, leaving yellow-white trails where their torches were too bright for the laptop displays.

"The Neanderthals waited for sunrise," Bowen said.

Emily glanced at his bunching fists. "Can we try our lights again?" she asked.

"No. They're too close."

"Then why did you bring me here?" *I can't watch this,* she thought, and yet her gaze remained on the computer screens.

She hadn't spotted P.J., although the resolution of the video feeds had improved. Their cameras were no longer on night vision. Bowen's recon teams were sighting through binoculars or using the cameras' own zoom power.

Her watch read 5:41.

The streets were black with ash and shadows. Even the men were smudges except for their firebrands. They shifted through the wreckage, circling, hiding, then creeping forward again. They'd almost reached the barricades.

"I don't want to kill anyone, but my first responsibility is to defend this stronghold," Bowen said. "Give me a reason to tell my sniper teams to stand down."

"If we try our lights—"

"Drawing them into the building would be insane. They're here to burn us."

"They might come close enough to talk!"

Bowen shook his head. "I was told your lab work is going well. Is that true?"

"Yes." Emily said anything she could think of. "I'm sure we'll see overexpressions of keratin and FOXP2. That's enough for a biomarker. We can use it for roughshod blood tests and the first steps of a new gene therapy."

"But we'll have to inject each man, is that right? You can't fix one person and have him spread it like a cold?"

"No. I'd insert tailored genes into a retrovirus, which would need to be individually delivered in a tiny amount of blood plasma with a hypodermic. Then the genes will make functional—"

He pointed at the video feeds. "Can you stop those men?"

"With what?"

"The virus you just talked about. A nerve toxin. Anything."

Emily swallowed hard, wondering if she had the courage to pick up a gun herself. What if the fighting came to that? "I don't know how to make bioweapons," she said. "Even if I did, we'd need more time and—"

"Get her out of here," Bowen said, gesturing at Walsh. Then he turned to another officer. "Snipers ready."

She couldn't protect P.J. anymore. Bowen needed to do anything necessary to stop the Neanderthals before they incinerated Silver Lake or drove everyone out of the hospital.

Walsh took her arm, but he was halfhearted in pulling her away. Maybe he'd expected more from her, too.

"Tell the engineers to move back," Bowen said.

"Sir, our claymores are off-line in sectors three, four, and eight," an officer said.

Somehow the soldiers had placed anti-personnel mines outside the building as a final line of defense. Emily could see the explosives marked in the sketches posted on the wall. Most lined the barricades to the south, but the sketches showed others at the back entrances on Silver Lake's north and west sides. Unfortunately, some of the mines had failed.

"I want squad weapons at every entrance," Bowen said. "Order grenades as a last resort. We don't want to bring this place down on ourselves."

"Yes, sir."

"Fire."

It was a simple word. It knocked Emily's breath away.

She heard muffled gunshots from the front of the hospital. Then the sound was lost as the refugees on the ground floor screamed.

On the computer screens, outside, a dozen men jerked back like puppets. One fell in a puff of red mist, his torch igniting his hair. But he wasn't dead. He thrashed and bucked.

Emily resisted the urge to cram her hand against her mouth.

Too much was happening too fast.

Was this really P.J.'s group? They'd last seen him near midnight. He shouldn't have needed six hours to bring torches from the city. Why would he come back at all? They were imprisoned in this building while he could travel at will. Fighting them was pointless, which meant the men outside might be a completely different group.

Maybe he's safe, Emily prayed.

In the parking lot near the south entrance, Nim staggered as something bit through his shoulder. It shook embers from his torch onto his arm, but he didn't stop. He redirected his momentum, lowering his arm and the torch's weight to send himself sideways and back. The barricades were a few feet behind him.

"Down!" he sang, calling to his survivors.

He saw three men retreat and take cover. Finally he knelt, peering into the open.

Inside the barricades, the hospital's main parking lot was lined with cars, but too much of the asphalt field was exposed. In it, eight men lay bleeding. Above, sunlight played through the hectic clouds.

One of the injured was Han. Encrusted in ash, Han squirmed on his elbows as if to find Nim. Blood ran in obscene puddles from his back.

Only luck had saved Nim when death took so many others, yet the killing force wasn't imperceptible. It had direction. It had originated from points to his north and east along the building's face.

The killing force also had sound. Seconds after most of his hunters were leveled by the first volley, Nim's eyes and ears had also detected four near misses where dust leapt from the ground or unseen objects slammed into the cars. In the pattern, he'd glimpsed safe zones where the Dead Men could not reach.

Perhaps those zones were changing?

He hadn't anticipated their magic where he'd been hit, so he waited, reevaluating every clue. He sang. "Nnnnnnnn mh!" he cried, finding his hunters.

"Hnnn!" En answered, then a second man, and a third.

Other survivors joined their song as Nim inspected his shoulder. The gash was no worse than other cuts and bruises he'd sustained as they pushed through the city, so he dismissed the pain. Who else was alive? Where were they?

Listening to them, Nim perfected the map in his head, swiftly calculating sixty-two positions—twelve able-bodied hunters, nineteen wounded or killed, and thirty-one reports of near misses. He saw how the dead meshed with the living. There were interlocking lanes of danger and safety.

He called new orders to his survivors, sending each man into a safe zone for their assault.

"What are they waiting for?" Emily shouted, but no one heard her in the torrent of voices.

The soldiers' discipline was unraveling. None of them had slept. Now their shouting grew wild. Bowen didn't notice Emily when she pressed in close beside him.

On their screens, behind the barricades at the southeast, human shapes and torches were briefly visible—a shoulder, two heads, a running man—and yet they went unharmed by Bowen's snipers. That was why the soldiers were yelling at each other.

"If we can see someone, we should be able to get a weapon on him!" Bowen argued with an officer, who said, "Sir, our cameras are farther out than our shooters. We don't have anyone directly above the south entrance."

"Move them up."

"Most of the armor is immobile, sir. We only had two welding sets.

We're using scrap where we couldn't rig boxes, but those shields aren't something our guys can carry. The shooters above us on the west end and the ground-floor units along the face of the building are locked in place. They don't have good angles at the south entrance."

"Goddammit!" Bowen yelled, jabbing his finger at the screens. "Get some rifles on those men!"

For an instant, Emily heard one soldier talking on his handset. "Copy that." He turned to Bowen and said, "Team Ten lost their shooter, sir. We're moving another . . ." Then he saw Bowen's expression and his own face went pale.

It was a bad moment. The chill on Emily's skin sank through her bones as she understood what everyone else in the command center had already realized.

We don't have enough guns in position to keep them back.

Another soldier's handset muttered, and the pocket of silence collapsed. They returned to their tasks.

"Use the lights again," Emily said. Daylight was growing fast in the video feeds, but she couldn't think of anything else. "They didn't like the lights. It might slow them down."

"Try it," Bowen said to one of his men.

"We should make more noise, too," Emily said. "If we get five hundred people banging on the walls or the floor . . ."

Bowen looked her up and down. Maybe he was swayed by her presence of mind. "Do you have a line to our security details downstairs?" he asked another Guardsman. "Give the order. I want everyone yelling. Each man on the ground floor will use his sidearm to fire one clip into the floor, but spread out their shots. Make 'em last."

"Yes, sir."

The strain was more than Emily could bear. She fidgeted with the hem of her filthy blouse and rocked on her feet like a child. How soon until the Neanderthals attacked?

Outside, Nim's song continued. Their voices were graceful and clean, unlike the wind, the ash, or the bent corpses of their friends.

Sprawled in the open, Han had quit moving. He'd bled out, but losing him did not spark impatience or reckless hate in Nim. Dead was dead. Only the living were useful, and Nim felt a very different passion now.

He was learning.

It was his single-mindedness that had led his pack into the slaughter. To preserve the rest, he needed to do better. He needed to grow. For hours, Nim had fought a second war within himself, an internal struggle to circumvent his ancient drives. Self-examination was alien to him, but his limitations had become obvious even before his tribe was decimated.

The night had passed because Nim got lost, not because he'd waited for sunrise, not because he'd deviated from his search for fire to find others of their kind. Because he got lost.

The hypermnesia that was his greatest strength was also a handicap in the city. Los Angeles was nothing like the terrain for which he was hardwired, eons before the planet changed along with its climate. At his ancestors' pinnacle, glaciers covered most of Europe. Even the regions that had been free of the ice, near the oceans, were affected by the cold. Rain was unknown. The sky tended to be frigid and gray. Consequently, there had been no forests, only sweeping, open plains.

Nim's reflex was to get beneath the wind. To him, any breeze was a threat that stole moisture from their bodies. Overexposure could mean dehydration and weakness.

Hiding from it now was pointless. The storms rushing over California were thick with water vapor from the Pacific. Nim could taste the wind's damp salt and heat, and yet during the night he'd sheltered his pack again and again without questioning this impulse. His decision to hide had also stemmed from a need to recover from sensory overload.

In the Stone Age, Europe's ecology had been unspeakably basic. No trees meant no birds. The cold meant few insects. Their world had contained only grazing animals such as horse and reindeer, a few hibernating rodents such as voles and mice, and meat eaters like cave lions, hyenas, bears, and men.

Foremost among his talents was the ability to scour the emptiness for any detail. The cold preserved spoor for years. The plains of the Ice Age had been marred by tens of thousands of hoofprints, dung, bits of fur, and old bones, each of which he could separate at a glance.

The cityscape was more complex. The human population alone was stunning, as were the birds, dogs, cats, vermin, and bugs. The endless geometry of buildings saturated his eyes. Memorizing this labyrinth would not have been beyond Nim, but the gale winds that flooded the streets—combined with so much life and wreckage—had left him baffled.

Survival demanded more.

Crouched behind the barricades, Nim pushed deeper into himself, sorting through his preset responses for a newer, more flexible mode of thinking. Part of him was still Laura's son Peter Joshua, a phantom interlaid with Nim's base personality. The modern human brain was a murmur that he could hear like a deaf man concentrating on the bass vibrations of an orchestra.

His other persona was an unexpected resource. Hints of imagination gave Nim the ability to divide his pack into *more valuable, less valuable* components, although he arranged them in trios again without realizing it.

The less valuable men would go first. The more valuable would follow. Sacrificing a few to improve the majority's survival rate was a small jump for a species that placed the whole before the individual, but including himself among those who would wait was a spectacular innovation. Nim had always led the pack. Now he chose not to risk himself, breaking with a fundamental instinct.

He rose on the balls of his feet, balancing his club and his torch in either hand. The wind gusted like knives through his hair. "Go," he sang.

His hunters charged the building.

"They're rushing the south entrance!" a soldier yelled. Five video feeds showed only cars and city streets. But in two of the computer screens, enemy shapes sprinted through the barricades.

They were bunched in threes again. Why threes?

Emily didn't know if Bowen's snipers fired on the men outside. None of the fleeting shapes were hit, and gunshots drummed through the floor beneath her, masking any shots overhead. Then the men vanished from the computer screens. They were inside the cameras' ranges.

"Spotter puts them at forty yards," an officer said. "Thirty. Fifteen."

"Claymores," Bowen said.

Explosions ripped through the din, painting one computer screen with fire and smoke. The blasts also silenced the noise on the ground floor, where the soldiers and refugees were much closer to the mines. Emily pictured them ducking for cover.

"Spotter reports two men still coming," the officer said as another Guardsman called, "A dozen of our mines misfired, sir!"

"Colonel, there are more combatants on the perimeter!" a soldier yelled. This time, six of the video feeds showed motionless scenery—but on one screen, a second wave of Neanderthals ran through the barricades.

Many of them went toward the south entrance. Others diverted toward the larger doors in the center part of Silver Lake, charging the main entrance beneath the big red EMERGENCY sign.

"They were testing us," Bowen said. His voice held equal parts fury and quiet awe. "They made us show our defenses before committing their reserves."

Oh no, Emily thought, identifying P.J. among the charge. He carried a torch like all of them.

"Can you bring the rest of those claymores online?" Bowen asked his Guardsmen.

"I'm trying, sir."

Bowen looked at Emily. "What will happen if our men shoot through the glass? The effect will come inside, won't it?"

"I don't think the glass is holding it back," she said. "We're shielded in here by all the steel and concrete. If your soldiers get too close to the windows, you'll lose them whether they shoot or not."

Bowen turned to his officers with handsets. "Tell them to do it," he said.

"You can't!" Emily embarrassed herself by protesting. Sending the Guardsmen to the windows, sacrificing them to protect everyone else inside Silver Lake, was like chopping off a man's hands and feet to save his body. Bowen had no choice.

Machine guns stuttered beneath her. Some were near. Some were far. What each position had in common was that every gun stopped within seconds. Soldiers were giving up their minds to fire those few shots. They must have run from the depths of the hospital to scan the landscaping or the parking lot outside, shooting even as they succumbed to the effect. Then where did they go? Had there been enough time or rope to provide them with tethers?

A man said, "Spotter reports two kills for Team One, sir!"

The conflict in Emily was hideous. She hoped P.J. wasn't among the dead, but did she have any right? The best thing might be if he was wounded and brought inside—if he could survive a bullet—if the hospital was ever safe again.

Alarms vibrated through the never-ending noise.

"Sir, we have smoke inside the main doors and the ER," an officer said as another man called, "We're on fire at the south entrance! I have a sergeant on the ground floor reporting enemy combatants inside, but most of his platoon is disabled and he can't engage or we'll lose him, too! He can only hear them!"

"Does he have grenades?" Bowen asked.

"Yes, sir! He threw them, sir!"

"Back him up with anyone we have available. Center our defenses on the middle part of the building. Is the sprinkler system on?"

"Sir! Yes, sir! I have reports of sprinklers activated across the ground floor!" the soldier said as another officer said, "Colonel, there are torches inside the main doors. Parts of the ER and the central lobby are on fire."

Despite their guns, despite superior numbers, they were losing. Emily guessed the same fight was repeating itself all over the world. Normal men were trapped inside or underground while the Neanderthals were free to burn or bury them, and the realization that struck her now felt evil.

P.J. might be better off outside, she thought.

Greasy black smoke rolled through the open door, spilling across the ceiling. Someone shouted before the sprinklers overhead burst like a squall of rain, drenching everyone and their paper maps and laptops. One computer shorted out. Its screen went dark. The soldiers yanked at their equipment in a tangle of wires, shoving their laptops beneath their desks.

Walsh charged the door. That alone would have been a selfless act, but he drew his pistol as he ran into the hall, shutting the door with his back to it. Emily heard him yelling on the other side.

Bowen shouted through the hissing sprinklers. "I want this water in buckets or any containers we can find! Move as much as possible above the fire! Be ready to shoot through the floor! Maybe we can coordinate with our men on the ground."

Wet and cold, Emily tried to help the soldiers sort cables in the downpour. A few of the video feeds were up again.

Outside, suddenly, she saw three people sprinting away. They ran south, dashing through one screen and then another. "Look!" she said. Were those soldiers who'd been lost to the pulse? Or were the Neanderthals retreating?

Seconds later, the crackle of the guns blended into a louder, heavy drumbeat. A rhythmic *whup whup whup whup* slapped at the sky.

"Spotters report a chopper inbound, sir!" a man yelled as another said, "Check that. It's an Osprey."

"I have no ident!" the first man yelled.

"It's ours," Bowen said, lifting his fist in triumph. "Thank God. It has to be ours."

Nim fled. The thing in the sky was too loud, too big, too unlike anything he understood. He wasn't sure if it was alive or a natural event like an avalanche.

"Follow me," he sang.

It hammered out of the north as he broke off his assault, calling for the hunters who'd run inside. Only two emerged. That left him with six men, and all of them were hurt.

As the thing in the sky swung closer, it scattered the pack. Two of his men ran into a danger zone. "Wait!" Nim called. They couldn't hear him. The vibrations were immense, and Nim glanced over his shoulder to see if death would strike.

Smoke twisted from the building in four places, concealing his hunters. All of them had thrown their torches into the Dead Men's caves. Maybe it would be enough. If the Dead Men burned, the battle was over.

If not, Nim would be back.

23

. . . .

LOS ANGELES

In the cockpit, approaching the southern face of the hospital, Drew didn't see the men running beneath his aircraft until it was too late. His attention was on the wind and the few clear areas in the parking lot.

Tnk. A bullet punched through the fuselage somewhere behind them and Bugle yelled, "We're taking fire!"

"What—"

People on the hospital's west end were shooting at the men outside. Drew had descended between them within eighty feet of the building, sending up great whirls of ash and smoke. He didn't think he was the target, but there wasn't enough fuel to abort, so he ignored the guns.

Lowering into the dark mess took all of his concentration. The V-22 Osprey was a vertical takeoff and landing aircraft just a few years off the drawing board. Equipped with heavy positional rotors on its snub wings, the Osprey's sixty-foot body was nothing like a fixed-wing fighter, and Drew had barely clocked fifty hours in test flights. If the wind tipped him into the building . . . If he hit a tree or a car . . .

"Kingsnake Eight Five, this is Romeo Nine!" Bugle yelled on the radio. "Kingsnake Eight Five, do you copy?"

"They can't hear you," Julie said on their ICS. She was in back.

Bugle sat beside Drew in the copilot's seat and flipped his middle finger at the hospital. "Quit shooting, motherfucker!" Bugle yelled as the radio answered through pops of static: "—manding officer Colonel Bowen. Say again?"

The gunfire had stopped. Bugle was only mouthing off because there wasn't anything better for him to do.

They were almost on the ground. Then a glittering hail struck the asphalt in front of them. Drew jerked the aircraft up and away. Glass peeled from the hospital in shards and larger panes, which was why he hadn't landed closer. He couldn't afford to get hit. Even if the Osprey wasn't seriously damaged, rents in its protective coating could leave its electronics vulnerable to the EMP. They'd need to patch the bullet hole. There were no aircraft left to replace this one.

The Osprey's tires jolted into the ground before Drew anticipated contact. The hard landing made someone shout in back. "Great," Drew said, trying to hide his tension—but it showed in his next words. "Ask them about Dr. Flint."

Bugle waved him off. Static was making both sides repeat their call signs, so Drew powered down the engines and pulled off his flight helmet, careful not to dislodge the silvery mesh cap beneath. His ears and cheeks itched. He rubbed with both hands, showering himself with gray flakes of dead skin.

ROMEO had drugged him again during the long flight from Japan to Edwards Air Force Base just north of Los Angeles in the desert. Vicious tail winds had carried their C-17 across the Pacific in record time. Even so, Drew's burns appeared two or three days old after responding to their salves and intravenous nutrients. Pink new skin had emerged beneath his dry blisters.

"Nice work," Julie said at the cockpit door. She wore a mesh cap, too, like a thin snow hat. Her smile was mischievous. Without that look, she was pretty, but the sly light in her eyes made her beautiful.

She turned her back on Bugle, concealing her smile from the co-pilot's seat before she bent down for a kiss. Her slender hand explored his chest as they nuzzled.

Drew tried not to ruin her happiness. Unfortunately, he'd almost killed everyone aboard the plane. He might have noticed the guns and the running men sooner if not for his blind spot, a hazy fleck in the corner of his left eye.

He hadn't told anyone his vision was permanently impaired. What would Julie think if he did? He knew he had trust issues, which was ironic, because by joining the Navy he'd committed himself to a larger ideal. It was the details of individual relationships that came harder to him. He wasn't good at sharing. They both enjoyed their little secret. Touching each other was a harmless diversion, but he couldn't ask her to lie for him.

He was right to fly. U.S. Command needed every pilot available, although Drew had been careful to volunteer for a lesser mission. He'd made his decision during their brief layover in Japan, where thirty agents and Special Forces soldiers had stayed behind in order to penetrate the Chinese mainland. Drew wanted to take part in the hunt for China's weapon programs, infiltrating their coastal sites, but he'd needed more time to heal.

Retrieving the geneticist at Silver Lake Hospital was a third-priority objective. Joint specialists with the NSA and DIA had been tracking Silver Lake's loop transmissions since last night, piecing together every fragment they'd gleaned, but they'd only sent Drew's team to snatch Doctor Flint because they were grasping at straws and she was nearby.

"All right, knock it off." Bugle smacked the back of Julie's leg when he might have slapped her butt in the close confines of the Osprey.

Drew thought his friend was intimidated by her, not because she was talented and smart. Bugle was talented and smart, but Julie shared something with Drew that Bugle never could. He hadn't even made a joke when the three of them were assigned together.

"Flint is here," Bugle said. "Someone needs to get her."

Drew removed his straps. "I'll go."

"You're the pilot," Bugle said.

"Then you go."

"I'm nav, comm, and electronics," Bugle said with a meaningful glance at Julie. "This aircraft won't function without you or me, so—Shit."

A line of people moved between them and the hospital. Drew reached for his console, hot-starting his engines as Julie peered through the cockpit glass on either side. "I see nine to our left and more by our tail," she said.

"Kingsnake Eight Five, hostiles are surrounding the aircraft!" Bugle yelled on the radio. "Can your snipers protect us?"

"Hold it," Julie said. "They're running away. Tell the Guard to stand down. Those people outside are their own people."

Drew glanced up as the rotors began to spin. *She's right*, he thought. The people in the open were nonaggressive. Most of them wore civilian clothes. Two were National Guard. They'd hugged the building, coming no closer than sixty feet to the Osprey. Now the fury of the engines chased them away. They ran into the barricades and the city streets beyond.

"Call off the snipers," Drew told Bugle, powering down again. He regretted the wasted fuel.

Where had those people come from? They must have been inside Silver Lake. They were so desperate to escape they'd convinced themselves that his arrival meant it was safe outside, exposing themselves to the EMP.

They were lost lives. Drew didn't have time to corral them, and they weren't the only people his team would leave behind.

"Let's move," he said. "Everybody out."

They filed from the cockpit into the body of the aircraft, where a Marine stood at the side door with an M4 carbine, his forearm encased in a fiberglass cast.

The four of them were it. ROMEO had no one else to spare. A Navy captain had told Drew to grab one man from a pool of unattached agents, so he'd taken the Marine he'd befriended aboard the C-17. Even with a broken arm, or maybe because of it, Staff Sergeant James Patrick looked like an incomparable fighter.

Patrick had shut the protective screen on the aft side of the door. Drew closed a second one behind himself. The Osprey had been modified with runners across its deck and ceiling, allowing metallic fabric curtains to isolate this section of the interior. Otherwise they would allow the EMP inside when they opened up.

Drew said, "Bugle, Sergeant, stay with the aircraft. Julie, you're with me."

"Oh sure, she gets all the fun," Bugle said.

Drew took an M4 from a duffel bag at Patrick's feet. He handed the weapon to Julie, then grabbed a backpack and another carbine for himself. "Buddy-check each other," he said.

Bugle stepped to Drew first, leaving Julie and Patrick to pair up. All of them would wear their flight helmets as additional armor, which made it difficult to verify that their mesh caps were seated across their foreheads and temples. Bugle had to lean close. His breath smelled like the beef noodles they'd gorged down at Edwards AFB.

"Watch yourself out there, dick hole," Bugle said.

Drew squeezed his friend's lanky arm. "We'll be back in fifteen minutes," he said.

In the command center, Emily gawked at the video feeds as a Guardsman said, "They're walking outside!"

The plane was low and fat, its fuselage barely off the ground. When the side door opened beneath its high wings, four people rushed out. They seemed immune to the effect. The first two ran toward the hospital. The others stayed by the plane, walking apart from each other with their weapons up.

"The sun must have stopped," the Guardsman said. "We can go out there!"

"No way," an officer said, keeping a handset at his ear. "We just lost thirty people from the ground floor when they ran for the plane."

"But those pilots—"

"They said they have some kind of armor. It's on the plane, too."

"Is that possible?" Bowen asked Emily.

"I'm not a physicist," she said. "I can't make anything like that."

"I didn't expect you to. You've done enough. Thank you."

"You're welcome," Emily said cautiously, wondering at his sincerity.

He sounded like he was saying goodbye to her.

Five minutes later, Emily hung back as Walsh escorted the Navy pilots into the command center. They looked clean. Their uniforms were new. The man hadn't shaved—his nose and cheeks were peeling—but the woman's face looked well-scrubbed inside her flight helmet.

The brims of their mesh caps fell to their eyebrows and formed broad sideburns, giving them both a hooded, bird-like appearance. *Could it be that easy?* Emily wondered, pressing her fingertips to the soft part of her temple. It was another clue.

The man saluted Bowen. "Sir, I'm Lieutenant Commander Drew Haldane. Under the Bighorn protocols, I'm authorized to draft as many as nine of your men."

"My men won't do you any good out there," Bowen said.

"I've been requisitioned ten spare caps, sir. One for her. Nine for reinforcements."

"I need five," Bowen said. "There are fires right now that we can't reach."

"No, sir. The caps are mine."

Bowen clenched his fists. "This building is on fire," he said. "I need to be able to put it out. We need to be able to repel attacks."

"No, sir," Drew said. "I'm sorry, sir."

Emily wasn't sure how to feel about him. He was forceful, even rude, and he held his body like someone else might hold a sword. His feet were set apart, balancing his weight to jump or fight.

"I won't go," she said.

Everyone turned in surprise. "I'm under orders," Drew said.

"I won't leave these people. Isn't that what you plan to do? Take their best men and go?"

Julie said, "There must be a thousand people in this building who'd trade places with you."

Emily wasn't sure how to feel about her, either. She felt like they were ganging up on her. She said, "If you can go outside, we need you here."

"No, ma'am," Drew said. "My orders are to take you and your equipment to a secure location."

"We have to go after the Neanderthals first."

"No, ma'am. That is not the mission."

"We need to communicate with them! Maybe we can stop the war."

"One of them is her nephew," Bowen said.

Emily stared. Why would Bowen undermine her efforts when she was arguing to keep as many resources at the hospital as possible? Because he was a good soldier?

Drew said, "Ma'am, everyone's lost family and friends. I'm sorry."

"Listen to me! We have a chance here that we might never see again. The Neanderthals won't—"

"We're aware of your theories. That's why we're bringing you to a safe location with other top scientists. We need your help."

He managed to sound respectful, but Emily wasn't convinced. "Don't snow me," she said. "If you don't believe any of the data I've put forward, why are you here?"

Drew bristled back at her, and Emily realized his clean, rested appearance was a mirage. How had he suffered the blisters on his face?

"I'm not paid to think," he said. "I'm under orders." Then he looked at Bowen. "Sir, nine men. Point me in the direction of her equipment."

Emily intervened again. "That means you have more of your armor," she said.

He stared at her. "No, ma'am."

"There must be bags or sheets of it in your plane. If you didn't, you couldn't carry the lab gear outside without exposing it to the pulse."

"We do not have armor to spare," he said, looking at Colonel Bowen. "I'm sorry, sir."

"The labs are in the north wing," Bowen said.

Drew turned to Julie. "Lieutenant, I'll take a detail to Dr. Flint's labs with her to make sure we don't miss anything. I want you to grab four men and see what you can do to stop the fires."

"Aye, sir." Julie's voice was crisp, but Emily didn't miss her fond, worried glance. Everyone else was distracted as Drew took off his pack and removed ten mesh caps.

"This is M-string, the culmination of sixty years of Cold War research and next-gen physics," he said.

Bowen's men huddled around him.

Emily watched Julie instead. Once upon a time, she'd looked at Chase the same way every time he left for work. The two pilots were in love.

Before he walked to the door, Drew made eye contact with Bowen and several other men. "Colonel, all of you, I need a vow on your honor not to say anything about the caps. If word gets out that we can protect ten people, they'll riot."

Bowen nodded to Walsh. "Get helmets on everyone," Bowen said. "Try to hide the caps."

In the command center, only Walsh and a Guard lieutenant had been assigned to Drew. Walsh would gather seven recruits from their recon and sniper teams, send half of them after Julie, then meet Drew at a stairwell en route to the labs.

Leading Emily, they stepped into the hall, where Drew steeled himself to let Julie go. The smoke had thickened. Screams surged through the hospital below them. Julie had no training as a firefighter, but he'd seen West Hollywood crews among the police and National Guard. With luck, they had some equipment with them, even air tanks, because Drew couldn't ask the people in this building to watch his team fly away while they burned alive. He had to send Julie to help because he couldn't give her cap to anyone else.

"Hurry," he said.

Julie saluted. He returned it. Her face was somber now, and he missed the elfin light in her eyes.

She ran west with the Guard lieutenant. Drew went east with Emily. Within seconds, they dodged a line of soldiers relaying jugs of liquid detergent from a laundry room. That must have been all they had left on this floor to douse the flames. Then he passed four Guardsmen gasping for breath as a medic cut away a female soldier's charred pant legs. She squirmed and groaned.

Emily shouted at him. "The Neanderthals came here twice! They might come again."

Drew didn't answer.

"If there's any chance of reaching them, it's through me. I'm his aunt. I know him. P.J. might recognize me if we can talk."

Drew stopped her to avoid a squad rushing in the opposite direction with armfuls of wet towels. The sight filled him with horror and respect. They had nothing better to wrap themselves in before approaching the flames, but Bowen's soldiers were a long way from giving up.

He was harsher with Emily than he intended. "You're not my only objective," he said. "We can't stay here."

"We have to! P.J.'s our best bet to understand what's happening. I can bring up his medical records if you can access local data banks. The rest of those men are John Does."

"Why do you need his records?"

"Identifying a biomarker is just the first step. I can develop gene therapies that will cure them, but I need more positive controls. My sister paid for newborn screening. That means we have P.J.'s genotype."

"You don't sound like you're sure about this Neanderthal stuff."

"Have you seen them?"

"Yes. We have video nationwide."

"Then you know how they breathe and sing."

Drew reached the stairwell where he would meet Walsh. Blocking the way to the ground level were two desks and four soldiers. They were yelling at a horde of refugees on the stairs.

Emily extended one hand as if to grab Drew's arm, then held back. *She's afraid of me*, he realized. But that didn't stop her.

Beneath the yelling, her voice was firm. "In early *Homo sapiens*, the larynx gradually dropped into the throat to allow for extra air intake for short-burst running. Neanderthals never made that adaptation. For them, surviving the cold was more important. That's why their bodies were shorter and thicker than ours. That's why they're breathing funny."

"It's eighty degrees outside."

"In periglacial Europe, wind chill might have put daytime temperatures at fifteen degrees Fahrenheit *in summer*. That's why they developed larger noses and larger sinus cavities. They inhale slowly to warm the air, then blow it out fast to make room for the next slow breath. It doesn't matter now that they're in a temperate climate. The behavior is hardwired."

"I've seen them run."

"The people outside aren't true Neanderthals, and that's not my point. Neanderthals could run. They probably just weren't as fast as us. Everything is give and take. They sang because they couldn't talk because they didn't need language because they're less individual than we are."

Drew blinked at her logic, trying to keep up. He'd heard Bowen's broadcasts of her theories. "You think they use ancestral memory," he said.

"Yes. Even more important than the cold was the geomagnetic pulse. *Homo sapiens* developed an elastic skull and huge frontal lobes, but at the cost of weak spots at our temples. The Neanderthals had much heavier bone in their foreheads and comparatively tiny frontal lobes—anything to preserve their brain core. They're more efficient than we are. We have more imagination."

Emily shrugged, and Drew liked her for her ability to skim through eons of growth and transformation in so few words.

"There was interbreeding," she said. "The Neanderthals are still inside us today, and I can prove it if you don't waste this chance."

The tenacity in her blue eyes was compelling. So was the fact that she wasn't a stuck-up egghead whose main goal was to save herself. She didn't even want to leave.

Drew understood what it was like to predict trouble before anyone else saw it. ROMEO had disregarded his initial warnings, too, and he didn't know enough about her field to argue.

Could he be wrong for the right reasons?

Drew had no doubt the Chinese were using an EMP weapon. Solar activity created diffuse "noise" on a wide spectrum. No one would confuse man-made systems with this noise. Even if most of the havoc had been caused by flares, the unusual pulses he'd detected above the South China Sea were artificial. The only question was how many EMP weapons China had deployed and if they had anything to do with the change in the sun, which seemed unlikely. Even DIA analysts had considered that a stretch.

Emily must have noticed the change in him because she hurried to say more. "Forkhead box binding protein two plays into a host of physiological attributes like wider chests and altered vocal abilities with increased range in tone. Who does that remind you of?"

"Cavemen. Singing."

"There will be overexpressions of FOXP2 in the men I've tested. I expect the same for keratin, SELEN BP1, the list goes on and on, but I need a larger sample base to verify my biomarker and I need known subjects."

"Why?"

"Positive controls. Listen to me. My sister paid for newborn screening, which means we already have P.J.'s genotype. In his case, a lot of the work was done years ago. That will save me days of work and *weeks* of computer time."

Drew had said he wasn't paid to think, but, ultimately, that latitude was inherent in every ROMEO mission. He was trained—authorized—to change his mind if the circumstances warranted it.

"All right," he said. "I'll take a squad to find your nephew."

"I'm coming with you."

"What?" He nearly laughed, and she saw it.

Her blue eyes sparked with anger and determination. "I can handle myself," she said. "I walked through fifteen blocks of burning city to get here."

"It's too dangerous."

"We can fly after him."

"No. I'm tight on fuel. Even if we located him, it's unlikely we'd find room to land. We'll go on foot. It's too dangerous."

She didn't back off, which he admired.

"Most of the Neanderthals out there are dead," she said. "The rest are badly hurt. You have guns. They have clubs. You need me."

"Why?"

"How else can you get close to him?"

"We could shoot him."

"You . . ." She visibly choked with new anger. "He's an eight-year-old boy!"

"He led an assault on an entrenched position held by hundreds of trained soldiers, and he nearly won. But you're right. He's down to a few men, most of them wounded. I'll trap them, Tase them, then bring 'em back. It's high risk. You're not coming."

"What will a Taser do to a child?"

"He'll survive."

"You need me. I'm the only way to catch P.J. from a distance. He might recognize me. I can distract him. I'll have the best chance of telling you where he's gone and how he thinks. It's a big city. How else will you find him?"

Drew studied her face, her certainty, her intelligence. He weighed her claims and her life against the millions of casualties outside.

What if Emily was the key to this whole thing?

Drew nodded and said, "All right. Come with me."

24

NORTHERN CALIFORNIA

Those people outside might be able to help," Marcus said in the silence of the electronics room. "I know some of them. Maybe they can be . . . trained."

The dim room was stifling and hot. It stank. Marcus had stripped down to his pants, walking the concrete floor in his bare feet, but there was no airflow and the buckets they'd used for toilets were overripe. Outside, the wind had quieted as the morning sun lifted into the sky, leaving a thick, muggy heat. Sweat trickled down his ribs.

"I see Kym again," he said, standing awkwardly on a wire rack loaded with processors. The metal cut into his foot. That didn't cause him to step off of the rack. He held himself steady against the pain, bending his neck to keep one eye at his spy hole.

The shafts he'd drilled through the reinforced walls were ill-placed. All five were against the ceiling, where he'd hoped these tiny openings would be shielded by the overhang in the structure's roof. He was afraid of allowing the phenomenon through the walls—afraid of losing himself.

"They don't look like they treat her differently," he said. "I mean because of her eyes or skin color."

The short Laotian girl seemed to be Chuck's lover, playing a game very much like tag with him. They ran through the endless dishes of the array. Chuck caught her, released her, and caught her again, never quite kissing Kym yet nuzzling her ears and neck as she laughed and pressed her round body against him, flashing her white teeth.

Her voice sounded like music. She used no words, only laughter and teasing.

They were both shirtless, and Kym's pants were undone, as if she found it too complicated to use the buckle sewn into the elastic waistband of her green calf-length pants. She wore no underwear. Marcus had seen too much of her when they darted close to the station. He was chagrined to find himself looking at all, but there was a sweet, unfettered sexuality in Kym's movements he'd never seen before. Maybe he was more cognizant of her physical quality because he'd slept with Rebecca Drayer so recently. Kym's every step was a dance. She seemed happy, almost intoxicated by her freedom.

Both of them were careless. Chuck's shoulders were burnt red. Kym was brown-skinned and black-haired, well-suited for the sun whenever it blazed through the unsteady cloud cover . . . and yet her chin was bruised and her back had been abraded, leaving dots of blood and new scabs.

There were also two men watching from the hillside beyond the white dishes. Marcus couldn't see their faces.

Was one of them Steve? Were they Rebecca's soldiers?

More important, he wondered if those men were guarding Kym and Chuck from harm or waiting for their own chance with her. What if they were rivals for the girl?

Kym might not have been given any more choice in the matter than Rebecca. Marcus couldn't guess if Kym had paired herself with Chuck because anyone else would be even more unbearable. She might be pretending her attraction.

She might have forgotten resisting him.

As far as Marcus could tell, the people outside lacked all but the most fluid self-consciousness. They lived in the moment.

What kind of society would emerge among men and women who possessed only shreds of memory? It would be tribal at best, and Marcus believed Rebecca and Kym were the only females in hiking distance, although Chuck's presence opened this assumption to question.

During the first interrupt, Chuck's car must have stalled before he'd driven Roell more than forty or fifty miles from the array. Then he'd walked back. Maybe other people were climbing into the mountains—people like Roell.

"I'm going to shout at them again," Marcus said. He leaned back from his spy hole and breathed slowly, making sure he had enough oxygen. The last time he'd started to yell, he hadn't been able to stop. He'd yelled and yelled until he nearly fainted in the heat. Without the AC units, the electronics room was a Dutch oven absorbing the sunlight, and he needed to ration the barrel of fuel for the generator.

I have snacks and candy, he thought. *Maybe I can push something through a hole and they can bring me water. Maybe, in time, they can do more sophisticated work.*

They could help me with the array.

"Kym!" he yelled against the tiny hole. "Kymberly Vang! Chuck! Hey, Chuck!"

They'd frozen in their game. Kym held one forearm across her breasts. Was that modesty or a more basic instinct to protect herself? So help him, she looked like a doe or a purebred horse or a gazelle, compact and graceful.

He called to her like he would coax a dog or a horse. "Kymmie Kymmie Kymmie! Kymmie!"

It was an effort to keep his tone light, but she smiled at his cajoling. She was curious.

Chuck didn't like her response. He took her arm and pulled her back.

"No! Wait!" Marcus's voice sharpened. "Wait!"

Issuing a command was the wrong thing to do. Kym's smile faltered. Then she turned and retreated into the array with Chuck.

Marcus scrambled to another spy hole, clattering sideways along the wire rack. He'd drilled three holes in the room's south-facing wall and two more on the west side.

"Kym! I'm sorry! I—" His voice skipped again, lurching from his terror to a false cheer so pathetic it wouldn't have fooled a baby. "I have food! I have yummy treats! If you . . . Kym!? Kym!"

He couldn't see them. They'd gone east, and the north and east walls of the electronics room faced into the station, which left him blind in those directions.

Why had they come here to begin with? Were they hunting in the squirrel-riddled field or did they remember the array as an important place in their lives?

The men on the hillside were gone, too, either leaving as a group or pursuing Chuck and Kym. Marcus watched impotently. At last, he stepped down from the rack into the gleam of a single flashlight lying on the floor. A watch waited beside it with a notepad and three pens and a red bottle of Gatorade.

"Kym smiled," he said hopefully.

Silence.

"They'll be back," he said, but there was no one else to hear him. He was talking to himself.

Rebecca Drayer had disappeared from the room before sunrise.

25

LOS ANGELES

As the day grew hotter, the wind increased. Warm currents raked the city. Spotted with rain, the gales whistled against power lines and storefronts. Endless garbage tumbled through the ash—plastic wrappers, plastic bags, paper trash. Nothing else moved. The fires and the fighting had cleared the streets of animals and primitives. Every species had fled from the burns and from the gunshots at Silver Lake. Now there were only buildings, scattered cars, and ash.

Six figures ran east with the storm.

As they jogged through the cars, they kept their heads up, listening to the wind. Behind them, the hospital remained a dull source of yelling and noise. Ahead, Los Angeles was quiet except for the sudden cacophony of barking dogs. The sound erupted north of their position.

"Down," their leader said.

They knelt between a blue Toyota and the beige stucco wall of a men's fashion outlet, weapons ready. In the middle of the group, Emily watched Drew—their leader—assessing him.

She was reminded of P.J.'s wary movements when P.J. first approached Silver Lake. Los Angeles was no longer home to any of them. Emily believed even the soldiers felt small and impermanent against this vacant concrete landscape, so, like the Neanderthals, they stayed close to each other—three members of the Navy team—two Guardsmen—and Emily. She was their nucleus. They protected her on all sides, and, joining her in the center of their formation, Staff Sergeant Patrick had attached himself to her hip as her personal bodyguard.

This was combat. Before she stepped outside with Drew's team, Emily had thought she understood the difference between war and the fifteen blocks she'd survived on her own. Then she'd confronted the three wounded men and the twisted bodies P.J. had left behind in the parking lot.

When they landed, Drew and Julie hadn't bothered to check for casualties, much less to administer aid. Emily had insisted on hauling the wounded men into the hospital, but Drew and Julie had come for her, solely for her, and they would kill or abandon anyone who interfered.

She envied their clarity and toughness, their ability to let go. She was loyal to a fault. First she hadn't been able to abandon her ideals or her plan to design a prenatal vaccine despite Laura and Ray. Now she'd half-fabricated reasons to go after P.J., gambling with her life, and, worse, the selfless heroes who'd accompanied her.

The barking faded.

"*Sst,*" Drew hissed, signaling Julie and a Guard corporal. He pointed north. The jitters in Emily's hands and chest increased as she prepared to follow them.

The soldiers looked so confident. Their faces were hidden by goggles or visors, but their body language was assertive. Were they all faking? Maybe that was the real trick of bravery, not wanting to be the first to complain.

I promised him I can do this, she thought, glancing at the other woman in the group.

Julie repeated Drew's hand signals and added another, swiping her finger above a map she'd folded into a square. He nodded. Then the squad rose together. The only sounds were a faint *clack* as the Guardsman repositioned his weapon and the scuffing of Julie's map as she tucked it against her own gun.

They advanced into the city.

Emily's right hand tugged at the rings on her left hand. She had so many good memories of Chase. She needed him now.

Abruptly, Drew gestured for everyone to kneel again.

Oh God, Emily thought. He approached a station wagon by himself, then quickly waved the group forward. As she passed, Emily saw two bodies behind the car, but they were old bodies, layered in ash, and had no obvious wounds.

At least one of P.J.'s companions was seriously hurt. Someone had left a blood trail. A few splotches were large enough for Emily to find herself. Mostly there were dime-sized drops obscured by the soot and light rain. Except when she stepped on one by chance, Emily didn't know how Drew was tracking the dark spots.

The two-story retail shops ended where Temple Street met Glendale Boulevard. Across the intersection, on the south side, were the first narrow homes of a residential neighborhood. It looked like a hopeless maze—small yards, fences, detached garages. On the other corner, where Glendale went north, a large green park stretched for two hundred yards until its trees and paths met a thirty-foot embankment supporting the high, flat line of Highway 101. Glendale ran beneath the highway. Shadows gathered among the cement pillars.

Drew led them toward the park, pausing twice to study the underpass or the nearest trees, a stand of sycamores with one scratchy palm tree reaching above them.

The light rain briefly turned to showers. The moisture worked like glue in the ash. Emily was glad for the skin of her leather jacket. Colonel Bowen had found some boots for her, but her pants had turned wet and black as soon as they left Silver Lake. Four blocks later, she was coated in grime.

She felt slow and bulky. Drew had outfitted her with M-string, a flight helmet, and a bulletproof vest. None of the gear weighed much, but it left her swaddled in layers. The back of her helmet rubbed against the vest, impeding her movements exactly when she wanted to be able to look eighteen ways at once. She wanted to be able to run.

"Sst," Drew hissed again, waving the corporal in close to him. Trailing the squad, the Guard lieutenant also adjusted his position, sweeping leftward behind Patrick.

The blood trail was obvious on the gray concrete surrounding the playground. Red spatters led into the grass and more sycamore trees, but Drew angled away from the trail. They were almost at the restrooms, a cube-shaped building with three doors. MEN. WOMEN. THIS DOOR TO REMAIN LOCKED.

Drew paced steadily around the corner at a distance of twenty feet. He held his carbine high and tight. Emily supposed that was to minimize the weapon's length, making it harder for anyone to jump out and slap it away.

"Clear," he said.

They walked past a red-and-white jungle gym mounted in an oval sand pit. Four swings creaked in the wind. Did she hear voices? Emily was nearly delirious with sleep deprivation. The warm, soggy weather also had her flustered. Her skin itched inside the heat of her jacket, but her feet and hands were cold, confusing her body with hot chills like a fever.

How much radiation were they taking outside? Would the solar flares make everyone sick? As part of her research into the chimpanzee genome, Emily knew atomic tests during the Cold War had been the first to prove it wasn't only lower primates who were more immune to radiation than human beings. Compared to men, every other species on Earth had reduced cancer rates.

Animals evolved for the pulse, too, she thought.

She missed Drew's next signal. Patrick grabbed her arm and pulled her down, banging her knee. It frightened her. She wasn't sure why they'd gone on alert. Each soldier faced in a different direction, maintaining their assignments, so she looked at Drew. He was studying the trees again.

"There's too much blood," the corporal whispered. "I can't believe this guy's still on his feet."

Drew shook his head. He didn't want to talk, so Emily debated with herself. *Maybe they're carrying whoever's hurt,* she worried. *Or maybe two or three of them are bleeding. If we hurt them more . . .*

Drew and the Guard lieutenant were equipped with Tasers. Whether or not 50,000 volts would kill an eight-year-old boy was open to question, but Emily didn't want them to subdue P.J. by shooting him with their carbines. Her job now was to act as a lure. She needed to bait or delay P.J. She hoped to attract him by singing. She needed to remember to breathe like him, too, and to hold her body in a crouch. Posture and sound were everything to his kind.

"Heads up," Julie said.

A man stood on the highway above the park. He was mostly concealed by dry brush and the edge of a sound wall, standing where the cinder block ended. His torn shirt flapped in the wind. He held a club with his left hand.

"Nobody moves," Drew said. "Not yet. On my mark, we run for the embankment."

"I don't like it," Julie said. "They have the high ground and we'll get hung up on that fence."

Six feet of chain link separated the park from the base of the embankment. Emily knew she could climb it, but they would be slow going over while P.J.'s group was well-positioned to stab or club them.

The man on the highway seemed to share her thoughts. He stepped out from the sound wall into the open, raising his arms on both sides. To Emily, he looked like a scarecrow or a vulture. He looked like death.

Patrick wasn't impressed. "Hah," Patrick grunted, laughing at the man's display.

Then the man turned and hooted. The rest of P.J.'s group were obviously hidden somewhere behind him. Emily should have been relieved, but this was the first time she'd seen them break their trios. One man alone was a change, and she felt a new, ominous thread of misgiving.

"This isn't a good idea," she said.

Drew glanced at her with irritation. "We're here because of you," he whispered. "You said we need prisoners."

"We do."

Drew turned to his men and pointed. "Let's take him," he said.

Nim looked up from the carcasses of four dogs when En's song reached him. Then he smelled their enemy. The Dead Men were permeated with the odors of cordite, soap, fuel, and gun oil—all things unidentifiable to Nim, but unique to the Dead Men—which was why he'd fled east with the wind. If he was pursued, he wanted as much notice as possible. His pack had only turned north to hunt the dogs.

Sating their thirst and hunger had been a challenge. Water was scarce. Nor were there large animals to follow to drinking holes or a herd's favorite grazing areas.

The park had helped Nim in two ways. He'd first seen the dogs gobbling at the trash from an overturned garbage can. The dogs had run, but the few bits of stale lunchmeat and popcorn left on the ground went into his men's bellies. Next they'd ripped up dozens of handfuls of grass, gaining quick energy from the thin, damp, sugary roots before following the dogs into the underpass. Nim had an innate phobia of closed-in or subterranean spaces, but the highway was only eight lanes wide. He could see the other side.

In the middle of the broad tunnel he'd felt particularly odd, his head banging with thoughts that didn't feel like his own. Fortunately the sensation went away, and, once through, they found an unexpected bounty. On the north side of the highway were two more sections of park. Buildings and roads boxed in each piece of land, and both were laid with concrete and benches, but the farthest section also held a pond.

The foul-tasting water revived them. These areas of dirt and plants were soothing, and Nim's people weren't the only living things who preferred this land to the cityscape. They saw birds and squirrels. The dogs tried to hide in a thatch of juniper bushes.

Nim trapped his prey with an age-old pronged attack, splitting his weakened group. Two of his men were nearly bent double by their wounds. He didn't believe they would live through midday. They knew it, too, but they gave their last hours to the tribe, using themselves to form the wall into which Nim and his able-bodied men stampeded the dogs.

The dogs were strange to Nim. Despite bunching together, they almost seemed to belong to different species. One was almost as large as him. Others were much smaller. Their fur also varied wildly—long, short, black, brown—and yet their insides were arranged normally. The loins and brains were easy to find, although removing these choice parts was sloppy with only a splintered hunk of wood for a knife.

But there wasn't time to feast.

"Here!" En sang as he scrambled down from the long straight hilltop of Highway 101. "Here!"

Nim dragged the dogs' carcasses into the open as bait, then quickly divided his hunters again. Did they have enough time before the Dead Men appeared?

"Hurry," he sang.

26

· · · · · · · · · · · ·

LOS ANGELES

Drew stopped his team on the highway. Thirty feet above the park, the storm was blinding. Channeled by the intermittent cinder-block walls, the wind rasped at his flight helmet, sneaking soot into his eyes and masking his ears with noise.

Where was the man they'd chased?

Due north, the parks spread out below Drew were a mess. A maple tree had crashed down across two picnic tables. Other trees had lost branches or most of their leaves. Except for the wet heat, it might have been autumn, which helped him. He was able to see more, and there were few places to hide.

"They're gone, sir," the corporal said.

"They ran into the city," Drew agreed, glancing at Emily with mixed feelings. She was in decent shape—probably a gym rat. She'd climbed the fence and the embankment readily, never lagging behind.

Now he had to tell her to go back. They couldn't follow her nephew all day. He just didn't have enough men to encircle the boy. He wished he hadn't left Bugle in charge of the aircraft. A stupid joke would have

242

gone a long way toward easing Drew's mind because he was beginning to think they'd underestimated P.J. The boy must be tired and hurt. Drew was perplexed that he'd hiked so far so fast.

"What's that?" Julie pointed at the second block and its man-made, crescent-shaped pond.

"There's something by the parking lot, too," the corporal said. "Bodies." He aimed his M16 at the northeast corner of the nearest block, sighting through the rifle's scope.

Drew slung his M4 and pulled his binoculars. "Those are . . . dogs," he said. "It looks like they cut 'em open."

"They're hunters," Emily said.

Drew looked back at the pond. "There's a man by the water, badly hurt. He might be unconscious."

"They must be close," Emily said. "We startled them before they could eat."

"Why are they eating dogs?" Julie asked.

Emily shook her head. "What else is there? Cats. Birds. Dogs are the biggest. We think their diet was almost entirely protein. There are enough vitamins in liver and marrow to stay healthy. Neanderthals were predators."

"We'll see if we can save that guy," Drew said. "Then we go back to the plane. I'm sorry. We can't keep running after them."

Emily said nothing. Strands of blond hair whipped around the edges of her helmet.

In silence, she nodded.

Drew wondered what she felt. *Maybe we can ID the guy down there and she'll find his medical records like she needs*, he thought. He wanted to say something to encourage her, but he had nothing to gain by allowing her to reopen their argument. She was too persuasive. In the hospital, she'd talked circles around him with words like *genotype* and *protein expressions*, so he turned to Julie instead.

"We'll move to your side," he said, pointing west.

The embankment descending from the highway was lined with another chain-link fence. At the east end of the park, an on-ramp rose from the surface streets to join the highway. Drew wanted to avoid that dark space. The underpass where Glendale reemerged on the west side of the park was also a potential hiding place, but his team had scouted it five minutes ago, which was why he led them down the embankment at a westward angle.

His boots dug into the moist earth. Weeds and trash covered the slope. Emily sent an old bottle clattering into the chain-link fence at the bottom, slipped, then caught herself. Everyone paused as she stood up with mud on her knees, brushing angrily at her hands.

The fence sagged in places. Drew chose his spot to climb and went over it in seconds. On the ground again, he faced north, covering his squad mates with his M4. Julie and the corporal climbed after him as Patrick, Emily, and the lieutenant waited to take their turns. They were separated from Drew by the galvanized steel wire.

Then everything went to pieces.

On the fence, clinging to it, Julie yelled, "Contact left!"

Drew swung west. P.J. and a dark-haired man had leapt out from the underpass less than twenty feet away. They'd run into his blind spot, gaining a crucial second.

Behind Drew on the other side of the fence, Emily screamed. The chain-link rattled as Julie and the corporal redoubled their efforts to climb. Beside Emily, the Guard lieutenant opened fire. His rounds clanged through the wire, grazing P.J.'s leg and the dark-haired man's ribs, but they never slowed, and he couldn't sweep his weapon without hitting Drew.

"Watch it, *watch it!*" Patrick yelled.

"Nnnnnnnmh!" P.J. shrieked.

Drew fired as P.J. darted past the barrel of his M4. The three-round burst took off part of P.J.'s scalp, the muzzle blasts scorching his hair.

Nothing stopped the boy. He slammed his thin arm into Drew's chest. Drew must have outweighed him by a hundred and thirty pounds. Nevertheless, P.J. lifted Drew off his feet, then chopped down with his club, a broken-off slat of wood. It cracked against Drew's flight helmet.

Staggering, Drew saw the dark-haired man lunge at him, too. The man was larger—quieter—stronger than P.J. He swung a heavy pipe.

Drew lifted his M4 to block it. Impact shattered his pinky finger and something in his hand, knocking the M4 from his grip. He felt no pain. The sensation was a bad sound like a *snap*. The blow drove him to one knee.

Somehow Julie flew past him. Had she jumped from the fence?

She struck P.J. first. They rolled into the dark-haired man's legs. Then the three of them collapsed. Julie lost her M4 in the scuffle. Drew saw her weapon disappear beneath the rolling bodies. P.J. bit and shrieked as Julie punched him.

Drew grabbed the 9mm Glock on his hip.

His broken hand wouldn't close on the pistol's grip.

The Guard corporal had also cleared the fence. He charged into the melee, swinging his M16 at the dark-haired man. Drew ran to join him. But on the embankment, Emily yelled, "Behind you!"

Drew hesitated. He saw three men sprinting from the east end of the park. They dashed toward him with crude spears and clubs.

Patrick cut them down. On the embankment with Emily, Patrick's M4 stuttered in short, controlled bursts, slashing through all three men.

Drew ran to Julie. The corporal had her arm. He tried to tug her free as she kicked at P.J., who held one of her legs. Drew caught P.J.'s filthy shirt. Drew meant to choke the boy—but his broken fingers slid off P.J.'s collar.

On the ground, the dark-haired man caught Julie's flight helmet in the crook of his arm, yanking at her. Julie bent awkwardly.

P.J. used the weight of his club like a pendulum. He cocked his arm behind his back. Then he whipped forward, smashing the wood slat into Julie's throat.

It snapped her neck. Her body twitched like a frog, lacking any dignity or grace.

"Noooooooo!" Emily cried.

Drew's insides felt like Emily's scream. He pulled his sidearm with both hands, wrapping his good left hand around the weapon with the busted fingers of his right.

P.J. turned with his club.

There was nothing in the boy's eyes except a cold reptilian light. Drew shot him twice. The bullets went high because Drew's grip was weak, but each 9mm round punched through the top of P.J.'s ribcage like a train, slamming the boy into the ground.

Drew shot the dark-haired man next. He put one round through the man's thigh. As the man flailed away from Julie, Drew fired four more rounds into his torso.

Finally reaction set in. Drew's head roared.

Somewhere, Emily kept screaming.

Drew knelt beside Julie. He set his hand on her distended neck, not believing there wasn't a heartbeat until Patrick shouted, "Commander!"

No time to mourn.

One of the men on the east end of the park staggered up again. His arm hung as if its tendons were cut. His chest was destroyed. That he stood at all was demonic. He moved like a resurrected corpse, fighting for one step, almost falling, then lurching forward again.

"Hnn!" the man cried.

Drew had ignored the signs of their preternatural strength. Even in cautioning himself not to underestimate P.J., he'd assumed he was pitting his team against a ragtag band of unarmed civilians. Stupid. Stupid. Emily had warned him. These men were more than human. They were powerful, fearless, and cunning. P.J. must have doubled back to the underpass on Glendale and sent his other men to the east side of the park, luring Drew into the middle with the dogs and the man by the pond.

Was that man also alive?

Drew wanted to kill everyone responsible for Julie's death, but his self-discipline had been built on years of ROMEO conditioning. He gestured at the walking man. "Lieutenant, Corporal, take that man prisoner," he said. "Patch him up. Then we'll check the man by the water."

"Sir," the corporal said. "Yes, sir." His voice was shaken, but he didn't protest. He waited for the lieutenant to climb the fence.

"Sergeant," Drew said to Patrick. "Cover the lieutenant with your M4. Stay with Dr. Flint."

"I'm sorry!" Emily cried. "Is she—? Oh God, I'm sorry!"

The corporal and the lieutenant ran across the park as Emily walked to the fence. She stood against the wire, holding her hands apart like a woman who'd been crucified. Then she began to climb.

Drew would have preferred if she kept her distance. He didn't want anyone to see his stinging tears.

He opened Julie's visor. Blood trickled from her mouth. Her eyes were huge, bugging orbs. He shut them for her. He wiped at the blood and caressed her cheek. He'd lost other people under his command. This was something more. In a short time, Julie had grown closer to him than he'd allowed anyone in years.

He would never know what they might have been together.

Emily stepped down from the fence in a numb haze. *My fault,* she thought. *This is my fault. Oh, P.J., I wanted to save you, and we really do need your DNA, but I should have let you run into the city . . .*

She was afraid to impose, but she couldn't just stand there. Kneeling beside Drew felt like the right thing to do.

JEFF CARLSON

"She loved you very much," she whispered. He glanced at her, and she was surprised by the surprise in his face. "I saw how she looked at you," she said. "I—"

"Movement," Patrick said. "Up the street." He remained on the embankment with his M4, which he'd aimed over their heads toward the northwest end of the park. He was no longer covering the Guard lieutenant and corporal, who'd jogged sixty yards east to the wounded man. He was targeting a new enemy.

There are more of them! Emily thought.

Northward up Glendale, nine strangers stood at the edge of a two-story home on the corner. They were partially camouflaged by the mulberry trees and the hedge in its front yard. Two were black. One was about sixty years old. All of them stood in an identical top-heavy pose, heads down, eyes up, their shoulders hunched as if their clubs weighed more than any chunk of wood.

Drew rose from his lover's corpse and matched the Neanderthals' stance. Emily thought he would attack. Instead, he barked at his two Guardsmen without turning his gaze from the Neanderthals. "Lieutenant, come back! Leave him!"

One of the men at the front of the new group raised his voice in answer, a wordless sound. Something about it seemed very familiar. What was it? But her pulse roared through her body like the wind. She was almost deaf with adrenaline and other questions—

Where were the Neanderthal women? In hiding? ASD affected four boys for every girl. Emily wondered faintly if these hybrids were exclusively male. If so, it could be another clue to saving them.

Meanwhile, the lieutenant and corporal hustled to rejoin Drew. In silence, the Neanderthals watched from a hundred yards away. They eased into the street, leaving the home on the corner. Each step was subtle, almost unseen. Their progress had the gliding quality of a nightmare.

248

"I'll carry Julie," Drew said, lifting up his right hand. Emily realized at least one finger was broken. The implication was he couldn't use a gun, so he'd let the others protect the team.

From the embankment, Patrick said, "Sir, do you want me on that side of the fence or are you coming over?"

Drew shifted his pistol to his left hand. "We'll run through the underpass," he said. "Lieutenant, you take point. Sergeant, Corporal, you're our tail. Fire only on my order. If they don't chase us, leave them alone."

Patrick's boots clattered on the fence. Then he landed beside Emily, rousing her. Suddenly she fumbled through her pocket for a blood kit. Drew bent to hoist Julie over his shoulder as Emily darted past him, jabbing a VacuCap into the dark-haired man's arm.

"What are you doing?" Drew asked.

"Give me a second."

"Move!" Drew began to leave with his burden.

Following him, the Guard corporal picked up Julie's M4 and then Drew's, slinging both weapons over his shoulder. Patrick caught Emily's arm and hauled her away from the dark-haired man. They stepped over P.J.

"Take the boy, too," she said. "Please. He doesn't weigh anything. You're so big. I can't—"

Their gathering speed triggered something in the Neanderthal pack. The nine men burst into a run. "Fire," Drew said as the Guard lieutenant yelled from in front, "Watch it!"

Emily saw more Neanderthals ahead of them.

Guns blazed on all sides, overriding her mind, overriding any concern for P.J.'s body. She screamed and screamed as Patrick dragged her into the underpass, where their weapons hammered and echoed.

"Clear! We're clear!" the lieutenant yelled, leading them from the south end of the tunnel.

Three men sprawled in the street. Emily barely noticed. Her panic was so total, her consciousness spread so thinly beneath her hysteria, she retained few details of their escape. Gun smoke. Gunfire. One ray of naked sunlight.

There was also the leader's high song amplified by the underpass. It was the same sound he'd made before.

More important, his voice dwindled behind them as they charged down Glendale Boulevard. Emily looked back before she turned onto Temple Street. The corporal was the farthest behind, skipping backward with his M16 at his hip. No one followed.

"They stopped!" she shouted. "They gave up!"

Drew growled at her from beneath Julie's corpse. "They might be trying to flank us," he said. "That's twice they've caught us in a pincer."

Emily's head rang with the leader's voice as she dodged through the cars and ash. She remembered how P.J. and the others had identified themselves at DNAllied. Every man had made his own sound—and yet P.J. had used this same drawn-out syllable. *Nnnnnnnmh.* What did it mean?

"I have movement on our right," Patrick said, holding his M4 sideways. At first Emily thought he was covering the two-story windows above them. Then, beyond the rooftops, she saw a running shape on the highway.

"They're following us," Drew said.

"We're almost there!" she said. "You don't have to—"

Another voice called from her left. Three men stood at the corner of a small restaurant. Their leader sang to a fourth man farther up the street. Eerily, he also used the same formless word as P.J.

"Nnnnnnmmh!" he cried.

"Hnn!" the fourth man answered.

"Fuck, they're coming out of the woodwork," the lieutenant said. He took one knee beside an Audi, leveling his M4.

Drew ran past him. "Keep moving! Don't stop!"

Emily's thoughts felt like a meteor shower. *It's the noise of the guns,* she realized. That was why the Neanderthals kept coming. The fight at the hospital had attracted every group in the vicinity, and now they were paying the price.

At least that was what she told herself. Her most insidious fear was she'd been more accurate than she'd known while arguing with Colonel Bowen.

How many people had turned? One in a thousand? More?

"Here," the leader sang. He was a tall man, six foot four, with gray hair, brown pants, brown loafers and a blood-stained length of pipe.

His name was Nim.

Two of his three men were Han. The last was En. They were accustomed to having many of the same people. The Neanderthals had just six base personalities, three male, three female, although some incarnations were more outspoken than the rest, allowing for a hierarchy even when a tribe held many Nims.

Their trios were an adaptation to a time when their species' numbers had grown precariously small. They paired two husbands with each wife in the same manner that they hunted—always in threes—an eternal, instinctive effort to break loose of their limited diversity.

"Now," he called, rushing into the street. The Dead Men were caught in a pocket among the cars. Nim did not understand the vehicles, which looked like metal boulders and burned at the touch, but he liked the traps created by the cars' haphazard arrangement.

His hunters swarmed the enemy. Somehow the Dead Men knocked them back in a deafening roar of fire and hail. Nim twisted as pain skewered his middle. He fell, his club banging on the street.

His last thought was that the Dead Men's weapons were too strong for his group, but killing one Nim was like killing ants.

There would always be more of him.

27

NORTHERN CALIFORNIA

The room had become too small for Marcus's fear. There was nowhere to go except deeper into himself, sitting on two blankets he'd folded on the floor.

His notepad was rumpled and marked with grungy fingerprints because he'd fussed with it dozens of times, first recording everything he knew about the flares, then adding personal information. Like a man in the grip of schizophrenia, Marcus had also written a short list of instructions to himself.

The electronics room was not entirely safe from the pulse. The most intense spikes penetrated its walls. After he'd regained his senses the first time, the door was open and Rebecca was missing. He'd screamed for her, but he hadn't run outside.

What if he had only seconds before this lull in the geomagnetic flux was over?

He'd shut the door, then wedged paperclips into the lock and stacked most of his supplies against the door, hoping to prevent himself from leaving if he suffered another blackout.

That decision was its own danger. If the pulse intensified again and remained at a high level, if he lacked the intelligence to pry open the lock, he would die in this room. But what was the alternative?

"You can't leave," Marcus said in the dark, suffocating quiet.

The notepad was his anchor. It was his last testament. He set it on his lap and studied the words he'd drawn and redrawn in ballpoint until the letters were dense black scars.

1) DON'T GIVE UP. WAIT.
2) YOU CAN STILL HELP ROELL.
3) READ PAGES 5 AND 8.

His handwriting was jagged on the pages inside. He hadn't been sure there would be time to complete this record. Once started, he'd also found he had more to say than he expected, drowning in nostalgia and pain.

He longed for things that had never been—a better relationship with his son—more time together—another chance. Why had work seemed so important while Roell was growing up without him? Nothing mattered more than family, yet he'd let the boy slip away, obsessed with the stars and other marvels he could never touch instead of the small miracle of his son's life.

Yesterday he'd wasted his best opportunity to find Roell, choosing to stay here instead. How much of that decision had been cowardice?

The truth wouldn't have hurt so badly if his choice amounted to something, but Marcus had not been able to bring the array online. Too many of the processors and signal converters had fried when the pulse came through the room. He had a toolbox and screwdrivers, even a power drill, but not the spare modules he needed to repair the electronics. That equipment was in the assembly shed across the field, and he wouldn't know if any of the extra modules had survived the pulse until he ran over there and checked.

If he lived, if he ever spoke to anyone again, he would never admit his first thought. He'd considered taking apart everything in the room—the processors, the shelves, everything. He could strip the ruined hardware for copper and steel, bolting another thin layer of armor to the ceiling. It might preserve him. But for what? His juice and soda wouldn't last two days. His food wouldn't last a week.

Even if he coaxed Kym and Chuck to the wall, he couldn't push candy or chips through his spy holes. They couldn't read or use words anymore. He had no way to pantomime *Bring me water* that they could see, and a hole large enough to show his face would probably allow the pulse inside.

1) DON'T GIVE UP. WAIT.

He needed to drink as little as possible without becoming so weak he couldn't run. If there was another lull, he could sprint outside and refill his bottles. Then he would rush to the assembly shed and gather what he needed. His notepad was crammed with checklists.

If he could bring the array online again, he might be able to analyze the sun's activity. He might even predict the course of the storm. Imagine if he could tell the world when it would be safe to find their families! A radio or a cell phone might work if the pulse stopped. More soldiers would come. So he didn't sleep. He didn't dare rest his eyes. His body was sluggish with fatigue poisons that caffeine and sugar couldn't wash away, but if he closed his eyes, he was afraid he'd sleep for hours and miss any hint that Kym and the others had turned normal again. They would yell or cry or there might be footsteps inside the station if he could only wait.

Despite everything he'd told Rebecca, Marcus had hoped the first interrupts were the peak of the solar max. With luck, the flares would stop again for years or lifetimes. He would be insane to hope for anything else.

"You're not insane," Marcus said. But there were more sinister thoughts inside him now than the prospect of starving to death in this lonely cage.

After Rebecca's team had commandeered the station, he'd never had a moment to open the files he'd received from NOAA. Today he'd examined their data closely before his Mac burned out.

Why are you reading about ice caps and lava beds? Kym had asked.

"Because solar flares leave nitrates in the ice, and cooling lava records some properties of Earth's magnetic field," Marcus said. He was barely aware that his conversation was one-sided. "There are sample cores from Antarctica dating back four hundred thousand years. The ocean beds are even older. Some of the lava fields under the Atlantic show fifty million years of magnetic shifts."

He looked down at his empty left hand, remembering the feel of Rebecca's fingers interlocked with his own when they first ventured outside. *I don't understand,* she'd protested.

"The pulse isn't going to stop," he said.

Marcus was not a fatalist. He had always been pragmatic, making the most of observable data, but there was no way to fight the sun. What if Rebecca had sensed his despair, shared it, and realized what might happen between them if they were trapped in this room forever? Starvation. Madness.

Could that be why she'd run outside?

For decades, NOAA's Paleoclimatology Program and the National Snow and Ice Data Center had gathered information from ice scientists and biologists everywhere in the world. Many of the contributing studies were focused on global warming or marine habitats. Others were more interested in the ancient pollens, dust, and insects preserved by glaciers and polar ice.

In the frantic hours before the pulse, all of this data had been reconsidered by specialists equipped with new theories posed by astronomers like Marcus.

Contamination disguised a lot of the clues they'd sought. Even the deepest ice was subjected to thermal heat, churn, exposure, and recompression. Throughout the past decade, as laser spectrometry allowed for ever more precise analysis, many researchers had doubted their own findings or were ridiculed or ignored—but the ice didn't lie. The ice didn't care about publishing, funding, or politics.

Nitrates filled the ice from prehistory all the way through its oldest layers. The story told on the ocean floors was even more uncompromising.

Some rocks, like basalt, were slightly magnetic. In 1963, a geophysicist named Lawrence Morley noted that although rocks on the planet's surface appeared to have been randomly magnetized, this was an illusion caused by erosion. Beneath the oceans were lava beds preserved from upheaval or decay, which, as they cooled, had been magnetized in lines consistent with the direction of Earth's magnetic field.

Modern-day equipment had found hundreds of anomalies in the basalt. There were subtle distortions caused by geomagnetic storms much like cold and heat affected the growth rings in trees.

These distortions weren't well-documented. It wasn't a mystery that had been glamorous enough to draw young minds, much less a lot of money, and yet NOAA had cobbled together a preliminary model and sent it out before communications ended. Other people would have this data, too. For all the good it did them, the human race had come close to recognizing the peril before it struck.

"Maybe now we know what happened to the dinosaurs," Marcus said. "But some of us will survive."

Not you. Not in this place.

"We can adapt," he said.

Cold-blooded life forms, especially large ones, would be especially vulnerable to the pulse, and no one had fully explained why the giant reptiles disappeared so abruptly.

There were competing theories about the dinosaurs' extinction; the Chicxulub meteor strike; years of darkness brought on by worldwide volcanic eruptions; the rise of small mammals who fed on dinosaur eggs. What they knew for certain was that at the end of the Cretaceous period, the only species to move forward were small birds, small mammals, burrowing reptiles like lizards and snakes, and creatures able to hide underwater like frogs, turtles, sharks, and fish.

That would mean the sun had been calm for eons while the dinosaurs ruled supreme, and perhaps that it had flared on and off again for thousands of years more.

Rapid climate change was only the beginning of what the pulse would do to Earth. As the warming oceans filled the atmosphere with rain, geomagnetic stresses would cause volcanic activity on a massive scale, adding ash and smoke to the swelling cloud cover. Plummeting temperatures would have doomed the great reptiles even as the cold enabled fur-bearing mammals.

Then the Earth had warmed again. Some mammals returned to the ocean. Why? To escape a new period of flares? Dolphins, whales, and seals were land animals that had evolved back into the water, losing their hair in the cases of the dolphins and whales, growing flippers over their five-fingered hands, yet never quite escaping the surface due to the lungs they'd developed in the open air.

Regular pulses might also explain why early humans appeared to have been stuck in a series of evolutionary ruts despite having a skull capacity equal to that of modern man.

As someone who was fascinated with history, anthropology, and the rise and fall of civilizations, Marcus knew this was the big question. Why had *Homo sapiens* taken so long to become what they were today?

For uncounted millennia, men had been brutes with the most simple tools and societies. Then in the space of four thousand years, they'd built empires and cities and wrapped the entire world in electrical grids, highways, agriculture, shipping lanes, and aircraft. They'd begun to understand the stars and the cosmos.

Too late.

Ignoring his thirst, restlessly adjusting his blanket on the floor, Marcus felt a sad, bitter irony.

He might die in this room, but his race would carry on. In fact, he believed the inconstant sun had pushed humankind in ways they barely realized. They owed their intelligence to sudden variations in Earth's climate, unknowingly responding to a cycle much larger than their own lives.

The geological record showed that Africa, the cradle of life, had been a lush jungle for two hundred million years. In that unchanging environment, the first crude primates had been a viable but static part of the biosphere.

Then something happened. The jungle became grasslands, which became desert, which grew into savannahs again. Huge lakes covered the land, then disappeared in more droughts until another volcanic apocalypse cooled the planet and Africa was swept by monsoons and new forests.

All of this occurred in two hundred thousand years, a very short period by evolutionary standards. The pressure to adapt had been unimaginable. Humanity's ancestors were those who *could* change. The survivors became problem solvers, tool users, and omnivores. Everyone else had died.

Using mitochondrial DNA, biologists thought they could trace every living person to a single female in 140,000 B.C. Doing the same with Y chromosome DNA, they found a single male between 60,000 and 90,000 B.C.

Repeated extinction events like the Toba supervolcano had lowered the human population to a few thousand individuals worldwide. From them, only one family line had persisted. One. That was how close *Homo sapiens* had come to annihilation, and it had happened at least twice.

Everything that made them great—their creativity, their initiative, and their persistence—stemmed from the need to outwit the next disaster.

They were a heroic species.

Most of them were doomed. Whatever was left of humankind would need to dig into the Earth, deep down, building new cities beneath the surface. They would be forced to give up the sky and everything else they considered their birthright.

"But someone might find your notes," Marcus said. "You can still help."

He wanted to recopy the messiest parts. He also hoped to miniaturize his handwriting in order to shrink the most important parts to no more than one page, which he would fold into a waterproof case meant to contain flash drives.

"*You* might find your notes," he whispered.

He'd tried to shy away from it, but this scenario seemed more and more likely, so he reached for his pen and read out loud in the shadows.

"Your name is Marcus Washington Carver Wolsinger."

Constant exposure would cause neurological damage like Alzheimer's disease. It would disrupt his memory, leaving only fragments of his past. He needed some way to hold on to himself, so he wrote his own history.

His voice was soft and trembling:

"You were born on July 21, 1969, a day after a spacecraft called *Apollo 11* brought a man named Neil Armstrong to the moon. He was the first human being to land on another world. None of your professional accomplishments meant as much to your mom, Marilyn. Even twenty years later when she was dying of cancer she liked to brag to you, to her nurses, to other patients, that you had been a moon baby. She made you feel special. She wanted to name you Apollo or Armstrong or Rocket, but your father said those were white names. His name was Ed, which he hated. He wasn't so proud of you for getting into MIT. He wanted you tougher, better at sports. He made you waste your afternoons throwing balls and running with balls, but he raised you well enough with your sister Korba in Atlanta, Georgia, which is very, very far from here. Too far to walk."

He choked up. He wasn't close to his family. He dutifully traded Christmas cards with Korba, and she'd flown out to visit last summer, but he hadn't seen his father for years and he regretted every minute of it. Worse, he couldn't deny that he'd hurt his own son as badly as his father had wronged him. He should have been more accepting.

He blamed Janet for Roell's attitude. She'd bought Roell his iPhone. She let him follow all of the latest hip hop, even the dirty stuff, often sharing downloads and CDs with her son.

Marcus disapproved. He was also jealous. He was still mystified by her. Janet had grown up in the inner city streets of west L.A., underprivileged and undereducated, yet she'd risen to become a full-time paralegal.

Nevertheless, she'd responded to something in Roell's posturing. She'd encouraged it. Roell's belligerence appealed to her even when it amounted to nothing more than immature, illogical stubbornness.

Janet was probably dead. Uncontrolled fires must have roasted entire cities alive, and San Francisco had already had its share of brutes and killers before people lost the ability to reason . . .

She might have been here with him and had some chance at survival if he'd been a better husband.

Survival. No one was going to live to a ripe old age if they were taking as much UV as he suspected. People might have another fifteen, twenty years, then slow and ugly deaths. That matched what he knew of fossil records. In the distant past, no one had grown old. There would be no doctors, no dentists, no optometrists, no police. Even for those lucky few who didn't develop skin cancer or cataracts, what kind of life would it be?

His mother had eaten a bottle of pills and he'd hated her for it. The doctors had said she had a good chance, but she'd refused to lose her hair or suffer through the cure.

He'd hated Janet for quitting, too.

He wouldn't give up. He'd never quit in his life, not on his scholarships, not on his Ph.D., and not on his son. But the thought was with him now. Sooner or later, he would drink the last of his water. Then he would have to go outside.

Would there be waking moments of confusion? That was why he'd written his messages to himself. He would tie the waterproof case to his waist.

What if he removed it in his animal state? Maybe he could carve enough information into his arms to remind himself. There was a box cutter in the tool kit. He could rub ink into his wounds, chancing infection but forcing the cuts to scar.

Or he could open his wrists with it.

Alone in the room, Marcus wept.

NORTHERN CALIFORNIA

An hour later, Marcus heard shouting outside. He leapt to his feet. Then he had to kneel again, grabbing for a wire rack as his head spun. It was so hot. His stomach rolled, but there wasn't enough moisture in his system to vomit.

Retching, he climbed the rack and pressed himself against a spy hole.

"Kymmie!" he yelled. "Kym!"

He couldn't see anyone. He moved to the next hole. A familiar shape scampered through the white dishes. It was Chuck. One of Rebecca's soldiers ran with him, calling ahead to someone else in a wary tone. Chuck looked over his shoulder once before they passed from view.

"Charles Keen!" Marcus yelled. "Chuck!"

The breeze rustled at the spy hole, taunting him with fresh oxygen and the dusty grass smell of the mountains. Was somebody coming?

"Don't get your hopes up," he said. "There won't be a helicopter if the pulse is—"

Another man paced into the field. His gait was different, heavier, sturdier, although he didn't look as if he weighed more than Chuck. He carried a short, bone-smooth branch with its bark removed.

Marcus realized the branch was a weapon and leaned back from his spy hole.

Hide, he thought, but he was concealed by the wall, so he pressed his eye to the hole again.

The man wasn't alone. Marcus glimpsed at least three others walking with him in a skirmish line through the stout white dishes. All of them were armed. More disturbing, every man in the battle group carried himself with the same stoop-shouldered pose.

Far across the array, Marcus also thought he saw Roell.

"Ruh," he said. His throat wouldn't open. He didn't want to draw those men into the station, yet he couldn't let his son pass.

Roell's obsidian features were unmistakable. Marcus's heart leapt with shock and joy, but Roell was too far away to guess if he was with the armed men or running from them like Chuck.

Then the skirmish line was gone. So was his son. They'd walked out of range of his spy holes.

Marcus yelled and yelled. "Roell! Rooooooooeeeeell!"

A new sound wafted back to him. One of the men called, "Nnnnnnnmh!"

Another man answered, "Hnnh!"

Marcus didn't know what that meant, but as a language, it was more complex than anything he'd heard from Kym or Chuck. It helped him decide. He couldn't stand here while his son left him behind.

Even if he had unlimited food and fuel, Marcus wondered what he'd hoped to accomplish inside this room. If he lost his memory, he would probably lose the ability to read, too, so what good were his notes? There was no reason to create a set of charts that no one would ever see.

His greatest fear wasn't that the array couldn't be fixed. It was that he would improve his shelter, jury-rig a permanent protected area, then sit alone in it as the sun flared forever. He would have his memories, but would there be any worth keeping?

The people outside seemed competitive, even violent, and yet he'd seen Kym and Chuck at their best. He wanted to be a part of their Eden for as long as they had left.

If he went outside now, he would gain as much as he lost. Life might be brutish and short, but at least it would be *life*. He would have Roell. They would recognize each other. He was sure of that, so he stepped down from the wire rack and ran to the door.

He took down the stack of boxes he'd set against it.

He cleared the lock with a screwdriver.

Then he opened the door.

· · · · · · · · · · · ·

NORTHERN CALIFORNIA

He dreamed. The images were fleeting—a kaleidoscope of white faces and brown mountain slopes—rain and wind—but his other senses made lasting impressions on his soul. He felt hunger. He tasted blood and roots. Friends were constantly around him, and danger, and with each step he walked a balance between those two states— sometimes safe, sometimes at risk. Sometimes he increased the risk to himself in order to protect his companions, but never was there a deliberate thought. He did not consider his choices. He acted.

The small pains that hounded him were unimportant, such as the gash in his ankle or the bruises on his forearm. If he scratched an itch, it was forgotten. If they were cold, they huddled together. More extraordinary was his passion for the woman. Their pleasure was ferocious. There was also the low, enduring thrill of the hunt and his rage in combat.

His tribe clashed twice with another breed of men. Each group tried to drive the other from a muddy creek, the best water source in the area, until their running war was ended by a larger threat. A monster thundered out of the sky. It scattered his tribe. He lost everyone in the noise, which followed him across the sparsely wooded mountainside. Finally he turned to fight. The thing was immense, and its breath pounded at him like a stone. *Whup whup whup whup whup whup whup.* He ran beneath its belly in order to inflict whatever damage was possible, giving himself to the monster. Maybe the rest of his tribe would escape. Then a square mouth opened on the monster's side. A man stood there with no eyes, no mouth, only a dark, smooth bulb in place of his head. Black wisps sprang from the man's hand and the world flashed with lightning—

Voices reached him inside his agony.

"Don't drop him."

"The fucker bit me! He—"

Awareness returned in fits and pops. He hurt on so many levels. It was difficult to see. His head swam, and everywhere his middle-aged body felt overexerted. Even lying in a fetal position was an ordeal. His knees throbbed. His skin was covered in small wounds.

One voice held the hard tone of a man accustomed to command. "Doctor Wolsinger?"

Marcus tried to open his eyes but reeled from the chaos of silhouettes and light. He realized he'd wet himself. His urine was even more pungent than his sweat, adding to the miasma around him, but he was too far gone to feel much embarrassment. His stink was only another form of suffering.

"Doctor Wolsinger, we're with the Defense Intelligence Agency," the man said. "I know you're in pain. We're giving you morphine. Coming out of the EMP can cause symptoms like a grade-two concussion, and we had to subdue you out there. Some of the discomfort you're feeling is joint ache from the Taser."

"Where—" Marcus said, but a single word was all he could manage. He swallowed and swallowed again, like a fish, unable to get past the roughness in his throat.

"You're aboard a V-22 Osprey currently on the ground near your installation. My name is Lieutenant Commander Drew Haldane."

"Where are the others?" Marcus gasped, struggling with his eyes again. He needed to see. Then he realized some of his blindness was caused by a soft fabric they'd pulled down to his nose. He reached for it.

Drew caught his arm. "Don't take that off. It'll protect you against the EMP."

Drew reseated the fabric on Marcus's forehead. The fingers of his right hand were swollen beneath an aluminum brace. Behind him stood a young woman with her face pinched in concern. He wore a uniform. She did not.

"I wasn't alone," Marcus said, trying to sit up.

Rebecca had been with him. He was certain of it. He could taste her unique salt smell as if his senses had been cross-wired. The memory of her scent was on his tongue and in his mind, and he'd seen Roell through his spy hole. Had they been together? So much was distorted.

"Easy," Drew said, helping Marcus with his good hand. "You're safe now. This is Dr. Emily Flint and Lieutenant Buegeleisen."

Emily nodded hello. Beside her stood a second man in uniform, a tall, lanky guy with a horse nose. He carried a pistol. Who was he guarding?

Me, Marcus realized. *He's guarding me.*

There had been fighting outside. His shoulder and back ached from sharp, wrenching movements, and the contusion on his arm was probably from blocking another man's club. None of this frightened Marcus as much as he would have believed. In fact, he felt a glimmer of self-worth.

Drew obviously felt wary of him. They all did. Their expressions were troubled, but they wouldn't underestimate him, and Marcus savored their respect.

He glanced from side to side through the fuselage. There were no seats, only the bare deck and a loading ramp at the back, where the plane was crowded with several pieces of lab equipment and a cardboard box secured to the deck with yellow straps. There was also a black body bag.

The lump was smaller than a full-grown man. It completely unnerved Marcus, and he moaned, "What did you do!?"

"That's not anyone you know," Emily said quickly. "We . . . We've been in Los Angeles, San Jose, and Berkeley, and it's awful out there."

"Where is my son!"

"Take it easy," Drew said. "It's been almost three days since the EMP started. You look like you were outside the whole time."

"Three days," Marcus said, trying to believe it.

"Today is the 16th. What's the last thing you remember?"

The most prominent emotion in Marcus was his conviction that he would reunite with his son. Before today, his temper might have gotten the better of him. This was almost a peaceful feeling like faith. Marcus welcomed it.

Something happened to me out there, he thought. *Something good.*

Certain aspects of his mind and soul had changed in ways he'd barely begun to perceive, and Emily seemed to notice his discovery of his own transformation. Her blue eyes soaked up every detail in his face until Marcus tried to deflect her attention.

"His name is Roell," Marcus said. "He can't be far away."

"We'll do what we can," Drew said. "Our orders are to find you and your staff. We didn't realize you had dependents in the area."

"I won't leave without him."

"That may be impossible," Drew said. "First we need to secure any data and gear you think is useful. Our instructions are to bring all assets to a designated bunker. Help us, and we'll do everything we can to look for your son."

Marcus didn't trust him. Drew never said *I*. Every pronoun was an impersonal *we* or *us*. Would he honor his promise to rescue Roell?

"First you need to find him," Marcus said.

"Mr. Wolsinger, there are only seven of us including yourself and Dr. Flint," Drew said. "I'm sorry. We don't have enough men, and we're under strict orders to save you. We'll send another team as soon as there's time."

"Why would you do that after you've taken everything you need?"

"Sir, we have to get this installation up and running again. The plan was never to strip this place. Our orders are to safeguard as many staff members as we can locate along with your most important data and hard drives. As soon as possible, we'll return in force." Drew pointed through the wall of the plane. "We can land C-130s on the road on the hillside. Then we'll bring in as much material as it takes to reinforce the station against the EMP."

"We need the array," Bugle said as Drew added, "We'll find your son."

Marcus stared at them, silently calculating his options. Then he nodded. "Most of what you want is in the electronics room," he said.

Feeling nervous on several levels, Emily signaled Drew before he left the aircraft. Outside, Staff Sergeant Patrick and the two Guardsmen patrolled the V-22 Osprey. They expected to be attacked. But she was anxious for another reason.

She couldn't imagine how he'd forgive her for Julie. It was her demands that had caused them to pursue P.J. into the city. She would never forget seeing Drew crouched beside Julie's body.

"Drew?" she asked, waving him toward her equipment in back. If necessary, she would pretend they needed to check something in order to get him away from Marcus.

She understood Marcus's sorrow. She might have been an ally to him. He must feel even more strongly for his son than she'd felt for P.J., but she could never ask Drew to look for someone outside. Not again. More than that, she didn't like the flat light in Marcus's eyes.

"Be careful," she said. "This guy . . . He worries me."

Drew met her eyes, something he hadn't done easily since Julie died. He worried Emily, too, because he hadn't blamed her. Instead, he was polite.

"We won't leave you alone with him," Drew said. "He's coming with us into the station."

"Thank you," she said. "But that's not what I meant. I don't think he's telling us everything he knows."

"He might not know everything he knows," Drew said. It wasn't a joke. "He was out there for a long time, and his pupil response is slow. He's concussed."

Emily shook her head. "He must have some sense of who he was."

They weren't positive if Marcus had been a primitive or a Neanderthal while he was outside. As they approached the Hoffman Square Kilometer Field, Bugle had spotted one group assaulting another on a distant slope. Both fled from the plane. Luckily, Marcus's skin color made him easy to single out.

Drew had used the aircraft like a giant hand, hovering and banking until he trapped Marcus in a hollow. Marcus had screamed when Patrick leaned through the side door with a Taser, but engine noise kept Patrick from discerning any clear sounds.

"He was wearing his shoes," Emily said.

"He's not the only primitive we've seen who kept them on. He's definitely not autistic."

"No." She frowned. "No, you're right."

Drew had been right every time since she'd met him. His one mistake had been in allowing P.J. too close, which was her fault, but her guilt was only the surface reason for her agitation. She liked Drew. He was competent, brave, and committed even after what she'd cost him.

Emily had grown sure she could rely on him. That feeling of security was dear to her, especially after they'd left L.A. without anyone else she knew.

Colonel Bowen and Captain Walsh were needed at Silver Lake. Nor was there room to spare aboard the plane. Emily, Drew, Bugle, Patrick, and the two Guardsmen were the only ones who'd flown away from the hospital. They'd also left the wounded and dead Neanderthals after taking blood, hair, and fingernail samples in addition to photos and fingerprints. If Drew had brought those men along, he might have been forced to care for them—or to turn them loose—because he needed to reserve his M-string for the experts on his list.

He'd been ordered to rescue more people than could fit in the aircraft. His target list included biologists at DNAllied and UCLA; engineers in Santa Monica; a famous astronomer in Oxnard; computer scientists in San Jose; geneticists in Berkeley and Walnut Creek. They obviously hadn't believed he would have much success, and yet Emily wondered. What if he'd found most of the VIPs? If some people had to be left behind, where did she rank? Could she have swayed him to keep her aboard?

Above the fast-moving storms, the sun was a mottled orange—and beneath the cloud cover, southern California was littered with burned-out cities, downed aircraft, wrecked trains, and jammed streets.

Maybe she was fortunate that none of the people on Drew's list were in shelters near their work or homes. In six cases, Drew hadn't even able to land. He'd circled above corporate buildings or government labs as Bugle and Patrick used binoculars to scan for anyone who matched the photos they'd been given. The only other option was to put the aircraft down and walk into the debris. With just five military personnel aboard the plane, which he couldn't leave unguarded, Drew could have sent three men into the ruins, but if something happened, he might never see them again. Emily was glad when he kept everyone with the plane.

They were also hampered by a steady downpour. For two days, the rain had come in torrents. Once they'd stayed on the ground for six hours because Drew refused to fly in heavy turbulence. The storm doused the fires, leaving rivulets of black sediment in the streets—but before the weather turned, San Jose had burned down to concrete and steel.

Hunting for the VIPs was like looking for needles in junkyards, except each junkyard was miles wide and the people they wanted actively avoided them, burrowing into alleyways and buildings to hide from the plane.

Worse, Drew had confided to her that America's standoff with China had turned into a shooting war. Both nations were hamstrung by the pulse. Neither could move its forces against the other, but they were barely able to engage in diplomacy, either. Most of their satellites were down. Landlines, cell towers, and Internet hubs were fried at key points. Radio frequencies were inundated by the pulse. Meanwhile, the Navy maintained its strike group in the South China Sea, including its nuclear submarines.

What if one side launched by mistake? Emily thought the leaders of both countries would be idiotic to start anything, piling disaster upon disaster, yet they were human, and human beings could be selfish and mean and delusional. Someone might think now was the perfect opportunity for an attack.

Drew should have taken her to safety first. His mission was a waste of time. With every hour, it became more and more unlikely they'd find anyone on their list, but she didn't know how to ask without sounding like a heartless bitch. Nor was there any way to argue with his superiors. Drew had been given his orders and sent on his own, and Bugle gleaned very few updates from his static-ridden satellite transmissions.

This morning, they'd caught a glimpse of another plane. Other teams had gone to find the crews at the Jet Propulsion Lab in Pasadena or the physicists at LLNL in Livermore. Drew's team wasn't totally alone. A skeletal remnant of America remained, and yet the six of them were a microcosm unto themselves. They lived inside the plane. At sunset, Drew landed. The men took turns resting while two stood guard.

What would they do if they were attacked? Fly away, she supposed. The Osprey had no guns.

Emily was amazed she'd been able to sleep. There were killers outside. Her bedroll was uncomfortable on the flight deck. She had no privacy. But her exhaustion was as constant as her fear and stress, and she trusted Drew to protect her.

Three times he'd filled the Osprey's tanks at abandoned airports, working carefully to take what he needed without being electrocuted by the static charges built up in the fuel trucks or other aircraft he used to siphon fuel. Emily was useless. The best she could do was to serve their meals and tidy up afterward. Stupidly, she'd almost scorched herself on the magnesium mix included with their Meal, Ready-to-Eat rations until Bugle showed her how to heat the food.

Bugle was a clown. Despite everything, he tried to make her smile, pretending to grab all the chocolate from the MRE pouches or talking about where they'd put a couch and a TV inside the plane if she wanted to play house.

Emily thought Bugle was hitting on her. She watched Drew instead. Once upon a time, she'd loved to be silly. Now it was Drew's serious, dedicated nature that appealed to her most.

After three days above the endless devastation, she felt closer to these elite fighters than she had any right to expect. They ate together, slept together, used the ridiculous port-a-toilet together—and meanwhile Julie's corpse lay in back. Any one of them could be next.

I have to keep doing my best, Emily thought, glancing at the filthy, beaten loafers they'd taken off Marcus. Bugle was tending to the man's feet, outfitting him with new socks and an enormous pair of boots.

Especially with the oversized boots, Marcus looked harmless. He was in his forties and heavy in the stomach, and yet Emily was afraid for her men.

"I should go with you," she said.

"No," Drew said. "Stay inside."

"You need all the hands you can get." She was mystified by his careful tone. Was he distancing himself from her? She touched his arm. "Let me help."

For a moment, he seemed to consider it.

"I can carry boxes or keep a lookout," she said, but reminding him of the hazards outside increased his caution.

"You're staying," he said.

30

• • • • • • • • • • • •

NORTHERN CALIFORNIA

M arcus breathed slowly as he followed the soldiers from the plane into daylight. The wet, swirling wind smelled far better than inside, which reeked of dirty people, guns, and jet fuel.

The array was beautiful. Marcus glanced over the white dishes, but the allure he felt was a mute whisper compared to the pride he'd once cherished. In order to use the array, he would need to return to his prison in the electronics room, so much like the cramped, stinking plane.

That was what they wanted.

That was why they'd saved him.

Drew said, "Dr. Wolsinger? Do you need help, sir?"

"I'm all right." Marcus was gruff. Had they seen him looking past the dishes to the scrub- and rock-covered mountainsides?

He realized Bugle and Drew were also watching the landscape, either watching for more people to save or anticipating an attack. Very little of their attention seemed to be on him, which was good, because he didn't think he'd concealed his pain.

A big soldier with a rifle pushed through the exit from the lounge. "They were set up in the back rooms, sir," he said to Drew. "There are some cots and duffel bags."

"Excellent. Stay here with Lieutenant Buegeleisen." Drew escorted Marcus up the ramp, leaving his men to guard the plane.

As they passed through the door, the air felt hushed. The wind continued to slide past the shattered windows, but it barely stirred the dust or garbage inside.

The familiar walls could have been from a dream. Marcus felt strange. This was more than déjà vu, the perception that he'd previously experienced this exact moment. The French also had a term called *presque vu*, "almost seen," the feeling of being on the verge of a premonition or great insight. The uncanny sense of it hummed through his thoughts.

"Wolsinger?" Drew said. "Excuse me, Dr. Wolsinger."

Marcus shook himself. "What?"

"I asked if you have any spare clothes. You'll feel better if you're clean."

"Yes." He clomped down the hall in his new boots. They were loose, and banged against the gauze pad on his ankle, but his body felt more attuned to the doorway to the office where he'd made love to Rebecca.

He went to it and looked inside.

Rebecca.

His relationship with her transcended any conventional norms. Outside, in the sun, their attachment to each other had been heightened by the competition for her within the tribe. At the same time, Marcus didn't think he'd resented his tribesmen for challenging him for her. It was okay to share. They were family. They'd had no concept of existing without their group.

Standing in the hall, Marcus rubbed his forehead before Drew grabbed his wrist. "What are you doing?" Drew said.

"I— My head aches."

"You need rest." Drew pulled Marcus's hand away from the M-string. "I promise you can sleep after we're through here, but we need to finish what we came for. Where's your stuff? This is an office."

"Okay. I know." Marcus turned and crossed the hall, entering another door.

The room where he'd bunked before the interrupts was also a pig-pen. The cot was overturned and his bags had been dumped out, the clothes strewn on the floor.

Marcus knelt. He found a shirt. There were shoes.

His memories of each unique individual in his tribe were the basis of his recurring *presque vu*. He could feel them if he tried.

"Sir, you need to hurry," Drew said. "Can I help you with something? What about your boots?"

"I'm okay." Marcus formed each word ponderously. For an instant, he closed his eyes and was far away. But he returned to himself with new urgency.

He fumbled into a clean pair of pants, then the shoes. Then he stood up. "Let's go," he said.

As they walked to the control room, Marcus gathered every bit of courage he'd built inside himself. He was only able to enter the electronics room by keeping his eyes on the floor.

"You want these," he said, pointing at a rack of IBM 5150 servers. Each was about the size of a desktop computer turned on its side. There were a dozen of them. "My laptop's over there. I don't know if anything is functional. The pulse came through this room more than once."

Drew looked at the supplies, the blankets, and the generator. "You tried to hold out in here," he said.

Marcus ignored the desolate feeling in his chest. "We'd better grab my notes, too," he said, finding the notepad on the floor. Some of those pages were extremely personal, but he wanted the government to have his summaries, for all the good it did them.

"Thanks, Doc," Drew said, relaxing for the first time. He reached for the notepad, but Marcus thumbed through its pages and said, "Let me make sure nothing's missing."

Drew led him back outside. Marcus walked down the ramp, tasting the wind again.

"Lieutenant," Drew said, "take Dr. Wolsinger inside the plane. Sergeant, I need help with some gear."

"Yes, sir."

The big sergeant went past Marcus. Bugle approached him and said, "Come with me, sir."

Marcus pretended not to hear, watching Drew, who took the sergeant inside. Then he showed Bugle the notepad. "This is important," he said before he dropped it.

Bugle bent to grab the pages. Marcus shoved him, then turned and ran as Bugle fell.

"Wolsinger! Stop!"

His shoes pounded on the damp earth, his blood thumping with exhilaration. Behind him, he heard the station door bang open and Drew's disgusted voice. "Get him."

They wouldn't shoot, would they? Marcus reached the first dishes. He dodged into the metal forest. They were young, but he knew the array better than anyone. He hoped they would give up if they couldn't find him immediately.

"Wolsinger!" Bugle shouted.

Another soldier called from Marcus's left and he heard more voices behind him. He increased his speed. He barely felt his ankle. He didn't notice his own heaving lungs. There was one thought in him, and one thought only.

Roell.

The superconsciousness he'd tapped beneath his waking mind felt like a puzzle whose pieces had stretched and melted. Few of its parts fit well, but those that touched each other were undeniable. He'd been with his son. They had been happy, which was more than he'd ever expected, and he didn't believe the soldiers would look for Roell. They might not come back at all. Even if they did, it might be days or weeks later, and by then Roell could have walked for miles.

"Here!" a man yelled.

Marcus saw him through the dishes, a soldier in camouflage, his head rounded by a combat helmet. Goggles hid his eyes. Marcus gasped. His sight blurred with the memory of another faceless demon. He could almost hear the *whup whup whup* of the plane, but the thundering sound was his own heart.

Suddenly the dishes seemed to be in his way. They didn't hide him. They obstructed him. He clipped one with his head and nearly fell, grabbing his temple and staggering on.

"I got him!" another man yelled. "Over here!"

They were cutting him off. Marcus glanced through the white dishes for an opening. A soldier flitted through the array on his right. He heard a second man ahead of him.

He'd hoped to be miles away before he removed his M-string, but his body acted for him. His palm was already set against the fresh bruise above his ear. Now his fingers bunched in the mesh fabric. *I'll find you,* he thought.

He pulled off the cap.

Drew and Bugle spread out as they followed the corporal's yell. "Bugshit crazy old man," Bugle said, and Drew shushed his partner.

"Quiet," he said.

From the sky, the dishes looked well-spaced, like pegs in simplistic patterns, but at ground level the array was a labyrinth. They could be ambushed too easily, especially because the blind spot in his left eye hadn't healed. It probably never would.

"Watch your back," Drew said as they reached a meadow among the dishes. The corporal stood across from them in the open space with his M16 leveled at Marcus, who crouched facedown in the weeds, propping himself on both hands and one knee. He shuddered and exhaled noisily.

Drew took one hand from his M4 and traded signals with the corporal. *Protect our flank.*

The corporal acknowledged. He turned to cover the endless white dishes as Bugle marched forward and bent over Marcus. "All right, fun's over," he said.

"Bugle, wait—"

Marcus surged up, driving his shoulder into Bugle's stomach, clubbing his arm through Bugle's M4. Bugle didn't let go of his weapon, but momentum threw him sprawling as Marcus rose over him in a low, hulking crouch.

Marcus's face was blank of human emotion. "Nnnnnnnnmmh!" he shrieked. Then he slammed his fists into Bugle's face.

Drew leapt on Marcus seconds later. He'd drawn his Taser. First he needed to separate Bugle from Marcus, so he kicked his boot into the man's head. This was no longer a middle-aged desk jockey. He was Neanderthal.

He heard a *crack* as Marcus's cheekbone imploded. Both of them fell away from Bugle, but Drew stayed on his feet.

Marcus thrust himself upright.

Drew fired and the Taser leads leapt into Marcus's chest.

Convulsing, Marcus stumbled back. Muscles corded in his neck. The voltage must have been excruciating, but he reversed himself, planting one foot forward, then the other, groping for Drew like a man in a storm.

The corporal aimed his M16.

"No!" Drew shouted. He triggered the Taser again, sending a second charge through the leads.

Marcus collapsed.

Emily was right, Drew thought. Marcus had none of the hallmarks of Neanderthal behavior, but somehow Emily had guessed. He'd been better prepared because of it. She might have saved their lives.

"Holy fuck," Bugle cursed, mopping at his bloody lip.

"Get up," Drew said. "Jesus. You couldn't take care of one civilian?"

Bugle's eyes widened. The rebuke obviously hurt him more than the violence to his face. It wasn't fair, but Drew was too frustrated to apologize.

"Let's go. Grab his M-string."

Inside the plane, Emily felt a fresh sting of adrenaline when the corporal threw open the side door. She retreated against one of the protective screens. Bugle and Drew wrestled Marcus inside. Bugle's mouth was swollen, and Marcus's cheek looked wrong. Part of it was crumpled while the rest of his face had puffed on that side, swallowing his eye.

Marcus jerked and moaned. He was semi-conscious, and yet Emily realized Bugle was treating him roughly. Bugle had Marcus's legs, which he dropped to the deck. Trying to compensate, Drew knelt, easing Marcus's head and torso onto his lap.

"Watch it," Drew barked.

"What happened!?" Emily asked.

Drew was focused on Marcus. "We can get your son," he said. "I swore we'd find him."

"You don't understand," Marcus groaned. "Put me back."

Drew stood up and looked at the corporal. "Sedate him," he said. "Let's load his gear. I want to move out."

"Don't!" Marcus tried to grab Drew's leg until Bugle pinned his arm against the deck. "Put me back!" he said.

"Crazy bastard took off his M-string," Bugle told Emily.

She stared at him with a flurry of emotions. Marcus's effort to reunite with his son was insane, but it was also courageous. It was suicide. It was a bizarre form of rebirth, bringing back whoever he'd been outside. In a way, she approved—and she definitely couldn't condone beating a middle-aged man.

"Why did you hurt him?" she asked.

"He turned Neanderthal," Drew said.

She didn't want to believe him, but the denial she felt turned to new horror. She trusted Drew. "Neanderthal," she said. It wasn't a question.

Drew nodded. "Absolutely. He stood like them, sang like them, and he did that to Lieutenant Buegeleisen's face."

Emily glanced at Bugle's mouth. Then her gaze returned to Drew's brown eyes. She wondered again at his quiet strength. His determination. His ability to perform his job in any circumstances.

The corporal knelt among them with a med kit. He removed a disposable hypodermic as Marcus wormed on the deck.

"Don't!" Marcus cried.

Bugle secured Marcus's wrist and biceps as the corporal jabbed the needle into his arm. The effect was swift. Marcus went limp.

"If he turned Neanderthal, all of my working theories are wrong," Emily said. "He doesn't have ASD."

"No."

"This changes everything," she said.

PART TWO
FALL

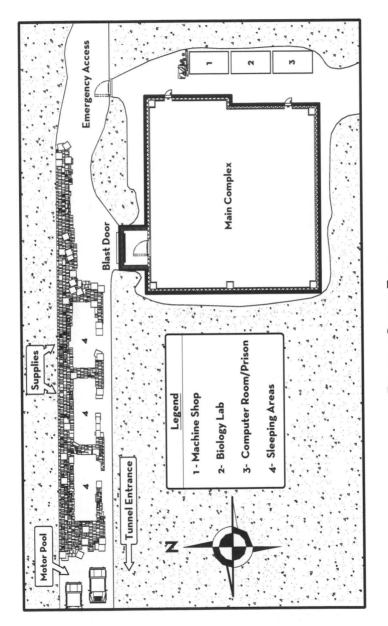

BUNKER SEVEN FOUR

31

. . . .

NORTHERN CALIFORNIA
BUNKER SEVEN FOUR

E mily's shoes rang on the lower deck of the complex, an unnatural sound like a steel drum, which she enjoyed. The complex was well-lit and clean. It felt orderly and permanent. The narrow corridor had white-painted walls, brown-painted floors, and evenly spaced lights mounted in wire cages. The floor hummed from the vibrations of a distant engine. She might have been belowdecks on a submarine or an oil rig.

In her white lab coat, Emily matched the complex nicely. Part of her wanted to stay inside forever. A smaller part felt claustrophobic and tense.

She entered an intersection, then stopped as a man called, "Halt."

She kept her hands where he could see them. "I have a pass," she said. She lifted a blue slip of paper. Tucked beneath her other arm were files and printouts. She was sure the uniformed man recognized her—they'd spoken several times—but as a Navy SEAL, he insisted on his protocols.

"Approach," he said.

Emily strode toward him.

Twenty-six days had passed since Drew and Bugle brought her underground. Bunker Seven Four sat a thousand feet into the side of a mountain fifty miles north of Sacramento near Beale Air Force Base. Budget cuts had closed the base years ago, but it had been mothballed like the bunker, housing a skeleton crew, until the solar flares.

Schematics of the bunker looked like a comma. The long entry tunnel led to a round cavern, which held an eighty-foot-long metal box—the complex—a three-story cube seated on steel coils meant to absorb the nuclear shock waves. Bugle said it was no accident that the inside of the complex resembled a submarine. Like the old NORAD base in Colorado, the Air Force operated Bunker Seven Four, but the Navy had designed and constructed it, maximizing its tiny footprint.

Emily had quickly memorized the interior layout. On the lower deck, the corridors formed a square-cornered 8 with two exits into the cavern on the east wall and one exit into the tunnel on the north. Most of the doors to the rooms inside the complex ran down the central corridor.

"Please tell Commander Haldane I'd like to speak with him," Emily told the Navy SEAL posted at the barracks door.

"Yes, ma'am." The SEAL didn't move.

"Can you do it now, please?"

"No, ma'am."

Emily cursed to herself. If she asked if Drew had left on another mission, the SEAL would stonewall whether he knew or not. Everything was top secret with these guys. "I'm going to leave a note," she said, rummaging through her printouts for a corner to tear off. "You put it on his bunk."

"Yes, ma'am."

The SEAL ignored her flash of impatience. Every day, the discipline among the military personnel grew tighter in response to the discord among the civilian refugees.

Emily supposed it was predictable that the two groups had drawn apart. The bunker was manned by thirty-one soldiers while there were sixty-four refugees. The soldiers felt outnumbered. They treated the civilians like a mess that could be tolerated but should be cleaned up if the mess would just cooperate.

The problem was the soldiers were highly trained like Drew and Bugle, and, even better for their morale, they had jobs around the clock.

Most of the civilians were experts of some kind. They were scientists or engineers or government or religious leaders, but too many of them were spinning their wheels to no purpose, waiting for equipment, waiting for their families, waiting to see the sky. They complained to the soldiers about the food and the cots they shared in shifts. They screamed at each other over slights like who'd kept everyone else awake, snoring or talking, or the unforgivable offense of stealing a clean pair of socks. Two women whose combined IQ must have exceeded three hundred were locked in a caustic dispute about who used too much of the toilet paper they'd been warned would overload the septic tanks.

Emily tried not to be drawn into the bickering. Everyone was frayed and petrified. She did her best to emulate the crew from the Osprey.

Self-discipline was the answer. Emily worked as much as possible. Unfortunately, she wasn't allowed in her makeshift lab more than two four-hour periods each day. Even then she had to share the room with three geneticists and a toxicologist because the science teams had nowhere else to set up.

Worse, they were given equal time on the computers, which had slowed her data processing to a crawl. She'd tried to tell General Strickland how critical her work could be, but everyone said their work was critical. Strickland had ordered them to work in rotation. The rest of the time, Emily was left scribbling on paper or pacing through the same cramped sections of the bunker, hoping to anticipate her next set of results—hoping for a breakthrough—hoping to run into a familiar face who was also off duty.

For a brief time after she'd reached the bunker, she'd relaxed. Now each day felt like the lowest point in her life. Somehow even the terror she'd experienced aboveground seemed better than Bunker Seven Four's stale, congested spaces.

The pressure to give General Strickland something he could use was a constant weight. Emily's shoulders ached with deep-set knots. Her mouth hurt from grinding her teeth in her sleep.

"Here," she said, folding her scrap of paper before handing it to the SEAL. "Thank you."

"Yes, ma'am."

Would he read it first? Probably. She had to assume Drew wasn't the only one who'd see her note, so it was friendly, yet short. *Please find me. Emily.* She had more she needed to say, but not for public consumption.

She turned and left, folding her arms over her chest against the cool air. Maybe she lingered too long. Behind her, the SEAL cleared his throat.

By decree, the corridors in the complex and other priority areas were kept clear of supplies or idle people. Guards had been posted to enforce the new rule after six civilians were caught making camp behind the enormous diesel tanks in the power room.

Emily relished the near-solitude of the corridor. She would have stayed if the SEAL allowed it because there were so few places to escape the crush of refugees.

At the intersection, she went left like the SEAL would expect if she was leaving the complex. Four soldiers passed, arguing about a radio transmission. But at the next corner, Emily turned left again when she should have gone to the exit, fighting a jolt of tension.

If they catch you . . .

She knew the complex better than most civilians because Bugle had taken her on three tours. Each walk had felt more and more like a date. Bugle was energetic and fun—and Emily missed Chase. She wanted to be with someone at night.

Why not Bugle? He wasn't right for her. More and more, she thought of him as the Scarecrow from *The Wizard of Oz*, a sweet, floppy-armed guy with a great heart. Bugle could be wise in his way, but he seemed more like a brother than a potential romance. Emily was careful not to lead him on.

She loved to laugh at his jokes. Nevertheless, she'd continued to wear her rings—her engagement ring and Chase's class ring—hoping Bugle would catch on. She wasn't sure if he could tell the difference between friendship and courtship.

At least he'd inadvertently shown her a place to hide.

The outer corridor led to two exits into the cavern as well as a low-traffic corner where their computer servers and utility controls were stored. The hiding place was a short, L-shaped branch to the locked door of the server room.

Emily ducked into the dead-end space and pressed her back against the wall. Her body wanted more oxygen, but she struggled not to gulp for air. More footsteps jogged through the corridor. What if someone heard her?

She knew it was crazy, but she needed this secret place. There was nowhere else for her to cry.

At top capacity, in the event of nuclear or biological war, Bunker Seven Four's air filters had been rated for thirty days, as were their food and fuel supplies, although the air was fine and Drew's squads were able to scavenge outside through the nearest towns. His raids had extended their ability to live underground almost indefinitely.

Day after day, Emily found the lack of space disorienting. Her longest view was in the tunnel, where the soldiers had left two hundred feet open for walking or jogging. The entrance itself had been blocked off to stop the pulse. The rest of the tunnel was crammed with vehicles, gear, and the thirty-foot pockets they'd created for sleeping areas. The complex didn't have room for so many people. Strickland had segregated his military personnel from the refugees.

Emily's spot was in the third sleeping area in the tunnel, which was wretched. No amount of blankets could keep her warm. It didn't help that many survivors woke with nightmares or couldn't sleep at all, especially after a series of earthquakes rattled the mountain. Each time, everyone thought Chinese missiles were detonating outside.

Two women were catatonic with sleep deprivation. Some people had given up on social norms. One man stared blatantly at Emily and the other women. Other people farted or burped no matter who was nearby. A few didn't bother to wash.

One thing the bunker didn't lack was water. Moisture seeped through the rock, leaving puddles, moss, and dribbling streams. Drains led to more pipes, most of which led to reservoirs in the deepest part of the cavern. Those ponds were full now. Outside, the rain had been constant. The mountain was a sponge.

Everyone was allowed cold showers as often as they liked and five gallons of hot water every fourth day. Too often, a hot rinse was the highlight of Emily's week. Fifteen minutes of privacy without her days-old clothes were a delight; the good smell of the soap; the clean, slick lather on her legs and neck. Emily supposed she wasn't the only woman masturbating in the plastic stall. Others had brought men into the shower with them one at a time.

The sexual tension was especially noticeable among young survivors like herself. Most were geeks and eggheads. They'd spent their lives being more cerebral than physical, but the urge to touch each other was the most basic imperative of any threatened species: to breed. No one actually wanted babies. That would have been ludicrous. But stress and close quarters generated pheromones—and lust—and quarrels and posturing and seductions and fights.

Some of the survivors had paired up, relieving their pent-up desires. For the most part, those couples seemed like the happiest people in the bunch. Others broke up as swiftly as they'd found each other, then nursed a grudge or carried a torch. Emily thought they were happier than the rest, too, absorbed in their personal dramas.

Like the Osprey, the bunker was a miniature world unto itself. This group was much larger, so they were taking longer to settle into their rhythm, but she hoped they would overcome everything that poisoned them—their trauma, their isolation, and their dread.

Drew had led a team outside to reinforce the bunker's communications array. They were in steady contact with other shelters, even the president. Emily had been allowed to send dozens of questions to biologists across the country, but reception was spotty. Everything had to be encrypted to keep it from being intercepted by the Chinese.

Reception was best at night, when the rate of errors could be as low as 40 percent. During the day, if the pulse was particularly intense, the error rate was total. Even if the soldiers hadn't reserved the lion's share of the radio time for their own codes, Emily couldn't successfully transmit her data. Her files were too large.

That meant she worked alone. She found it impossible to build relationships with experts she knew only as transcripts on paper. Too many people had come and gone. Sometimes she still thought of Michelle, Colonel Bowen, and the other men and women she'd met in the hospital.

Silver Lake had fallen silent. They were lost.

As much as Emily hated being underground, most of the safe places on the surface hadn't lasted. The survivors had been forced to abandon their shelters for lack of water and food or they'd been driven out by fire.

The Neanderthal attacks were escalating.

If anyone had a solution, the time was now—before the last hold-outs were destroyed—but not everyone agreed on the evidence. Some of the science teams in Bunker Seven Four were looking for a viral trigger as the cause for the attacks. America's military and intelligence leaders couldn't let go of the idea that China might be responsible. Most of the geneticists agreed with Emily's theories, but they were pursuing their own lines of research.

Her own work was muddled. The light seq tests she'd started at the hospital had been pointless except as quick, unreliable indicators. Then she'd lost six days helping the soldiers set up their labs and cobble together enough servers scavenged from outside to handle the workload.

Emily had taken three weeks to analyze, assemble, and compare the deep sequencing of her RNA samples—and she wasn't happy with her results.

She needed to talk to Drew because it was vital for her to join him on his next raid. That's what she told herself. How much of her anxiety stemmed from the need to walk in fresh air and sunlight? Her new plan was definitely an excuse to see Drew.

Her hiding spot didn't last. A few minutes later, the sound of boot steps reverberated in her dead-end corridor. Sitting on the floor, Emily made herself smile as an Air Force captain nearly tripped over her feet. He glanced at the server room door. "What are you doing here?"

She showed her pass and her paperwork. "I needed somewhere to think. I'm one of the biologists—"

"Ma'am, this section is off-limits. Get up." His tone reminded her of Drew, who used the same formality as a shield. But this man was rough. He grabbed her elbow and led her away.

"I wasn't doing anything wrong," she said. "I just . . . I need somewhere to work."

"Security!" he called at the intersection. "Security!"

He's overreacting, Emily thought as the Navy SEAL ran into view. Another armed guard appeared behind him. Emily felt her cheeks burn. General Strickland would learn she'd bent the rules.

"What is your name?" the captain asked.

"Dr. Flint. I need somewhere to work."

"Get her out of here, then close the hatches," he told the SEAL.

"Honestly, I . . ." Emily said, but the SEAL gestured rudely. Did they really think she was up to something? What? Stealing food?

The SEAL escorted her to a hatch, which was where she'd entered the complex. The stairwell was hardly more than a short ladder. Voices rose from the cavern outside. She felt a breeze caused by the temperature differential. The cavern was always colder than the complex.

"Go," the SEAL said.

Emily climbed down, leaving the white corridor for a rocky hollow full of shadows and machinery. The SEAL shut the hatch above her. He locked it with two resonant *bangs*. The complex towered above her, partially concealed in the dark and by the sweeping contours of the rock. Emily stopped on the ladder, fighting her loneliness and more tears.

Don't cry. Goddamn it, don't cry.

Her hand discovered some kind of graffiti on the outside of the third step. Otherwise she wouldn't have seen it. An inch-long crucifix had been etched into the metal plate beside a formation of four notches like an H.

She ran her thumb over the carving, wondering at its ridges and divots. Was it the beginning of someone's name?

Graffiti had been outlawed by General Strickland, although it continued to appear throughout the bunker. Clean-up details had been another source of conflict between the soldiers and the civilians, with accusations that some of the obscenities, prayers, and artwork must have originated among the soldiers themselves. No one else had access to the spray paint used to sketch a blue landscape on the wall near the water reservoir.

Bishop DeSoto had gone so far as to assert that some graffiti was a positive outlet. Paintings like the landscape should be allowed, he said. Privately, Emily agreed, but if she was going to argue with Strickland, she wanted to argue about better lab conditions.

The graffiti intrigued her. Some people had been stupid enough to etch their initials into the steel, masonry, or naked rock. They were discovered and disciplined. Even the vandals who left anonymous marks or drawings risked punishment. Why?

They wanted ownership. They wanted control. Emily had felt the same compulsion when she'd written Chase's name on the hospital's list of known dead. Oblivion was too close. Everyone was afraid of being forgotten. If Emily hadn't had her work to occupy her, she might have scratched her name into the rock herself.

Maybe I will anyway, she thought, ducking her eyes from the crucifix. It was so puny and helpless. Then she jerked her hand from the ladder as a man approached. She stepped down.

"Emily," he said. "We're having a meeting in the tunnel in fifteen minutes. You should be there."

"I . . ."

"We need more votes if Strickland's going to listen."

Emily nodded. At the barracks door, she'd been angry with the SEAL, but the soldiers expected foolishness from civilians. She needed to be more politic in how she treated her fellow refugees. Whether she liked it or not, she was one of them.

"Sure, Jake," she said. "What are we voting for?"

"Rooms. There's no reason we can't arrange the supplies to make our own rooms."

A thin man in his thirties, Jacob Leber was a mechanical engineer with too little to occupy his time. He worked in the machine shop, building armor to suit Drew's needs outside, but it wasn't enough, so Jake had usurped the role that should have belonged to Senator O'Neal or Mayor Reaves. He'd harnessed the discontented factions among the civilians with attainable goals like less-restricted access to ibuprofen or an extra TV to watch movies.

"I'll vote for private rooms," Emily said. "Can you tell everyone, please? I'm late for a follow-up." That was a lie, but she would scream if she had to sit through another meeting. "God knows we've been packed in this tunnel like sardines."

"Good. We can count on you?"

"Yes." Emily sidled past Jake into the cavern, which was an odd combination of bare rock and technology. Bundles of pipes and conduit ran along the passageway: water lines, sewer lines, forced air, heat, and fuel. The floor was concrete, yet spattered with dirt. Emily smelled ozone and grease, but beneath the man-made smells was the dank, wet scent of the earth.

Silhouettes walked in twos and threes past the lights on the wall. They were going to Jake's meeting. Emily moved in the opposite direction, faking a smile in response to each questioning look. She pointed apologetically at her paperwork. "Thanks," she said.

"You need to come with us," a woman answered, her face set in a stubborn frown.

"I can't. I'm sorry."

The woman had walked past Emily, but started to return. "I don't think you realize—" she said until one of her friends caught her arm.

"Karen, don't," he said.

They left. Emily stood looking after them with her heartbeat shaking through her chest. First there had been peer pressure to attend their meetings. Now they were openly intimidating her. Emily resented it.

I'm closer to solving this than you'll ever be, she thought. *Let me work. I can save you if you let me work.*

Ahead of her, the tunnel was blocked by the front end of an eighteen-foot trailer, scrap metal, and acetylene tanks. Between the trailer on one side and the pipes on the other, the path narrowed to four feet.

Emily hurried through the tight space. Beyond this trailer were two more trailers lined up like train cars, their windows caked with years of moisture and grime. The lights were off in the first trailer. It was Jacob's machine shop. The next trailer had been transformed into the science labs. People should have been inside if they hadn't left for the meeting. Emily considered entering herself, but if anyone caught her using the equipment out of schedule, they'd have another reason to ostracize her from the group.

She rapped on the door of the third trailer. It had been divided into a computer room and the bunker's only jail cell. A soldier opened up. He was often on duty here. "Dr. Flint," he said.

"I'd like to talk to him, please."

"Sure. Let me call it in."

Securing permission was standard operating procedure, but Emily worried she might be denied because of the misunderstanding inside the complex.

She paced restlessly between the trailer and another stairwell into the complex. This hatch was always locked except when the prison guard changed shifts, yet Emily paused, then moved closer when a familiar shape caught her eye.

A tiny cross had been etched into the third step from the top. This cross had a formation like an A alongside it. Her first thought was someone had found a new way to carve their initials, separating the two letters while uniting them with the crucifixes, but she couldn't think of anyone whose initials were A. H. or H. A.

The slashes might not be letters at all. What if they were hash marks? Was there anything to count except the movements of the soldiers . . . ?

You're being paranoid, she thought. *You're tired.*

But some of the people in this bunker were *very* smart, and others were sick with grief. What if they were planning something dangerous?

Standing at the ladder, Emily's mind raced like a stopwatch flickering down to zero. Suddenly the Air Force captain's shouting made sense. He'd acted like she was a rat because the base personnel were concerned. She wasn't the only one with personal ties to the soldiers. Other informants might have passed on rumors or clues.

Emily knew there were civilians who wanted into the complex. Eight days ago, she'd overheard a group of men whispering that Strickland should empty the tunnel and let everyone live behind the blast door. The crowding would be insufferable, but there was a larger issue.

If the war with China boiled over, nuclear strikes outside the mountain would kill everyone in the tunnel, which was designed to absorb and deflect blast waves away from the complex. Emily had expected a noisy meeting on the subject. Nor could she blame them. A few VIPs had been rescued with their dependents. Among the sixty-four civilians were five children, a wife, and two husbands with no strategic value, merely the good luck to be rescued. The need to protect them might have twisted someone's thinking beyond the normal instinct of self-preservation.

If a few conspirators were using Jake's meetings to cover their own activities, that could explain why his votes were increasing. If Emily was plotting something herself, she'd push Jake to raise as much hell as possible. He was a diversion.

What did they want? Did they have guns?

You can't let anyone see you staring, she realized, whirling from the crucifix. She couldn't get inside the complex to warn the soldiers until they unlocked the doors, but maybe she could use the prison guard's phone.

She ran to the trailer. "Sir?" she asked. "Sir?"

If someone was plotting a takeover, she'd missed the signs. She was definitely not welcome among the innermost circles of the refugees. They'd seen her with Bugle and Drew—and no one was sure what to make of her friendship with Marcus Wolsinger.

32

. . . .

BUNKER SEVEN FOUR

The guard waved for Emily to come into the trailer. He was alone, although the small front room held two chairs, two desks, and a coffee maker with several mugs. A space heater sat on the laminate floor. Old paperback books, DVDs, and a thirteen-inch TV filled a table in the corner. An ordinary telephone hung on the wall.

"Can I use your phone?" she asked. "I need to talk to someone in charge."

"I thought you were here to see Dr. Wolsinger."

"I am. I . . . Please. It's important."

The guard looked her up and down. She must have sounded as nervous as she felt. He went to the phone and lifted the handset without turning his back on her. It was a direct line. He didn't need to punch in a number. "Holding cell," he said. "Dr. Flint is asking for an officer now." His eyes narrowed. "Copy that."

What were they telling him?

He hung up and said, "Ma'am, we're on alert. Everyone's occupied."

"Some of the people in the tunnel are planning something," she said. "I don't have much proof, but you guys need to know. There might be trouble."

"You mean Jake?"

"I don't know. I hope it's nothing."

"I'm going to ask you to go into Wolsinger's room," he said. "You'll be safe there."

Right, she thought. *Then you'll have me in jail, too.* Maybe it was her best move. If she went into Marcus's cell, the guard would realize she wasn't a threat.

Emily walked down the hall as the guard reached for his phone again. Sign-in sheets hung on a nail. Many of the signatures were hers, although plenty of people consulted with Marcus. She recognized Drew's tidy handwriting among the names. Apparently she'd almost run into him two days ago.

Where was he now? Hunting more blood samples for her outside?

As she entered her name on the list once more, she prayed it wouldn't be the last time. She couldn't believe the situation was that bad—but on the phone behind her, the guard said, "I may need backup."

Marcus's door wasn't locked. He had a bathroom and they brought him food, so he had no excuse for leaving. If he did, he'd meet the guard in the front room. His sole window was inches from the rock face of the cavern.

Emily knocked, then knocked again. He didn't answer. She opened the door an inch and leaned into the gap without looking. "Marcus? It's Emily."

"Hey, girl."

Good, she thought. *He sounds good today.* "Can I come in?"

"I'm not going anywhere," he said without humor.

She stepped into the neat, narrow room. He sat on his cot. She stayed by the door. There had been a time when she was physically afraid of Marcus and required an escort. He wasn't eating, so he'd lost most of his desk belly, but he would always outweigh her, and her first impressions of him had been as he recovered from his Neanderthal state.

Even now, they never engaged in contact like a handshake. He had become a sounding board and a mentor to her—a father figure—yet she hadn't let go of her suspicion. Today his expression was open and coherent. Sometimes it wasn't.

When he turned sullen, Emily could only guess what he was thinking based on the things he'd told her and the reports of science teams worldwide. Did he remember being Nim and yearn for it? Or was his anguish for his son too much to endure?

Emily would have been interested in having a neurologist examine Marcus and run CT and MRI scans. Had he suffered permanent brain damage during his three days in the pulse? Or would a psychologist be more useful in treating him?

"I'm sorry I haven't come for a while," she said.

"I know you're busy."

"Yes."

"How are things outside?" he asked, allowing her the charade of chitchat.

For him, *outside* meant the larger space of the bunker.

Shells within shells, Emily thought. His room was a minuscule box inside a cave beneath a mountain on the surface of a planet circling a violent sun lost in one measureless stretch of the galaxy. It made her feel insignificant.

"I have new data," she said, showing him the files under her arm.

Marcus wasn't looking. He glanced at the door, easily reading her tension. Emily realized she was standing on the balls of her feet.

"Something's wrong," he suggested.

"I—" Emily cleared her throat and took her usual chair in the corner. Marcus stayed on his cot, where he leaned against the wall with his blankets up to his waist. Maybe he'd been napping. He slept a lot. The television they'd provided didn't interest him because it was slaved to the TV in the front room, where the soldiers watched action flicks. Emily had talked to them about playing funny movies, for which Marcus thanked her, but he had even less taste for gross-out comedy like Adam Sandler or *South Park* episodes. Too bad. Emily would have stayed for hours just to have a chance to smile.

Marcus had one interest. The pulse. He read reports from everyone who provided them, not only the astrophysicists and engineers but also biologists like Emily, climatologists, geologists, NASA techs, and M.D.s.

They said he was weird. Emily agreed, although she also saw the sad, wounded man behind his calculated front. A lot of people didn't. They envied the way he lived like a king with his private room, private cot, and private TV. They didn't care that he was a prisoner. Everyone felt trapped, so they belittled him even as they kept coming back for advice.

Marcus was as smart as any three of them put together. He pointed out discrepancies in the astrophysicists' data and argued with the climatologists. From the doctors and biologists, he asked for more. Their reports fascinated him. Meanwhile, he advised the team of astronomers at the Hoffman Square Kilometer Field and offered his own forecasts on the solar max. In every way, he seemed to be participating in their survival—but he was inconsolable.

The bunker was more than a hundred miles from the array. Three weeks ago, Bugle had been unable to capture Roell or Rebecca while leading a second rescue mission, which made Marcus bitter.

Marcus was correct in believing the soldiers hadn't given many resources to this attempt. Drew had kept most of his team at the array, guarding their precious Osprey, unloading steel and cinder block to reinforce the station, while Bugle led four men into the surrounding landscape. Roell hadn't even topped their list. Bugle's main objective had been the other ES2 astronomers like Steve, Kym, and Chuck. Bugle hadn't been able to find them, either, but Emily didn't think things would be different if Roell had been imprisoned with Marcus.

He would despise being trapped in here no matter what we did for him, she thought.

"Why don't you tell me what's going on?" Marcus asked. He was mild, biding his time. "Is it something we're not supposed to know?"

Emily shook her head.

"If it was, who would find out?" he asked, indicating the walls.

Emily glanced at the door again, wondering how long she had before the soldiers came to question her. "There's more graffiti than usual," she said.

Marcus wrinkled his brow. He'd expected to hear the new development in her research.

"You know how I feel about cave art," he said.

"Yes."

"Nobody's going to stop because Strickland said so."

"This is different," she said, uncertain how much to share with him as his mood changed like a lightbulb switching on. He became agitated.

"*Homo sapiens* developed their own strengths like the Neanderthals," he said.

"Marcus—"

"They're responding how they're made to respond. Strickland can give as many orders as he wants."

"Marcus, this is different," Emily said in a firm voice.

He visibly struggled with himself. Then his smooth face returned. How much of his self-control was real? She worried it was a facade. Every glimpse of the commotion beneath his bland face made her wary.

Marcus thought the prehistoric totems and cave paintings found in Europe had been early *Homo sapiens'* attempts to withstand the interrupts. They had surely left drawings aboveground, too, during the long intervals between geomagnetic storms, but those had worn away in time, whereas some of their totems carved in horn still existed today.

Some anthropologists cited mystical purposes for *Homo sapiens'* cave murals of reindeer and other large game. Chips in the walls were proof that men had practiced hurling spears into the drawings. Marcus agreed those people hoped their magic would bring them food, but he'd also taken this idea a step further. Had they carried their totems with them as reminders during the interrupts? Natural selection would have favored the hunters who increased their ability to train themselves, mimicking the Neanderthals' focus.

Thousands of years later, prodigies like Emily and Marcus were the culmination of *Homo sapiens'* talent for abstract visual representation— and yet both of them also had Neanderthal genes in their families.

What if early *Homo sapiens* had purposefully bred with their cousins in order to become more like them?

So-called "normal" people exhibited any number of traits that were borderline autistic—fussy with clothes—fussy with belongings— digestive allergies to grains and dairy—and a preternatural ability to concentrate on certain stimuli. Like Marcus, Emily was neat and quick with numbers. In their individual cases, the combination had made for powerful intellects.

We belong together, she thought. *Marcus could help me solve the discrepancies in my data. But I can't trust him.*

Most of what he said was useful and right. She'd also learned to listen for his lies. He slanted everything in his own interest. Each time she visited, it felt like a mental tug-of-war. She needed him. He was an incredible asset, yet Emily questioned his motives even as she sympathized with his pain.

What if Marcus had been coaching some of the other scientists through the first stages of a rebellion? He didn't want the bunker to last.

He wanted to find Roell. If he could cause the collapse of this stronghold, or merely introduce enough mayhem to escape his jail cell, Emily didn't suppose he cared what happened to the rest of them.

"I think someone's planning an attack inside the bunker," she said. If he reacted, she might be able to give the soldiers better information.

"Who?" he asked.

"Some of the civilians. It looks like they're counting the soldiers going in and out of the complex."

His face showed nothing.

"Why would anyone do that?" she asked. "We have so many problems already."

"People need trouble, Emily." He waved at the blank TV. "Look at our entertainment. We like to be scared because we have a huge capacity for fear. The most basic element of storytelling is conflict because we respond to it. If nothing's wrong, we'll create new conflicts."

"I don't believe you." Her world had been full of greed and infidelity, but the game she was playing with his ego depended on her appearing naive. It helped that she was younger and female.

He smiled. "Emily, our most innate phobias can be traced to early survival traits. Fear of heights. Fear of open space. Fear of blood. Fear of strangers. You're a biologist. You know nobody is ever afraid of paper or shoelaces. They obsess over things we're evolved to guard against. They want to have these things to worry about," he said, shifting and bending his left hand as he spoke.

She didn't think he was aware of his fidgeting. His brown eyes were distant and insane.

He felt an echo in his mind. On the surface, he remained Marcus Wolsinger, but he rolled his arm again and again compulsively. The muscle memory went beneath his waking thoughts. He almost remembered.

No one who hadn't felt that superconsciousness would understand. He wished he could show Emily, but she wasn't one of the chosen.

Most of the people in his old life would be strangers to him now. Marcus thought of his ex-wife. All of the excuses Janet gave for divorcing him had been why she'd loved him at the start—because he paid the bills on time, because he remembered birthdays and anniversaries. He'd provided the stability she'd lacked in her childhood, but it hadn't been enough. He was too awkward at participating in the excitement she craved, crowds, dancing, gossip, drinks. Eventually she'd left their perfect lives for a new adventure.

Roell had felt directionless for the same reason. Life had been too easy. They'd complained about gas prices and food prices and their wireless bill, which were fantastic luxuries. Even on Marcus's middle-class salary, before Janet went to work, they had been richer than 99.99 percent of human beings who'd ever lived. The grocery stores were loaded, their nation had the industrial might to roll off three cars per household, and every other family had the money to feed two pets in addition to their kids.

We were so lucky, he thought. *Too lucky.*

Every day had been a fleeting treasure. They should have cherished their time together. Instead, they'd quarreled and looked away from each other in discontent.

"Marcus?" Emily asked.

He tore himself from his memories, blinking at the bare walls of his cell. "We're programmed for hardship," he said. "People are happiest when they're working themselves to the bone."

"No. Everyone in this bunker is stressed past the breaking point."

"We're evolved for less food, more exercise, less sleep, less security, more paranoia. The irony is that as a species, *Homo sapiens* was stupendously successful. It became normal to have more food, less exercise, more sleep, more security, less paranoia. Why do you think so many people were prone to obesity and depression? Insomnia? Drug addiction? We were stagnating."

"I, uh . . ."

Emily hesitated, and Marcus knew why. She'd told him about her work before the pulse. As part of her autism research, she'd brought forth new data that indicated a weakening gene pool. The discovery ate at her as if unearthing the trend made it her responsibility. Now he used her guilt against her.

"Widespread illness and cognitive disorders, our disaffected youth—these were symptoms of overpopulation," he said. "Our lives were too soft, too cerebral, too different from everything we were meant to be."

He believed it. Otherwise the decay in his relationships would have been his fault.

Putting the firmness back in her voice, Emily said, "A lot of people think the pulse may be intermittent. Bill Elledge swears it will stop."

"He's wrong."

Emily wanted to slap him. She controlled herself. She fought down her helpless rage and said, "Even if the flares last, that doesn't mean we should give up. We can do something about it. We're safe in here."

"For how long? Barely half of you are breeding age. That's not enough to sustain a viable population."

"There are other shelters," Emily said. "If the flares last, we'll figure something out. The men could rotate. We'll make these caves bigger."

She'd just proposed an insemination program as casually as she might have discussed tonight's dinner, but Marcus ignored her.

"For the past month, the oceans have been steaming," he said. "The rain at sea level fell as snow in the mountains and at the poles. It's counterintuitive, but intensifying solar heat will cause a cooling effect. There's too much moisture in our atmosphere. The ice caps are growing, the higher elevations have turned white, and Earth's albedo is increasing at an exponential rate. More and more of the sun's heat will reflect back into space. Soon the balance will tip. The cold will create new weather patterns, drawing more water from the oceans. There will be more and more snow."

"But that's exactly what I mean," she said. "I don't understand how you could want to leave this bunker. I know you want to find Roell."

"It's more than that."

"Marcus, people are dying out there."

"Some of them. They'll either adapt or they'll disappear. You and I both know who's best suited for another Ice Age."

Emily lowered her gaze in disgust. It was one thing for him to say they should walk outside. He belonged to the dominant species, whereas she would be vulnerable, especially with her looks.

Biologists attributed the appearance of blond hair and blue eyes in Caucasians to sexual displays like parrots' feathers. Their diet and their environment had allowed for those small mutations, which persisted, then spread.

Colorful differences to attract mates would be even more important among people in a primitive state. If she was forced outside, she would never be alone—never have a choice—and she would probably give birth to children with the same physical allure.

Emily couldn't keep the resentment from her voice. "People like you aren't real Neanderthals," she said.

Marcus was implacable. "Their children will have children who will be," he said. "The rise in background radiation will accelerate the change. Then the best of them will breed with each other."

Emily winced. Eons of heightened radiation, ash, temperature changes, and the necessity to survive at times on weeds or bark might explain why humankind had so many digestive and blood-screening organs that no one fully understood.

The adenoids, the appendix, the gallbladder, and the spleen were all filtering organs that could be surgically removed without fatally affecting the patient.

Under enough environmental pressure, those organs might become vital again.

Short, furiously evolving generations, she thought, envisioning the future in her mind. It was an empty feeling. The die-offs would be steep in all living things. But like a crucible, the storm-swept environment would purify the hybrid Neanderthals, leaving only their strongest.

Would they grow thicker and shorter until they physically resembled their ancestors? They were already more cohesive than *Homo sapiens*. If they also regained their musculature, every war across the planet would be brief. *Homo sapiens* would be driven from the best territories and left to persist in the deserts, the barren plains, and the rotting old concrete cities.

How could Marcus be so heartless? Because he was right?

Emily had one last card to play. "What if I could cure you and Roell?" she asked.

Marcus's gaze sharpened on her for a moment. Then he turned away again as if drawn by something inside. His left hand continued to flex. "You can't," he said.

"I can. I'm getting close."

"Emily," he said. "Let me go."

She stammered in surprise. He'd never asked outright before. "Th-that's not up to me," she said.

"You could talk to them. Let me go. There's so little time."

"You mean because something's going to happen," she said, finally drawing him back on topic. "What are the marks on the hatches into the complex?"

Marcus sidestepped her question. "Do you know the Fermi Paradox?" he asked.

I shouldn't have come to see him, she thought. He kept hammering at her, kept trying to coax her over the brink. She needed an anchor instead. She needed Drew to talk some sense into her because Marcus's obsession was catching.

"Years before the SETI Project, a physicist named Enrico Fermi pointed out Earth should have been overrun with aliens if we weren't alone," Marcus said. "There are as many as ten to the twenty-first stars in the universe."

She knew *10 to the 21st* meant 1,000,000,000,000,000,000,000—a stupefying amount.

"Many are yellow suns like ours," Marcus said. "Most of them have planets. But if G-stars aren't as stable as we thought, there may not be anything more advanced than bacteria in galaxy after galaxy after galaxy."

"That's impossible. With so many stars, there must be other living worlds."

"All of them burned." His voice was mixed with fervor and despair. "I wasted my life looking for something that doesn't exist. I should have known."

"Marcus, this isn't you talking."

"I want to be with my son as long as I can."

"You were hurt! Even before Drew saved you, you were starving and hurt."

"We were fine. Let me go."

The wall shook against Emily's chair as the front door of the trailer banged. Footsteps thumped in the hall. Then two soldiers entered the room. Emily stood up.

Marcus also rose. "What's happening?" he asked.

"Stay where you are, sir," one of the soldiers said.

Emily stepped toward the armed men. She didn't know if they were rounding up suspects or if they'd come to protect her, but she wanted to leave if Marcus intended to yell or fight. She saw an indelible hint of the top-heavy Neanderthal pose in him, menacing and strange.

"Emily, wait," he said.

This is who he really is, she thought. *I've been fooling myself wanting him to be something he's not.*

"Wait!"

She turned her back and left, second-guessing herself with every step as the soldiers led her through the trailer.

We can never let him outside, she thought. *Not unless we've given up.* If Marcus retained even half of his cunning after turning Neanderthal again in the pulse, he could become their greatest Nim.

Right now, the Neanderthals seemed disorganized. Each tribe was its own entity. What if one man united them?

Emily shuddered at the notion as she followed the soldiers into the cavern's chill air and shadows. Another soldier waited at the stairwell into the complex. She heard no other people or sounds. Were they taking her prisoner?

"I need to talk to General Strickland," she said.

A soldier closed his hand on her arm. "Let's get you inside," he said. It wasn't an answer, but Emily didn't argue. Entering the complex seemed like the right direction, and she didn't have the energy to fight.

From the day they'd met, the fact that Marcus turned Neanderthal had destroyed Emily's working theories. He was borderline OCD with a high IQ, yet he didn't fit her profile. Neither did his descriptions of Roell or Rebecca.

Other labs had proven that not everyone with autism became Neanderthal. Conversely, not everyone who turned Neanderthal was autistic. A far more subtle combination was at play in the human genome, so Emily had begun a new line of research, abandoning her initial efforts and starting over.

This morning she'd seen results at last—results that were too disturbing to share with Marcus. Her results were why she'd tried to find Drew.

She remembered thinking P.J. was better off outside the burning hospital. From there, it had been a short jump to questioning herself, and her self-doubt had been fertile ground for even greater misgivings. Originally, she'd hoped to fix Marcus and everyone like him. Now her misery held a darker thought.

If the geomagnetic storms were permanent—if she was their only salvation—Emily might be able to reverse-engineer her gene therapies. She could unlock the protein expression patterns that would make *everyone* Neanderthal, including herself.

NORTHERN CALIFORNIA

Shh, boy," Drew said, scratching the ruff of Orion's neck. The golden retriever crouched between Drew and another man on a hillside above the Feather River, which had overflowed, creating a broad, muddy current dotted with tall cottonwood trees. Incongruously, the top of a SPEED LIMIT 35 MPH sign also rose from the water. A road lay beneath the flood.

Across the valley, dozens of homes sat in the river, but those shapes were difficult to see through the gray drizzle of the rain.

Drew kept his 17x SSDS sniper's scope aimed upstream, watching the people in the mist with his good eye. Four hundred yards away, a Neanderthal tribe bunched together among more cottonwoods and walnut trees. "I count thirty," he whispered.

"Shit."

"Don't move. We'll let them go first."

"Shit. Oh shit." The man on the other side of Orion scribbled on his waterproof pad, then tucked it away and shouldered his M4.

The three of them lay on their bellies, the two men and the dog. Drew had steadied his 7.62mm M40A5 sniper's rifle on a broken oak branch with one hand in order to sink his other fingers into Orion's fur.

He was careful not to tug at the custom-fit mesh sleeve on the retriever's skull. Like both men, Orion wore M-string. His trainer said he'd removed it once under controlled circumstances. Orion had turned feral, snapping at his trainer and the other observers. If he hadn't been leashed, he would have run. Like cats and horses, dogs were smart enough to lose something in the pulse. Higher mammals such as apes and elephants were surely affected, too.

In his right mind, Orion enjoyed contact. So did Drew. Golden retrievers were sweet dogs and eager to please. Drew took as much comfort in Orion's loyalty and warmth as in the canine's heightened senses, which reached much farther than Drew's ears and nose. Orion was like a living radar unit even in the storm.

Sleet pattered through the willow brush and the tangle of the uprooted tree he'd chosen for their hiding place. The icy rain drummed on his helmet and soaked through his jacket collar and his pants, drawing away his body heat everywhere except his scalp and his torso, which was wrapped in the firm, clammy bulk of a Kevlar vest. His boots were wet. His gloves were wet. His fatigues and long johns and underwear were wet.

He knew he shouldn't love it out here, but he did. The freedom he possessed on each mission came with many risks, and yet the desolation held undeniable beauty.

Rain slashed at the slow-moving water. The wind whipped through the trees. There was a timeless Zen quality to the landscape, in part because the clouds reduced the light to a constant heavy gloom except at dawn and sunset. Every day felt identical.

It was the enemy that was changing.

Something's not right, Drew thought, moving his scope from the Neanderthal group to the river.

The trees and brush submerged in the flood were snarled with natural debris and garbage—plastic bags, bottles, cans, and more eye-catching things like a toy robot and a blue sofa cushion. Much nearer, several cars had lodged themselves in the shallows, adding steel-and-glass boulders to the mess.

But in places, the junk looked like it had been stacked or fitted together, creating handholds for anyone trying to cross the river. Why would the Neanderthals bother to construct something so permanent unless more of them had come through here or were on their way?

"I think other tribes have crossed here before," Drew whispered. "The water must be shallower than it looks, and check out the bank. There are too many footprints in the mud."

"Shit."

"How close could someone get behind us before Orion smelled him?"

"In this wind? A hundred feet. Closer. Oh shit."

Orion's handler, Bob Macaulay, had been a civilian trainer attached to a sheriff's unit before the pulse. He was brave and willing, but wholly out of his element.

As a pair, Macaulay and Orion were certified in wilderness, avalanche, and urban search and rescue. Now they ran combat ops with Drew. Their shattered nation had been reduced to using every available resource to evaluate and track the Neanderthals. Sometimes they also engaged the enemy, harassing scouts or entire tribes away from valuable sites. Operatives like Drew were also collecting blood and hair samples, not only to develop vaccines or cures but also for bioweapons specifically designed to incapacitate or kill the Neanderthals.

He hadn't told Emily about the weapon programs, some of which were under way in Bunker Seven Four directly alongside her own research. There was a lot he hadn't told her. She would despise him for taking any part in genocide even if it wasn't his decision. He was under orders. In any case, those programs were classified, which meant instead of arguing with her, he could enjoy her smile each time he went back inside.

Emily was dependable, sensible, and brilliant, not as hard as Julie, yet equally tough. She was unselfish.

The influence of her example had made Drew a better leader. He glanced past Orion at Macaulay, wanting to encourage him. Macaulay's skin was pale beneath his helmet, especially in contrast to his red beard, although most of his lack of color was due to his Irish heritage and a month without sun. Macaulay's eyes were steady, if frightened.

Drew nodded in approval. He'd tried to drill it into all of his men that they were no longer lions. They were mice. They had aircraft and firepower, body armor, binoculars—and they would be overwhelmed in a toe-to-toe fight.

They were the minority now. Just today, including this new group, Drew had spotted half as many Neanderthals as the total population of Bunker Seven Four. The maps in his breast pocket were scrawled with circles and arrows projecting the locations of twelve known tribes.

The enemy was on the move, heading east and north. Despite the weather, the Neanderthals were hiking into the foothills of the Sierra Nevada range. Aerial surveillance indicated that some of them had gone deep into the mountains. Apparently they'd mobilized across the continent. No one was certain what they were doing, but their migration kept them in constant contact with the ROMEO and Army squads outside. The platoon of Special Forces at the Hoffman Square Kilometer Field had been brushed aside twice, surviving only because they fell back. The array would have been lost if the Neanderthals had any interest in destroying it. Instead, the enemy merely passed through.

Marcus said the Neanderthals were drawn north because modern-day America was too warm even with the rain. Their instincts were geared toward colder climates.

Independently, Emily had pointed out the geographic similarities between California and Europe. The oceans were to the west, the wind came inland, and there were mountains visible in the east. This place was a lot like the Neanderthals' ancestral home. Maybe they were more fixated on the West Coast because of it. Drew had never seen anything like this dogged human tide. Nothing stopped them—not the flooding; not the dense wreckage on the highways; not the hundreds of thousands of primitive *Homo sapiens* in their paths.

More and more, they also looked the part. Their hair was long and knotted. The men wore beards. They'd found canvas and leather in the abandoned towns, fashioning rough vests, kilts, and leggings. Their weapons were bone and rock.

"Okay, the tribe's getting up," Drew whispered. "Scouts first. If I say so, run."

"You think they saw us?"

"No. But if they circle into these trees, they might. Leave your pack. Weapons only."

Macaulay looked at Orion. His first priority was his dog. The two of them were like brothers. The golden retriever's fur was lighter than Macaulay's red-brown hair, but not by much. Consciously or not, Drew supposed their similar coloring was why Macaulay had picked Orion as a pup.

I'm sorry, Drew added silently, watching six of the Neanderthals trudge in their direction, then split in half. One threesome angled away. The other trio came straight at them, probably to gain a vantage point on the hilltop.

Drew had been too aggressive in sneaking closer when Orion detected a human scent. He owed it to Julie. If he didn't succeed, her sacrifice was a waste. That was why he'd overcommitted. He'd hoped Orion had found a lone trio of hunters far from their tribe, so he'd left the rest of his eight-man team on the other side of the hill in order to minimize noise and movement, crawling after Orion through the oak and brush. Both Drew and Macaulay carried Tasers for subduing the enemy at close range. They could have handled three hunters. A tribe was too much.

What could he do? He had no way to call in air support. They'd left the Osprey at Beale AFB to conserve fuel and wear and tear, hiking the seventeen miles to the river, and radios didn't work in the pulse.

There also wasn't as much cover as he would have liked. At this elevation, a few hundred feet above sea level, the environment was in jeopardy. Week after week of rain and near-freezing nights had confused the oaks and cottonwoods. Their leaves had browned, then ripped away in the storms. Then the heaviest trees pulled loose from the sodden earth as the hillsides crumbled and slid.

The mud should have been an equalizer, also slowing the Neanderthals, but Drew knew how tireless they could be. More unsettling, he'd also heard of several cases in which Neanderthals had been identified as handicapped people who'd risen from their wheelchairs or other medical assists. Something in the brain was making them stronger. They were rewired for incredible endurance.

Drew guessed he had two minutes before the scouts either discovered his position or went past.

Two minutes was an eternity. He settled even more fully into the mud, growing still. If he couldn't gather hair and blood for DNA, his next objective was to record individual details. Across the world, mathematicians were running stats in every effort to help the geneticists and mission planners.

"I see two women in the group," he whispered. "They've also got an old guy about fifty."

Macaulay squirmed behind his M4. "I don't have my pad out," he hissed.

"Just help me remember." Females were rare. So were adults older than forty, like Marcus. "One of the women has Down's features. I think she—"

Macaulay began to rise. "They're too close!"

"Shhh." Drew scrunched his fingers in Orion's fur again as if doing so might calm Macaulay. The dog had started to growl inside his chest, reacting to his partner's fear as the nearest scouts reached the base of the slope.

This game of hide-and-seek would have been different in the mountains, where evergreens were adapted to winter temperatures. Snow levels were fluctuating between four and six thousand feet elevation at night. When the seasons changed to autumn and winter, it would come lower. Much lower.

What would these valleys look like in two hundred years? Marcus said the pine forests would expand as deciduous species like walnut, oak, and cottonwood retreated all the way to the ocean, persisting only in the warmest regions along the coast.

There were Christians inside the bunker who called the deluge another Great Flood. Marcus said flood myths appeared in most cultures around the world. A few were stories of natural disasters like Atlantis, which some geologists attributed to the Thera volcanic explosion and tsunamis in the Mediterranean in 1600 B.C. or the catastrophic flooding of the Black Sea four thousand years earlier. More common were accounts of divine punishment visited upon mankind by various gods, such as the Biblical and Quranic accounts of Noah's ark or the much older Sumerian epic of Gilgamesh. Places as diverse as Fiji, Iceland, South America, North America, and Asia all had legends in which only the righteous survived or in which human beings first arose from primeval waters that had cleansed the planet.

Drew thought that sounded a lot like people who'd woken up after a period of flares. Seismic and volcanic activity caused by the pulse, in tandem with rapid climate change, must have slammed Earth again and again—and it wasn't only plant life that was fading.

He'd seen flocks of birds clinging weakly to rooftops and trees. Others lay dead by the hundreds like wet leaves made of feathers and claws.

A few birds would survive and adapt. They'd done it before. They would do it again. Drew was a long way from giving up. Like men, animals were tenacious. Some of the reptiles would hibernate out of season, trying to outlast the rain, and he rejoiced each time he spotted a dripping wet coyote or mud-faced raccoons. Countless rodents lay drowned in the fields or jammed like driftwood on the riverbanks with larger creatures like cattle and human beings.

The primitive *Homo sapiens* were starving. They were sick. Drew estimated the death toll in the tens of thousands. No one could keep fires burning in the rain, and the drowned animals were rotting and contaminated.

The worst part was they were surrounded by homes and supermarkets, but they didn't understand cans or boxes or bags. In the first few days, they'd devoured the fresh produce and bread. Then they began to go hungry or ate raw meat or grass or leaves, which wasn't enough. Again and again Drew had seen the primitives huddling together like birds—thirty of them on a farmhouse porch, ten of them on the lee side of a ridge—listless and weak, dully waiting for a break in the downpour.

Only the Neanderthals were thriving. They were better at scavenging edible roots and bark. They also hunted more successfully.

If the Neanderthals were going to hike the distance to Canada and stay there, Drew was inclined to let them. Living in separate worlds seemed like the only solution, because in several areas, the Neanderthals had made a campaign of killing every primitive they could find. U.S. Command thought they might focus on American bunkers next. The enemy appeared to be moving north, but several trios had returned to the Sacramento Valley either as guides or observers.

These envoys joined the tribes still finding their way through the floods. Drew had identified six envoys himself and, in theater briefs, had been given descriptions of nine more in the area. All were young males.

They were the hardiest scouts. There was no question they carried messages such as *I can show you where we crossed the river* or *We found shelter here.* What if they were also firming up intel like *There are* Homo sapiens *in that mountain?* Organized war might not be far off, which was another development Drew had been ordered to keep from Emily and everyone else who didn't wear a uniform. The civilians inside Bunker Seven Four thought they had it bad. He'd heard their complaints. But the reality was much more bleak.

"Fire on my command," he whispered.

The scouts were almost on top of his position. Rain swirled between them.

At the last moment, the Neanderthals angled east, detouring around the deadfall. The crown of the giant oak tree had shattered over an area of sixty feet, covering the ground with branches and heavier sections of trunk.

"Nnnnnnmh," one of the scouts sang. Maybe the deadfall looked impassable. Drew thought they'd seen him.

Then they were gone. Macaulay exhaled and Orion ducked his muzzle into Macaulay's ribs and armpit, avoiding Macaulay's M4, yet sharing the man's relief.

Drew aimed his scope through the trees to the east, making sure the scouts weren't doubling back. Finally, he stole another glance at the riverbank. The main pack had left the stand of cottonwoods. A sagging fence barely slowed them. In front was a man who must have been their dominant Nim. At his side was a young black man, tall and well-muscled with four distinctive scabs on his cheek where he appeared to have been clawed by a human hand.

Drew had seen the young man twice before with other groups. "They have an envoy," he whispered.

Macaulay nodded as he rubbed his gun hand in Orion's fur and watched the trees, making no move to bring out his notepad. Macaulay was done. He didn't want more information. It wouldn't have meant as much to him in any case because he had no personal connection with the tribe.

The envoy was Roell Wolsinger.

Drew had to let Roell go. Watching him was fascinating. As the tribe walked with the blowing rain, they maintained a circular formation in order to protect their women, their injured, and their oldest. The wind was unable to breach the line of hunters on the outside. Even the rain must have been less for those in the middle.

No one seemed to question their place in the circle. If healthy, the men took the outside positions. If hurt, they moved inside and stayed inside until they healed or until there was a need. When the tribe was threatened, or when they sent hunters to find food, even the injured and the old stepped up, replenishing each gap in the ring.

During the first days of the pulse, the Neanderthals had weeded out any hybrids who misunderstood this fluid dance. Position, hierarchy, response, and reset were ingrained in their best people. Now the tribe was silent. They were as pure as they could be in modern bodies.

"Let's get back to our team." Drew slung his pack, grimacing at the weight. He was exhausted, but there was no help for it. The forty-pound rucksack held rations, clean water, ammunition, blood collection kits, and chemical cold packs to keep any samples cool.

Drew let Macaulay and Orion take the lead as they slogged from one oak tree to another. The ground was sturdier above the roots. The trail they'd left pinged back and forth from tree to tree, providing cover and traction.

Ten minutes later they rejoined their team, an unconventional mix of three Air Force commandos, one Army Ranger, Bugle, and Patrick. Drew traded fist jabs with Bugle as the other men rubbed Orion's neck for luck.

Bugle had a cold. His eyes and long nose were red with irritation. "What's the scoop?" he asked.

"Good news, bad news," Drew said. "We found a place where the tribes are crossing the river, so this area will be good hunting. The bad news is there's thirty of 'em over the hill right now, circling east. Their scouts might have seen us."

"We have news, too, sir," Patrick said, pointing southward. His arm had healed and his cast was gone. "There's another tribe behind us about three klicks out. Northbound. I think they'll miss us."

"How many?"

"Fifty."

"We'll evade," Drew said, pulling his map from his pocket. "Let's boogey off this hill and sit down on the next one in case the first tribe comes looking for us. We'll wait out both groups. If the second tribe comes close enough, we can write more stats for the math guys."

Bugle laughed.

"Commander?" Macaulay said. "You don't think they're boxing us on purpose, do you?"

"I don't know."

Sometimes it seemed like the enemy was capable of long-distance communication, one group attracting another from miles away. If Emily was right, it was because they all thought the same, so they made the same decisions as they fended their way through the landscape.

The rain increased as Drew's team angled across the slope, riding the weight of their packs. Going down was harder than hiking up. In his wet socks, Drew's feet had blistered and half-healed and blistered again and rubbed raw. Bruises covered his elbows and knees. Each of them walked with his own suffering. Small pain was unimportant. They topped the next hill in five minutes and organized a perimeter.

Drew carried his rifle to the east side, where a clear patch in the oaks and buckeyes allowed him to gaze out at the rolling terrain.

Brown creeks. Brown ponds. Brown trees. Brown earth. There was no sign of either tribe. That made him nervous.

"*Sst!* Bugle," he hissed.

His friend ambled through the rain like an overgrown spider, both arms extended to let the water run from his shoulders and neck. "They were past the ridgeline," Bugle said.

"What if Macaulay's right? We've seen them do too much spooky voodoo."

"Amen to that."

"Fifty Neanderthals are probably two or three tribes that merged together. Maybe one of them is that group we hit last week. Either way, if they join the tribe that just came across the river, the whole pack will probably know we're here."

Bugle nodded. "Emily would say bet on it."

Drew didn't want to talk about her. Bugle had been hot for Emily since the beginning, chatting her up, cracking his jokes. Drew couldn't compete with Bugle's noise. Did she like Bugle? She definitely laughed with him. The dude was a ray of light. He was also Drew's best friend, and Drew felt bad for entertaining his own thoughts about her.

"Maybe we'll get lucky and hit another interval," Bugle said. "That guy Elledge swore it'll happen again."

"Maybe."

The greatest secret they'd kept from the civilians was that the pulse had stopped three times in the past eleven days. The first interval lasted eight minutes. The third lasted twenty-six, but so far the second break had been the granddaddy of them all. It lasted seven and a half hours.

The sun was sputtering.

Would it stop altogether?

Some of the astrophysicists said the intervals could mean an end to the flares that caused the pulse, and yet U.S. Command decided this information was strictly need-to-know. General Strickland had censored the data from the Hoffman Square Kilometer Field to keep any sign of the intervals from Marcus and other consultants because he was concerned that the civilians in the bunker would demand to be let outside.

There was never going to be anything they could do about the sun except wait. A few geeks had talked about sending rocketfuls of nano-tech into the photosphere and reconfiguring its composition. Other jarheads wanted to launch hundreds of nukes at the sun. They thought a few thousand megatons could disrupt the flares, but the nanobot guys admitted they were years from being able to design anything like what they'd proposed, and the jarheads didn't realize how goddamned careful they needed to be with their arsenal.

With each break in the pulse, as soon as they were able to bring their remaining systems online, the U.S. went from DEFCON 2 to maximum alert, watching for Chinese missile launches. In the South China Sea, the *America* and its strike group prepared to repel enemy planes or destroyers.

The diplomats had initiated attempts to meet via radio or satellite, but China's government and military appeared even more damaged than their U.S. counterparts. Communications were sporadic. Their chain of command had fractured. Neither side had much left except its network of bunkers and silos, and the personnel inside those holes were trained for war, equipped for war, and ready for it.

When the pulse stopped, what the Chinese saw was the Western world on full alert. They responded. Then U.S. forces escalated in kind. It was a reflex scenario. The deadly seesaw of early warning and targeting systems was like an out-of-whack Rube Goldberg machine designed to bang away at itself until it erupted in nuclear fire.

That's who we are, Drew thought, shifting in the cold. Twenty minutes had passed without any sign of the Neanderthals, but he was patient.

He brooded.

Nobody could argue that the Neanderthals weren't better suited for the pulse than the primitives—the millions of poor, stupid, inarticulate *Homo sapiens* who'd been caught outside without M-string. But in some ways, the Neanderthals were also better than thinking men like himself.

The Neanderthals didn't bother themselves with self-induced conflicts like power grabs or arguments of any kind. As far as anyone could tell, they had no politics or religion. Unlike primitive *Homo sapiens*, the Neanderthals weren't interested in race, either. They identified each other in more profound ways. Most of them were white, but Roell was hardly the only minority Drew had seen. Drew believed they would be supremely peaceful if left alone.

He worried that by stalking the enemy, teams like his own were attracting attention to themselves. That would be a very human predicament, monkeying with a situation for the sheer sake of monkeying with it when the best thing might have been to keep their distance.

One benefit of the intervals was that the Neanderthal armies had been slower to form. Each break disrupted the enemy, scattering their tribes when they regained their normal personalities.

During the longest interval, American strongholds had been forced to hide from or repel their own people. Bunker Seven Four was too remote to have been swarmed by refugees. Only a few survivors reached their fences and were driven away, and yet the awful, bloody, recurring equation of condemning a majority to save a few had hardened Drew's resolve.

Outside, he was pitiless. Inside, the warmth he fought to protect meant everything. He'd warned himself that he didn't need the complication of a relationship with a civilian, but he thought about Emily constantly.

Her fiancé was dead. Julie was dead. All of them could die any day if the sun went supernova or in Chinese or Neanderthal attacks.

How long was it right to wait?

And . . . what if she learned about the decisions he'd been forced to make? Emily was a good person. She wouldn't approve.

Seven hours between interrupts could have been enough time for Drew to lead the survivors to shelter and treat their wounded. Operatives like himself could be rescuing people every day. Instead, he danced with the enemy. During the longest interval, his team had gathered more blood and hair samples than in the past three weeks combined. For her. He did it for her.

Movement, Drew thought. He straightened behind his rifle, bringing the scope back to his left.

Nine hundred yards east, three scouts had emerged from a seam in the rolling grassland. They hurried north through the rain. Minutes later, their tribe appeared behind them.

Nothing else moved on the brown earth but brown water. Then another, smaller tribe jogged from a gully. Roell's tribe. They were headed straight for the larger group.

"Bugle," Drew whispered.

His friend had been catnapping but woke in an instant. "What do we got?" Bugle asked.

The leader of the larger group was a kid. Skinny and blond, the boy looked like he was crippled. One arm hung at his side. Drew nearly dropped his rifle. "Oh fuck."

"They coming at us?"

"No. Look at the front of the larger group."

Bugle lifted his M4, which was also mounted with an SSDS scope. "I see 'em. So what?"

The boy must have been critically wounded. Was it possible that he'd stood up again, recovered, and walked all the way from Los Angeles? Drew knew the answer was yes. He'd confronted the Neanderthal super endurance again and again, and yet he clenched his hands on his rifle as if trying to pull himself away from what he was witnessing.

"P.J. is alive," he said.

BUNKER SEVEN FOUR

Drew looked for Emily as he limped into the tunnel without his pack, jacket, helmet, or vest, carrying his rifle and a waterproof satchel. The electric lights were comforting. So were the sounds of his men's boots on clean, dry concrete. Unfortunately, leaving the ready room had been complicated. Their debriefing officer had been less interested in their reports than in advising them of the developments inside the bunker.

I can't believe it, Drew thought.

At least eight civilians had plotted to take control of Seven Four and push the soldiers outside. Interrogations were under way. The debriefing officer hadn't told Drew all of the conspirators' names, but two of them had acquired handguns. Several more had hidden knives or metal bars among their belongings.

As his team shifted through the Humvees parked near the tunnel entrance, Drew nodded to a pair of Air Force sentries. Then he reached a forklift and the first stacks of pallets and crates. Beyond these fat blocks of supplies, the civilian living quarters formed three open rooms.

Shadows stretched over the uneven ceiling. Some were cast by the bumps in the rock. Most were the distorted shapes of the supplies. From deep in the tunnel, human sounds reached through the gap between the ceiling and the crates. Drew heard tense voices and a scraping metal-on-concrete noise like someone dragging a cot against the floor.

Two more Air Force sentries stood at the mouth of the walkway that led down the tunnel. They'd barred five civilians from intercepting Drew, making room for a Navy captain to speak to Drew instead.

"Commander Haldane!" one of the civilians called, a geneticist he'd met in Emily's lab. "Sir? They said you had the blood and hair samples."

"We want to get the purple caps under refrigeration before the RNA degrades any further," another man said.

Drew ignored them and saluted the Navy captain. Word had obviously spread that he'd returned, but he didn't see Emily, which made him antsy. *What if she's one of the people in lockup?* he thought.

"Good afternoon, Commander," the captain said.

"Sir."

"I need a few minutes. The rest of your team is dismissed until sixteen hundred. Then you'll rotate into the guard shift. We're stretched thin, so make sure you get chow and hot showers. They also have a tub ready for your K-9."

"Thank you, sir," Macaulay said, extending his hand to Orion.

All of them smelled like sweat and mud. Orion's damp, matted fur exuded a dog stink that wasn't unpleasant to live with, but the odor must have been staggering to the bunker personnel—and Drew's team had been ordered inside the complex, where they'd be in closer quarters than in the tunnel.

The military and civilian populations of Bunker Seven Four were under total quarantine from each other. If Drew was going to find Emily, the walk into the complex was his best chance unless he volunteered to stand watch immediately. That would seem odd after a five-day mission outside.

"Give the eggheads our samples," Drew told Bugle, handing him the satchel as one of the scientists called, "Are there notes describing each sample donor?"

"No," Drew said. "I've got a lot of shorthand, but I can make sense of it for you as soon as I sit down and eat."

"Excellent," the scientist said. "We're in Lab One."

"I'll meet you there," Drew said. He hoped he'd find Emily in the trailers, of course. That was why he hadn't given them his notes.

The tunnel echoed with footsteps and voices as Bugle and the rest of his team left. The scientists hurried after them.

"Walk with me," the Navy captain said.

"Yes, sir." Drew followed the captain through the irregular stacks of crates, boxes, plastic-wrapped pallets, and the loose items on top like sewing machines, lawn mowers, garden hoses, lamps, and coffee tables. When his scavenging crews hadn't been able to find food or fuel, they'd taken everything else the aircraft could carry. Someday they might need motors or furniture—the furniture could serve as firewood.

Captain Fuelling was a short man with a knot in the bridge of his nose where it had been broken and healed poorly. He was also the senior ROMEO contact inside Bunker Seven Four.

It's bad news, Drew thought.

Fuelling had only spoken to him in private twice before, first to establish their bona fides, then to share a covert assessment of Seven Four's viability. The DIA considered the installation highly unstable, yet no one could spare the aircraft to relocate Seven Four's civilian element. Not even ROMEO had tried to muster a relocation force. They'd instructed Drew to scavenge as many luxuries as his team could find, simple things like chocolate and shampoo, in hope of calming the refugees.

They should have done more.

Maybe our agency is actively taking charge, Drew thought. They might run damage control in order to keep the imprisoned scientists working. But how?

ROMEO operatives were sanctioned to act outside the military justice code. Technically, they were federal agents. As such, they weren't beholden to the Navy or U.S. Command.

Drew was not a thug. He would refuse to torture anyone if that's what his superiors wanted, but he wasn't above intimidating the eggheads who'd organized the conspiracy. *A walk outside might be exactly what they need,* he thought as Fuelling led him into a pocket of darkness where he remembered light.

One of the sleeping areas had been shut down in order to pack the civilians into fewer spaces. They didn't have enough military personnel to secure more real estate.

In the empty space, Fuelling stopped Drew. "I have new intel and contingency plans for your ears only," Fuelling said. "Lieutenant Buegeleisen and Sergeant Patrick are unauthorized for these directives."

"Aye, sir."

"Some of it may be hard to hear."

"Is this about the civilian takeover?"

"Affirmative. There's something you need to know," Fuelling said, watching his eyes.

Drew waited.

Whatever Fuelling saw in him—anger, commitment—it was the correct response. Fuelling said, "The civilian insurrection wasn't limited to this bunker."

"I don't understand, sir. How could they talk to each other outside this shelter?"

"I need your oath before I tell you more," Fuelling said. "I want your word as a ROMEO operative."

"Aye, sir," Drew said.

Standing in the shadows, Fuelling spoke for ten minutes in a low, insistent tone. He raised his voice once when Drew objected. Then he returned to his fierce tone. His eyes gleamed ominously. His gestures were short and clipped.

Finally, Drew nodded. "Aye, sir," he said.

Near the blast door into the complex, Drew found Bugle waiting for him. Floodlights lit the massive steel slab. Bugle rested against the pallets that separated the door from the third sleeping area in the tunnel, which danced with shadows and noise. Drew couldn't see the civilians on the other side of the pallets, but the ceiling flickered as they gestured or paced through their lights.

"You knew!" a woman shouted. "I think you knew and now we're stuck in here!"

They were tearing themselves apart.

Feeling uneasy, Drew walked toward his friend. He stopped when he realized Bugle's height obscured Emily. She sat with Bugle. Darkness hid her face, but Drew would have recognized her profile and her ponytail anywhere.

"Drew," she said from Bugle's shadow. She stood up.

"Are you all right?" Drew said.

"I'm so glad to see you." She lifted her chin to look at Bugle as she spoke, including Bugle in her sentiment even as she approached Drew.

Drew felt happy, too—happier than he'd anticipated. He'd been almost certain she hadn't taken part in the conspiracy, yet he'd worried when she wasn't at the front of the tunnel when he returned. "I, uh," he said.

"Em's the one who tipped off our guys about the mutiny," Bugle said, rising from the pallet to stand close to her again. He nudged her shoulder, and she smiled, but her body language was uncomfortable. She didn't want Bugle's affection.

Why hadn't Drew seen it before? Emily had put up with Bugle's flirting because the two of them were buddies, nothing more.

She and I are a better fit.

Drew couldn't articulate what he was thinking. "You're the one who warned General Strickland?" he asked.

"I didn't . . . It wasn't anything special," Emily said.

If there was shooting, we could have lost you, Drew thought. He extended his arm as if for a handshake. Instead, she hugged him abruptly, and Drew glanced past the blond halo of her hair at Bugle, his heart pounding. Could she hear it?

Bugle's face had tightened. The manner in which she'd embraced Drew, leaving Bugle, couldn't have made her preference more clear. Drew wondered how he was going to make it up to his friend as his arm tightened on her waist.

He tried to catch Bugle's eye, but Bugle wouldn't look at him.

Bugle walked to the blast door, which hung open just enough to admit people in single file. The touch of a button would close it in 1.4 seconds, locking fifty tons of concrete and tempered steel against the bulkhead of the tunnel wall.

Drew stayed with Emily. Hugging her, he remembered Julie, which felt awkward and strange. Was she worth any rift between himself and Bugle?

Worse, being with him would put her in new danger.

Emily deserved to hear that P.J. was alive, but Drew couldn't share any of the information Captain Fuelling had told him.

He's so nervous, Emily thought with a faint smile. *Me, too.*

In a normal world, the two of them might have been separated forever by duty and sorrow. Now, in his arms, she was exactly where she wanted to be.

His uniform smelled like fresh wind and rain and dirt. Beneath it, he stank. Drew hadn't bathed in days, but even that was a good smell, healthy and genuine. Emily thought of the rumors of the men taken into the women's shower. Then she flushed and kept her face nestled in the crook of his neck. Was it too soon?

She'd lost Chase. He missed Julie. She still wore her rings. But with so much turmoil and death, everyone needed positive relationships.

"Let's go inside," he said. "Is there coffee?"

Despite her emotions, she balked. She wasn't ready for a date. Not yet. Dating inside a doomsday bunker seemed unreal.

"It's just coffee," he said.

Emily sensed the tired grin in his voice and looked up. "I know." She knew what she wanted. Reassurance. Safety. Friendship. More.

Drew motioned toward the blast door. "Let's go."

Emily kissed his cheek, then separated herself from him. She wondered if he'd sensed the conflict of attraction and guilt in her eyes.

They slipped past the blast door and its thick locking bars, which protruded from its side like cylindrical teeth. Inside, the entry room was a smooth concrete box except for its rock ceiling. Like the tunnel, the entry room was a buffer meant to deflect shock waves from the complex. A second, smaller door like a bank vault stood across from them.

"I need to tell you something," Drew said.

Involuntarily, the fingers of her right hand gripped the rings on her left. What was he going to suggest? More than coffee? Emily tried to head him off. "Let me talk first," she said. "Please."

"It's about P.J."

Less than coffee, she thought. He'd changed his mind. Too much had happened between them. Her words came out rushed. "Shooting P.J. wasn't your fault, and I'm so sorry about Julie. Please don't say you and I can't—"

Drew stopped her. "Two days ago, my team saw P.J. outside," he said. "Your nephew is alive."

The reversal left her stunned. "But you shot him."

"He's one of the dominant Nims. He looks like his left arm hasn't healed. Except for that, he's fine."

"Here? How did he get here?"

Drew held her hand tighter. "You can't tell anyone I told you."

A bright new optimism woke inside her. "You need to save him!" she said, but Drew shook his head.

"Promise me," he said. "This is dangerous information. Right now, just us being together is dangerous."

Emily stared at their intertwined hands. "What do you mean?"

"You have to trust me," he said.

"I do." She would have followed him anywhere.

"My team couldn't reach him. Believe me."

"I do."

"If there was any chance of getting him, I would have tried," Drew said. "We had eight men. They had ninety. But there's more. Roell is in the area, too."

"Marcus's son?" Emily was astounded.

"Actually, it's not a huge coincidence." He told her about the massing Neanderthals and their envoys. "The flooding, the mountains, and the snow are bringing them through the middle part of the state."

She met his eyes. "Can I ask you something?"

"Anything."

Kiss me, she thought, but what she said was "I've completed my biomarker. I can tell you who'll become Neanderthal in the pulse and who won't. That's the first step in designing a cure, but there are more things we could do with it. Scary things."

"I'm sure," Drew said.

He didn't seem upset by the idea, so Emily was cautious. "We could screen for Neanderthal tendencies in unborn babies," she said. "It might be possible to remake humankind. We could abort fetuses who exhibit those traits."

"And you're not sure that's . . . ethical."

"I'm not sure it's *desirable*," she said. "What if the pulse lasts five thousand years? What are we going to do? We can't hide in here forever."

"You've been talking to Marcus."

"I wasn't, I," she stammered.

"Marcus is crazy. You know that, don't you?"

"I think he's seen things we haven't."

"He's crazy, Emily. Don't let him get to you." Drew tried to embrace her, but she pulled free with a fresh pang of guilt.

She couldn't ask Drew about developing a gene therapy meant to turn everyone Neanderthal. Drew would never quit. No matter how few of them were left, no matter how many years it took, Drew would fight.

He was who she needed to be with. Could she honestly claim the reverse was true?

I'm no good for you, she thought.

She needed to decide which direction to go. She could try to cure the Neanderthals. Or she might bring peace if she awakened that ancient mind in everyone.

To Drew, the choice must be obvious. But to her, the cost remained unclear. Was P.J. better off as a severely autistic boy muted within himself? Or was he happier and more productive as a functioning Neanderthal? Even a healthy kid like Roell appeared to become everything he desired during the pulse, competent and powerful, and Marcus had already made his decision, wanting the strong relationship with his son.

"What did Marcus say to you?" Drew asked.

"It's nothing."

"If we're going to . . . You said you trusted me."

"It's nothing," she said. "I know what I have to do."

Drew cupped both sides of her jawbone in his hands and kissed her. Emily rose against him, tugging down his forearms. She directed his palms to her hips before she wrapped her arms around his neck.

She wanted to feel his body against hers. She wanted to be as vulnerable as possible. Her breathing was shallow and quick when they broke for air.

"Emily," he said.

I know a private place, she thought, but he said, "I had twenty minutes before I needed to meet someone. I wanted to get coffee with you."

"We can."

He shook his head. "Don't come inside with me. Are you supposed to be in the labs? Either stay there or go back to your sleeping quarters."

"I won't."

Drew smiled, both sad and proud. Of her? "This isn't a joke," he said. "Go."

"Let me help."

"No," he said. "There's going to be more trouble."

35

· · · · · · · · · · · ·

BUNKER SEVEN FOUR

"Captain Fuelling ordered me to keep this information from you, but we've had each other's backs since day one," Drew told Bugle and Patrick. "I can't let you walk blind into our next mission."

"Thank you, sir," Patrick said.

The three of them stood in the central corridor on Level One. The complex felt deserted. On top on Level Three, a full crew occupied the command center. On One, nine men slept in the barracks behind Drew. The remainder of Seven Four's uniformed personnel were in the tunnel or at the labs, guarding their prisoners and the other civilians. Drew might have led Bugle and Patrick into a supply room for privacy, but if anyone noticed them, it would look funny. As long as they spoke in whispers, the empty corridor would suffice.

Standing in the open should also make it easier for them to believe my orders are legitimate, Drew thought. His head thrummed with anticipation. He was accustomed to prebattle nerves. What he didn't like was his own reluctance, so he concealed his doubt with a staunch tone.

"The Chinese EMP weapons are real," said. "Our ships and armored ground assets are failing at a higher rate than we can reconcile with the pulse, and the same thing is happening with our hardened aircraft. They're burning us off the map."

Patrick cursed. "What are we doing about it, sir?"

"DIA analysts found a pattern in the burnouts," Drew said. "They've linked it to attack satellites in polar orbit."

Bugle was unusually quiet. He held a Pop-Tart in one hand and used it as an excuse, chewing instead of talking. Drew hadn't had a chance to apologize about Emily. He'd found Bugle and Patrick in the cafeteria, and bringing them up to speed was more important than anyone's love life.

"Here's where we earn our pay," Drew said. He wanted Bugle to make a stupid remark like *Pay? When was the last time we got paid?*

Bugle inhaled the last of his Pop-Tart, stuffing his cheeks.

He really likes her, Drew thought, but they didn't have time to bicker. "The evidence is soft," Drew said. "Most of our satellites are gone, and the people at the Hoffman array are talking about probabilities instead of hard targets. The Chinese might have two attack satellites. They might have three. We know they're in low Earth orbit, but intercepting them will be a guessing game."

"We have more than three missiles, sir," Patrick said.

"The president and his advisors aren't convinced of the threat. The risk-reward is for shit. If we launch ASATs, China might think it's the front end of a full-scale attack and retaliate. Nobody wants a nuclear exchange."

"What about our generals, sir?"

"They're split. Their decision was to hunker down and wait."

"Sit and take it, sir?"

"My information is we've tried reprisal air strikes, but we don't have enough fighters off China's coast or long-range bombers at home. They've burned almost forty of our hardened aircraft out of the sky. Who knows how close they came to hitting our Osprey."

Patrick frowned. Drew had made it personal, which was his intent, because he was about to ask them to cross the most personal line of all. Nothing was more sacred than a man's loyalty—but the pulse had done more damage to the nation than any war. ROMEO's leadership would never have dreamed of taking matters into their own hands if America's last holdouts weren't scattered and separated.

As much as Drew sympathized with Bugle's indecision, they had a responsibility. They'd sworn to accept the toughest jobs even if the cost was their lives.

"The three of us and Fuelling represent the largest bloc of ROMEO operatives in any single bunker west of Colorado," Drew said. "There are also four Navy SEALs under Fuelling's command. He thinks the Marines will side with us, too, especially if you talk to them. They respect you, Sergeant."

"I'm not sure I follow, sir," Patrick said.

"We need to hit the Chinese satellites before we don't have the ability to launch at all. Captain Fuelling and I have been ordered to lead a bloodless takeover."

"Oh, fuck me," Bugle said.

Drew's voice sped up like a salesman's, desperate to convince his friend. "Fuelling was behind the civilian conspiracy," he said. "Fuelling talked to their ringleader early on and let him steal a pair of handguns—after removing the firing pins. The conspiracy fell apart sooner than Fuelling wanted, but it brought most of the bunker personnel out of the complex. No one's left inside to stop us. We take the command center, take General Strickland, and the place is ours. Nobody gets hurt."

"This bunker doesn't have any launch capacity, sir," Patrick said.

"Four weeks ago, PACOM sheltered two Aegis cruisers in the San Francisco Bay, the *Nickels* and the *Randolph*," Drew said. "They've both suffered some systems degradation, but the *Randolph* has jury-rigged repairs to its AN/SPY and the *Nickels* is carrying SM-3s."

The RIM-161 Standard Missile 3 was a battle-tested satellite killer. Their AN/SPY radar would be severely hampered by the pulse, as would the missile's in-flight communications with the *Randolph*, but Drew could match real-time solutions with data provided by the Hoffman array and other assets nationwide.

"We'll fly assault teams onto both ships under the guise of bringing in food and gear," he said. "Bugle and I are Navy officers. ROMEO also has a man on the *Nickels*. He'll help us take the bridge. Fuelling is in possession of the launch codes. We'll hit the Chinese satellites. Then at least we'll have a level playing field again."

"And after that, sir?"

"After that, we stand down. We get the job done, then we surrender. Then there are very good odds all of us will face courts-martial."

"Right. I just wanted to be clear, sir." Patrick might have laughed. He made a grunting sound in his throat, which Drew acknowledged with a nod. Patrick's unflappable nature made him a bulldozer of a man.

Drew's guts were in a knot. He was caught between two oaths, one to the Navy, one to ROMEO. His honor was at stake—and his memories of Julie.

It wasn't too late to warn General Strickland instead of helping Captain Fuelling. If he warned Strickland, Drew could ensure he wasn't lining himself up for a jail sentence. He wanted his life to count for something. But he was convinced it was for the greater good.

"Why us?" Bugle asked.

He's tired, Drew thought. *Me, too.* "The original data on China's EMP weapons was ours, so they knew we'd believe it. More than that, the other bunkers in range of Aegis ships are too secure. ROMEO didn't think there was any way to break a team loose."

"But the president—"

"We have to do this," Drew said. "If China keeps scratching at us for another month, or for a year, there won't be any working electronics in North America even if the pulse stops."

Patrick said, "When do we go, sir?"

"Three hours. The men sleeping in the barracks will relieve the guard shift outside. Our SEALs are ready to secure the complex doors. There'll be no one inside except us and six or seven men in the command center."

"Why can't we just grab the Osprey when we go back outside?" Bugle said.

"The bunker personnel will know we took it. They'll alert everyone else in the area. We need to control communications before we take off."

"Mutiny isn't the answer," Bugle said.

"I know what you're feeling—"

"We're supposed to be the good guys."

Bugle had never argued with him before, and Drew felt a glint of pride. He nearly grinned. In the moment, his reaction was perverse, but he liked this new Bugle. The angel who'd always sat on Drew's shoulder wanted to steer him true.

"I know what you're feeling," Drew repeated. "This sucks. But stepping outside the normal chain of command is what we're trained to do."

"Not now," Bugle said. "Not with millions of people lost or dead. You said it yourself. If we launch, the Chinese might empty their silos before they realize we're only hunting their satellites. There'll be a holocaust."

"Our guys can hit those satellites as they pass directly overhead, so the SM-3s won't lift far enough to look like nukes. They'll never reach suborbital trajectories, much less turn and reenter the atmosphere. Each strike will be done before China can react."

"They're on a hair trigger. We both are. You might cause our own guys to launch if two of our ships go dark."

"You have your orders, Lieutenant," Drew said, emphasizing Bugle's rank. "This is a ROMEO directive."

Bugle retreated from Drew and Patrick. In doing so, he cleared room for his hands, but Drew couldn't believe his friend would pull his sidearm. "Stop," Drew implored him. "I know this is tough. I don't like it, either."

"Then why—"

"We need you."

"Let me finish," Bugle said, chafing at the interruption.

Drew was willing to let him have his say, but Patrick shifted to one side as far as the corridor would allow. A second later, footsteps walked lightly on the metal deck behind Bugle. Bugle glanced over his shoulder. Then his hand settled on the 9mm Glock at his hip.

"Don't do it," Drew said.

Emily walked into the intersection. Level One had a simple pattern of corridors in a square-cornered 8. The men stood in the central corridor. She'd entered from the east side of the complex facing the cavern and the labs.

Her blue eyes were round with trepidation. "Drew, I'm sorry, I know you told me to stay below," she said. "I—"

Patrick lunged at Bugle.

They crashed into the wall as Emily leapt back, screaming.

Bugle cracked his pistol against Patrick's head, once, twice. Patrick toppled. Bugle shoved his weapon at Drew and shouted, "We don't have to do this! You can tell Fuelling no if we—"

Patrick groped at Bugle's legs, almost dropping him. Drew saw his opening. He'd drawn his own gun. But he couldn't shoot his friend.

They stared at each other in the white corridor.

The standoff tipped in Drew's favor when Patrick regained his feet, pressing one hand against his bleeding scalp. "Don't fucking move!" Bugle shouted. His face was hectic with emotion, yet he held his ground.

On the level above them, the floor clanged beneath other men's feet. Behind him, Drew heard shouting in the barracks. He'd planned to approach their teammates one at a time with Bugle and Patrick, ganging up on each man, using their camaraderie to convince Macaulay and the others. Now that seemed impossible. The corridor would become a mob scene when the bunker personnel responded to their yelling.

"It's not too late for you to help us," Drew said, aiming his pistol at the floor.

Bugle's eyes widened.

Drew thought he could bring his friend back into the fold, but his mouth was working faster than his brain. "We can tell them you two threw some punches about something stupid," he said. "A girl."

The word must have punched the wrong buttons in Bugle. He'd viewed Julie as a danger to their friendship. Then Emily had also chosen Drew.

Bugle shook his head violently and yelled, "Security! Security!"

Emily was extraordinary. She whacked her arm into Bugle's hands with a simple *kihon* maneuver, knocking the pistol from his grip.

Somehow Bugle caught the weapon as he crouched and bent. Drew and Patrick rushed him. Bugle's gunshots were deafening in the narrow metal shaft of the corridor. Two bullets rocked through Patrick's side. He grabbed Bugle's uniform as he sagged, hauling Bugle down. Their momentum smashed Drew's fist into Bugle's cheek like a hammer. Bugle's head snapped back. In the collision, all three of them dropped their pistols.

Patrick's blood was warm on Drew's chest.

Bugle sat up, groping for a weapon. Emily snatched it first and kicked another pistol away from him. Drew grabbed Patrick. The huge Marine weighed two hundred and fifty pounds. He coughed red splatters onto Drew's leg.

"You stupid shit!" Drew shouted at Bugle. "Get back!"

The pain in Bugle's eyes was more than physical. He stayed down.

"Help me," Drew said to Emily. "This way."

"Why you are fighting!?" she cried.

On the west side of the corridor, five men charged into the intersection. They stopped in the skirmish line, one kneeling, four standing.

Three held assault rifles. The other two brandished handguns. They were Air Force and Army, not his teammates. Drew knew them—but not well enough.

"Freeze!" a soldier screamed as an Air Force major yelled, "What's happening!? Commander Haldane! What happened here?"

Drew shoved Emily away from them—east—the direction she'd come. He was slowed by Patrick's bulk. "Go. Don't stop."

"I said *freeze!*" the major yelled.

Drew thought he could reach the command center before anyone sent a warning from Bunker Seven Four to U.S. Command. Radio transmissions were always hampered by the pulse. First he needed to rendezvous with Fuelling and the SEALs, but he was ten feet from the bend in the corridor. He couldn't move fast enough with Patrick. The nearest door led to an AC unit. Drew glanced back at the armed men.

"Don't make me shoot!" the major yelled.

Bugle must have had second thoughts or, at least, he didn't want to see Drew killed. He rose between Drew and the airmen.

"Drew!" he shouted.

He bought them enough time for Emily to reach the corner. Only Patrick and Drew remained in the corridor when the major ran after them.

The major shoved past Bugle and opened fire.

In his trailer, Marcus eased through his door as the guard shouted in the front room. The linoleum floor squeaked. But the guard didn't hear.

"Say again?" the guard yelled. He was on the phone.

Outside the trailer, people were shouting. Marcus had heard two dull *bangs*. He hadn't been sure if those noises were pistol shots until a rattle of gunfire drifted through the thin trailer walls, but the sound was muffled. Someone was shooting inside the complex.

"I don't know, sir!" the guard said. "I'll check, sir!"

He would have seen Marcus if he'd turned. Instead, he juggled the cordless phone in one hand as he grabbed his M4 and flicked off the safety, moving toward the trailer's window, which faced the complex.

General Strickland did not station his best people in the trailer with Marcus. The soldier was a castoff from a Guard unit who'd been rescued in Sacramento almost as an afterthought. He probably considered Marcus an old man, and he was absorbed with the phone. "I see our guards at the complex hatch, sir," he said. "There are no civilians in the tunnel."

Marcus took three more steps up the short hall, testing for creaks. Once he pulled his toes back from a soft spot. Otherwise his feet settled perfectly into the linoleum. His thoughts were a quiet gulf completely unlike the guard's excitement.

"Roger that," the guard said. "Where was—"

The shouting outside increased.

"I have men pointing weapons at each other, sir!" the guard said. "Our men! They're ordering each other to stand down! The two soldiers at the hatch— Yes, sir. The men who jumped them are Navy SEALs. I count four against two if— The soldiers at the hatch surrendered! Oh, Jesus. They surrendered. One of the SEALs has them on the floor. The other three SEALs ran into the complex. Yes, sir."

The guard set the phone on the windowsill, perhaps needing an instant to steel himself. Marcus thought he'd been ordered into the fight, but whatever was happening, Marcus did not want the bunker personnel to regain control. Marcus wanted chaos.

A short lamp rested on an end table by the TV. It looked like the desk lamp he'd used as a club on the first day of the interrupts.

He reached for it.

36

. . . .

BUNKER SEVEN FOUR

Behind Drew, the major's rifle blazed through the corridor. Impact tore Patrick from Drew and knocked them off their feet.

Patrick made one sound. "Guh—"

He thudded into the floor. Drew rolled with their momentum, losing his knife as he scrambled forward.

The corridor ended in a T. Emily was behind the corner. She latched onto Drew's sleeve with her left hand. She held the 9mm Glock in her right. He would never forget her face. Most of her hair had sprung loose from her ponytail, framing one cheekbone. The rest of her hair sprouted in an unruly knot, but it was her eyes and mouth that held him. She bared her teeth and roared: *"Get up!"*

Drew wasn't hurt. A bullet had creased his left wrist, but Patrick had taken the other rounds. Blood pooled from Patrick's motionless corpse.

In seconds, the barracks personnel would follow him.

Drew leapt up, clapping his hands on Emily's pistol. He crushed her fingers against the trigger, firing twice. Both shots went low. Drew wasn't aiming. He wanted to delay the people behind him.

His second shot took an airman in the chin as the man ducked around the corner with his M16. Drew's bullet swatted him back in a hideous burst of gore. Someone else yelled behind the airman, who warbled, "Aaaayaa—"

The thrashing airman stopped the others as Drew wasted precious seconds in horror and remorse. He ripped the Glock from Emily, firing four rounds into the ceiling as they ran.

They were up against the east wall of the complex. An exit into the cavern stood behind them. Another was in front. And beyond it, at the southeast corner, was a stairwell to the command center on Level Three.

"Go!" Drew shoved Emily toward the stairwell. Captain Fuelling would join him in taking the command center if Fuelling and his SEALs were able to enter the complex.

If not, this would be a short fight.

"Stop! Stop!" Emily cried. "Why are we—"

Ahead of them, out of sight in the exterior corridor on the south side, weapons blazed. Drew recognized the chatter of an M4 and the higher pitch of two MP5s, the submachine guns preferred by Navy SEALs.

Fuelling is inside! he thought with jubilation. Anything except victory would be a sin. If they didn't take the command center, Patrick had died for nothing.

But the submachine guns were retreating. Who was there to oppose the SEALs?

The people on Level One were Drew's teammates. He couldn't hurt them.

Then there was a lull in the gunfire. A man sobbed, badly hurt. Drew heard Orion barking. In a whiplash of adrenaline, his confidence became dismay. He might reach the SEALs before he and Emily were caught, but then what? The SEALs would be outnumbered and pinned from both sides.

The hatch leading into the cavern was open. Drew decided his course of action as a man backpedaled around the southeast corner with an MP5. He was one of Fuelling's SEALs. He swung his weapon at them.

Drew shoved Emily down and shouted, "Navy! Navy!"

The SEAL didn't fire. Instead, he yelled at someone out of Drew's sight. "Hold 'em! Hold 'em! We got reinforcements!"

Drew stayed with Emily, crab-walking her to the hatch. She tried to stand. He shoved her down again into the fresh air curling through the gun smoke. "Get outside," he said.

"What about you!?" she yelled.

He didn't answer. He pushed her through the hatch, intending to run to the SEAL. If she was out of harm's way, he could help turn the tide. The battle for control of the complex might not be lost—

An M4 raked the SEAL at the corner.

The SEAL crumpled, his chest heaving as he bubbled and choked. Shouting men advanced on him. Behind Drew, two airmen dodged into the other end of the corridor. Bugle was with them. Drew began to throw down his pistol and raise his hands, but he wasn't fast enough.

The airman on point screamed, "Don't do it!"

The other airman opened fire.

In the cavern, at the base of the complex, Emily stood shaking with her hands covered in blood. She'd fallen down the five-foot ladder from the hatch to the cavern floor, where she'd landed on two bodies.

She didn't see anyone else. People were shouting somewhere in the pools of darkness. They sounded like they were near the emergency access from the cavern into the main tunnel.

So much blood.

The slick fluid was on her arms and knees. It was in her hair. The dead men were a soldier and a SEAL. They sprawled in a heap.

Emily lifted her eyes to the trailers along the cavern wall. The nearest was the trailer that served as the labs' computer room and the jail. The door hung open. Another soldier lay in the entrance. She couldn't see more than his arms and head, but she realized his skull had been crushed. The dent behind his ear was as large as her fist.

Spent cartridges lay around him, glinting in the light. An M4 was on the concrete floor of the cavern. Someone had emptied the weapon from the doorway, probably after clubbing the soldier and taking it from him.

Where is Marcus? Emily thought with a deep welling of loathing and fear.

She reached for the ladder. Her instinct was to climb back to Drew. Then a spray of gunfire banged against the inside of the complex above her as someone hurtled through the hatch. His boot smashed into her shoulder. Emily fell. She scrambled up again, frantic to get away from him and the slick bodies. But it was Drew.

"Marcus got out of prison," she said urgently.

He pulled her into the shadows. "They'll think we did this!" he said, stepping over the dead SEAL's bent legs.

Emily was still staring at the dead men when a soldier crouched in the hatch with the wicked silhouette of an M16. She saw him take in the bodies, sweeping his rifle down and sideways to cover each human shape.

Emily and Drew were fifteen feet away. Her shoes scuffed against the concrete.

The soldier at the hatch fired. The muzzle flashes were blinding. Emily felt more than heard the 5.56mm rounds zip past her head.

Drew dragged her beneath the complex. A two-foot gap existed between the raised structure and the steel pipes running along the cavern floor. Emily cracked her temple as they ducked in. Then they were through. The flat space was almost four feet tall between the cold dirt and the steel beams overhead. Thick steel coils stood every five yards, bearing the one-hundred-ton weight of the complex. There were no lights. Fifteen feet from the gap, she could barely see.

"Do you have a weapon?" Drew hissed, leading her forward.

The coils were a mathematically precise forest of smooth, ribbed tree trunks. Emily cut her palms on the gravel as they scrambled into the oppressive space.

Claustrophobia made her paranoid. She thought she heard someone else crawling ahead of them, but every sound rustled and multiplied. She stopped in despair. "You took my gun and there wasn't time to look for—" she said.

"Give it up, motherfucker!" a man yelled behind them. "You're trapped!"

"Shh," Drew whispered. "Over here."

Emily dodged after him and they hid by a coil, huddling together. He opened his arm. She pressed her bruised temple against his chest. *There wasn't time to look for a gun by the dead men,* she thought. In fact, neither body had seemed to have a weapon except for their sidearms, which felt wrong.

"Get some lights!" the man yelled.

Emily made sense of the missing guns at the same moment she became certain she and Drew weren't alone beneath the complex. Her voice was hoarse with terror. "Marcus took their rifles," she said. "He's in here."

"What are you—"

Emily pointed through the dark space, remembering her comparison of Bunker Seven Four's layout to a comma. The cavern was the round body, containing both the complex and the trailers. The tunnel to the world outside formed the comma's tail.

Two exits led from the cavern into the tunnel—the blast door at the front of the complex and an emergency access directly through the rock.

"He'll sneak beneath the complex to the far side," she said. "Then he can surprise the guard at the emergency door."

The shouting behind them grew louder as two men scrambled beneath the complex.

Drew moved away from her, preparing to intercept them.

"We can't let Marcus get outside!" she said. "That must be where he's going. If he's even half as smart out there as he is now—"

He might help P.J. stay alive.

"Marcus could be the most dangerous hybrid on the planet," she said as Drew glanced back at her. They were stuck. It was too dark to read his face, but Emily felt his indecision in the rigid muscles of his shoulder. She could hear it in the sharp rhythm of his breathing.

Behind them, the bunker personnel were coming in. In front of them was a madman with at least one automatic weapon. Drew couldn't protect her from both directions, so Emily made the decision for him. She scrabbled past the nearest coil, using it to prevent Drew from stopping her.

Marcus might help P.J. stay alive, but he could also become the Neanderthals' greatest general.

They'll kill us all.

A man rose in the darkness forty feet ahead of her. Emily saw a gleam of metal seconds before he squeezed off the entire clip in his submachine gun.

Bullets chewed through the thin space.

37

. . . .

BUNKER SEVEN FOUR

rew jumped for another coil as ricochets thunked into the rock and dirt, filling the air with dust. *Emily!* he thought.

If he knocked out the gun, he could save her.

Sneezing, giving himself away, Drew tried to circle to Marcus's side. The weapon had a flash suppressor—but in the shadows, orange light lanced and popped among the coils. The sustained chatter of the gun was deafening.

Then it quit. Marcus's weapon was empty.

Drew heard a shifting in the darkness. Drew was twenty feet away, but he thought Marcus might have dropped the submachine gun in favor of another weapon. Then he saw Marcus's silhouette. Marcus had retreated to the edge of the complex where there was more light, framing himself against the gap.

To his right, beyond the complex, Drew heard running feet and yelling. Marcus slipped up into the noise. Drew might have scrabbled after him. Instead, he went back for Emily, listening for the other men. Had they retreated?

He found Emily pressed against the ground in the dark.

"Are you hit?" He felt along her torso and leg. Her clothes were torn and damp with blood. But he couldn't find a wound. The blood wasn't hers.

"My face," she gasped. "I'm all right. My face. Where is he?"

Drew bent closer. Her cheek was bleeding. It wasn't a gunshot wound. She'd taken a spray of shrapnel, probably rock kicked up the bullets. "You're all right," he said with more calm than he felt. She'd nearly lost an eye.

"Where is he?" she asked.

"He crawled out."

They started after Marcus, and Drew realized the gunfire might have worked in their favor. Behind him, he recognized a voice yelling, "No! No, sir!"

Macaulay had refused to enter the crawl space. They didn't know Marcus was free, or, if they'd put that together, they didn't know Marcus had ducked beneath the complex before Emily and Drew. They thought Drew had fired.

His team probably hadn't discovered who they were chasing until a minute ago. Inside the complex, in the heat of battle, his friends would have joined the barracks personnel as a matter of course to repel the SEALs' invasion. Now they were arguing.

Drew heard incredible confusion in the cavern, although most of the voices weren't behind him. A crowd had gathered between the complex and the trailers lined up against the far wall of the cavern. That was useful. As he led Emily beneath the complex to the gap where Marcus had climbed out, Drew expected to emerge behind the crowd.

Who were they?

He glanced through the equipment stacked against the complex. Two fat rolls of chain link, a Bobcat, and a big Craftsman tool chest blocked most of the gap.

Ahead of him was the emergency access from the cavern into the tunnel. It was another steel door like a bank vault. It should have been closed and under guard, but four bodies lay twisted on the concrete. The door had been opened manually.

"When I say *go*, run for it," Drew whispered.

"Marcus killed them!" Emily said. Her shock was muffled by the hand she'd clamped against her cheek.

"No. Marcus didn't fire until we crawled in after him," Drew whispered. "Those men were dead before he got here."

What was happening in the tunnel? More fighting?

One of the uniformed bodies was Rick Fuelling. Another man was a civilian. *What a cluster fuck*, Drew thought, trying to make sense of it.

ROMEO had planned to seize the bunker in order to control all communications as they flew their teams to the destroyers in the San Francisco Bay. Meanwhile, the civilian population was under lockdown—most of them innocent—because of a few desperate men and women who'd hatched their own scheme to take control, exile the soldiers, and keep the bunker for themselves.

When the shooting started inside the complex, Fuelling must have subdued the guards at the emergency access. Then he'd led his SEALs into the cavern. At the same time, the ringleaders of the civilian conspiracy had seen an opportunity. Apparently they'd overpowered the guards in the tunnel, taking their weapons and running to the emergency access.

Had Fuelling schemed with the ringleaders? He might have tried to enlist them as reinforcements. If so, he'd underestimated their selfishness and their angst. Close-range gunfire had killed Fuelling, two guards, and the civilian sprawled in the emergency access. Then the civilian rebels had stormed the cavern.

Listening to them yell, Drew thought there were more civilians in the cavern than uniformed personnel, although he had no doubt the civilians would quail when met with an organized military force. The divided soldiers and airmen would unite against the civilians. Then they would disarm or shoot them.

Right now, no one else was coming through the emergency access.

"Go," Drew said, helping Emily out from beneath the complex. He brought the empty submachine gun. A bluff was better than nothing. He might find a spare clip on Fuelling.

They charged the access, where Drew paused to rummage at Fuelling's body. The civilian rebels had stripped him clean.

Drew looked up and saw at least eight civilians in the cavern. They were spread to either side, taking cover as the bunker personnel hollered at them from deeper in the cave. One woman had already given up. She pressed her back against the complex wall with her hands on her head. Another man cowered against a vertical band of pipes, removing himself from the fight.

The soldiers would get through in seconds.

Drew chased Emily to the door. Where was Marcus?

This far into the mountain, the tunnel narrowed to a width of fifteen feet where a knob of granite had been left to shield the emergency access. The other side of the rock would be the perfect spot for Marcus to set a trap, shooting them point-blank.

But they couldn't slow down. Behind Drew, the soldiers' commands were overwhelming the civilians' disorganized shouts.

He and Emily sprinted into the main tunnel, where most of the civilians had stayed. Two men were helping an Army sergeant with a head wound. Ahead, a wall of crates and supplies blocked the width of the tunnel. To their left, the primary blast door was sealed.

"What happened to Marcus?" Emily whispered.

Drew didn't answer.

The guards assigned to forward points by the entrance had probably mingled with the noncombatants by now, taking new positions to secure the tunnel. The good news was those guards would stop Marcus. The bad news was Drew and Emily couldn't wade into the pandemonium. The crowd would be like a minefield, hiding soldiers and airmen.

Something rattled above Drew.

"There!" he said. A desk fan dropped off the highest crate, pushed by a foot or a knee. Marcus had scaled the wide blocks of pallets and crates onto the loose items on top.

Drew hurried to the wall. "Stay here!" he said.

But Emily ran with him. Blood trickled from the wounds peppering her face. The bruise in her temple had grown into a goose egg. "Boost me up," she said, latching onto the rim of the first crate with both hands.

Drew remembered how well she'd climbed the fence at the high-way where Julie died. "Stay here," he said. "Let them capture you."

"We can't. Marcus is too dangerous to let outside. If he's a Nim—"

Drew set his hand under Emily's backside and pressed the submachine gun against her. The weapon must have hurt her, but she got up. She climbed the next two layers of crates herself. Drew climbed after her. Then they were twelve feet above the floor of the tunnel.

Below them, shadows mixed with the beams of flashlights. Drew also saw a well-lit area. About twenty people milled through the pathway and the closest sleeping area as he led Emily to his right, hurrying in the same direction Marcus must have gone.

The long, high surface of the crates was a nightmare. Thousands of crevices lurked in the darkness. Sharp-edged bolts and wire covered the ceiling, and the uneven rock was never more than six feet above them.

The maze was worsened by odd groupings of bikes or PVC pipes or appliances like microwave ovens and toasters. Drew's blind spot made every other step a game of Russian roulette. He stepped on a card-board box that collapsed. Then he crashed into the pallet next to him, a plastic-wrapped bundle of bulk-buy children's mac and cheese in purple boxes.

"Shit! It's like walking on—"

A bullhorn overrode his frustration. "THIS IS MAJOR WHARTON OF THE UNITED STATES AIR FORCE! ALL CIVILIANS GET ON THE FLOOR! GET ON THE FLOOR!"

The voice came from the tunnel behind them. The bunker personnel had won. Now they would spread out, hunting for Drew.

"Marcus will go for the entrance," Emily said. "If we—"

"LAY FACEDOWN ON THE FLOOR!" the bullhorn shouted. "LAY FACEDOWN ON THE FLOOR OR YOU MAY BE SHOT!"

Drew clambered forward with Emily. The beam of a flashlight stabbed at them from the next room down among the pallets and crates. "Someone's up there!" a woman cried. The beam of light danced over Emily, lost her, then lit her blond hair again.

"Keep running," Drew said. He braced his feet. Then he hurled his submachine gun like a large, badly weighted knife.

Below him, the woman shrieked. Her light tipped away.

The bullhorn continued deep in the tunnel, but Drew heard the bunker personnel running closer. Hysterical civilians quit talking as the soldiers and airmen hustled into the sleeping areas. Here and there, other loyal troops stepped forward, shouting recognition codes.

"STAY FACEDOWN ON THE FLOOR! STAY FACEDOWN ON THE FLOOR AND YOU WON'T GET HURT!"

Drew wasn't sure he could reach the front of the tunnel before the other men. He caught up to Emily and took the lead again, moving faster than was wise. From one step to the next, he fell and cracked his knee.

"We have to hurry," he said. "The civilians aren't going to hold—"

Rifle fire hammered through the tunnel ahead of them. The uncontrolled burst was Marcus's signature, emptying his weapon in seconds.

Drew began to run again, slipping and banging through the supplies. Behind him, dozens of civilians screamed. Someone fired a pistol into the ceiling—once, twice—but if the gunman meant to silence the crowd, the shots had the opposite effect.

The ambient light dimmed as someone knocked over a lamp in one of the sleeping areas. Drew heard another pistol shot. Hysteria inundated the tunnel again, which would impede the soldiers.

But the rifle fire meant Marcus was at the entrance. He might have ambushed the guards from above.

Drew was fifty feet from joining the fight. The distance between him and Emily had grown as he raced ahead, yet she didn't call out for him.

He dropped into a fissure between two pallets, scrambled up, and worked past a loose heap of insulated picnic coolers. He caught himself on the brink of a ten-foot drop where the crates ended.

Their motor pool of four Humvees and a Dodge Ram lay below. Beyond the vehicles, Drew saw the trailer that served as their ready room. It contained most of the gear for their recon teams. Every light was out except one over the trailer door. Beyond it stood the military bus and iron bars they'd used to plug the mouth of the tunnel.

He detected no movement. If there were footsteps or whispers, those sounds were lost in the reverberating screams behind him.

The bullhorn continued. "STOP! STOP WHERE YOU ARE!"

Drew couldn't let Marcus go. He also didn't want to meet the next soldiers to reach the motor pool. After the killing inside, those men would be twitchy. Drew wanted to believe Bugle would give him a chance to explain, but the bunker personnel might shoot first and ask questions later . . .

But if Drew got outside, very few people could follow.

Emily was behind him. "They're catching up," Drew murmured to her before he jumped. He landed with a *thud* and ran to the nearest Humvee.

Emily was louder climbing down. Drew watched for a response in the dark. Nothing. They started toward the trailer before he saw the brittle glass on the floor and a human form. The Dodge Ram had been strafed across its roof and hood. An M16 lay on the concrete.

Drew lifted the rifle and pulled the magazine. Empty. It was Marcus's M16. The soldier had been hit in the leg, chest, and neck, killing him instantly, after which Marcus had taken the man's weapon and sidearm.

Emily swore softly. "That son of a bitch."

Drew led her to the steel door welded into their blockade. A damp wind stole through the seams in the iron and sheet metal jammed around the bus. Their shield didn't need to be airtight, merely dense enough to deflect the pulse.

Outside, rain pattered against the shield. Neither of them had jackets, and the temperature wouldn't rise above fifty even in daytime. Drew glanced at the ready room. The lockers were hung with weather gear.

Outside, distantly, a man howled. His voice was triumphant and insane. It curdled Drew's blood.

"Nnnnnnnnnnnmh!" the man screamed.

"That's Marcus," Emily whispered. "He made it."

Drew had only one mesh cap with him. They never left their M-string in the ready room. The armor was too precious. ROMEO and General Strickland had both ordered Drew's team to maintain personal possession at all times. The spare M-string was in the Osprey, which they'd sheltered at Beale AFB to minimize its exposure to the pulse. The hangar was 1.6 miles away.

Drew put his mesh cap on his skull. "We need to run to the plane," he said.

"I can't."

"I'll keep you from getting away."

"No. Oh, no."

"You're not strong enough to hold on to me or I'd give you mine. But I can hold on to you."

Emily nodded suddenly. "Don't let go."

Drew felt a roar of affection. Emily was risking her soul. If he lost her while they were outside— If she was killed—

He kissed her and she threw her arms around his neck.

"Clear," a man said distinctly behind them. The soldiers would enter the motor pool in seconds.

Drew opened the door with one hand. His other fingers were locked on Emily's wrist. The thin corridor through the pile of iron and sheet metal went left, then right. He reached a second door.

Rain skittered against the cement and the razor-tipped fences on either side of the tunnel entrance. To the right, above him on the mountainside, the communications array was insulated from the pulse and Neanderthal scouts by a series of tall steel clamshells and more fences— but he would need several minutes to hike to the cluster of dishes and antennae. Bugle or another man in M-string would catch him at the fences before he could disable the antennae. That meant U.S. Command would learn of ROMEO's treason.

He saw no sun, only the wet haze and the road curving down the rocky mountainside. Yellow grass and brown shrubs clung to the slope. The runways, fences, and buildings of Beale AFB were a distant collection of geometric lines. Old barracks and family residences spilled away from the base's southern side like white bricks.

Emily stumbled.

Drew hauled her up again.

She began to fight. Her eyes rolled as she tugged and bent. She bit him like a cat. "Stop it," he said, hoping his sharp tone would scare her, but she tossed her head and snarled, keening with a soft, insistent ferocity.

The rain soaked through her clothes, plastering her shirt against her small breasts and her jeans to her hips. Her blond hair darkened. So did the color of her eyes.

A 9mm Glock pistol had been abandoned on the road. Drew grabbed it, darting his eyes left and right, but Marcus wouldn't have set up to shoot. Drew had expected to find both of the man's weapons. Emily would have dropped them in her primitive state. Marcus was a more advanced tool user. He must have kept the rifle as a club. With luck, he'd shoot himself.

Emily tried to run away across the hill. "Aiee!" she cried, whipping her free arm at his shoulder and face. "Aiee!"

Drew cuffed her. The blow reopened the cuts on her cheek, but it also knocked her out. Then he bent and slung Emily's slim frame over his shoulder.

It wasn't fair. Today's events could determine whether or not Emily was a success. If she was deemed an outlaw and locked up, or if she was hurt, she would never have time to develop her cures. Now she wasn't even a participant in the fight, so he would succeed for her.

I swear it.

He'd bring her to the plane before her precious mind was damaged. Then he'd track Marcus and execute the murdering son of a bitch. Marcus's corpse might be enough for Emily and Drew to win their way back into the bunker in one piece.

The thought gave him strength, which he needed to bear Emily's weight. Soaking wet, she was a hundred and ten pounds. The cut on his wrist throbbed. He'd sprained his knee.

Limping, Drew ran into the storm.

Men emerged from the tunnel before he'd gone two hundred yards. Their voices cut into the wind. Was it Bugle and the rest of his team? They were shouting at each other, not him.

Drew collapsed behind a broad fin of rock, nearly throwing Emily against it when his knee twinged. He'd left the road for the mountain-side. Running on the asphalt would have been faster, but he couldn't afford to get caught in the open.

"Drew!" Bugle screamed. "Drew, come back!"

What were they arguing about? If they should let him go? Their uncertainty was a small advantage. It sounded like they hadn't moved from the bunker entrance. Drew thought he knew why. Bugle had rushed two or three men outside in their M-string caps, hoping to catch Drew while the rest of the team threw on their Kevlar vests, jackets, and helmets. When those men emerged, Bugle would duck back inside for his own jacket and other equipment.

Drew shoved himself up beneath Emily's weight and began to jog again, sliding in the mud. As soon as the men inside had their gear, they would run him down without Bugle in command.

He felt a creepy shiver in his brain, a sixth sense like someone was watching him. He looked back.

No one was standing on the roadside. Bugle might follow its bend to the north while Drew continued southwest. There shouldn't be any boot prints where he'd left the road. He'd hurried out onto a cracked slab of granite until it broke away with the mountainside—but they must know where he was going even if he had no intention of stealing the Osprey.

The irony was it would be useful to have Bugle's men outside. Drew couldn't let them catch him, because if they marched him back inside, they would be paralyzed by accusations and arrests—yet on his own, he probably couldn't cover enough ground to find Marcus. He needed their help.

If Marcus joins the Neanderthals . . .

Breathing hard, his neck hurting beneath Emily's waist, Drew ran another four hundred yards before his knee crumpled and he spilled her headfirst into the rocks and brush.

He lay dazed. He'd ripped open his chin and his left palm. Nearby, Emily moaned and stood up, swooning.

Her face was matted with mud and hair. One sleeve had torn, revealing an ugly scrape.

Drew jammed his bloody hand against the ground and groped for her with his good arm. But she moved no farther except to lower herself into a submissive crouch, staring past him with a quiet wail. Drew thought she was looking at soldiers and airmen from the bunker.

They caught us.

He couldn't locate his pistol. It had bounced into the weeds and rock. "I give up!" he said, spreading his arms. Then he turned, prepared to lunge at Emily if she ran.

Standing in the rain behind him were eighteen Neanderthal hunters.

38

. . . .

NORTHERN CALIFORNIA

Each man was a heavy, dripping shadow elongated by a club or a spear. In front stood a blond child with a bad arm. It was P.J. The darkest shape was Roell.

Drew staggered back. *They came for Marcus,* he thought before he realized, *No, that's impossible.*

If they'd heard Marcus yell, they were looking for him now—but Drew didn't believe the Neanderthals were telepathic. P.J. must have led his best hunters into the area, tracking Drew's team. Then the gunfire in the tunnel had brought them right on top of Bunker Seven Four.

P.J. gestured silently, deliberately. It startled Drew, who'd heard too many battle cries.

The gesture caused P.J.'s hunters to spread out in an enveloping half circle. The eighteen of them could certainly kill Drew, but they must have recognized that he was also a warrior. They wanted as few injuries to themselves as possible.

Their caution allowed Drew another instant. Sidling closer, they took the high ground above him, pacing up the slope. In hand-to-hand combat, the taller man often won, but Drew had spotted his pistol in the weeds. The black muzzle protruded from a clump of yellow grass on the far side of Emily's slim, trembling body.

Roell was among the nearest hunters. If they attacked as soon as Drew jumped, Roell would surely reach him before he grabbed his weapon, so he tried to distract them.

"Nim!" Drew yelled.

Roell's dark eyes never changed. If Drew's cadence or his pronunciation were wrong, there was no time to try again. His shout brought different voices through the wind.

"Nnnmh!" Marcus screamed in the distance as another man called, "This way!"

The men from the bunker were almost on top of them. All of the Neanderthals turned slightly. "Bugle!" Drew shouted as he lunged for his pistol.

Roell spun back to confront him, swinging a wooden baseball bat in a crushing overhand. At the same time, behind the Neanderthals, the drizzle erupted with yelling soldiers and rifle shots.

Drew's feet tangled with Emily's legs as he slapped his fingers onto the pistol. He rolled away with it, knocking her downhill. His palm found the weapon's textured metal grip.

Roell smashed his club into Drew's elbow. Impact snapped the joint and sent a wave of agony through his chest. His numb hand released the Glock. Then another hunter loomed above him, a larger adult carrying a broken flagpole.

This is it, Drew thought, rising a few inches. The feeble movement toward the larger man was the last thing he could do to protect Emily. She might escape while they killed him.

A bullet punched through the man's head, shoving his body into Roell. The cold rain turned hot. Drew's eyes were seared by the man's blood. He couldn't spare a hand to wipe his face. He wrenched himself onto his knees, lifting the Glock with his good hand.

The Neanderthal tribe had divided. Most of them charged the soldiers on the road above, but there was a third hunter who'd rushed Drew along with Roell and the larger man.

There were always three. Drew was already looking for him. He slowed the man with a wild shot, opening a superficial wound on the man's hip. The man swung a pipe at Drew's skull, but he was off balance. Drew dropped the man with two rounds in the belly. The pipe clanked into the ground.

On the hillside, P.J.'s hunters ducked through the brush and rock, sifting toward Bugle. Drew spotted his friend's tall figure among the gunmen. Several hunters lay dead. Bugle's squad had secured the high ground that the Neanderthals had wanted for themselves. Half a dozen M4s blazed from the roadside as Bugle's squad leaned into the slope, shooting down at the tribe.

Some of the hunters were very close. Drew saw them where Bugle's squad could not, hiding against every scrap of rock. The Neanderthals' grasp of timing and patterns had led them through the soldiers' few blind spots.

Drew couldn't help. On one side of him was Roell. Behind him was Emily. The three of them were momentarily forgotten in the larger fight.

Roell stood up, but it was an awkward motion. He'd been wounded in the burst of rifle fire that killed his companion. Coursing with rainwater, his face had a gruesome white tinge. An exit wound gaped in the middle of his chest.

Drew retreated to Emily. His right arm throbbed uselessly. If he was going to grab her, he needed to holster his weapon—

Roell lurched as he attempted to lift his club, then fell. Even the Neanderthal super endurance had failed him.

Drew tucked his pistol into his belt and caught Emily.

Seconds later, more Neanderthal hunters ambushed Bugle's squad from behind. Drew saw a small horde collide with the soldiers on the edge of the road, led by a familiar shape.

Marcus.

"Contact left!" a man shouted as the regular volleys of gunfire quit. There was a larger fusillade as Bugle's squad let go with everything they had, and yet some of the M4s never rejoined the rest. Marcus's attack eliminated a few soldiers. Then the rest were overrun.

Bugle's squad disappeared from the roadside, falling back.

It was the opening P.J. needed. His hunters leapt up the slope, sprinting to reinforce Marcus's group.

How many of Bugle's squad were left? Eight of them? Less?

In desperation, Drew yanked viciously on Emily's arm, needing to control her. "Run!" he shouted, driving her with his fury and his pain.

The fence surrounding the base was twelve feet high and topped with barbed wire. Drew might have been able to climb it with one hand, but not without letting her go.

He jogged four hundred yards to the nearest gate, wrestling Emily with each step. She didn't like the wire or the buildings inside. She knew the base was man-made, and even without her intelligence she was a stubborn little sparkplug.

He worried about Bugle. He wondered if P.J. was alive. Minutes ago, the battle on the mountain had ended. Drew didn't think Bugle's squad had been wiped out. They'd fought their way back into the tunnel. The gunfire had petered out, but someone continued to take sporadic shots. Shouldn't there have been more weapons in play?

Drew wondered if some of the Neanderthals had abandoned the fight at the tunnel entrance and were roving for survivors like himself. Their instincts were fantastic. Marcus had swiftly found his kin, perhaps meeting a trio of scouts from P.J.'s tribe. Then he'd guided them like a spear into Bugle's flank.

"Get down," Drew said, bending Emily's wrist until she fell to her knees. His fingers had squeezed bruises into her skin.

Left-handed, it took him three shots to break the lock on the gate. Even if the Neanderthals had stayed by the bunker, the noise would be all they needed to locate him.

He couldn't hold Emily and close the gate again, much less tie the chain into a knot.

"Move," he said.

Maybe the two of them could come back with a new lock once she was wearing M-string. But then what?

They crossed the field where he'd buried Julie. Neither the bunker nor the mountainside had any soft ground, so they'd used this corner of the base. Six graves lay beside her. A lot of good people had given their lives delivering the civilian experts and supplies to the bunker, and Drew guessed at least twenty more had died today.

"We're almost there," he said gently.

Emily seemed to notice his change in tone. Her blue eyes flickered, almost meeting his gaze.

Hangar Twelve was secured like the gate. Drew spent two more rounds destroying the lock. His pistol was almost empty. Inside, the Osprey was a welcome sight. In some ways, the aircraft felt like home, but there was no way they could hide in it until the fight was over.

Pain stitched through Emily's head. "Oooh," she said, squinting at the interior of the plane. She was sitting down. Drew held her, cradling her in his lap as she suffered through vertigo and nausea. She hated for him to see her retching, but she was glad for his hand on her hip. The gesture wasn't brotherly. It was intimate and possessive.

"Try to breathe," he said.

"How long were we outside?"

"Thirty minutes. Longer."

A neat mesh cap covered her head. Drew had placed his own armor on her, using a flight helmet to secure a roughly cut sheet of M-string on himself. Tasers and a submachine gun sat beside them on the flight deck.

He told her about Bugle, P.J., and Marcus. "I don't know if any of them are alive," he said.

Emily closed her eyes, searching for every last reserve of strength. "Let me put some kind of a brace on your arm before we go back outside," she said, and Drew smiled sadly.

"I love you," he said.

"Don't joke about it."

"I'm not joking. I love you."

Emily seized his good hand. She was filthy, hurt, and utterly wrung out, and yet the fire curling through her heart was worth it. She glanced at the paired rings on her finger. Maybe it was time to remove them at last.

"I love you, too," she said.

They strode back through the gate like a pair of killers, jangling with equipment and weaponry. Emily wore an Army jacket that was too big for her. Inside it, she shivered with cold and adrenaline. She carried the M249 submachine gun. Drew had an M4 slung from his shoulder with his good hand steadying its grip. Both of them wore sidearms and Tasers. Her backpack and his belt held extra stun guns.

Emily also carried a walkie-talkie. "Seven Four, this is Romeo One," she said. "Seven Four, do you copy?"

Her transmissions were almost certainly futile. Drew had tried to contact the bunker from inside the Osprey, using the aircraft's much stronger radio. Even at a distance of a mile, the pulse was too strong, but they might catch a break if the interference let up for a few seconds.

"Seven Four, this is Romeo One," she said.

Drew had told her they'd run into Beale AFB through the same gate, which was why the lock was shot out. It was a secondary entrance to the base. The road was only a lane-and-a-half wide, and there was less open space on either side of the asphalt than they would have liked. A brown swamp covered the earth. Dead brown trees and dead brown brush rose from the water, partly concealing their view of the mountain.

The wind and the rain rushed at their backs as they edged forward together. All around them, branches rubbed and scratched. Raindrops whispered in the swamp.

"Stop here," Drew said.

Emily nodded. She'd walked through the gate for P.J. Drew's motives were different, and she accepted that he was right. If the two of them had any expectation of not being jailed or banished, they needed to bring Marcus to justice. But she'd walked through the gate for P.J.

"Seven Four, Seven Four," she said.

She nearly dropped the 'talkie when it answered: "Who is this?"

"Bugle?" Her feelings for him were especially confused, but she let him hear her joy. "You're okay!"

His voice was rigid. "Are you alone?"

"No." Emily held the 'talkie to Drew, who said, "Not so loud." He never took his eyes off the swamp. She lowered the volume. He said, "This is ROMEO Agent Andrew J. Haldane, authorization code Quebec Hotel Four Golf Niner Four."

"It's too late for that," Bugle said as the 'talkie squealed with white noise.

This must be so hard for him, Emily thought. *For both of them.* She turned to watch the trees and mud.

"I have Priority One targets outside," Drew said.

No reply.

"Bugle, do you copy? Marcus Wolsinger is outside. I repeat, Marcus Wolsinger is outside and he killed most of our people in the bunker!"

No reply.

Long minutes passed as Emily called again and again. At one point, she was certain she heard a blip of a voice through the static.

The longer they waited, the more her shaking increased. She held her M249 in both hands, steadying the weapon against her ribs, but she couldn't let go of the 'talkie and it clattered against the weapon's dark steel. She didn't think she could have walked more if Drew had wanted to march farther from the gate.

"The Neanderthals will come from two sides," he said.

"Yes."

"Keep your eyes moving. Don't assume it's safe behind us. They might climb over the fence anywhere in the base."

"Yes."

"Remember I love you."

"Yes." Even that answer was rote. Her stomach churned, weakening her. The two of them were bait. Standing in the open should bring a trio of hunters for sure.

Drew wanted the entire tribe. "Nim!" he bellowed. "Niiiiim!"

"Someone moved on the hill," Emily said immediately.

"I see four people," Drew agreed. "Five. Six."

Emily slipped the walkie-talkie into her pocket and lifted a pair of binoculars. "There's Marcus," she said.

"Good."

"He looks . . . more verbal than anyone else I've seen. He's giving orders." Emily couldn't make out his face, but his body language was confident. He gestured and the other men moved like puppets, dividing into two groups. Marcus led the smaller bunch to one side.

Emily exchanged her binoculars for the walkie-talkie again. "Bugle, are you there?" she asked. "Bugle!"

It issued only static in her hand.

39

· · · · · · · · · · · ·

NORTHERN CALIFORNIA

f I say so, run for the plane," Drew said as six men hurried through trees in front of them.

Emily pointed. "There's P.J.!"

The boy lingered behind a screen of two hunters, near enough to create a trio, yet far enough behind that his small, ruined body wasn't a weakness for an enemy to exploit.

"Please try not to kill him," she said. "Can you shoot his legs?"

He might die anyway, Drew thought. In the movies, people blasted someone in the thigh or the foot to bring them down. In reality, a leg was packed with arteries. The feet were 80 percent bone. If he shot P.J. in the thigh, the boy could die. If he shot him in the ankle or the foot—if P.J. lived—he would have a bad limp to go with his crippled arm.

Three of the Neanderthals were bleeding. One man was wounded seriously in the abdomen. Another looked like he'd lost his teeth. They moved at the front of P.J.'s skirmish line like expendables. They would soak up as many bullets as possible to bring P.J. and the other men to Drew.

"Steady," he told Emily. He pressed his clumsy right arm against his M4, using the shoulder sling and his forearm to pin the weapon. Firing left-handed from the hip wasn't ideal, but he needed the carbine's power and thirty-round magazine.

Beside him, Emily gasped. She dropped her walkie-talkie to embrace her M249.

The first hunters emerged from the trees.

"Fire," Drew said as she screamed, "Marcus!"

Drew couldn't look. P.J.'s expendables sloshed through the muck, closing fast. Drew knocked down one man but missed the next two. "Shit, I can't—"

Emily's M249 chattered.

Recoil pushed her into Drew's swollen elbow. Twisting in pain, he let his M4 swing free and pulled his Glock. Four shots stopped the two men.

Then he thrust his Glock at P.J.

P.J. was within thirty feet, running from the water onto the asphalt. It was unlike Drew to think twice, yet he glanced at Emily to see if she needed support. He intended to turn back. Maybe he could wing P.J. or disarm him.

Another hunter crashed into Drew. The man had thrown himself beneath Emily's M249. His weight cut Drew's legs out beneath him and they tumbled onto the road, the M4 smacking against Drew's neck. Somehow he kept his pistol.

Drew slammed his knee into the man's groin, once, twice. Then he cleared his arm and fired three quick rounds at the man's feet. One connected. The man howled.

It was Marcus.

He clawed at Drew's eyes until Drew rammed his pistol grip into Marcus's neck. Marcus tottered. When Drew shoved him aside, he saw Emily screaming at P.J. as the boy ran at her with his club. She'd lowered her weapon.

"P.J., please!" she cried.

Drew's mind slowed to a single thought of protest. *No.*

Beyond her, four more hunters littered the roadside. One man was on his hands and knees. Another sat on his bottom like a child, cupping the bloody mess of his intestines. She'd blunted the second prong of Marcus's assault. She'd done it by herself. But shooting P.J. was too much for her.

Drew couldn't raise his pistol fast enough. He could only stare.

Emily stepped toward P.J., impeding his stride by kicking her foot at his shin. She redirected his club with her left arm. Her right hand lifted from her side. She held a Taser.

She jammed the stun gun into his ribs and discharged it. P.J. jerked. He collapsed, whacking his skull on the road.

Marcus was half-conscious, groaning, but Drew refused to take any chances. He put his own Taser against Marcus and jolted him, too. Then he hurried to Emily. She knelt over P.J., weeping. Amazement and relief swelled inside Drew, but there wasn't time to compliment her.

"I need the ties in your pack," he said.

"Yes." She didn't move to take it off.

"Help me reload and keep watch." He shoved his Glock at her. "I can't help their wounded unless you cover me."

"Yes."

He hugged her clumsily, turning his head to watch the swamp. After a moment, Emily shook herself as if waking up.

She'd slid a new clip into Drew's pistol before Bugle's squad filtered out of the trees. She could have handed the loaded pistol to Drew. Instead, she set the weapon down and called to them, "It's over. You got us."

The hunter sitting in the road died before the medic finished his cursory examinations of Emily and Drew. The other Neanderthal was unconscious, so was P.J., and Marcus couldn't stand on his own. Emily and Drew were barely able to move themselves.

Hiking back to the bunker was slow going. Emily shivered uncontrollably, too close to shock and hypothermia.

Her head was tangled with emotions. Hatred. Love. Dismay. Optimism. She'd been through too much with Marcus, P.J., and Drew. She would have given anything to walk alongside Drew and share their new closeness.

Bugle had separated them while arranging his column. Macaulay was on point with Orion. Emily came next, followed by two soldiers bearing the unconscious Neanderthal on a jacket they'd fashioned into a crude stretcher. Another man carried P.J. in his arms. Drew followed with his good hand secured to his belt with a plastic slip tie—the same ties they'd used to bind P.J. and Marcus. Three more soldiers hauled Marcus between them in another jacket.

Bugle marched alongside their column instead of being part of it, either waiting behind or pacing to the side, attempting to cover every direction at once. There was no one else left. Marcus's ambush on the road had killed four guys in Bugle's squad, and Bugle had yet to recover their M-string. First he'd run to help Drew because he'd intuited the trick Drew had played on the Neanderthals even if he wouldn't admit to such a strong connection with his old friend.

By making themselves a target, Emily and Drew had lured the Neanderthals from the bunker. Otherwise the soldiers might still be trapped inside. The best they'd managed was a few potshots at the Neanderthals as Marcus pried at the rock above the tunnel, starting a landslide, trickling gravel and dirt across the shield. Then the soldiers had realized Marcus and his tribesmen were gone. The Neanderthals had outraced Bugle's squad down the mountain, but in the end Drew had exploited the Neanderthals perfectly.

Their downfall was being predictable. They were so finely attuned to themselves and to any threat to their tribe that they couldn't decide not to attack. Yes, Marcus had used P.J. as a decoy exactly as P.J. had used his wounded men. They were clever. Nevertheless, they'd allowed Drew to bring them into the open swamp.

The memory of the gun shuddering in her hands wouldn't leave her. Emily's fingers fluttered and clenched as she trudged after Macaulay. She moved like a sleepwalker, utterly spent. Her thoughts felt as distant as the static on Bugle's radio and the muffled sounds from the end of the column, where Marcus had been gagged as well as tied.

That P.J. had been spared was a godsend. She prayed his mind would clear once they were inside. Would he remember her? What if he'd been permanently altered?

Orion was growling. The noise reached Emily as Macaulay said, "Movement. Left."

The soldiers dropped the unconscious Neanderthal to the ground, kneeling in the brush as they brought up their M4s. Bugle shoved past Emily. "Where?"

"Two wounded men eighty yards across the hill," Macaulay said. "They're hardly moving."

"Okay, I see 'em."

One of the human shadows crawled feebly on its stomach. The other lay on his back, either dying or dead.

Bugle dismissed them. "Let's go."

"Wait," Emily said, rousing from her daze. "It's Roell."

"We'll come back for him if we can."

"Do you know who that is? Roell is Marcus's son, and we need Marcus to cooperate with us!"

"I'd have to leave your nephew to bring anyone else."

"I'll carry P.J. myself. I can do it." Emily turned to find P.J. and stumbled. Her legs felt wooden and she shook herself, desperate for more energy.

"All right, all right," Bugle said. He chopped his hand sideways at the hill. "Heads up," he told his men. "We're gonna see if we can grab more of these fuckin' cavemen."

Orion and Macaulay led the short column of soldiers and prisoners through the brush.

Overhead, two birds darted through the rain.

Roell's eyes were open. He bared his teeth when they approached. "Hnn!" he sang, biting as Bugle and Macaulay held him down, keeping their hands from his face.

"I can't help this guy," the medic said. "There's too much damage. Lung. Ribs. Liver. Spleen."

"He's going to die?" Emily asked, looking at Bugle for empathy.

Marcus and Roell were only a few feet apart, and yet that space might have been wider than a thousand miles. It was as big as a lifetime.

"You have to let them talk," she said.

Bugle shook his head. "You fuckin' traitor. You really are crazy."

"I'm not. Marcus was one of the top astronomers on the planet. He helped design the Hoffman array. If he's ever going to work with us again—"

"Drew says he killed at least five of our guys!"

"You should give him this much. It might help us."

"How?"

"We can afford to show a little mercy. We won this time. But there will be more fighting. If we want to stop the war, someone needs to go first. They need to see that we can forgive—that we can be good. We need to find a way to make peace, and you don't know what we might learn here."

Bugle studied Roell's gray face. "Shit," he said. "All right. But I'll shoot them if I have to."

"I know. Thank you."

The soldiers carried Marcus to his son. At first, Marcus struggled even more. He calmed when they set him on the wet earth and removed his gag. He examined Roell, looking down at his son before sweeping his eyes toward Bugle and the rest.

"Nnnmh," Marcus sang.

"Hnn," Roell whispered.

"Nnnnnmh," Marcus sang again. Then he stopped. It was as if he'd taken Roell's measure and realized the teenager could not help him escape.

"Hnnnh," Roell whispered as Marcus ignored him.

To Emily, the scene was unbearably tragic. She couldn't say that Marcus didn't recognize his son or that they hadn't spoken of love or loyalty—but as Neanderthals, they seemed too limited to do more than study their enemies.

"This is stupid," Bugle said. "Let's go."

"We have to try something else," Emily said.

"It's not safe. What if they sent runners for more men? We need to get M-string on more guys and regroup."

"I have cargo sheets in my pack," Emily said. "Let's put M-string on them. Marcus needs to know what we've done for him."

"We'll tell the motherfucker inside."

"Bugle, please." Emily wasn't sure it was the right thing to do, but she would have wanted to be in her right mind if she were in Marcus's place.

It took three men to hold Marcus as Bugle belted a sheet of mesh fabric onto his head. Roell did not resist when Bugle repeated the procedure.

M-string was a trauma to them both. Roell went into seizure. He swiftly wilted, and his breathing grew shallow and erratic. Beside him, Marcus slumped over, unable to prop himself up with his hands tied behind his back.

Roell was in the pulse for weeks, Emily thought. *What will happen to P.J. when we bring him inside?*

"Dah," Roell said. It wasn't a Neanderthal sound. His eyes had brightened. Staring at the soldiers, he was obviously terrified and confused.

Marcus responded to his son's voice. His first answer was incoherent, a humming noise like *Nnnnmh.*

Roell's gaze shifted to his father. "Dad," he said.

"Cut his ties," Emily hissed. "Bugle. Cut his ties."

"I can't."

Marcus and Roell paid no attention to anything except each other. Marcus hunched closer, trying to embrace his son without falling onto his bloody chest. "Roell," he said. "Roell."

The boy might have smiled. "You were with us," he said.

"I'm with you now," Marcus sobbed. "Oh God, I'm with you now."

They murmured together like a duet, exchanging soft, meaningful words. It didn't last. Within seconds, Marcus was the only one speaking. Roell was gone.

Nobody moved.

Cold rain pummeled the hill.

"I'm sorry," Emily said, reaching for Marcus, but he thrashed and screamed and tried to throw off his M-string.

NORTHERN CALIFORNIA

Emily sat in a corner of her jail cell, pressing her forehead into the narrow slot between two bars. Her hunger felt like a rat inside her. It gnawed at her belly, pulling her midriff tight against her ribs. Even her face felt taut. She'd lost ten pounds she'd never had to spare. Her hair fell lank and unwashed against her shoulders.

The holding cells were in a sublevel of a California Highway Patrol station. Four lightbulbs lined the corridor ceiling. Everywhere else was in shadows. Their cells were dark and loud and disgusting, fogged with the stink of unwashed people, urine, and the ever-present ash and smoke smell of Sacramento.

Emily's hand reached through her bars. Her left hand. Without rings. She couldn't see Drew in the next cell—a cinder-block wall separated them—although if they both leaned against the wall, they could talk without being overheard. They could also touch fingertips by stretching their arms into the corridor.

"I wish we'd made love," she said.

"Stop." But his tone was interested, so her voice grew slow and erotic.

"I remember both times we kissed," she said.

"There were three times," he said.

"Once while we were outside?"

"I should have." His fingers tried to curl around hers and Emily laughed, straining to reach him. She was beyond feeling self-conscious or embarrassed. They'd forgotten those hurdles by the third day.

Emily and Drew had been transferred south from Bunker Seven Four during an interval that lasted nineteen hours, maybe longer, aboard a single-engine Cessna that was not armored against EMP weapons or the pulse. They'd listened closely as the pilot radioed twice for updated forecasts.

Most of the other inmates had arrived during the same calm. Then two days had passed before another, smaller group was escorted into the jail block. Those men said they'd been moved during a four-hour interval.

Since then, they'd had no information. The guards who brought two small meals a day were indifferent to the prisoners' questions. It didn't help that too many of them shouted for more food. Even Emily had lost her self-control on the fifth day, pacing against her bars and banging on the steel, demanding water, before she realized she'd cost herself dearly by breaking into a sweat.

She was so thirsty.

More insidious than her physical needs was their fear that America was at war. If the Chinese satellites continued to probe through U.S. and NATO strongholds, crippling their silos, burning their aircraft . . . At some point America's generals would realize they'd acted too late. Like a wounded dog, their ability to fight might be limited to one last all-or-nothing nuclear launch.

No one in the prison could say how much time they had left, so Emily had told Drew about her temptation to develop gene therapies that would turn everyone Neanderthal. He'd told her about the intervals, the predictions from the Hoffman Square Kilometer Field, and his blind spot. He'd admitted that he blamed himself for Julie's death.

Maybe talking was easier because they couldn't see each other, like confession, although the other prisoners had hooted or jeered when they started holding hands.

Emily shared her cell with two women, an Army lieutenant who'd stolen food for the primitives outside her shelter and a geologist who'd murdered a man who raped her. They were jealous of Emily for having a friend nearby, yet watching her with Drew had helped the three of them form their own supportive relationship. Maybe they would have helped each other simply because they were the only females in the jail block.

Every cell across the corridor held five or six men. So did the rest of the cells on Emily's side. Fortunately, Drew wasn't the only federal agent or soldier in lockup. He'd organized fifty-five prisoners by calling down the corridor, establishing rank and reforming squads among the disgraced men.

Emily wasn't surprised it had worked. Most of them weren't criminals. They were people who'd made mistakes like she had, often for the right reasons.

Listening to their different stories, she'd been struck by one similarity. All of them were high-value prisoners. They either had education like the geologist or military training like the lieutenant. There were no ordinary fools among them.

Drew's leadership was exactly what everybody wanted except in one defiant cell across from Emily. Those stupid bastards liked to yell. They'd begun a campaign of cursing, spitting, and exposing themselves. They were animals. Emily and her cellmates had to hold up a blanket as a screen whenever one of them used the toilet, which was a nasty, waterless, lidless steel bowl. The three of them also tended to gather in the right rear corner of their cell, where those men were unable to see them.

It was the left front corner where Emily could reach Drew. As she toyed with Drew's hand, one of the bastards shouted, "Hey, babe! Over here! Hey, I got something for ya!"

She was done crying or acknowledging them in any way. Even flipping him off was a waste of time. What she cared about was Drew. "Did I really forget a kiss?" she asked. "Our first time was inside the blast door when you grabbed me."

"Who grabbed who," he said easily.

"Then we did it again before we left the bunker," she said, smiling at her choice of words. Teasing him was the best she had to offer. She could barely stand it herself—eight days of talking—only talking—but at least her fantasies took her away from this place.

He'd fallen silent in the cacophony of voices.

"Hey?" she asked.

"You, uh, you're missing our best kiss," he said. "Inside the Osprey. I think I got to second base." His tone was light, but she heard the concern beneath it.

"Tell me," she said.

"We're just torturing ourselves."

"No. Tell me."

As long as they lived, fragmented memories would be a problem for anyone who'd gone outside without M-string. Two of the men imprisoned with Drew and the geologist in Emily's cell were dealing with their own confusion, sometimes extensive. Emily had held the other woman at night when she woke with nightmares.

In the geologist's case, it might be therapeutic to wipe the slate clean. Was that possible? Walking her outside would affect her short-term memory, which was how her assailant had intended to get away with his crime, but she'd retained too many impressions and now the act of knifing him was ingrained in her mind. She would never forget unless the soldiers sent her outside forever.

What if that's what they decide to do with all of us? Emily thought.

In their first few days behind bars, she and Drew had whispered about their fate. He'd also made the observation that everyone in the jail block was either a scientist or a soldier of one kind or another.

If U.S. Command was holding run-of-the-mill thieves and killers, those people were being kept somewhere else or, more likely, they'd been banished. Or executed.

Emily suspected the experts and warriors gathered in this jail block were closer to banishment than she wanted to believe. They'd only seen four different guards. Their rations were one step above starvation. Nobody had come to fix the plugged toilet in the cell at the end of the corridor, and two-thirds of the lights were off.

To her, it looked like U.S. Command had consolidated their high-profile troublemakers for final evaluations. They wouldn't waste food or electricity on people they decided they didn't need.

And if the bombs fell, it seemed unlikely that anyone would bother with fifty-five prisoners. This jail was more than death row. It could become their tomb.

Drew let go of her hand. "Listen," he said.

The noise level rose as the men by the entrance started shouting. Emily heard the locks *clunk* and then the familiar whine of the door hinges.

"Attention on deck!" Drew yelled.

He stood up and Emily matched him, rethreading her arm through the bars. Beside her, the lieutenant and the geologist moved to the front of their cell.

Three soldiers strode into the corridor, not the prison guards but new soldiers. Accompanying them was a man in a blue business suit. Under one arm, incongruously, he held a wide-brimmed jungle hat. His face glistened with sunburn.

Sunburn! Emily thought. That meant the clouds were gone unless he was a pilot. He looked like a bureaucrat.

He held a clipboard in addition to his hat. He stopped in front of Drew's cell with his three soldiers. "Haldane," he said. "Front and center."

"What is it, sir?" Drew asked.

Emily groped helplessly for his hand and couldn't find it. "Drew!" she said.

The man glanced at her. "You're Flint," he said. "Step back. Haldane, there's no need for you to fight."

"No, sir."

She heard Drew speak to his cellmates. Then the soldiers let him into the corridor.

"Wait," she said, drinking in the sight of him. Drew was pale, but he'd regained the use of his dislocated elbow and he looked good with a dark scruff of beard.

The sunburned man walked toward her. "You, too," he said. "You're both coming with me."

"What?"

"The pulse stopped three days ago. Our best projections are that the flares are done until the next solar max, maybe longer. Maybe a lot longer."

"What about China, sir?" Drew said. "Are we at war?"

"Not yet," the man said, increasing his volume. The prisoners had started hollering again. He waved his clipboard with a mix of weariness and excitement. "Shut up! Shut up and I'll tell you! Almost everyone here will be paroled as soon as we can process your records, but I promise you, this is your last chance. Martial law is in effect, and we are shooting criminals and looters!"

"These are good people, sir," Drew said. "I can vouch for most of them."

"We'll see." The man unlocked Emily's door, gesturing for her cellmates to move back. She took an instant to hug the geologist and the lieutenant.

We made it, she thought. *It's over.*

Then she was in Drew's arms. She pretended to be deaf to the catcalls up and down the jail block, but in her heart, the noise felt like a celebration.

41

. . . .

LOS ANGELES

Standing at a fence in the afternoon rain, Emily rolled up her jacket sleeve to display the *DIA, C-004,* and *E-3* tattoos on her forearm. A Marine sergeant rubbed his thumb on each mark. Then he nodded. "Okay."

The Marines at the fence lifted the gate to the secure area inside Camp Ninety—a dense, hodgepodge collection of tents and aluminum sheds.

Emily entered the maze of homes.

Not many people were outside. Earlier today, the sun had broken through the clouds for an hour, but the drizzle must have sent them back under cover.

A young man stood in the muddy path with his eyes closed. Despite the rain, he only wore a T-shirt and jeans. Emily wondered if she should ask him to get out of the cold. Then a voice piped behind her. "Hi!"

Framed by the open flap of a red tent, a ten-year-old girl stared at Emily's feet.

"Hello," Emily said.

"Hi! Hi!"

The noise brought an adult from the next shelter, a pup tent he'd enlarged with two canvas tarps. "Dr. Flint," he said. "I told you we need more to eat. We need blankets. You can't keep us here if you don't—"

"You can leave any time, Mr. Womack," Emily said roughly.

She'd changed. In another life, she might have haggled with him. Instead, she adjusted her sleeve with a conspicuous tug before she walked away, leaving her forearm exposed as a sign of rank.

Southern California hadn't recovered enough of its industry to bother with print shops. Rumor said the government was issuing photo IDs in Denver and Flagstaff. Here on the coast, they had a thousand more pressing needs. The military had instituted a system of tattoos, using U.S. Treasury ink to thwart the explosion of forgeries.

Some people bitched about it, of course, comparing the marks to those forced on Jewish victims of the Nazi Holocaust, which was absurd. Mostly the complainers were people who resented the fact that they hadn't been given top ratings.

Emily's tattoos were ugly as hell. They also permitted her inside the labs, the Marine barracks, and the cafeteria. The fenced area inside Camp Ninety had its own soup kitchen, but hot tea and soup were about the extent of their menu. Yesterday, they'd had powdered eggs. Otherwise, the inhabitants ate uncooked food from cans—and they were the lucky ones.

Five weeks after the last sporadic pulse, twenty-six fenced camps existed in California. The majority were in the southern part of the state where a few Navy and Marine Corps bases had weathered the disaster with losses as small as 40 percent. As fighting units, the naval and Marine forces had been devastated—but as peacekeepers, they were the best available option until civilian police forces could be reassembled.

Outside the camps, anarchy reigned. A few survivors had organized their own villages, claiming various city blocks or suburban streets. Others thrived as raiders or nomads in tribes much like they'd formed during the pulse. People also gathered by the thousands around every military post or fenced camp, looking for family, begging to be let in, subsisting on garbage and scraps.

Inside this fence, two hundred hand-picked children, women, and men were as healthy and well-fed as anyone could expect. Navy doctors and specialists like Emily paid steady visits, delivering care and medicine in exchange for hair and blood samples.

Camp Ninety was a VIP installation in Long Beach. Most of the city had avoided destruction because it sat directly against the ocean, storm winds driving the fires inland.

Despite being surrounded by the ruins of the L.A. basin, even because of the wreckage, Long Beach had been deemed an unusually functional place to rebuild. First, the oil refineries on the peninsula had been spared. Second, the burned areas prevented too many refugees from overrunning the Marines before they'd cordoned off essential sites. The refugees who did come found abandoned homes, and a high school's baseball diamond had provided most of the fence line for Camp Ninety. The school buildings housed the Marines and lab personnel. Across the street were the dead, open spaces of a golf course where helicopters could land, and five miles east was the Los Alamitos Army Airfield with two runways for fixed-wing aircraft. The Navy was also docking ships at Long Beach's commercial harbor, not only to bring in cargo and men. A nuclear-powered destroyer provided electricity to the labs, the barracks, and the refineries.

Emily felt as if she'd come full circle. She believed her apartment in Pasadena had burned, and she'd personally helped a platoon of Marines turn DNAllied into a ransacked shell, stripping it of equipment and computers—but Long Beach was close enough to call home.

I should be happy, she thought. *I am happy.*

She understood Mr. Womack's selfishness. He had a son to protect. In other people, parental instincts compelled them to volunteer for the work crews, contributing to the greater good, but not everyone could see the larger perspective, so Womack fixated on expanding his tent and hoarding as many snacks and clothes as possible. Even if she personally disliked him, the human race was richer for its diversity.

Individuality was the price of free will. *Homo sapiens* tended to work against themselves, yet it was because they clashed that they were successful.

They pushed each other.

Maybe I'm being selfish, too, Emily thought as she emerged from the tents into a clearing near one of the baseball field's dugouts. The space was dominated by the camp kitchen, which consisted of two garden sheds and a plastic awning.

Protected from the rain, several people stood over short barrels of water, scrubbing pots and bowls. Among them was a honey-haired woman accompanied by a spindly boy.

Shaking off her irritation, Emily smiled. "Laura!" she called to her sister.

"P.J., it's Em," Laura said, tugging at her son.

He didn't respond. It might be years before P.J. recovered from the strain and deprivation of his days as Nim. He was scrawny, hurt, and drained, and yet Emily detected a spark of the bright-eyed child he'd always been. He slapped a plastic serving spoon on the water's surface, whispering under his breath.

Laura met Emily at the corner of the awning. Her face was haggard. Emily wanted to hug her, but settled for patting her shoulder. Laura had a horrible new aversion to being touched. When the pulse quit, she'd discovered herself with a man who was a stranger. He hadn't hurt her. They had been mates. Now she was eight weeks pregnant.

Meanwhile, her husband Greg remained missing. Laura was far from alone in mourning lost family, but her pregnancy had unhinged her. She wanted Emily to tell local commanders to place Greg on their priority list. Laura herself had been plucked from the refugee hordes after repeating P.J.'s and Emily's names to every soldier she could find.

During the four weeks of the pulse, Laura had roamed seventy miles from West Hollywood, moving east into the San Bernadino Mountains.

Six days ago, she'd been flown to Camp Ninety on an Army transport. Ever since, Laura and Emily had fought—about Greg—about their parents—about the reasons why U.S. Command had gathered certain people inside the baseball diamond.

Camp Ninety held fourteen young men and boys like P.J., six girls, and fifty-seven adults with thick dashes on their forearms. Emily imagined a lot of quick worrying had gone into the decision not to tattoo them with N for Neanderthal. Too many refugees wanted targets for their rage and grief. If these people left the camp, an N might get them killed, although a dash amounted to the same thing. They were marked for life.

The rest of Camp Ninety's inhabitants were caregivers. Most of them weren't family members. They were people with backgrounds in health care or education. Laura and Mr. Womack were two of the very few parents who'd been reunited with their children, which gave them a certain moral power. Laura was grateful for her son's life, but she'd also yelled at Emily when Emily admitted their research had little to do with an autism cure.

Standing at the awning, watching P.J. instead of her sister, Emily said, "I talked to the admiral."

Laura must have sensed her answer. "Did he say no?" Laura asked. "You should do it anyway."

"We're under a lot of pressure from higher up."

"You can't—"

"Shush." Emily faced her now. "Originally I was close to developing a cure," she said. "A biomarker to identify Neanderthal traits is the first step toward stopping autism, but I can't do whatever I want, Laura. This is a government facility, it's their equipment, and things are moving fast. We're talking with the whole country again. Most of Congress is back in place in Washington."

P.J. smacked the water with his spoon—*splat, splat splash—splat, splat splash*—introducing variations to his drumbeat with his whispers. "Blom. Blom."

"My job is to develop gene therapies that will make ordinary people invulnerable to the pulse," Emily said. "That's the priority. We don't have the resources to set up another line of research. Not yet."

"There are twenty doctors in this place," Laura said.

"Most of them are combat medics, not biologists."

"What if there's another interrupt? Em, I can't lose him again."

What if you're supposed to? Emily thought. Laura was a good mother. She'd overcome her own trauma to defend P.J., but Emily was tired of running from the truth.

"There's a reason for who P.J. is," she said. "Even if we could change him, I'm not sure we should."

"What does that mean?" Laura said.

"You never saw him. I did."

"He's not one of your experiments!"

"Laura, we can't deny what happened during the pulse. Outside, in the open, P.J. was better than us."

"They say he was a monster."

"No. He was perfect."

Ultimately, Emily felt a profound respect for the tough, simple Neanderthals. She was willing to refuse Laura for something larger than all of them. In time, maybe her sister would forgive her. At the moment, she saw revulsion in Laura's eyes.

"Get away from us," Laura said.

"I won't. You want special treatment and favors from me? You've got them. You have food and shelter and your son. You're safe. That's more than most people."

For the first time in her life, Emily had stood up to her sister.

"I'm not sorry," she said, walking past Laura to P.J.

Laura tried to catch her arm.

Emily shrugged her off and said, "Don't. Let me talk to him." Then she softened her tone. "Laura, I love you."

Her sister shook her head.

Emily went to P.J. He hadn't noticed her until then. Ducking his head, avoiding her eyes, he tried to explain what he perceived in the water. "The sound is one three, isn't it?" he whispered. "One three, one three."

"I hear it," Emily said. Her heart ached with the sad, sweet, majestic wonder of him.

In so many ways, they were similar. Emily felt the same magnificent hope for herself. Life was difficult—messy, painful—and beautiful and rewarding.

"I hear it, P.J.," she said.

An hour later, walking with Drew inside the school building, Emily said, "Laura hates me." She needed more than a hurried conversation, but they'd been called to the east wing, Emily from her lab, Drew from his office. She was glad he'd waited for her at the security checkpoint.

On the ground level, the filthy windows showed the wire and sand-bags protecting the outside. Drew's boot heels clacked on the white tile floor. Emily's footsteps were softer. P.J. could have read their moods by the sound alone, a thought that struck Emily with fresh pain.

"Tell me what happened," Drew said. He stopped her and cupped his hand on the back of her neck, tipping his forehead against hers.

The intimate pose reminded her of murmuring in their jail cells. She almost liked the pose better than a kiss because it was unique. When they were in bed, after sex, she often leaned her face into his like he'd done now, re-creating their tiny, private space.

"Laura said . . ." Emily swallowed. "She said she can't lose P.J. again, and I'm afraid I'm going to lose her."

Drew nodded. "This is harder for Laura. It's always harder to sit and wait." His fingers curled in Emily's hair. "Let me talk to her."

"Thank you."

The sound of her footsteps became a better match for Drew's stride as they approached a second checkpoint.

Four Marines stood in the corridor. Behind them lay the secret heart of the labs.

Maybe if Laura knew what we were doing in here, she'd cut me some slack, Emily thought. But telling her sister was forbidden. It was bad enough she'd shared the real direction of her research. Too soon, rumors would spread through camp.

At the checkpoint, Drew and Emily displayed their arms to a captain who inspected each tattoo. "Sir," the captain said, waving them past.

Drew's clearance level was higher than Emily's. His C was followed by 002 instead of 004, but he wore just two marks compared to her three. Emily had been assigned a low-ranking Army pay grade in order to account for her billet and meals. Drew was no longer a Navy officer. He'd received a dishonorable discharge after ROMEO's attempt to take Bunker Seven Four. Now his sole allegiance was to the Defense Intelligence Agency. He was a federal agent and a civilian.

The corridor ended abruptly in a raw concrete bulkhead, which did not match the school's cream-colored walls and burgundy trim. Emily thought it looked like a gray block had dropped from the sky into the two-story building. The concrete stretched from ceiling to floor, which were cracked and roughly patched.

Set in the gray block were a steel door, keypad, and phone.

Drew lifted the handset. "This is Agent Haldane. I'm with Dr. Flint." He hung up and said, "They need a minute to open the baffles."

Emily nodded as the floor vibrated with a distant, grinding squeal. She took his hand.

She knew his dishonorable discharge haunted him. He'd served in the Navy since he was eighteen, but he had good reason to hold on to his pride.

Shaken by ROMEO's attempt to commandeer the USS *Nickels* and launch its anti-satellite missiles, the president had revisited their intelligence briefs dealing with the existence of China's EMP weapons. Some of that data had originated with Julie, Bugle, and Drew.

Before the pulse tapered off, while Drew and Emily were in jail, the order had been given. The *Nickels* had fired eleven ASATs over the course of two days, destroying all three of China's attack satellites.

Without that edge, the Chinese agreed to negotiations with the U.S. and Vietnam. China continued to deny responsibility, claiming the satellites were Iranian or North Korean, but war had been averted in part because of Drew. Emily wanted to tell everyone she met, although it suited him fine that his heroism was never publicly acknowledged. He only cared that his superiors knew—and Emily—and men like Bugle and Macaulay.

Bugle had vouched for Drew in his reports, pinning the blame for the mutiny on Captain Fuelling. The trail also led higher up. ROMEO's director had been jailed for instigating the mutiny, but the agency itself was too valuable to shut down. Field operatives who'd dealt with the Neanderthals were especially in demand, so Drew had been put in charge of the four-man ROMEO team at Camp Ninety.

It wasn't a glamorous assignment. It was better than prison.

It also left Emily and Drew in Bugle's debt.

The three of them might never be friends. Maybe someday they'd talk. For now, Bugle had been sent to D.C. to liaison with ROMEO's new leadership as they reestablished their networks on the West Coast. The job was a prominent national position. He'd earned it.

Emily had learned she could resent Bugle and wish him the best at the same time. Like her relationship with her sister, nothing was black and white.

The worldwide disaster couldn't have a pat storybook ending. Millions of people were dead. The very face of the planet had changed. Some astrophysicists thought they could predict the next spike in solar activity before it happened again—if it happened again—but humankind would be rebuilding for generations.

Worse, the physicists couldn't guarantee that the flares were over.

What if Laura was right? If the pulse returned today . . . If Emily might have changed P.J., yet sank her time into other research, leaving P.J. to become Neanderthal again . . .

"Ready?" Drew asked. The rumbling in the floor had stopped. The light on the keypad turned green.

"Ready," Emily said.

He opened the broad steel door. The hall behind it didn't fit. The door was five feet across, whereas the hall was three, as if the concrete walls had squeezed in farther than planned. The narrow hall also looked too short. After six feet, it bent to the right.

They went inside. The air tingled with invisible energy. Emily shivered at the preternatural charge as they reached a four-inch seam in the concrete where a steel disc had partly retracted into the wall. The first baffle was often stuck. They squeezed by.

The next baffle was fine. Once they'd gone past, Drew hit another keypad. The baffles scraped shut behind them. The electric feeling dissipated.

A steep row of stairs led into the basement level, where two men occupied a dimly lit floor. Behind them, in an equally dim glassed-in room, a woman sat at a bank of computers. In front of the men was another pane of glass. It shone with light.

They glanced up as Emily and Drew descended. "We had a breakthrough sooner than expected," one man said. "I was sure you'd want to see it."

Emily nodded. She was too nervous for small talk.

Construction had been under way for three weeks before the initial tests began. Unseen in the floors above, ROMEO engineers had installed a bevy of flux compression and magnetohydrodynamic generators. The power required was the real reason for the Navy destroyer berthed at the Long Beach docks. Emily's labs, Camp Ninety, and the Marines aboveground were important, but they were also a cover for ROMEO's new Phoenix Project.

The dimly lit floor was packed with easels, folding desks, recording equipment, and odd things like toy balls and handfuls of dirt.

The project director tried to intercept Emily at the base of the stairs. "Dr. Flint, if you'll look at our memory cards . . ." he said.

"I know." Emily dodged past him into the clutter. She and Drew had been included in the meetings to set their agenda, and she'd already noticed her own face among the photos clipped to the easels.

She walked to the bright window.

Beneath the generators, beneath an insulating layer packed with coupling antennae and conductive materials, the engineers had run lights, air ducts, and plumbing for a thirty-by-twenty-foot shelter. On three sides, it was a heavily shielded cage. In the wall facing the observation floor, they'd erected a screen of triple-pane glass with microphones embedded in M-string.

ROMEO had been able to mimic the electromagnetic noise of the pulse.

Inside, Marcus had noticed the activity among his captors. He stood at the glass, his dark eyes smoldering with Nim. He was calm. His posture was lopsided, affected by his bad foot, but he looked as if he could wait for eternity, studying them for any weakness or opening.

After Roell's death, he'd wanted atonement. He'd volunteered himself for the project. More than anything, he'd yearned for the Neanderthal mind and a lasting connection with everyone like himself.

Emily glanced at the easels. Roell's photo was there, too, and P.J., and less provocative images of things like water, hills, animals, and plants. Through a smaller set of baffles, the linguists could give Marcus objects such as the toy balls and color swatches. The amount of information they'd prepared might have dumbfounded anyone else. Marcus had soaked up this knowledge in a twentieth of ROMEO's most radical projections, memorizing and reiterating every test.

Emily's gaze connected with Marcus's eyes through the glass. At her side, Drew offered his hand. She clenched it tight, letting his love for her keep her grounded despite the ungodly tension.

"Can you hear me?" she asked.

Marcus cocked his head.

"We were friends," Emily said as their computer programs attempted to translate. Inside his cage, a speaker sang in a man's voice. Then he replied. The speakers on the observation floor uttered one word for him.

"Nnnmh," Marcus said. "Yes."

The two cousin species were learning to communicate.

ABOUT THE AUTHOR

Jeff Carlson is the international best-selling author of *Plague Year* and *The Frozen Sky*. To date, his work has been translated into fifteen languages worldwide.

Readers can find free fiction, videos, contests, and more on his website at www.jverse.com, including special art galleries with nanotech schematics and images from the *Voyager 1, Galileo*, and *Cassini* spacecraft.

Jeff welcomes email at jeff@jverse.com.

He is also on Facebook and Twitter at www.facebook.com/PlagueYear and @authorjcarlson.

Reader reviews on Amazon, Goodreads, and elsewhere are always appreciated.